NEW YORK TIMES BESTSELLING AUTHOR

NICHOLAS SANSBURY SMITH
AND ANTHONY J. MELCHIORRI

WILD FIRE

THE NEW FRONTIER BOOK 1

aethonbooks.com

WILD FIRE

©**2022** Nicholas Sansbury Smith and Anthony J. Melchiorri

To my good friend Ben and all those who have spent their nights and weekends as volunteer first-responders. You risk your life to keep others safe. Thank you for your service.

-Anthony

"I have seen that in any great undertaking it is not enough for a man to depend simply upon himself."

- Lone Man (Isna-la-wica), Teton Sioux

READER NOTE:

New Frontier is a brand-new series set in the Trackers universe by Nicholas Sansbury Smith. For readers of Trackers, this spin-off written with Anthony J. Melchiorri takes place two years after the end of *Trackers 4*. While Trackers was an EMP/war story about the destruction of the power grid in America, and the chaos that followed, New Frontier is a story about the aftermath. We focus on the recovery, but also on a part of the country that has yet to recover, a place with many names: the Badlands, Wild West, and the New Frontier. For new readers, you can dive into New Frontier without reading the four Trackers books.

If you would like to go back and start with Trackers, you can get the entire series in a box set here for a major discount. Again, this is not necessary to enjoy or understand New Frontier, but we thought we would present the option just in case you would like to explore the beginnings of the Trackers universe.

Thank you for reading!

-PROLOGUE-

THE COOL SUMMER BREEZE CARRIED THE SCENT OF smoke over the mountains. Moonlight bathed the mountaintops.

Crouching, former Marine Staff Sergeant Sam "Raven" Spears sniffed the air. A few feet ahead, his Akita, Creek, was doing the same. After losing an eye during the Collapse, the dog relied even more heavily on his nose than before.

Hard to believe it had been only two years since the event, Raven thought.

It simultaneously felt like the longest and the shortest two years of his life.

The power grid across the United States had been virtually destroyed in the North Korean coordinated electromagnetic pulse attack. That attack started with the strategic detonation of multiple nuclear warheads high in the atmosphere and another in a port outside of Washington D.C leading to the Collapse.

Not long before the bombs went off, Raven had returned home to civilian life from the Marine Corps. It wasn't an easy transition, especially with the demons he carried from combat that often led him to drink. But thanks to his sister Sandra and her daughter Allie, who lived nearby, Raven had settled into a new life in Estes Park, Colorado. His experience as a Recon Marine and the traditions he learned from his Sioux and Cherokee ancestors helped him launch a successful tracking business guiding wealthy wannabe hunters into the mountains. When he wasn't babysitting the clients, he spent time with his sister and niece.

While Raven had plenty of problems back then, including addictions and run-ins with the law, life at least had settled into a kind of comfortable normal.

Until the Collapse.

Since then, the country had spiraled into a new dark period of chaos. Entire regions were still without power. The western states had been hit particularly hard. Large swathes of Wyoming, Colorado, Arizona, Utah, and New Mexico continued to suffer.

Raven and his dog were out in one of those dangerous stretches of Wyoming. He had taken a job to find an older couple lost during the Collapse. They were last seen at their winter home in a small town called Elk Mountain. He only had three miles to go, but three miles was a long way when you were beyond the boundaries the US Government had drawn to mark off the so-called New Frontier—colloquially known as the Badlands.

That smell of smoke he'd detected meant he and Creek might not be alone.

Sometimes smoke came from an unmitigated wildfire.

Other times, it came from campfires.

The latter was what Raven feared the most.

People rarely lit campfires unless they were looking for trouble. Only the bravest well-armed people, or the dumbest, lit them to keep warm or cook what they had hunted down that day. Anything from squirrels, pikas, or even other people.

Raven focused on the drifting smoke, sniffing for the odor of charred flesh. It was a scent he knew all too well. There was a distinct gut-churning gaminess to it he would never forget.

Another gust of wind carried a heavier scent. Savory. Salty. Maybe some sort of stew. At least it didn't smell human. It seemed to be coming from the northwest, somewhere in the hills ahead.

Creek trotted back to him, tail between his legs.

If the dog was worried, then so was he.

Raven switched his crossbow with his suppressed M4A1, slinging the bow over his rucksack. The pack contained his survival gear: dried food, extra water, batteries, a flashlight, ammunition for his suppressed Sig Sauer P365, and gas mask.

Extra magazines were stuffed in the front MOLLE pouches of his vest along with his radio, Geiger counter, chemlights, two stun grenades, and a sheathed buck knife with an antler handle. Two hatchets hung from loops on his pack.

Under his rainproof hoodie, he wore a stab-proof Kevlar vest.

It was a lot of gear, but he still packed lighter than most other mercenaries, soldiers, or trackers that ventured into the Badlands, especially those that traveled alone.

Unlike most people, he knew how to work the land. Food, fire-starters, shelter. It was all there if you knew how to use it.

Raven considered his options to move forward. The quickest route would be to hop on Highway 30 and skirt around the campfire. Still, he usually avoided roads whenever he could. Far more likely to find an ambush there than in the woods. A serpentine detour through the forest would cost time.

But losing time was better than losing your life.

Raven set off into the woods, guided by the moonlight and Creek while memories burned through his mind.

So many had died in those first few weeks following the Collapse. Even more had died in the two years after. He was lucky to still have his sister and niece. Without them, he wouldn't have much to live for besides Creek.

His best friends were dead. Those that hadn't died had become estranged. Like former Estes Park detective, now Colorado Rangers sheriff, Lindsey Plymouth. They'd had a falling out a few months ago about the strong-armed tactics used by her people. Tactics that often meant shoot first and ask questions later.

He shook away the thoughts to focus on his mission.

The chances of the man and woman he was searching for still being alive weren't good. But the twenty-five-year-old woman who hired him, their daughter Chelsea, had been insistent. She wanted closure. Even if that meant finding a pair of charred corpses.

She had agreed to his ten-thousand-dollar fee in hopes he could tell her what happened to her parents. And assuming the worst, she asked him to at least come back with any family photos he might find along with a gold and turquoise necklace belonging to her mother—if it hadn't already been stolen.

A family heirloom, he presumed.

Creek bounded ahead, vanishing into the underbrush.

Raven maintained his same diligent pace, selecting each step carefully. The forest wasn't too thick here. He didn't have to cut down tangled vegetation or duck under swaying branches, but loose rocks and gnarled roots could still trip him.

Moving at night was always difficult, especially without a

flashlight. But flashlights, like fires, were something only ignorant people used. Or people that *wanted* to be found.

Raven preferred to use the moonlight, keeping his finger along the trigger guard of his rifle as he crept through the forest.

He divided the terrain horizontally into thirds like he had learned as a Recon Marine, systematically searching the dark canvas from left to right.

But nothing moved out here.

He'd even lost the scent of smoke in the shifting breeze.

Creek emerged from the brush a few minutes later, panting.

Raven bent down, strapped his M4 over his back, and poured water into a cupped hand so Creek could lap it up. As soon as the dog was satisfied, he scratched Creek behind his ears, then took a swig of water for himself.

After tucking the bottle away, he followed Creek through the final stretch of forest. Their improvised trail came out at a bluff overlooking Interstate 80.

A sprawling metal fence with locked gates formed a barrier below. Metal warning signs swung against the chain link, spaced out every quarter mile.

Raven made his way down the slope to one. The rusting sign read:

DANGER.

THIS TERRITORY DOES NOT SERVE UNDER ANY LEGAL JURISDICTION.

ENTER AT YOUR OWN RISK.

In other words, this was the Wild West.

Even the foreign aid groups that had helped get America back on her feet wouldn't venture past this boundary without major armed escorts. They had lost too many civilians and peacekeepers over the past two years trying to help the US restore law to these lands.

Raven didn't need to go far to find a panel of chain-link fence that had already been cut. He pushed the chain-link flap back to let Creek through, then ducked under.

The next thickly wooded area was about a mile away over an open stretch of road and rolling, rocky fields.

Creek ran ahead, sniffing the ground, and then stopped to raise his snout.

He turned to Raven. Whatever had spooked the Akita before no longer seemed to bother the animal.

Raven kept low as he ran among the tall weeds blowing in the breeze. Leaves rustled on the skeletal limbs of sporadic trees. He searched the terrain again.

Medicine Bow River bordered the field on his left, and O'Mara Creek flowed on his right. He started toward the creek. Maybe he would find boot prints in the mud and gravel if someone was using it as a thoroughfare.

Plus, the trees were slightly thicker there, giving him more cover.

Creek led the way toward the gurgling water. Raven didn't see any tracks in the moonlight and kept moving.

Finally, he spotted the boxy shapes of houses bordering a small town. According to Chelsea's direction, the one he was looking for was on Medicine Bow River right after O'Mara Creek fed into it.

He trekked toward the homes slowly, his senses on high alert.

Most had broken windows, dislodged gutters, and drooping roofs. Overgrown grass and weeds carpeted the landscape.

He kept close to the water. Creek finally stopped before

they reached Bridge Street, tail frozen, eyes pointed ahead, waiting for Raven's next command.

It had rained the day before. Enough to turn the dry ground to mud for a few hours. Good for Raven too; it helped him see what Creek had already spotted—tire tracks over the asphalt left by dried mud.

They appeared to be off-road tires from a four-wheel vehicle. The tracks headed east across a bridge that connected East Main Street.

Raven motioned for Creek to follow him down to the edge of the river. From there, they hugged the shoreline and moved under the bridge. Raven waited in the shadows, listening for signs of human activity.

He heard nothing, so he signaled Creek to forge ahead. They pushed onward toward the house, now only about a half mile from their location.

As he proceeded, he finally saw footprints near the water's edge.

Boot tracks. Several sets. They reminded him of his Marine-issue variety.

Raven stood, scanning both sides of the river.

Someone was definitely in the area. Or at least they had been recently.

He considered abandoning his hunt, the hair on his neck prickling. Even with the M4, could he afford to get pinned down in a firefight with some backwoods wannabe militia?

No, you're so close...

Something about the look in Chelsea's eyes had gotten to him the day he accepted this mission. Her desperate desire to know what had happened to her parents.

Raven understood that all too well.

He climbed up the hill and used the meager woods for

cover as he continued. He took each step carefully, sweeping the darkness for contacts.

And then he saw it.

A brown house with a metal fence overlooking the river. Just like Chelsea had described.

That was his target.

Raven guided Creek along a retaining wall for cover to get to the side of the house.

The back door was already kicked in, the wood around the deadbolt splintered.

Not good.

Undoubtedly, the people he was looking for were gone or dead. The question was, would he find their bodies and the items Chelsea wanted?

He had his doubts, but he hadn't come all this way to trudge back to Estes Park empty-handed.

Raven cleared the yard and street for hostiles. Seeing and hearing nothing, he moved through the busted door. Leaves, dirt, and debris were scattered inside the kitchen.

There were no recent tracks, though.

He crossed into a living room. Filthy floorboards creaked under his boots.

Using a finger, he motioned for Creek to stay and watch their back. Then Raven took a set of stairs covered in tattered carpet up to the second floor.

At the top, he cleared the hallway and then entered the first bedroom. A bed and dresser furnished the small room. It looked mostly intact. He hoped the same for the master.

Those hopes were dashed quickly.

The nightstands were toppled. Mold covered the walls. Part of the ceiling had collapsed onto the bed. Clothes and personal items were scattered on the floor among the heaped bed sheets. The closet doors were open, revealing a few hanging shirts and even more on the floor.

He went to look for the safe Chelsea had told him was hidden behind an older family portrait stored in the closet. He guessed the picture was the one that now lay smashed on the floor. A pile of shirts covered the broken frame.

Behind cracked glass, he found a photograph of a man and woman, each with a head of graying hair. Standing in front of them was Chelsea, much younger than she was now. Maybe in her late teens. They all wore smiles. A perfect image of innocence before the Collapse.

Raven wiped off the glass. The picture was still in decent shape. He carefully removed it and then inserted it into a plastic envelope in his pack. Then he searched the drywall, finding a hole where the safe had been removed.

"Son of a bitch," he whispered.

Creek suddenly burst into the room.

Raven heard the rumble of an engine a moment later. He rushed over to the window. Through the dusty glass, headlights speared across the river.

The low rumble of that engine had to belong to a truck. It sounded like a throaty V8. Maybe the same truck that had left the tracks he'd seen before.

He brought up his rifle scope. Through the moonlight, he could see at least three people in the bed of the pickup headed his direction.

"Shit, this isn't good, buddy," he whispered to Creek.

The dog whined.

So much for an easy in and out.

Moving his scope from the truck, Raven searched the town for the best escape route. The most direct way seemed to be along the river. As he looked for a path down the steep bank, he noticed what looked like a body in the shallow water just below the fence.

On the ground-level, he'd missed it, thanks to the large rocks breaking up the river. But up here, he could see the corpse perfectly. He had a feeling the body belonged to one of Chelsea's parents.

Creek followed him out of the room, down the stairs, and back outside. They moved around the house and down toward the river. The truck engine was idling now.

A voice called out, "I saw a dog. Went this way."

"You sure it wasn't a coyote?"

"Ain't no coyotes left out here, man. You ate 'em all, fat ass."

Laughter rang out.

The truck rolled onward, engine gurgling over the chuckles.

Someone *had* been watching this town. A perfect trap for unwary travelers.

Raven started down the bank toward the water. As he neared the body, he spotted a second stuck against a rock. His stomach turned over.

With only moments to escape, he moved into the shallow water with his rifle hanging over his chest. He grabbed both bloated, decaying corpses and dragged them to the opposite shore, gagging at the scent. Even with the gruesome signs of decomposition, he could see the bullet holes in the back of their skulls.

They'd been killed, execution-style.

A man and a woman.

Were these the people he'd seen in the family portrait? Hard to tell with their bodies gripped by rot.

Pulling up his bandana over his nose, he searched their clothes for anything that he could use to identify them. He felt something metal in the woman's jacket. At first, he thought it was in her pocket, but he found nothing, turning her jacket inside and out.

Then he realized how it was hidden and why it had been missed by whoever killed these people. He ripped at a hand-stitched seam inside the jacket. It was a secret pocket, meant to thwart thieves.

He pulled out a gold necklace with turquoise on it.

Holy shit.

It was exactly like Chelsea had said.

The sudden screeching of the truck jolted his eyes back toward the house.

"Someone's with that dog!" shouted a deep voice.

Raven cursed. They must've discovered his footprints in the house.

He pocketed the necklace and ran across the shallow river. Creek bounded next to him. They loped up the hill and into the woods.

"There!" someone yelled.

Flashlight beams chased them through the forest. A rifle cracked, a bullet cutting through the air.

Raven had to find a way to lose these people and hide again.

He directed Creek deeper into the woods, running hard for ten minutes. The sound of the truck faded, replaced by the soft rustle of the breeze. No vehicles could follow him through these trees, but he could still see the flashlight beams lancing through the darkness.

Every half-a-minute or so, he checked over his shoulder, seeing them farther behind.

There was a clearing ahead. Raven saw an old homestead with two standing pole barns and a house set between a semi-circle of pine trees.

The voices behind him grew louder again. Those flashlight beams danced frantically between the trees as his pursuers spread out, trying to encircle him.

Raven couldn't risk trying to outrun them with the truck out there. The only way to escape was to hide and holdout. Let them pass him by—or at least take them on, one-by-one.

But first, he had to kill his tracks.

Raven bent down and quickly unlaced his boots. Pulling them off, he secured them to his pack. He motioned for Creek to head toward the homestead.

Raven ran after the dog.

His lungs heaved with each breath, the taste of blood on the back of his tongue. His muscles burned as he sprinted, pushing himself as hard as he could.

It wasn't until he got to the first pole barn that he smelled it.

A campfire.

This time, the scent wasn't an innocent stew.

Creek had sensed it too, his tail between his legs.

Raven peeked around the side at the source of the overwhelming odor—a smoldering fire crackled under a spinning metal spike skewered through a charred human arm.

Lights suddenly hit the road, leading into the homestead.

Raven signaled for Creek to hide in the underbrush at the edge of the homestead then took off to hide behind the closest tree. He aimed at the truck with his rifle. Through the open cab window, he spotted the driver.

Three flashlight beams bounced in the woods about a quarter mile behind.

Of all the bad luck... his attempt at escape landed him right at what appeared to be the hideout of some cannibalistic monsters. Perhaps the very people running after him.

An idea sparked in his mind. Raven swapped out his rifle for his crossbow.

Holding in a breath, Raven waited until the vehicle was within range. Lining up the sights, he moved his finger to the trigger, knowing he would only get one shot.

He raised the sights slightly and squeezed off a single, silent arrow. It zipped through the open window and straight into the driver's neck. The truck swerved and went into the ditch. Grass and mud kicked up as the rear wheels tore into dirt.

Raven ran toward the vehicle, switching to his hatchet.

The driver was dead behind the wheel, the arrow sticking out of his neck. But a man stumbled out of the passenger seat. He aimed a rifle at Raven before he could throw his blade.

A deafening blast forced him to hit the road. He rolled away, prepared for bullets to puncture his body when a wicked growl exploded from the darkness.

Creek sprinted at the rifleman and leapt at him, pinning him against the hood of the truck, and sinking his teeth into the man's neck. He took the man to the ground, ripping out flesh and blood vessels.

Raven replaced his hatchet and switched to his M4 as the man let out dying moans.

"Over there!" someone yelled.

Raven looked around the front of the truck in time to see three more men approaching the ditch.

A hailstorm of lead blasted his direction, forcing him to duck down next to Creek.

Raven waited for a respite in the gunfire, then got up and aimed at where he'd seen the muzzle flashes. With several squeezes, he fired calculated bursts at the heads illuminated by each flash.

One of the bullets found a target with a crack, the man crumpling from the headshot.

Raven ran to the other side of the truck. He aimed at a shooter, firing from a tree nearly fifty yards away.

Another pull of the trigger, and another man lost his life.

Raven fired at the other man, forcing him down. He lowered his rifle, whistled, and pulled the dead driver out of the truck. The engine was still on, but the front wheels seemed stuck in mud with the rear wheels grinding away.

Creek jumped in as Raven slammed the four-wheel-drive truck in reverse, engine growling. Mud flew for a few seconds until the rear wheels bit into the soil again. After shooting out of the ditch, he slammed the shifter into drive and crushed the pedal to the floor.

Bullets punched into the truck bed and pinged against the bumper.

The truck burst forward, kicking up a rooster tail of dirt and grass. Rounds tore into the rear windshield. Glass exploded into the cab, raining down on Raven and Creek.

He swerved so he wouldn't be an easy target. A couple of rounds cut through the cab, dangerously close to his head. He leaned down until they made it to the muddy dirt road. Gripping the wheel with both hands, he mashed the pedal, accelerating wildly. The back end of the pickup fishtailed in the mud.

When they were around the next bend, Raven looked over at Creek. The dog was panting again, blood dripping off his maw.

"Thanks, boy," he said. "You saved my ass."

Creek licked Raven's arm and then curled up on the passenger seat.

Raven let out a deep breath and focused on the road.

Until he got back to Estes Park, he wasn't going to let his guard down.

This was the New Frontier, the Badlands, a place that could swallow even the most hardened warriors without a trace. And tonight, Raven and his dog were lucky to be alive.

1

THE SOUNDS OF TRAIN ENGINES IDLING FILLED THE humid air of Union Station. What had once been a majestic structure in Washington, DC was now nothing but skeletal support columns and piles of scree. The former restaurants and shops had all been gutted, leaving husks of what had once attracted shoppers and tourists.

In some ways, the train station was no different than what most of DC looked like after the North Korean strike two years ago. But despite the devastation, this place had become a vital part of the nation's recovery.

The US Corps of Engineers and the Civilian Volunteer Recovery Task Force—CVRTF—had repaired much of the train station and tracks, turning it into a hub to aid in the rebuilding efforts across the country.

Calvin Jackson was just a small cog in the machine that kept that recovery going. But no matter how many times he walked through this place, he still found it hard to believe it wasn't dangerous to his health. Even with assurances the radiation levels here were minimal, he sometimes wondered.

Having served as a Navy SEAL for over a decade prior to

the Collapse, he was no stranger to deadly field agent exposure. Neither was his close friend and fellow SEAL Steve "Mouse" Gomez, who walked with him toward the train being loaded on Platform A2.

Despite his nickname, Mouse stood six-foot-four and had the physique of a gorilla that spent every day in the weight room. He was a freak of human physiology that looked like he could bend a steel I-beam between his thumb and finger if he was mad enough.

The two of them marched between the roughnecks whose job it was to load the precious cargo. Sweat poured down their leathery faces, the sun beating down on them as they hoisted crates and barrels of medical supplies and food.

This was the Angel Line, one of the many trains originating on the East Coast that fed goods throughout the country, earning its name by delivering life-saving cargo. Like so many other trains, it traveled on a hodgepodge of routes cobbled together from the well-worn and well-known lines prior to the Collapse.

But not all these trains made it to their destination.

Especially when they traveled through the New Frontier, or the Badlands, or whatever people wanted to call it.

To Calvin, it was simply the shithole landscape filled with murderous ass-wipes.

The only upside for him was the existence of such a place meant he had a job as a Steel Runner assigned to protect the Angel Line.

Even if the SEAL Teams no longer had room for him and his bum spine.

Still, that experience from his time in the SEALs had earned him a spot as Iron Lead, more or less the equivalent of a Troop Commander. He was responsible for a solid eighty-some Steel Runners at any given time. The numbers assigned to his group, known as Iron Team, fluctuated, depending on the contracts of the people working under him and the size of the trains they were protecting. Mouse was Calvin's Senior Officer. If Iron Lead was comparable to a Troop Commander, Senior Officer was equivalent to the Troop Senior Enlisted on the SEAL Teams.

"Heat like this makes my balls stick to my legs," Mouse grumbled.

While Mouse talked like a jock in a locker room, the guy was one hundred percent professional when shit hit the fan. Of course, all the pent-up pressure of being a professional warrior meant when he could let off steam, he sure as hell did.

"Thought your wife took your balls years ago," Calvin replied in a gruff voice.

The huge man let out a belly laugh.

The sound rolled out like a gentle thunder—if thunder could be gentle.

"Giving Maureen my balls was an even exchange for Raquel and Frankie. A *great* trade if you ask me."

Mouse smiled from ear to ear.

"They're beautiful, smart kids, Cal," Mouse said. "When we get this next load to the West, you ought to come down and see them."

Mouse's wife, Maureen, lived near San Diego with their seven-year-old daughter, Raquel, and five-year-old son, Frankie. Mouse had been a West Coast SEAL stationed out of Naval Amphibious Base Coronado, which was where Calvin had met him during training. The big guy spent his time down there when he wasn't running steel with Calvin.

"Wish I could, but I got too much work to do," Calvin replied.

They paused and stepped aside as a forklift carried a pallet with steel barrels past.

"You've got a cabin outside Tahoe that you live in year-round by yourself," Mouse said. "You got work to do? Come on, hombre. Fishing, shitting, and sleeping don't count. Get your ass down south with me and the family. Just one weekend. Then you can go back up and play mountain man all you want."

Calvin shook his head, running a hand through his wiry, black hair. For a moment, he saw what appeared to be pity in Mouse's expression.

He hated pity.

"Nah," Calvin spat. "One more job, then I got to get the place ready for winter. Maybe next spring."

Calvin straightened out his spine as they pushed on. It didn't hurt that bad anymore except for the occasional flare-up. So long as he didn't try sprinting or lifting anything too heavy, he was golden. The spinal fusion had worked, but the docs still signed off on his medical discharge and that was it for his spot on the teams.

Then the Collapse hit.

Suddenly, the government got a hell of a lot less picky when it came to who they hired as contractors and enlisted in the various new services. If you could aim and fire a gun, you could get a job. A decent one at that.

He knew what it was like when they *weren't* available. When people didn't have options. He had grown up in the rough streets of inner-city Baltimore with very few ways to get out. Options were limited to somehow affording an education, joining the military, a fast track to prison... or worse.

He went with the Navy and never looked back.

The combination of a Pell Grant and Navy ROTC had gotten him a degree at the University of Maryland, Baltimore County. Then blood, sweat, and tears earned him a spot on the SEAL teams.

But bad luck derailed his plans. He was on a Black Hawk that went down in Afghanistan, breaking his back in the crash. Then the Collapse had eventually led to him joining the Steel Runners. With so few good jobs for someone in his condition to go around, maybe his luck wasn't so bad after all.

The Steel Runners were a bit like the rugged riders of the Pony Express. A private contractor group that worked with the government to protect and deliver goods—if the Pony Express had to deal with hordes of outlaws with automatic weapons and explosives.

"'There she is," Calvin said, letting out a whistle.

They had made it to the front of the Angel Line train.

One hundred ten cars long, her two-inch-thick armored plates glinted in the sunlight.

The train wasn't pretty. Far from it.

She had been scrapped together like so many other pieces of machinery following the Collapse. Underneath the armor, she was nothing but a normal freight train powered by an old Union Pacific Railroad locomotive with a 6,000 horsepower GE diesel electric engine. All the extra weight of the armor meant the train wasn't as fast as she'd been when she was just a cargo hauler, but at least she was protected. The steel plates buttressing the locomotive made it look reminiscent of the first jury-rigged Mine-Resistant Ambush Protected vehicles that Calvin had seen in Afghanistan and Iraq.

To prevent the heavily armored boxcars of the trains from being top-heavy, they were filled with cargo as usual.

Every ten cars or so was a Steel Runner Car—SR Car, for short. They looked like mobile pillboxes, complete with ammo boxes and bunks inside. A small turret fit for an M249 was situated on top of each car.

But those cars offered limited sightlines when traveling

the rails. Most of the time, the Steel Runners preferred to have higher vantage points, even if it meant less protection.

On top of the boxcars were the rest of the defensive emplacements affectionately known as nests. Because of bridge and tunnel height limitations along the rails, there wasn't much room to work with. As a result, the so-called nests were mostly just steel walls a couple feet high.

During a long ride, the nests gave the Steel Runners a chance to enjoy the fresh air. And on a dangerous ride, it gave them alternative shooting positions with a modicum of protection.

A series of ladders connected each nest and SR Car to the thin catwalks near the bottom of the boxcars, making the train one long moving fortress.

Calvin strode past stacks of crates to where his group of eighty-five Steel Runners from his Iron Team crew gathered. The hardened men and women noticed he was approaching and made room.

A woman named Anna in gray fatigues and body armor smiled when she saw Calvin. "Good seeing you, Chief."

Another man, Travis, with scars gnarling both cheeks, grinned at Calvin. "When's this show starting? Sooner we get out of here, sooner I can make that cash."

"And lose it," Mouse replied.

Travis spat on the ground. "What I do with my money is my own business."

The guy was a solid Steel Runner, but also a well-known gambling addict. He rode steel whenever he was out of money —which tended to be often.

"Wait here," Calvin said to Mouse. The big man did as Calvin ordered, standing beside Travis.

Calvin climbed up on top of a crate, ignoring the protests from his spine. "All right, all right!"

The idle chatter and talk between the Steel Runners quieted as all eyes turned toward him.

From his pocket, he took out a memo. One he'd just received this morning from the board of executives who ran the Steel Runner Union and managed their contracts.

"Iron Team, listen up!" he bellowed over the groaning engines belching fumes.

The ragtag group of men and women between the crates clicked their heels together, their chests puffing out, and their arms slapping against their sides. Most Steel Runner teams didn't follow anything close to military decorum.

Hell, these people were dressed in everything from hiking pants and technical shirts to hunting camo. Whatever they could scrabble together or whatever the Steel Runner Union higher-ups decided to give them.

But Calvin liked to run a tight ship, and the people who joined Iron Team fell into line.

"I got good news, Iron Team," Calvin said.

"What? We're getting paid *before* we run steel?" asked a slightly rotund, bearded man who went by the apt nickname Redbeard.

That drew a few laughs.

Okay, so Calvin *tried* to run a tight ship, but these people were still mercenary civilians.

"Cut the shit." Calvin shot a look that would melt train tracks at Redbeard. "Per usual, you do not get your payment in full until *after* we make it safely to our destination. If you want off the ride for any reason and aren't on Iron Team when we reach Salt Lake City, your bank account isn't getting any bigger."

No one bitched about it. They knew the rules when they signed up. No hopping off the train early because you felt like it. Only folks who made money for a half-ride were those who got taken off on a stretcher or a body bag. But none of their families really wanted hazard pay or compensation when it meant their loved one wasn't coming home.

"But here's the deal," he continued. "We got medical shipments from all our allies. The UK, the EU. Even China is sending goods from several medical companies on this run. Our Steel Runners' Union overlords want us to take extra care of these goods."

Calvin could practically see the looks in their eyes. *What's new?*

"This time, we're not getting our usual pay," Calvin said. There were a couple groans before he continued. "We're getting bonuses."

Hoots and hollers rang out, along with some applause.

Calvin let them celebrate for a few moments.

"How much we talking, Chief?" Anna called out.

"Fifty percent in addition to the usual," he replied. "The desk jockeys say these goods are important to bring in more business, and the companies shipping them have agreed to fund these bonuses as part of a new incentive program."

The demeanor of Iron Team changed almost instantaneously. Now people shared nods and brow raises. Extra money meant they could afford more food for their families, better shelter, even better armor and weapons for themselves.

"Rest assured, this could be the best haul any of us has seen in a long time," Calvin said. "But it will also be the most dangerous. We're headed straight through the Badlands to Salt Lake City."

That didn't seem to deter anyone from what he could see.

"Let's go, Chief!" Anna called out.

"I'm in!" Travis yelled.

Not a single face looked away.

"I won't blame you if you want to step back from this one," Calvin said. "But now's the time."

Everyone remained standing, eager and ready.

Money went a long way toward boosting morale.

"Then get your shit on that train," Calvin said. "Smooth rails, Steel Runners!"

The motto rang out all around as he stepped down from the crate. He watched the Steel Runners disperse, joking and laughing while climbing up into the nests or loading into the SR Cars.

"Well, that is some welcome news." Mouse clapped Calvin's shoulder as the former SEAL joined him again. "But with this kind of pay, it's going to be a *lot* more dangerous, right?"

"Maybe. But what else is new?"

"Dead men don't get bonuses."

"I don't plan on dying," Calvin said as they made their way toward the front of the train. "You?"

"Nah, man. I plan to make death my bitch as usual." Mouse gestured toward the other Steel Runners. "But you know, I worry about these guys."

"Me too, brother," Calvin said. "That's why I'm sleeping with one eye open this entire trip."

Mouse scratched the side of his head. "Never did figure out how to do that."

"Yeah, but you got the hang of babysitting all these roughnecks."

"And babysitting you." Mouse slapped him on the back with a chuckle.

They made their way to the frontmost nest situated above the main SR Support Car, right behind the main locomotive. The Iron Team's kitchen and comms station were there, all within easy reach of Calvin. He had a bunk there, which most of the Steel Runners were vocally envious about given the proximity to the food.

But he didn't care about spending his time locked up inside the Support Car. Just like in the SEALs, he liked to lead where his people could see him. At the front line—or in this case—atop the lead nest.

It gave him the best vantage of their surroundings along with the rest of the train.

As Calvin got situated against one wall of the nest, clanging sounded from the ladder. He turned to find Anna and Travis climbing up.

"Cannot wait for that bonus," Anna said. "My sister's kids are actually going to have a nice Christmas this year."

"And where are you going to spend yours?" Mouse asked Travis. "Roulette? Poker? Blackjack?"

"I'll save it," Travis said. He took out a White Sox baseball cap from his pack at the corner of the nest—his supposedly lucky cap—and pulled it down over his wrinkled brow.

"That's my man, Travis," Calvin said. "This could be the start of a new life."

As he looked down the train, he saw groups of four Steel Runners scattered along the top in nests like this one. Gun barrels poked out of the machine gun turrets.

The burden of leadership sank in as the engines fired and rumbled. He could almost feel the targets on their backs as the train rolled out of Union Station.

It was a long way across the New Frontier, and it was his job to make sure everyone survived the journey to collect their pay.

Like Mouse had said, dead men didn't get bonuses.

———

Lindsey Plymouth loved living in the idyllic mountains. Except for when it snowed. But even then, she appreciated the peaceful quiet. Growing up, she'd spent so much time— wonderful time—in Rocky Mountain National Park. It definitely felt more like home to her than her modest two-bedroom townhouse in Golden, Colorado. She had only moved down to Golden because of her Sheriff position with the Colorado Rangers.

Sure, she could see the mountains from Golden, but seeing them was different than being *in* them.

Like now.

Lindsey led a group of four Rangers under her command into the sunlit peaks, hiking to meet up with a group of UK Royal Marines helping them on this mission. The Colorado Rangers was the first statewide law enforcement agency and had a storied history of taming what had once been the Wild West. The rough men with her now were a testament to that history. They all had combat experience, and they were certainly helpful in tracking down the outlaws. But none of them were Sam "Raven" Spears.

She could have really used his skills on this mission.

They were searching for a group of bandits suspected of killing two CVRTF workers when they raided a supply depot outside Eagle, Colorado. Eagle was the hub of major restoration efforts, where the state government was working on a station to restore power and bring clean water to parts of the New Frontier.

Lindsey and her team had followed the outlaws up a trail for a couple days through Lookout Mountain Park just east of Glenwood Springs to an area that had been ravaged by wildfires.

She bent down to check the tracks of the alleged bandits in the ash. These marauders had been using the cover of darkness to travel, then setting up camp during the day, making them hard to locate.

Finally, the Rangers were closing in. But they would need to move quickly to ensure they didn't escape.

She flashed hand signals and three of the men crouched in the tall, swaying grass poking up from the ashen soil.

Deputy Sheriff Cody Palmer advanced a couple yards to the cover of a thicket of Rocky Mountain maples sprouting around a bullet-pocked, rusted-out old pickup.

Palmer had his sleeves rolled up to reveal tattoos of a bald eagle tracing down one arm and the American flag on the other. Lindsey had often heard the phrase "bleeding red, white, and blue." If there was anyone who *actually* bled those colors, well, it was definitely Palmer. He was the epitome of a Colorado Ranger, and she always felt better having him by her side.

Most of the Rangers, like Palmer, were former law enforcement officers (LEOs) who had jumped back into service following the Collapse. The men carried their own equipment ranging from M4s and modified AR15s to single-action revolvers and Glocks. They got by with whatever equipment they could get their hands on, making do with what they had available, thanks to the broken supply lines they were working to restore.

Due to her leadership during the Collapse, Lindsey had the honor of being assigned as the Rangers' Sheriff, which meant she was responsible not only for the more peaceful eastern side of Colorado where people were working hard just to get by, but also the side of the state that fell squarely within the realm of the New Frontier. A place that attracted evil men with zero interest in rebuilding society—only taking what they wanted.

Fortunately, it wasn't just the Rangers with her on this mission. Crunching sounded as a second team in their expeditionary party joined them. Lieutenant George Blair from the United Kingdom's Royal Marines pushed through the underbrush to Lindsey and Palmer's side.

One of Lindsey's old allies from the start of the Collapse, the Secretary of Defense herself, Charlize Montgomery, had worked with the Brits to get Blair and his Royal Marines assigned to work with Lindsey in Colorado to clean up the New Frontier.

So far, they had proved to be a valuable addition, but what Lindsey really wanted was American troops, something not even the Secretary of Defense could convince President Diego to send. So far, the government seemed only willing to send rifles and ammo like those her people carried now. That was great, but she needed more people to use those weapons

It was almost like this region wasn't seen as part of the country. And Lindsey had a feeling that wasn't going to change until it was purged of the evil that had taken root here.

"We're close," Lindsey said.

"We spotted them," Blair said with his crisp Northern London accent. He was a strikingly handsome man with a thin mustache and a serious face.

"Show me."

The Rangers and Royal Marines fanned out toward a ridgeline overlooking Glenwood Springs. Blair stayed next to Lindsey on the short walk.

Accompanying him were four Royal Marines. Each carried SA80 A2 ACOGs. On their thighs, they had L131A1s holstered. Lindsey didn't much like having foreign military men working alongside her, but they had helped protect her and her people enough times to help her get over her personal reluctance.

On the ridgeline, a cool mountain breeze brushed Lindsey as she surveyed the wild terrain around Glenwood Springs through a pair of binoculars. She turned them on the remains of the Glenwood Hot Springs Lodge, charcoaled by a forest fire.

The air still smelled like smoke.

Beneath fallen beams, she spotted a few sleeping bags and backpacks lined up inside part of an exposed hotel room. The entire outer wall had crumbled, but the ceiling had miraculously survived, providing some cover.

Much of the town was charcoaled. Brick walls jutted up from blackened timber where the innards of buildings had been gutted by flames. New growth grass and maples had started to give life to the once-charming town.

"There," Blair whispered. He pointed at a man acting as a lookout on the hillside overlooking the lodge.

"I see him." Lindsey roved her binos over the rest of the grounds.

Under a leaning awning, a handful of men lingered, drinking or catching some shuteye. A couple were smoking. She zoomed in on the empty cigarette boxes next to the guys and AK-47 rifles leaning against the blackened walls next to the men.

"Yup, these are our guys," she whispered.

"How do you know for sure?"

Lindsey passed her binos over to Blair for a look.

"Those cigarettes were at the supply depot these guys robbed, ready to be shipped out," she explained. "And those AK-47s were described from the shootout. Not your average rifle out in the Wild West. They probably stole them from a previously deployed foreign peacekeeping force."

"Good eye. What's the plan? It will be dark in a few hours."

Lindsey shook her head. "I'm not waiting until dark."

Blair tilted his head.

"Not giving them a chance to see us or escape," she said. "Besides, we don't have the equipment to hunt in the dark safely. Unless you can requisition some NVGs for us from your Marines next time."

"Maybe next time, but you know how it goes with lending out equipment like that."

She nodded and used her scope to survey the area again.

"Have your best shot take out the lookout, then move in from the eastern approach, crossing the river by foot," Lindsey ordered. "I'll take the southern approach up through town, right across the pedestrian bridge. Remember, we want to bring in one or two of these assholes alive for intel."

"Yes, Sheriff," Blair said.

At her signal, Blair split off with his four soldiers down the side of the mountain. They used the tall grass and leafy trees as cover.

"Palmer, hold rearguard," she said, returning to her deputy. "If things get dicey, we'll call in reinforcements. Our evac shouldn't be far if we need it."

"You got it, ma'am," Palmer said.

Then she gestured for her Rangers to follow her single file down a path out of view from the bandits. In the urban setting, it was easier to find cover, ducking behind the husks of what used to be sedans and SUVs or walking at a hunch alongside walls that listed precariously in the mountain wind.

When she made it to the narrow pedestrian bridge, she stopped to crouch. She raised her rifle and aimed at the lookout she'd seen before. It was a lone skinny man in hunting camouflage cradling a scoped rifle. The wind tugged at his long, stiff beard as he watched I-70 for interlopers.

After a gust bit into him, he reached down and pulled on a coat with dark stains that looked to be from dried blood. It wasn't just any coat either. Lindsey zoomed in on the gray "CVRTF" logo of the Civilian Recovery Task Force. The exact evidence she needed to know this monster was not just responsible for stealing from supply depots, but probably one of the murderers who'd killed the civilians at Eagle.

It was amazing he was dumb enough to wear the evidence in the open, but a lot of these raiders weren't the sharpest tools in the shed, as her father used to say.

She tensed up as she transitioned from the judge and jury to the executioner.

"We have him in our sights," Blair reported over the radio, his voice coming in hushed.

"Permission to fire," she replied. "Check his coat if you still have any doubts."

There was a pause.

A moment later, a single crack of suppressed gunfire echoed over the river. Even with the suppressor, the walls of rock on either side made the sound reverberate. The men around the campsite started yelling.

"Target down," Blair confirmed.

"Moving in," Lindsey said. "Cover us."

Lindsey surged over the bridge with her men. Their boots pounded the concrete as they passed over the Colorado River to the resort.

The bandits rushed for cover and weapons. A couple dropped beer bottles, glass shattering over cracked concrete. Others tripped over themselves trying to get away from the side of the pool where there was no shelter.

"Don't move!" she bellowed. "Drop your weapons!"

The bandits weren't listening. She raised her rifle and sighted up the first man she saw with a rifle behind a cracked column of the pool house building. Three squeezes of the trigger sent bullets stitching into his side.

The other Rangers fanned out across the bridge, firing while they moved. Concerted shots slammed into their targets with surgical precision.

Three bandits fell from the onslaught.

From what Lindsey could see, there were only five hostiles left. Two moved out from cover to fire on the still exposed Rangers.

Before they could squeeze off a shot, the Royal Marines opened fire from their position east of the pool. Bullets sparked against the pavement and punched into the two men.

One of the raiders hit the ground, writhing in his death throes.

The other man fell backward into the pool, kicking up a spray of wet algae.

All three of the surviving men went down on their knees and put their hands up.

"Don't kill us!" one begged.

"Then don't move," Lindsey said, stepping forward toward the long pool. The three outlaws that were left did exactly what she had asked. "Cuff them."

Blair's men surged up alongside the hot springs pool as the Rangers started securing the prisoners.

"That was bloody easy," Blair said.

"Too easy," Lindsey agreed.

She studied the scene and the dead. Most were young. She had expected grizzled, hardened men for the surgical strike on the secure supply depot.

Despite the heat and the sun beating down on the back of her neck, goosebumps prickled along her arm. She wasn't one to look a gift horse in the mouth, but this had been far smoother than she had expected. Now she was starting to question what she had been convinced of a few minutes earlier.

Had these men really raided that supply depot all by themselves?

Lindsey turned to Palmer. "Call in evac."

The deputy radioed their backup forces waiting on the other side of Lookout Mountain on I-70. The four SUVs, each operated by a two-man team, had been waiting out of sight and earshot of Glenwood Springs, ready to swoop in.

The growl of the SUV engines boomed in the canyon.

Lindsey moved to the three surviving prisoners sitting on the concrete under the watch of the Rangers and Royal Marines.

One of the assholes stared at Lindsey as if she were a piece of steak and he hadn't had a meal in a week. He grinned a mouthful of yellow teeth and licked his lips.

She ignored him and focused on the other two. They were both glancing up at the mountains. At first, she thought maybe they were trying to avoid eye contact, but then a chill traced her spine.

As soon as she turned to see what they were looking at, the crack of a sniper rifle sounded over the canyon. She ducked instinctively, looking for cover and hoisting her rifle back to her shoulder. Palmer dove in front of her, ready to protect her from incoming fire.

Another shot echoed from atop one of the mountains to their north. She thought she detected movement in the brush and trees.

The Royal Marines and the Rangers scattered for cover, searching for the shooters.

Lindsey found a rock and pulled out her radio. "We need eyes on the canyon walls and immediate fire support!"

The roar of gunfire filled her ears, nearly deafening. She couldn't hear the response from the backup team racing toward their position.

All she could do was fire at whatever shapes she thought were flitting around the mountaintop and do her best to find cover in the wreckage of the hotel.

The gunfire continued for a good minute, but she quickly realized it was only her side doing the shooting now.

"Hold fire!" she shouted.

The gunshots echoed away to silence.

She stared at the mountains, narrowing her eyes.

The SUVs skidded to a stop with reinforcements. The Rangers got out, using doors for cover while aiming up at the canyon walls and mountain peaks.

"Anyone got eyes?" Lindsey asked.

Everyone reported a hard negative.

Maybe the ambushers had been spooked by the arrival of the reinforcements—or maybe one of the Rangers or the Royal Marines had gotten a lucky shot.

"Anyone hurt?" she asked.

"Rangers are good," one of her men reported.

"We're all tiptop." Blair rose from behind a rusted metal table and tangle of metal poolside chairs.

"Sheriff," Palmer called. He pointed at the three prisoners.

All three were down, their hands still cuffed behind their backs. Blood spread around them like growing shadows. Chunks of skull and brain matter peppered the ground, a combination from all three of the men.

An eerie sensation prickled across her skin as she

surveyed the mountains, no doubt being watched by whoever was really responsible for that attack on Eagle.

The sniper had fired only three shots. Each a headshot.

That was who she was really after.

And whoever it was, they were far more dangerous than any of these dead men had been when they were breathing.

2

THE PART RAVEN HATED MOST ABOUT BEING A TRACKER for hire wasn't the solitude or danger. He was used to that. Hunting and tracking in the mountains with his dog Creek wasn't usually bad either.

But what he had to do now always felt like an arrow to the gut when he returned after a mission to a family that had hired him to find loved ones.

He missed the days of being able to reunite families. At the start of the Collapse, he helped save then US Senator Charlize Montgomery's son from a group of neo-Nazis. That had earned him and Sheriff Lindsey Plymouth considerable favor with the now Secretary of Defense.

Raven didn't talk to Charlize much anymore. She was out East, at the One World Trade Center, which seemed like an entire world away. Inside the tower of steel and glass, she served President Ron Diego, a career politician who had climbed the totem pole the night of the North Korean attack that killed the majority of his colleagues.

If you asked Raven, career politicians always seemed like a bad thing for the country. They often seemed to lose touch with the people they served over time. Diego was doing just that with the New Frontier. He didn't seem to care much about what happened out here. He seemed far more concerned with isolating the sector and keeping it from spilling into the rest of the country than actually going in to cleanse it of bad guys and restoring the law.

With the presidential election coming up in the fall, Diego didn't seem willing to risk any strained resources in a place most voters didn't seem to care about either.

It was politics.

And with polls pointing at a landscape victory for President Diego, the official New Frontier policy wasn't going to change anytime soon.

That meant the men and women upholding the law in the Wild West were mostly on their own. And it also meant Raven would continue returning home from missions without much to show, like today.

In his vest, he carried what little was left of yet another family shattered by the Collapse.

Raven had parked his Jeep and walked along a rutted, narrow road lined with small cabins in Allenspark, a bedroom community firmly situated on the safe side of the Rocky Mountains. With Creek tagging along, he waved at a man who was mowing his lawn with an old manual push reel mower. The man gave Raven a friendly wave, then mopped his brow with the sleeve of his shirt.

A few children were kicking around a soccer ball as two mothers watched from a front porch. Bicycle wheels crunched over gravel behind Raven. He turned to see a man riding a bike with a teenage boy and girl he assumed were the man's kids. Just out for a morning ride.

This was the type of community that had come back in the aftermath of the Collapse.

But no matter how safe and happy these people seemed, each was still recovering from the losses that had touched every soul in America.

A few birds sang noisily from the fir trees outside the cabin to welcome the morning sun. They quieted as Raven got closer.

As soon as he looked up at them, they took flight, squawking like he was a mountain lion ready to pounce.

He didn't exactly blame them.

His boots and pants were still caked in dried mud. He'd driven straight from Wyoming after swapping the truck for his Jeep, all the way to Chelsea's place. Despite the peaceful neighborhood, he still had his Sig Sauer holstered at his hip.

You never knew when you might walk to your neighbor's house, and instead of finding the friendly person that helped get you through the Collapse, you found a grizzled bandit with a bloodstained camo jacket and a rifle in his grimy paws standing over your neighbor's body ready to steal whatever the hell you had on you too.

He sighed as he approached her cabin. Then he rapped the back of his knuckles against the door.

A few seconds passed. No movement inside.

He reached into his pocket and toyed with the gold-and-turquoise necklace.

He knocked on the door again. "Anyone home?"

Creek whined.

The hairs on the back of Raven's neck stood straight. He reached for his pistol.

Chelsea, the woman who'd hired him to retrieve her parents' belongings, had looked like a tough gal. But if someone had snuck past her neighbors and broken into her home...

Raven tapped one more time.

This time, he heard shuffling inside. "Sorry, sorry, just a second!"

He moved his fingers from his holstered pistol just as the door swung open.

Chelsea appeared, dark bags under her eyes. Her wavy brown hair looked greasier than last time he saw her. She reared back slightly when she saw him, before forcing her expression into a soft smile.

"Sorry," Raven said. "Probably smell about as bad as I look."

She eyed him up and down. "Sorry, you must have gone through—"

"It wasn't too bad," he lied.

Raven opened his palm to reveal the necklace before she could ask questions.

She stared at it a moment before gently picking it up as if she was handling an invaluable archaeological find from an ancient civilization.

A glossy film formed over her eyes. She knew what it meant that all he'd brought back was the necklace.

"I'm really sorry," Raven said.

Her lips trembled slightly. "Did you... did you find their remains?"

Raven hung his head low and placed his hand on the back of his neck. He couldn't look in her in the eyes. Even Creek let out a whimper.

"Yes, I did," Raven said.

She shook her head. "I told them to leave. To come live with me instead, and..."

Her words trailed off as Raven pulled out the thin plastic protector he'd used to transport the family portrait he'd found.

"Here." He handed it to her.

She took the photo and stared at it. The tears in her eyes

finally spilled over, dripping down her cheeks. A couple landed on the plastic covering the portrait.

"How did they die?" she finally asked, looking up from the picture.

Raven paused.

"It's okay," she said. "I want to know. That's what I paid you for."

"They were shot." Raven sighed. "It was probably over very fast. I found them in the river. Together."

He paused for a moment. "I looked for the safe, but someone had already found it."

"But the necklace—"

"It was in your mom's pocket. Guess the thieves didn't look 'em over that good."

Chelsea kept shaking her head. "They would've been safer here. So much safer. But they loved the mountains too much. They thought... they thought... It doesn't matter anymore."

An image of their bloated, rotten faces appeared in Raven's mind again. He'd seen death more times than he could count and knew how to compartmentalize it.

But sometimes dark memories broke free of the prison in his mind, releasing images that had a way of coming front and center when he least expected it. Especially now.

Judging by the state of those corpses, even in the cold, pure mountain waters preserving them, they couldn't have been more than a few weeks or months old. Which meant her parents had clung to life for a while out there.

If only Chelsea had sent him earlier... but he wouldn't tell her that. It would only make her grief worse.

"I'm sorry," he said again.

"No, no, don't be." She reached out and touched his forearm, squeezing slightly. "I wanted closure, and you gave it to me."

The fingers of her right hand still gripped his wrist as she examined the necklace in her left.

"You sure you don't want to come in for a minute?" she said. "I was just making some food, and well, I could really use the company right now."

Chelsea looked bedraggled. Probably put through the wringer while she was waiting for news of her parents. Underneath that exhaustion was a pair of high cheekbones and a subtle, dimpled smile. There was a small gap in her front teeth that Raven couldn't help but find endearing.

In another life, he would've accepted her offer. He wasn't sure where it would lead. Maybe to nothing more than a single shared meal as she told him stories about her parents to cope with her grief.

Or it might turn into something more. She might ask him to spend the night...

All that Raven knew was that he'd learned his lesson on situations like this.

In the New Frontier, you didn't make friends if you didn't have to. Every person in which you invested time and emotion was just a risk of needless heartbreak later. Death and disappointment were more common than lifelong relationships and joy.

"I really need to get going," Raven said. "I'm sorry, but I've got another job."

"I understand, and I'm sorry for whatever you went through. For what it's worth, I can move on now."

"Good. I'm glad to hear that."

He turned, but she reached out. "Hold on one more minute; I need to get your payment."

Raven remained outside as she crossed her living room to

her kitchen. She returned a few minutes later with something wrapped in a dish cloth.

"It's just some shortbread I made." She held the bread out toward him with an envelope of cash. "And here is the rest of your fee."

Raven could smell the warm aroma from the bread as he took it with the payment. His stomach churned with hunger.

"Thank you." He took the items from her. "I'm sorry for your loss, ma'am."

Then he turned with Creek and left. He felt guilty on his way back to the Jeep, something his dog sensed. Creek looked up at him with his single remaining eye and whined once they were inside the vehicle.

"It's all good, bud." He scratched the dog behind his ears.

Raven drove between the pines whispering in the wind. A few of Chelsea's nosy neighbors poked their heads out of their cabins, watching the mud-covered Jeep pass. He waved at a policeman parked at an intersection.

The man didn't wave back. Instead, he stared at Raven until he curved around another bend, putting the woods between himself and Allenspark.

After all he'd done for the area, the lawmen still seemed to have it out for him. At least, when the rest of his world seemed to have changed, that one part hadn't.

He thought about going home to shower and clean up.

But what was the point?

What he told Chelsea about having another job wasn't a lie.

He drove back into Estes Park to a neighborhood with a view of the Stanley Hotel.

At least, what had been the Stanley.

The hotel had been the victim of arson during the Collapse.

He parked at a two-story home with big windows and brown siding. After confirming this was the place, he killed the engine and went to the wraparound porch.

After a couple knocks on the door, a wizened lady with curly white hair answered.

"Mrs. Lithgow," he said.

"You must be Raven. Please, call me Joanne."

Raven nodded. He looked down at his clothes again. "Sorry, I know I look bad. I just got back from another job."

She walked out onto the porch and took in a deep breath.

"You got something for me?" Raven asked after a beat.

She let that breath out. "Yes, it's half now, half later, right?"

He nodded.

"It's just inside, but first, can I tell you about the job before you accept?"

"Yeah, please."

She looked at the mountains.

"It's my son, Richard Lithgow, and my granddaughter, Lara. They were camping out near Kremmling, somewhere north of San Toy Mountain, at the start of the Collapse. She was only fourteen when they first went out, but she'll be sixteen now."

"Two years ago?" Raven asked. He didn't like the odds of finding anyone missing that long. Any evidence would be harder to find than Chelsea's parents.

"Yes, that's right. I sent a few other trackers out there. One never returned. Another said he had to turn back. A group of armed men scared him."

"It's a bad area."

"One man did make it to Kremmling, but didn't find anything at the campground, or so he said." She paused. "I didn't really believe him, but he insisted on payment."

"I won't take your money, ma'am. You have my word, and it's as good as those that vouch for me."

A wet gleam shimmered over her eyes. "I know your reputation. That's why I'm willing to pay your hefty fee."

After wiping at her eyes, Joanne went inside and returned with the down payment and some photos.

"Hopefully, this helps if you find them."

"You got any of their clothes for my dog? He can track scents."

"After two years?"

"It's not likely, but possible. Just trying to give us the best chance of finding—"

"I understand. I'll be right back."

Raven tucked the photos carefully into his bag while Joanne went to retrieve the articles of clothing. She came back a few minutes later, holding a plastic bag. "I picked one of Richard's shirts that still smells like him, and a sock from Lara that I never washed."

"Perfect. Thank you."

"I know you don't think they're alive," Joanne said. "No one else did either. But Richard is an outdoorsman at heart. He was an Army Ranger too. If anyone knows how to survive in the wild, it's him. Lara, too, was pretty good in the outdoors and has some Native American blood in her from her mother's side."

"I'll do my best to find them, ma'am, I promise you."

She nodded.

Raven went back to his Jeep with Creek.

He drove away, watching the woman as she turned to the mountains. She was right. He doubted Lara and Richard had survived, but he was going to do his damnedest to find them.

And who knew? Maybe this time he'd be proven wrong. Maybe they would actually be alive.

Calvin sat on the top of the SR Supply Car against one of the short steel walls marred by scars from incoming rounds. Mouse leaned against the wall next to him. The wall looked far too small to protect his massive frame from bullets. But so far, they hadn't taken a single shot.

They had already passed through mountainous West Virginia and were fast approaching Ohio. Forested mountains had given way to rolling green plains. Travis and Anna had since fallen asleep in the nest.

Calvin looked out over the rolling hills. As night approached, the landscape just kept getting blacker, like they were no longer on land but traveling through the ocean.

Before the Collapse, this stretch probably would've been lit up with small towns and farmhouses scattered in the distance. It would have looked as if hundreds of tiny stars had fallen to Earth.

Now he saw only blackness. Sure, there were a couple lights from people that had generators or fires going, but the restoration efforts of the US and its allies hadn't quite reached all the rural areas.

The only promise of civilization was from the soft glow of Cincinnati on the western horizon. It was getting brighter by the minute.

Looking down the train, Calvin spotted other Steel Runners in nests like his and Mouse's. Some were peeking above the walls, watching the landscape go by, taking turns while their comrades rested.

No one looked particularly stressed or worried. They still had a few days on the tracks before things got really risky. Nights when you didn't want to shut your eyes.

Calvin pulled a bandana up over his nose as black smoke

belched from the engine, puffing back their direction. He had long since grown used to the oily smell.

The train engines weren't always in great condition. Not with the abuse they took being run constantly across the United States and often taking damage from outlaws.

The armor helped, sure. But just like the race to develop better Mine-Resistant Ambush Protected Vehicles in Iraq and Afghanistan, the Steel Runners and train officials were constantly trying to scrape together better armor to deal with new improvised explosives and all manner of small arms fire. Trying to maintain the engines themselves was a whole different matter.

Each bump on the tracks, each jolt shaking through the train sent a slight wave of pain through Calvin's damaged spine. He tried to ignore it, reminding himself he could have it a hell of a lot worse. He was still breathing, after all, and he needed his focus for the long trek ahead.

"West Virginia's one of my favorite parts of this trip," Mouse said. "Just like the old John Denver song, mountain mamas and almost heaven and all that stuff."

"Yup," Calvin said.

"Especially in the summer. Hot, but beautiful."

Calvin raised his canteen as if to make a toast. "And the people don't shoot at us."

"Usually," Anna piped in, eyes still closed.

Turned out she was awake after all.

"Not like the yokels that like to take potshots at us in Nebraska," she said. "I could go and wring their necks."

Mouse rifled through his pack and pulled out one of the sandwiches the train's cook had passed out earlier. He took a bite of the ham and cheese, chewing with his mouth wide open as he spoke.

"The hell else is there to do in Nebraska?" Mouse asked with a mouthful.

Anna shrugged. "Cow tipping, getting laid, drinking moonshine, I don't know."

She opened her eyes. "You think we'll be okay, Chief?"

"What?"

She combed a hand through her thick, dark hair. "I mean, I like the idea of bonuses, but I never knew private companies to be so generous."

Travis was awake now too, and started unwrapping his sandwich. "She's right. Maybe they don't think we'll make it. Or maybe they want us to fight harder 'cuz they know shit's getting worse on the rails."

"The raiders just keep getting smarter," Anna went on. "You know how they used to sabotage the rails, firing on us and the train conductor."

"I'm more worried about the remote-controlled IEDs," Travis added. "Nothing we can really do to detect them. Just got to hope the train survives against a blast."

"Every time we adapt to them, they adapt to us," Mouse chimed in. He stuffed the empty sandwich wrapper into his bag and wiped his mouth off. "Feels like we're fighting Al Qaeda all over again."

"Only this time, it's in our own backyard," Anna replied.

"Fuckin-A." Travis scratched at one of his long scars. "I keep thinking about what's next."

He took a solemn bite from his sandwich.

"Some of my buddies told me Cincinnati was going to shit," Anna said. "More crime, more murders. The recovery efforts aren't working. People are getting desperate. Rioting and looting supply depots. Maybe we got more to worry about than the New Frontier."

"Take it easy," Calvin said. "You guys are getting ahead of yourselves."

Lightning flashed across the horizon.

It was so far that they could barely even hear the thunder.

"Another summer storm," Mouse said. "Looks like it's a good thirty, forty miles or more north."

All the same, Calvin recalled where he had stowed his poncho in his pack just in case it started pouring.

Anna and Travis looked worried, despite Calvin's assurances.

"Relax," Mouse rumbled, sensing what Calvin had picked up on.

"You two are in the best seats on the train riding with us," he said. "SEALs, baby."

Anna scowled at him. "Don't call me baby."

"It's a figure of speech," Mouse said. "Trust me, I ain't callin' *you* baby."

"Yeah, he's calling me baby." Travis winked

Everyone laughed.

It brought Calvin back to the banter he and Mouse had shared with their former teammates. The two of them had been together for a long-ass time. In fact, they'd been swim buddies since BUD/S or Basic Underwater Demolition/SEALs training.

Anna rubbed the back of her neck. "I just got to survive this run."

"Why's that?" Mouse asked.

She shrugged. "If this bonus really comes through, this will be my last ride. I'm going to buy myself a place in New York and stay near my sister with money I've saved up."

"How about you, man?" Mouse grumbled to Travis.

"Still got to figure out my life." Travis took another bite of his sandwich. "Get my shit back in order."

"Well, you got plenty of time to think," Calvin said. "Going to be a long ride."

"What about you, bud?" Travis asked Mouse.

"I'm running steel as long as Calvin does. Someone's got to look out for the boss."

"I don't need protecting," Calvin said. "You can retire. Find a different job in San Diego. Stay with the family. I'm sure Maureen would like it if you weren't kicking your own ass by running steel forever."

"Someone's got to do it," Mouse said.

"Someone doesn't have to be you."

"Trying to get rid of me, Cal?"

"Nah, man, you know that ain't it. It's the fact you've got a family." Calvin grinned, again recalling their time on the teams. "Remember how Ricky and Williams could never keep a steady girl. *I* sure as hell couldn't. Not when we were at the beck and call of Uncle Sam, never knowing when we'd be on a C-130 flying overnight to go nab an HVT or run a security op for some VIP."

"It's been tough." Mouse was quiet for a second. "Maureen and I almost didn't make it, because I think in a way I'm addicted to the action. Plus, this is great pay, and we need the money. What the hell would I do in San Diego? Sell bicycles?"

Anna chuckled.

"What about you?" she asked Calvin. "You going to keep doing this forever?"

"I don't think I'm the type that can sit at home either," he replied. "I got to work. Got to keep my hands and mind busy."

Another flash of lightning cut through the distance.

This time, the low rumble of thunder rolled over them louder, reverberating through the walls of their nest.

"Until you get the cabin in Tahoe finished and you decide

you're doing nothing but fishing and tossing back beers, I'm in this nest with you," Mouse said.

Mouse was like that. A guy with more loyalty built into his genes than a Doberman. It was why, after Mouse had gotten out of the teams too, he'd followed Calvin right into the Steel Running job.

For Calvin, this job gave him a purpose. For Mouse, it was a paycheck to take care of his family, and it helped him feel alive again. And while steel running wasn't exactly like being sent overseas to stomp terrorists, it made them both feel like they were doing something to help their country.

Plus, there was something about serving together, even as a Steel Runner, that couldn't be replaced: brotherhood.

This type of comradery was irreplaceable. Trusting someone with your life, and knowing they would take a bullet for you, and you for them, was something that no cabin on the lake, no matter how perfect, could replace for Calvin

Another fork of lightning tore across the black canvas. The thunder followed almost immediately.

"Looks like that storm is gonna catch us after all," Mouse said.

Calvin reached into his pack and took out his poncho. The rest of the group followed suit. The first few drops of a gentle rain suddenly gave way to a downpour that rang out against the steel nests in a percussive din.

A long metallic squeal sounded as the train neared Cincinnati. Water had puddled under their boots by the time they got their first clear view of the city.

Power had been restored in most sectors, illuminating the destruction from the Collapse. Entire blocks had burned during the power failures from a combination of electrical issues to gas lines breaking and riots born out of desperation and fear.

Many buildings were nothing but rubble. Piles of broken concrete and charred support structures were everywhere. Abandoned vehicles with busted windows and flat tires filled the streets. The iconic Ferris wheel near the river leaned precariously.

As the Angel Line rolled toward the train station, Calvin noticed armored vehicles driving through the slick streets framing the rails. French and British flags whipped in the storm. It was good to know their allies were working day and night to help restore order, but that didn't mean they were completely safe either.

Calvin took out his radio. "All Sierra Romeos, Sierra Romeo One here. Keep your eyes peeled. I repeat, keep your eyes peeled and weapons ready. We aren't expecting trouble, but with the storm, I don't want to get caught with our pants down. Over."

A flurry of affirmatives came back over his radio.

He peered out over the nest wall with his rifle at the ready. Mouse, Anna, and Travis did the same, their weapons already loaded and charged.

The train finally roared to a halt at a busy railyard.

All across the top of the Angel Line, the Steel Runners lifted their rifles to their shoulders. The turrets atop the SR Cars swiveled, looking for hostiles.

No one had ever attacked them in Cincinnati, but any time the train stopped, they were vulnerable.

Yard workers immediately started unloading crates and depositing new ones. Calvin watched them all suspiciously.

Those workers weren't the only ones to notice the train's arrival.

Civilians crowded the chain-link fences alongside the tracks, reaching through toward the Steel Runners and rail-yard workers. Rain poured over them, making their clothes stick to their flesh so tightly, Calvin could see their protruding ribs.

Many of these people were starving.

The foreign aid wasn't quite enough. Poverty was about as common as any other disease in the neglected slums plaguing so many of America's rebounding cities.

Calvin gulped, raising his rifle as the fence swayed. The barbed wire atop it didn't thwart a couple of young men who climbed through, even at the cost of their shirts and bits of their skin catching on the jagged barbs.

"Food! We need food!" one of the young men yelled as he ran toward the train.

A yard worker shouted for the guy to get back.

The Steel Runners in the closest nest shifted their aim toward the runner.

"Back up!" one of the Steel Runners screamed.

He didn't stop, and a yard worker tackled him into the gravel.

"Stop! I'm sorry!" the guy yelled.

The worker got off him. "Get out of here. Now!"

Calvin got a good view of the desperate civilian. The young man was looking up at him. He couldn't be older than fifteen, maybe sixteen. Dark skin gleaming with rain drops. Tall, thin, and full of rage.

Just like Calvin had been at that age.

"Hold on!" he yelled, lowering his weapon.

The burly yard worker turned around and looked up at Calvin as he reached into his pack and took out his sandwich. It was supposed to be his dinner, but he couldn't stomach it knowing so many others were begging for crumbs.

He tossed the plastic-wrapped sandwich down toward the kid. He caught it in one hand. As he unwrapped it, he nodded at Calvin.

"You always did have a soft spot, but we can't save them all, Cal," Mouse said.

"No, but at least that kid gets to eat tonight," Calvin said. "And if we get this train to Salt Lake City, a whole lot more hungry people are going to get to eat too."

3

RAVEN TURNED OFF THE HEADLIGHTS OF HIS JEEP JUST after he passed San Toy Mountain and parked along the side of a gravel road. He'd been searching for evidence of the Lithgows for the past day and a half. So far, exploring around Kremmling along with the land north and east of San Toy had been fruitless.

Frustrated and running out of options, he decided to check a new location: the Pumphouse Campground, just west of the mountain.

He turned off the engine, scanned the area, then slowly got out of the Jeep. Creek climbed over the front seat and hopped out, tail wagging.

As the dog patrolled, Raven pulled out the camouflage netting from the back and threw it over the Jeep. It didn't make the vehicle invisible, but it helped disguise it.

When he finished, he removed everything of value, bringing all the supplies he needed in his pack or the MOLLE pockets of his vest.

Once again, he carried enough dried food, water, and ammunition to continue the search for a few days. His M4A1 was strapped over his back, his hatchets were back in place, and he cradled his crossbow as he hiked down to the Colorado River with Creek bounding ahead.

A few wispy clouds drifted across the moon, but the stars were out in full force. The cool night air was made all the chillier with the snowmelt-fed river flowing by him like natural air conditioning.

He headed alongside the water toward the campground. The area was once a popular launching point for rafters back when Gore Canyon was safe.

Raven made his way from the rocky shore up into the cover of the trees. He couldn't imagine a man and his fourteen-year-old daughter would have fared well if they were out here during the Collapse, cut off from civilization. Not unless they had some kind of mitigation from the nuclear fallout, and outdoor skills to last two years.

And if they had survived all of that, then why not just head back to civilization. Surely you wouldn't want to stay out here...

No, Raven knew that Richard and his daughter were dead. He was almost positive of that. His job, like it was for Chelsea, was to bring Joanne closure.

As they got to the edge of the campground, he motioned for Creek. Then he held up the two pieces of clothing Joanne had given him. A shirt that belonged to Richard, and a sock that belonged to Lara.

Creek sniffed them in turn and then took off.

Raven began the trek slowly, looking at every gnarled tree along the gorge while his dog trotted ahead, nose down to the dirt.

Walled in by two sets of mountains, the river here wound through a mostly barren landscape broken up by pines and patches of swaying wild grass.

Raven used the cover of the sparse trees, but if someone with a discerning eye was watching from high up one of the slopes, they would likely see him. Not much he could do about that. He had to rely on his intimate knowledge of the land, and hope Creek detected anyone, before *they* were detected.

The dog's tail swished back and forth as he continued to sniff. He seemed to have already picked up a trail.

Maybe it was another person who had traveled these parts not too long ago.

As they got closer to the campground, Creek suddenly froze. His tail curled between his legs, and he pointed his nose up.

Raven raised his crossbow, searching for movement in the dark. He listened to the branches rustling in the wind and the bustle of the flowing river.

Everything sounded normal.

No cracking branches. No whispering voices.

Problem was that the people he wanted to avoid also knew how to read the woods. They knew how to hunt and how to build a shelter and how to escape the law.

But the difference between them was that he didn't view nature as a one-way relationship where people greedily took what they needed. He viewed his connection with nature as more of a conservational role, where he took only what he needed and did no damage wherever possible. He had learned to watch, respect, and even listen to the plants and animals that called these mountains home.

The more he paused and listened, the more that the environment spoke to him.

A lone howl erupted over the mountain, carrying through the gorge.

The hairs on the back of his neck prickled. Creek backed up toward him, tail still between his legs.

The first howl was answered by four more ghostly howls drifting into the night.

Raven held his breath.

Wolves.

His ancestors used to say the voice of a wolf was the voice of the gods.

He wasn't used to hearing them out here.

Before the Collapse, Colorado Parks and Wildlife had been discussing reintroducing gray wolves to the region. But they hadn't had an opportunity before the power went out.

The exodus of people from the New Frontier and the die-off of so many more had given the wolves a chance to come down on their own.

They were clearly enjoying hunting in their new territory.

Raven pushed onward cautiously along the river, listening to the occasional howl. The wolves didn't seem to be getting any closer. Maybe they were after some poor mule deer or an elk.

Raven didn't fear them coming after him, as attacks on humans were rare, even in today's new ecosystem. They would definitely attack Creek, though. He would hate to kill one of the magnificent creatures if that happened, but he would defend his dog with his own life.

A plasticky flapping sound drifted on the breeze as they neared the campground.

Sure enough, a pair of deflated rafts were caught on the branches of a tree. Those trees were directly next to the small concrete bathrooms.

A few rusted-out SUVs and sedans were covered in grime in the nearby parking lot. Raven scanned the ground but saw no sign of recent tire tracks. He kept heading toward the rafts.

He paused when he noticed a thin white string at about ankle height. Kneeling, he examined the thread and followed it to a tree. A cluster of empty beer cans hung from it like a wind chime made of trash.

The more he examined the ground, the more he noticed other strings tied up to similar improvised alarm systems.

When he got to the rafts, he realized they weren't blown up here by a heavy wind. Someone had used bungie cords and climbing rope to sling them up as a kind of tent. There was a sleeping bag inside too.

He avoided every string, careful not to disturb the crude alarm.

Raven motioned for Creek to stay.

The dog whined slightly but obeyed, keeping just beyond the spider web of strings. Raven snuck up to a tree and took out a buck knife from his utility belt. He sliced through a few of the strings, gently tying them on the tree branches so he didn't have to move the cans.

With the tension on the strings safely broken, he gestured for Creek to join him at the makeshift tent. Inside, Raven knelt next to the sleeping bag as Creek buried his nose in it.

He glanced up with his one eye, tail wagging.

The Akita definitely had a scent. Whether it was Lara or Richard's, he wasn't sure.

Raven felt the bag for warmth, but could tell no one had slept here tonight, at least. He noticed a thin layer of dirt and dust covered most of it. An aluminum-framed hiking backpack leaned up against one of the tree trunks stabilizing the raft-tent, but it was empty.

There was a stick propped up against one wall of the tent. Someone had carved it so that it appeared to be a rifle.

Interesting.

He found a pair of mildew-covered hiking boots that had been worn out. The sole was separating from the shoe.

From a distance, even during the day, this campsite might've fooled other people who thought it was being used. That immediately set off warnings in Raven's mind.

To make matters worse, he realized the wolves hadn't howled in a couple minutes. Maybe something—or someone— had scared them.

He started to sift through the campsite to see if it by chance belonged to the Lithgows. The lack of noise sent a shiver through his flesh.

He hunched down, listening for something, *anything*. It felt like something or someone was watching him. His heart hammered.

Raven shouldered his crossbow and continued the search. After another thirty minutes, he still had yet to find any concrete evidence of the Lithgows.

Creek took point again as they pushed through the camp. Judging by the way the Akita looked back and forth in the darkness, the dog couldn't quite tell what or who was out there, much less where.

Raven halted when he saw something unusual ahead.

"The hell..." he whispered.

He indicated for Creek to get behind him before approaching a scaffold of branches and sticks in a thicket of trees. A couple of deer skulls hung from two corners. Atop it was what Raven guessed to be a body shrouded in an animal skin.

He was intimately familiar with this scene. Or at least, he knew it from the stories his grandfather had told him when he had grown up on the Sioux Rosebud Reservation in South Dakota.

This was a Sioux burial ritual.

He approached the body, careful to watch his surroundings, feeling a warm reverence approaching the corpse. Traditionally, bodies would be left on just such a platform for a year after death. People still treated the deceased as if they were living, showing the same respect they would any other person. Joanne Lithgow definitely wasn't Sioux and neither was Richard. But she'd mentioned that Lara was part Native American.

Could this be Lara's doing?

He couldn't help himself. He felt drawn to the sight.

Creek walked beside him, tail down like he could feel the spirit of this person still lingering nearby.

Raven didn't want to disturb the body. There was no telling how long the person had been out here, and tradition said it could take days or longer for the deceased's spirit to take the right journey after their death.

Disturbing the body meant disturbing someone's carefully planned ritual.

But if this person had anything to do with Richard or Lara, then he couldn't just walk away either.

He paused by the body, asking forgiveness to the person's spirit.

I'm sorry to disturb your rest, but I'm looking for a man and his young daughter.

Then he took out his buck knife and started to carefully cut the seams along the shroud to reveal the person's face.

Before he could even cut more than an inch of the shroud, he heard the familiar twang of a bow. He ducked instinctively. A second later, an arrow struck the tree next to his hand.

He turned right as a second arrow hit him in the chest, punching into the stab-rated Kevlar vest. The air burst from his lungs as he fell backward.

Keeping low, he staggered away.

A third arrow whizzed through the air, narrowly missing his carotid artery but slicing off a chunk of flesh that burned on impact.

Creek barked ferociously as Raven fled.

"Run, boy," he choked out. "Get out of here!"

"Thanks for the lift," Lindsey said.

She got out of the forty-year-old Bronco that her deputy drove.

"Good luck," Palmer said. "I'll be up as soon as I get parked."

"Thanks. Be sure to bring in all those weapons we confiscated too. The Council needs to see what we're dealing with."

It was late in the evening. Just past nine.

But she didn't want to wait until morning to meet with her Foreign Advisory Council. Not after the mission in Glenwood Springs, and thankfully, they, like her, tended to work all day.

With a wave at a guard, she strode past the layers of chainlink fences topped with razor wire into the complex that had once been the Jefferson County Sheriff's Office and County Jail. With much of Denver destroyed, the complex had become the central waypoint between eastern Colorado and western Colorado. The building was now a hub of activity for both military and LEO matters.

The people who worked here called it Fort Golden for good reason.

She headed toward the round cylindrical buildings with their sheer glass windows behind concrete block walls and Hesco bastion barriers. Looking up at the guard towers at the complex's corners, she saw the snipers and men manning the machine guns looking out over the foothills. They were mostly locals up there, some without much training at all. Most of the foreign peacekeepers were out of sight. It was another reminder how little help she had out here. It was also a reminder her request for additional support from Governor Wyatt Anders had been denied. He was more concerned about protecting some of the bigger cities like Denver, and no matter how much Lindsey warned him her problems could become his, he held strong.

And after what she had seen out there with the raiders, she feared her threat would become a reality. With no one else to turn to, she decided to reach out to her best ally, the Secretary of Defense.

Lindsey took the sat phone from her belt as she walked.

"Lindsey?" Charlize answered.

"I'm sorry to bother you at this hour, Madame Secretary, but there's a situation in the New Frontier that needs your immediate attention," Lindsey said.

She quickly went over everything that had happened, including how the prisoners they'd tried to bring in were assassinated by a sniper.

"My God," Charlize said. "This stinks of conspiracy. Do you have any idea who the ringleaders are?"

"Not yet," Lindsey replied. She gave a brief wave to another Ranger heading toward Fort Golden's entrance. "I was hoping you might have an idea."

"Nothing I've heard of, but I'll keep my ear to the ground, so to speak. Perhaps you might want to start pressing your Foreign Advisory Council. They might be able to devote more manpower and money, along with their own country's intelligence agencies, to this specific task."

Lindsey let out a sigh. "I can try convincing the FAC to

help, but it would really help if I could get some US troops to help me out here. I appreciate the weapons and supplies you've all sent, but we're stretched thin here. We need more trained soldiers."

Charlize paused for a moment. "With the election coming up, I really don't think that is going to happen. I'm sorry, and part of that is because of how well you have done."

"Some days, it really doesn't feel like that, and now I have a bad feeling we're going to see something worse than before."

"You can handle it. I have faith in you."

"Thank you, Madame Secretary." Lindsey strode past an SUV that two Rangers were loading with weapons and ammunition. "Faith doesn't secure our borders, though."

"All those Front Range communities of yours have survived the past couple of years. That counts for something. President Diego has said as much to me, and to be honest, he's reluctant to send more aid your way because you've done so well keeping things under control."

"All due respect, but I'm not sure I buy that. Can I be honest?"

"Of course."

"To me, I think this is more about how bad it would look if US troops died out here before the upcoming election." Lindsey tried to keep the anger out of her tone, but President Diego was really getting on her nerves.

"And now I will be honest, Sheriff."

Lindsey braced herself, hoping she hadn't offended the Secretary of Defense and her best ally.

"The President has decided to let the FAC deal with the New Frontier, in tandem with your office and other allies," Charlize said. "I know you didn't sign up to deal with these people when you became sheriff, but these Councils have accelerated the recovery efforts across the US."

"Indeed, they have, but if I could have just a small fraction of the troops that have secured other areas of the country, I could bring back law and order to the New Frontier."

A guard held open the door to Fort Golden for Lindsey, and she entered the hall, giving her a moment to consider her next words. If anything, she needed to keep the Secretary of Defense an ally, and not rub her the wrong way.

"I'm sorry, I understand you are in a pickle, and I will do more with less without bringing this up again," Lindsey said.

"Trust me when I say you aren't alone in this. While the New Frontier is the worst in terms of lawlessness, we have threats to the recovery of our nation all over the map, and that is why the FAC is so important. There is no telling how long we will have their assistance."

"Oh?"

"I've heard rumblings that some of the countries helping us aren't sure how much more they can devote. The Collapse crushed the world economy and many of our allies are still hurting back home," Charlize continued. "President Diego is not the only one that doesn't want to lose troops, and we've already seen some of our support pull back for that very reason."

Lindsey had witnessed that firsthand. Most of the foreign troops deployed to the United States for recovery had pulled out within the first year due to the violence. China, for example. They were still here helping with aid, but their soldiers were almost all gone.

All that remained were peacekeeping forces, but they rarely left their posts.

Lindsey felt her stomach churn with anxiety. She knew where this was going. And while the FAC wasn't over-the-top helpful, she did need them.

"We barely have our highways back together, and we sure

as hell don't have reliable supply lines figured out or funded yet," Charlize said. "The United States' recovery will stall if we don't get that aid."

And it will stall if there is something more sinister going on out here... Lindsey thought.

She started up the stairs to the fourth floor, dodging past a pair of Rangers rushing down with rifles strapped over their backs. "The FAC is a necessary, bureaucratic evil. I get it, and I will work with them."

"Good, because until we're on our feet, we do what we have to so we can survive."

"Sometimes surviving is all I feel like I'm doing here."

"You're doing great. Keep it up and keep me updated on your situation."

"Thank you, Madame Secretary."

Lindsey ended the call and made her last-minute preparations for the FAC meeting.

Talking to Charlize usually made Lindsey feel more confident, but today not so much. The country seemed in worse shape than she realized, and if they lost the support of the FAC, they were going to have major problems.

That meant she had to handle things here more delicately.

Before she went to the conference room, Lindsey grabbed a cup of coffee. She savored it, hoping the caffeine would help her perk up. She was running off just a few hours of sleep. Everyone stood when she entered, but she motioned for them to sit.

"Just a few minutes and we'll get started," she said. "Just waiting on Deputy Palmer."

Lindsey took another sip of coffee and discreetly scrutinized the faces of the people she needed to convince to continue helping her.

Lieutenant Tiankai from China was seated in a rigid posture. He wore his familiar green uniform. The jacket and trousers were somehow always perfectly pressed. He and his people had been helping the United States since the beginning of the Collapse. It was remarkable who had come to help when America was at her weakest. Former enemies were now allies, and allies had become even better friends.

Next to Tiankai was Captain Juan Martinez from Mexico. The man wore a mottled green camouflage uniform with a matching cap. A black pendant with a silver star on the cap signified his rank. The man had a round face that gave him a soft, almost boyish appearance despite the wrinkles at the corners of his eyes and the graying hair peeking out from under his cap.

Representing the United Nations was Lieutenant Faustin Uwase of the UN Police Force. He'd made the long trek from Rwanda months ago and was generally one of the quieter members. He had a receding hairline and thick-framed black glasses that sat atop his round nose. A neatly trimmed beard traced his lips. The guy looked as exhausted as Lindsey, which was unusual for him. But she chalked it up to the long hours they'd all been working lately.

Second Lieutenant Delphine Piard from Canada sat across from Uwase, wearing the brown and green camouflage of a Canadian army combat uniform. Her blue eyes always carried a certain heat like she was ready to dress someone down if they so much as looked at her funny. Coming from Montreal, she had a slight French accent.

Lieutenant Blair was dressed in yet another variation of a camouflage combat uniform, representing the United Kingdom's interest in helping secure Colorado.

Two years ago, the last place Lindsey thought she would

be was in a room full of foreign military and police officers discussing how they were going to save her state.

But here she was, and she needed them more than ever.

The door opened, and Palmer walked in. He dropped a large bundle on the table wrapped up in a green sheet, and then took off his cowboy hat.

Lindsey cleared her throat. "I know we're late, but that's because we just got back from a very important mission, and I've been dealing with the aftermath since," she said. "As you may have heard, we took out ten men who were part of the gang that robbed the Eagle supply depot a week ago."

"You're sure it was them?" Martinez asked, his brow scrunched up in concern.

"Yes. Palmer, show them."

He clicked on a projector. Images of the stolen cigarettes, a couple damaged crates marked FOREIGN AID, and other goods showed over a screen at the back of the room. "We recovered some of the goods. These crates and items were all confirmed to be on the inventory list for the Eagle supply depot."

"Maybe they bought these items off the black market," Piard suggested.

"Doubtful," Lindsey said.

She motioned to Palmer.

Next came a photo of the dead lookout wearing a CVRTF jacket.

"Judging by the stolen clothing and images recovered from the supply depot, these guys were one hundred precent part of that raid," Lindsey said.

A new set of pictures showed a selection of men, both from images captured on the few security cameras outside the supply depot, along with drawings provided by sketch artists from witnesses. Each sketch or picture captured by a security camera was shown side-by-side with an image of a dead raider.

"Do you have any idea who these people are?" Martinez asked.

"No," Blair said. "They didn't have any IDs, of course."

"Maybe some survivalists working as mercs," Palmer chimed in.

Lindsey nodded. "We might've taken these guys out, but there's a bigger problem I think we may have uncovered... You see, we didn't kill all these men."

"What?" Piard asked.

"We took three prisoners, but before we could talk to them, a sniper blew off their heads," Lindsey explained.

That got everyone's attention. The Council members exchanged glances and raised brows.

"Palmer, the rifles," she said.

Palmer pulled back the sheet from the bundle he'd put on the table and revealed the fully automatic AK-47s they had recovered from the bandits.

Lindsey picked one up. "These match the weapons used at the depot raid too."

"I know where you're going with this, but maybe they got these from the black market." Uwase gestured at the weapons. "There has been a flood of military-grade weapons since the Collapse."

"Yes, and we've done our best at tracking down arms-trafficking rings with no luck."

"So we still have work to do to stop these rings," Uwase said.

"Maybe we need someone besides the Rangers to get the job done," Martinez said, always the most curmudgeonly of the group.

"It's not an easy task," Tiankai said.

"Look, this is beyond arms trafficking." Lindsey felt the anger rising inside of her but remembered what the Secretary of Defense had said.

They needed the FAC, and while she wanted to tell Martinez to get his ass up and help, it wouldn't do any good.

Lindsey held up the rifle. "This isn't what matters most. It's the fact someone didn't want us to bring those raiders in. Someone is covering their tracks. Probably the same someone who organized the raid on that supply depot in the first place."

Lindsey studied the worried faces before continuing.

"If this *someone* had access to weapons like these, doling them out like candy to bastards willing to do their dirty work, we're facing something far more insidious in the New Frontier than we thought."

Blair nodded. "The snipers who brought down the three prisoners took them down at distances that would make our own snipers proud."

"Do you think this is a foreign threat?" Piard asked.

"Could be. Or maybe it's a US-based militia that is equipped and organized better than any we've dealt with before," Lindsey said.

"This is an important question to answer," Tiankai said.

"Yes, and I need your help answering it."

Blair gave her a reassuring nod, making it clear the British were behind her one hundred percent. The others were silent for a moment.

She wanted their unwavering support, and she knew just how to press their buttons, hopefully without making them mad.

"Martinez, Piard, we share a border with your countries, and I know none of you want our problems crossing those borders. Perhaps it's time for your peacekeepers to help us keep the peace."

Then she turned to Tiankai. "The US used to be China's largest trade partner. I'm sure we'd both benefit if the US were back to consuming everything your country is dying to export again, right?"

Finally, she looked to Uwase. The man was kind and patient. He truly seemed invested in making Colorado a better place. He even brought his wife, Agathe, and six-year-old son, Emmanuel, to the state. Lindsey had met them a number of times over the past year. The boy had a contagious smile, and Agathe was kind.

"Uwase, it's been a few weeks since I've seen your family," Lindsey said. "How are they?"

Uwase hesitated, almost like he was scared to say. "Fine. Just fine."

"Imagine all the loving families in Colorado like yours who are at risk right now. We need your help to protect them."

"Yes, I understand," Uwase said, evidently still nervous to be put on the spot.

Lindsey surveyed the group again. "You all came here to help, and I am forever grateful for that. Truth is, we need your help more than ever. I hope I can count on you, because our success is your success."

Raven crept through the woods, following Canyon Creek up the side of the mountain nearly a mile away from the camp with his rifle. His neck throbbed from where the third arrow had glanced across his flesh, but he kept his hands on the weapon.

He hadn't had time to bandage the wound. Blood still trickled down over his vest. Fortunately, it wasn't bad enough he needed to stop. Spending even a second to patch it up would mean the person that shot it would have another chance to hit him, and this guy was good with a bow.

If it weren't for the vest, Raven would be dead.

For that reason, he wanted to put enough space between him and the shooter to plan his next step. The person had gotten the best of him once, but not again. Especially not with Creek out there prowling to warn Raven.

He finally stopped to rest under a rocky outcropping. In the shelter, he listened for the telltale crunch of footsteps while keeping his rifle up and ready to fire.

Creek emerged from the surrounding brush a few minutes later, tail up.

They were clear.

For now.

Raven took a few minutes to patch up his neck. Half of the arrow that had hit him in the chest was still sticking out of his vest. He plucked it free and looked at the tip. This wasn't some store-bought hunting arrow.

This was homemade.

"The shit..." he whispered.

After taking a drink of water, he paused to think.

From the burial site to the arrow, he knew now whoever was chasing him likely was Native American—or had for some reason adopted some Native American practices. That explained what he saw in the camp too, with the traps.

This definitely wasn't like any outlaw hideout he'd seen.

Was it worth going back to check the body on the chance it could be Richard? If so, why the hell would he have stayed *here* all this time?

Raven let out a sigh that hurt his ribs.

"We'll scope it out, okay, boy?" he said to Creek.

Creek wagged his tail.

Then they were moving again.

Raven took a different route back to the camp, watching the forest through the moonlight. Creek had a scent now, but Raven didn't want his dog leading the way with a hostile out here.

As they got closer to the river, Raven stopped to listen and scan the woods. Whoever was out there wasn't far, judging by Creek's posture.

The dog was looking back down toward the river valley.

Raven went that way, moving slowly and silently.

It didn't take long to find tracks. Smaller than he'd expected, but he followed them down to the river, keeping the high ground as he searched.

Creek kept next to him, sniffing right toward a cluster of trees. Raven stared for a few minutes before the moonlight revealed an opening in the rocky mountainside. He could vaguely hear someone or something moving around inside. Whoever or whatever was in there had drawn Creek's scent.

If it was a person, they had to know something about the camp. And as a result, there was a decent chance they had encountered the Lithgows.

"I know you're down there," Raven said. "Come out with your hands up."

In the dull moonlight, Raven saw the silhouette of a person standing with a bow and arrow, creeping to the edge of the opening and turning toward the hill Raven stood on.

"Don't move!" Raven called out.

The person took a step anyway. Raven fired a suppressed shot into the dirt in front of what looked like a thin, lanky man.

"Next one will be a bullet to the head," he said.

Whistling, he ordered Creek to flank their quarry.

"Drop the bow," Raven said.

The thin man did not respond.

Raven took a step closer. "I'm not going to ask you again."

Creek ran over, growling from the other side a minute later.

His target finally dropped their bow and moved into the moonlight.

That was when Raven realized the person he was after was not who he had envisioned them to be at all. It was definitely no man.

"You shouldn't be here," she said.

Raven lowered his rifle slightly and took a step toward her.

She didn't answer, instead staring at him with eyes radiating anger, even in the dim moonlight. If he added two years to the pictures Joanne had given him, then he could almost recognize the once innocent young woman now hiding behind those spiteful eyes and the long hair. She was dressed in animal hides and pieces of a tarp that had been cut and fashioned into clothes.

"Lara?" he asked, taking his finger off the trigger. "Lara Lithgow?"

She suddenly stiffened.

"Your grandmother hired me to find you," Raven said. "To find you and your father."

At that, Lara looked away for a moment, back down the slope toward the burial site Raven had uncovered.

Apparently, he had already found her father.

Of course.

If he had peeled back that shroud, he would have almost certainly seen the distinctly aquiline nose and light brown hair of Richard Lithgow.

"How do I know my grandma hired you?" she asked, tensing again. She looked like a frightened doe ready to spring into the woods.

"I wouldn't know your name and where to find you if she hadn't," Raven said.

"I thought she..."

Raven waited for her to finish the thought, but Lara remained silent.

"Your grandma sent up other search parties, but my guess is they took her money and never searched very hard," Raven said.

He approached cautiously, lowering his rifle completely now. He was close enough he could see a wet sheen glimmer in the girl's eyes.

"You've been up here all this time?" he asked.

"I thought everyone forgot about us."

"Your grandmother never did," Raven said. "I think she spent every last dime she had trying to find you and your father."

Guilt suddenly ate at the back of his mind for taking the woman's money.

He'd deal with that later.

"I tried leaving here with my dad after everything collapsed," she said, "but we got sick and... We came back, trying to survive until he got better. He never quite got well enough to leave the mountain, and with all those dangerous people out there..."

"I'm sorry. I'm sure it's been hell."

"*I* tried to leave again, but there are men in these mountains. Evil men. With guns and vehicles and... all I have is a bow."

"I know, but I'm not one of them."

She took a step back. Her arm shook like she was about to raise the bow again. He also noted the roughly carved stone dagger jutting from a belt that looked to be made from handmade leather.

"How do I know that?" she asked.

Creek let out a growl as the howl of a wolf pierced the night.

"I know you don't trust me, but I'm here to help you," Raven said. "Come with me. I promise I'll get you back to your grandma safely."

She hesitated, glancing back down at the burial site again. "What about my dad? I can't leave him there."

Raven had a feeling that was why she had attacked him. She had been protecting her father's spirit, which meant she'd been the one to make that burial scaffold.

"You're Sioux?" he asked.

"On my mother's side."

Raven put a hand over his chest. "I'm half Sioux and half Cherokee, actually. Your father's spirit will find his way. But I can tell you that his spirit won't want to leave this earth if his girl is killed on this mountain."

Lara seemed to think about it for a second. "Fine. But I have a few things I need first."

"Sorry, but I'm not sure I want you going back in that hole of yours." Raven figured if he let her out of his sight, she'd run. And this time, she wouldn't be found so easily.

She shook her head. "That's not my camp. I just use it to hide sometimes. My stuff is somewhere else."

"All right." Raven held her gaze. "Just stay close."

She went to pick up her bow, but he shook his head.

"I'll carry that," he said.

Lara paused again, then turned to Raven.

"I'm sorry for shooting you," she said. "It's just... I thought you were another one of those men."

He grunted.

She reached down to her bow.

"Easy," he said.

"I'm not going to nock an arrow," she said.

The weapon looked crude but appeared to be carved from an ash tree. The string was definitely the sinew of an animal.

"Please don't take it," she said.

Raven thought on it and then nodded. "All right. But please don't make me regret this."

She slung the bow over her back and walked up to Raven. Creek followed, tail wagging.

"Your mother must've taught you a lot about our heritage, huh?" he asked as they trudged from the river and into the trees. Maybe if he kept her talking, she'd let down her defenses and trust him a bit more.

"My dad liked to take me camping, but my mom was the one that taught me about nature," she said. Her voice was weak and hollow, like she wasn't used to speaking to another person. "She showed me how to survive off the land, and my dad taught me how to survive."

They walked the rest of the way to her camp in silence. It was so well-camouflaged, with branches and leaves covering everything from a small firepit to scavenged camping supplies and two sleeping bags. One must have been her father's. He felt another pang of sympathy.

Around the firepit, Raven noticed tools made of animal bones.

She gathered up a few of her belongings and put them in a dirty hiking pack that she slung over her shoulders.

"Are we walking all the way back to the Front Range?" she asked, fear visible across her face.

"I've got a Jeep parked not far," he replied. "It'll just be a couple hours walk."

Together they started down the side of the mountain with Creek leading. The howls of the wolves drifted in the still night air.

"Have the wolves been here long?" he asked Lara, in part to keep her mind off running away.

"Sure, but they don't bother me," she said. "I think their spirits know who I am. They leave me alone."

Raven didn't doubt that, and he wasn't particularly worried about the animals coming after him or Lara, but he kept a close eye on Creek.

As they hiked, Raven noticed Lara looking at his neck.

"What?" he asked.

"You're bleeding through your bandage."

"It's fine."

"Fine until you get an infection." She could hardly meet

his gaze when he looked at her. "My mom always said you should clean a wound immediately."

"Who was sent to rescue whom?"

She snorted, and Raven thought he had even drawn the tiniest hint of a smile from the frightened kid for the briefest moment.

"Come on. Let me have a look," she said. "After all, it's my fault."

Raven decided maybe it wasn't a bad idea, so long as she wasn't trying to trick him again. He paused and knelt, keeping an eye on the knife at her belt. "I've got some bandages and—"

"No need." She was already scrounging through her pack. She withdrew a small pouch filled with a poultice of leaves and flowers. The smell was extremely fragrant and familiar.

"Yarrow?" Raven asked as he pulled back the bandage.

"That's right." Lara rubbed it on his wound.

It was supposed to help stop excess bleeding and clot the blood. Sure enough, the oozing blood began to coagulate.

"I mixed it with prickly pear cactus too, to help stop any infections," she added.

The cactus was native to the drier parts of the mountain and could be used as an antiseptic.

"Your mother taught you very well," Raven said. "And your dad too."

"I miss them very much," Lara said quietly, almost dreamily.

The distant howls of the wolves almost became a welcome background melody, during the trek.

Raven could hardly believe his luck. Finally, he was returning with good news for a family. Someone who was alive.

It was a miracle.

"You know how I can tell you're a good person?" Lara asked after a while.

"How's that?" Raven asked.

She pointed to Creek, who was bounding through the underbrush.

"Your dog," she said. "He looks happy and well-fed, even though he's missing that eye. Most of the guys up in these mountains with dogs don't take care of them like you do. A person who treats an animal well is probably a good person."

Raven smiled.

Creek had helped him again without even knowing it.

———

Calvin was lying down on his bunk in the SR Supply Car, trying to keep his eyes closed. He wiped the sweat off his forehead with a sleeve.

The hot, humid summer air was nearly suffocating, making sleep difficult. It didn't help that Travis snored like an eighty-year-old man in the adjacent bunk. Nor did the fact they were sleeping next to the kitchen.

The cook, a bearded man named Zach, turned toward him, his bald head glistening with sweat, illuminated by the glow from the oven and stove. The smell of a salty stew drifted from a pair of massive pots. He was surrounded by crates of food and ammunition that lined the car's walls. There was a small space between the supplies where the train's comm officer, a woman in her early thirties, worked at a radio.

Calvin nodded at the cook.

"Can't sleep?" Zach asked.

"It's the heat."

"Don't I know it."

Zach used a sleeve to wipe his brow before turning back to the stove.

Calvin climbed up a ladder in the center of the car. He opened a hatch that led to the nest and took in a breath of fresh air.

"Yo, Boss," Mouse said. "Didn't think my shift was up."

Mouse stood at the side of the thigh-high steel wall on top of the train car. Anna was there too, on watch. She stared off over the darkened landscape. Pinpricks of light winked across the fields from fireflies.

"It isn't," Calvin said. "Just got tired of listening to Travis's snoring and dealing with all the fire of Hades down there."

"You know Hades is the god of the Underworld," Anna said. "He isn't like another name for Hell or something."

"Thank you, Miss Jeopardy," Calvin said as he settled against one of the nest walls.

"My pleasure," she said. "It's a small token of my gratitude for putting me on a sleep shift with Mouse instead of Travis, who sounds like a shitty chainsaw."

"Ahem." Mouse cleared his throat. "Much as I like seeing you try to dress down the boss, Hades *can* be another name for Hades. So I should get the points for this one. Not Anna."

Anna rolled her eyes. "Oh, you can go straight to Hades then."

Calvin chuckled, then moved over to look at the gentle blink of the fireflies across the black. "That view almost makes you forget the world is going to shit."

"Almost, huh?" Mouse asked.

Anna settled into her spot at the wall again.

For a few moments, they all just sat in silence. It was especially unusual for Mouse to be quiet. To the guy's credit, he knew when that was needed.

Back when they'd been serving together, Calvin's mom had passed away while they were on leave. He didn't expect Mouse to show up to the funeral. The guy only had a few days with his wife and daughter before they were supposed to roll out to Afghanistan again.

But sure enough, Mouse was there in Baltimore, having flown straight from San Diego. In his SEAL dress uniform, he stuck out like a sore thumb amid the other native Baltimoreans attending from Calvin's childhood neighborhood.

After the service, they'd gone back to Calvin's mom's place. It was just like when Calvin had grown up there. A half-working TV, a couch with a protective lace sheet, and a refrigerator full of Natty Boh beer, the local cheap brew. He took out two cans and tossed one to Mouse. They exchanged a few words, but mostly, Mouse just sat with him.

He wasn't sure if Mouse truly knew what that day meant to him.

"Almost back in my stomping grounds," Anna said, breaking the silence.

Calvin didn't need to check his GPS. He had this route practically memorized. They were almost in Iowa.

With the moonlight, Calvin could vaguely make out the rolling plains filled with crops.

"So good to see a decent crop," Mouse said.

"Do you know what looks decent?" Anna asked. "'Cause that isn't it. Soil is still shit from the toxic rain after the Collapse."

Mouse shrugged his huge shoulders. "Looks okay to me."

The fireflies continued to flicker over gently swaying cornfields. Interspersed between those were vast fields of soybeans.

In the warm air, Calvin smelled something else. Something that made his nose wrinkle. "Damn, Mouse, is that you?"

Mouse let out a rough guffaw. "I'd tell you if it was. Iowa was known for their pigs before the Collapse, right? Guess pork's back on the menu."

"Are you telling me that's *all* from a pig farm?" Anna asked.

"You don't believe me?" Mouse lifted his rifle up to his shoulder and stared through the scope. "Let's see. If you look just over there, you'll see the—"

He stopped midsentence. All the casual humor in his voice disappeared. His posture went rigid.

Calvin's exhaustion vanished in a second.

Mouse's seriousness reminded him of when they'd been riding through the Helmand province, and the big guy had spotted a Taliban fighter settling into a sniping position.

His quick reaction and even better perception had saved a life or two.

"What's wrong?" Calvin asked.

"No fireflies in that field over there," Mouse said. "The soybean plants are moving like a storm wind was cutting through them. Fast-like. Not the slow way all the others are going back and forth, know what I mean?"

Calvin thought he had scoped in on where Mouse was indicating, but he didn't see anything. "All I got is blackness. Am I—"

A spark lit up in the night. If he hadn't been zoomed in on the spot, he might've even thought it was nothing but a bright firefly.

But he knew better.

"Down!" he yelled.

Mouse threw himself flat in their nest, and Calvin pulled

Anna to the floor. The staccato rattle of bullets hitting the side of the steel wall erupted with a violent intensity.

Calvin snagged a radio from his pack lying against one of the nest's short walls. "Sierra Romeos, this is Sierra Romeo One. Taking fire. Keep all heads down. If it's just snipers, we can outrun them."

The acknowledgements came back frightened and terse. No one else seemed to have expected the sudden attack in the middle of the farmlands either.

More incoming fire slammed into the side of the train with a metallic din.

"Angel Line Engineer, Sierra Romeo One," Calvin called to the train's operator. "I have all Sierra Romeos in defensive positions."

"Copy that, Sierra Romeo One," the engineer called back. "We're going full ahead. We'll skip past these guys, no problem."

"What if they got explosives?" Anna said, her voice raised to be heard over the train engine.

"Just hang on for now!" Calvin said.

"The hell is going on?" Travis asked, climbing out of the hatch.

"Get your weapon close, and just stay low," Calvin called to him.

He felt the train speeding up. Often, their best defense was to keep on moving. That didn't always work well in areas with torturous curves or filled with IEDs, but right now, they had no choice but to run.

Gunfire filled the night with incessant cracks. It wasn't all coming from the cover of the fields, though.

Calvin risked a glance back down the length of the train.

While bullets sparked against the side of the train, the

flare of gunfire burst back in response to their invisible attackers. Rifles barked from several nests.

"Frigging rookies," Mouse bellowed, following Calvin's eyes.

"Hold your damn fire!" Calvin yelled over the open comm channel.

Most of the Steel Runners weren't as experienced at engaging in firefights. They didn't have the mind for ammo conservation. They just pulled their trigger whenever they were spooked, unloading dozens of rounds a minute at unseen targets.

Might as well have been firing at ghosts.

The gunfire lancing into the side of the train was erratic at best.

He fought the adrenaline plunging through his blood vessels, telling him his only options were fight or flight.

Most of the Steel Runners were giving in to those instincts.

But not him or Mouse.

They chose the third option, instilled by years of training to overcome baser human instinct.

Wait, and stay calm.

"All Sierra Romeos, hold your fire!" Calvin yelled over the radio again. "You're just wasting ammo shooting at an enemy we can't see."

This time, they followed his instructions.

Calvin listened to the enemy fire now that his teams had stopped shooting.

Judging by the volume of gunfire, he guessed there were at least a couple dozen people spread between the fields.

"This place is supposed to be safe!" Anna yelled between shots.

Travis was holding on tight to his rifle with one hand and

his White Sox cap with his other, frightened by Anna's statement.

Anna was right. Something was wrong. They weren't used to attacks out here.

Not in these numbers, especially.

Usually, an attack like this was coupled with an IED blast derailing the train first.

So what was the point of this assault? Were they just trying to pick off Steel Runners?

Calvin didn't much like that idea.

The gunfire continued to grow in intensity as they passed more scattered snipers. Rounds smacked into the train's armor, pinging off in ricocheting blasts. He peeked over the side of the wall again. Most of the sparking gunfire seemed aimed at the slots in the sides of the SR Cars or at the openings the turret gunners used.

These people were definitely after the Steel Runner blood.

But if his people just kept their heads down, they should be okay.

Then came the sudden flare of fire closer to the train.

The brief light was enough to reveal two men near the tracks as they lit what appeared to be a Molotov cocktail.

Shit!

Calvin didn't hesitate. He squeezed the trigger, sending gunfire lancing into the man with the bottle. The man fell, and the bottle cracked against the ground. It shattered, spreading flames around the edge of the field as the train shot past.

"Sierra Romeos, they're using Molotov cocktails!" Calvin called over the radio. "Fire at anyone using one!"

All throughout the darkness in front of the train and beside it, more fire blossomed to life. Molotov cocktails flew at the armored hull, flames licking over the steel. Most of them burst harmlessly.

Except for one.

He watched almost as if in slow motion as one of the improvised weapons was lobbed into SR Car 10, just nine cars back from the SR Supply Car. Fire splashed across the deck of the nest, erupting up past the steel walls. Screams pierced the gunfire and the rumble of the train engine.

"Oh, shit," Calvin said. The flames weren't going out on their own, catching on the wooden deck of the nest's flooring. They would burn the Steel Runners in the nest or force them out into incoming fire.

He could already picture the four Steel Runners trapped there. Redbeard, Maggie, Otto, and Sean.

Any of them trapped inside might be asphyxiated by smoke beneath the fiery roof.

Calvin knew exactly what to do.

He swung down into the SR Supply Car, through the hatch.

"Fire extinguisher!" he yelled at Zach.

The cook took a second to respond, then unlatched the extinguisher near the oven and gave it to Calvin.

Slinging it under one arm, Calvin lunged back atop the train.

"Cover me!" he yelled. "But stay put!"

"Boss!" Mouse shouted.

Calvin ignored him as the trio began firing at their faceless enemies. He wasn't sure how much good the cover fire would do when they could barely pinpoint the snipers, but at least the train was moving quickly.

He prayed he'd be a small target.

Sprinting at the rear wall of the nest, he focused only on his own speed. He hurled himself over the wall, then landed and ran across the next boxcar. He had eight more cars to go. The gunfire might have finally started to weaken, but the flames on SR Car 10 continued to spread.

The screams of someone in horrible pain erupted from the fire.

Calvin sprinted and jumped again. Over and over, he ran and jumped until he made it onto the burning nest.

Flames licked up at him, catching on his jacket. Black smoke threatened to choke him as he pulled the pin to the fire extinguisher, then sprayed white foam over the deck, pushing against the conflagration. The foam smothered the fire, revealing two Steel Runners whose skin was blistered and red, their eyes closed. Sean and Otto.

Calvin ran to each, checking their pulses. Neither had one.

Fuck.

He used his gloves to yank open the hot metal hatch to get inside the car. Most of the deck boards had been burned but didn't seem to have fallen through into the car yet. When he opened the hatch, black smoke billowed out.

He pulled his shirt up over his nose, coughing into it.

"Anyone down there?" Calvin shouted.

Maggie and Redbeard should be down here, assuming they were still alive.

Someone coughed in the smoke.

"To me!" Calvin yelled. When no one came, he dropped into the hazy car. "Follow my voice!"

Someone lurched through the darkness toward him, coughing. It was a woman. Maggie, he realized. He guided her toward the ladder and made sure she was headed up.

If his memory served correct, the last person in this train would've been Redbeard, the crotchety old Steel Runner with the eponymous facial hair.

"Redbeard?" Calvin called into the smoke. It was beginning to clear, but it still scratched at his throat.

He pushed through the smoke until he saw a limp form at the corner.

Rushing to the man's side, he felt Redbeard's wrist for a pulse. This time, he felt a gentle thump.

The man was alive. For now.

"We got to get out of here!" Calvin yelled. He prodded Redbeard, dragging him toward the ladder where the smoke was beginning to clear.

The large man began to cough.

"Up, brother, up!" Calvin called. "You need air."

Finally, Redbeard opened his eyes. He apparently understood just enough to clumsily grasp the ladder and start pulling himself up. Calvin steadied him from behind, pushing him until they were both outside, coughing next to Maggie.

All three of them leaned against the side of the nest, sitting on the charred deck. Mouse was nearby, chest heaving, next to the two downed men.

"Sean and Otto," he said between gasps. "They're both... They're both..."

Calvin fought a pang in his gut as he looked over at the two burned bodies. Sean and Otto, both just in their mid-twenties, were dead.

Maggie began to cry. Redbeard simply stared into the darkness, coughing.

It was then Calvin realized the gunshots had stopped. He slowly raised his radio to his mouth.

"Sierra Romeos," he managed to say, his throat scratchy. "Status report."

In came the calls from the other cars. Two more Steel Runners had died. Another eleven in addition to Redbeard and Maggie were injured. A mixture of burns and even a couple unlucky bullet wounds.

Calvin issued orders based on the info, making sure the medics stationed at various SR Cars were headed to the men and women that needed their help the most.

"Is it over?" Redbeard asked.

Calvin looked out into the fields and brought the radio back up.

"Everyone, stay alert," he said.

He kept his rifle up, anticipating an IED or more gunfire, but it seemed the attack was done.

"What do you think?" Mouse asked.

Calvin wasn't sure what to think.

An attack like this outside of the Badlands was nearly unheard of, especially one as fierce as this.

"Why not go after the cars?" Mouse asked. "I don't get it."

Calvin replayed the attack, from the snipers to the Molotov cocktails.

"They're trying to thin us down," Calvin muttered.

He looked back out into the now calm darkness.

Fireflies once again had reclaimed the night. He stared to the west, shuddering to think what hell awaited them when they entered the unforgiving mountains of Colorado. His only hope was that he could at least make a call to the Steel Runners' Union. Maybe they would send some extra help to get them through the mountains.

If not, then Calvin and his crew would be on their own against God only knew what kind of forces.

-5-

THE NIGHT AIR GREW CHILLIER AS RAVEN AND LARA hiked back to his Jeep. Creek continued to sniff at the wind, guiding them cautiously between the trees and boulders. Every time Raven looked back at Lara to make sure she was following him okay, she avoided his gaze.

"You doing okay?" he whispered.

She nodded.

Even in the dim moonlight, the dirt smeared over her face was visible. She smelled awful too, but he didn't exactly smell like roses either.

He still couldn't believe how long she had survived out there. The stories she had were probably remarkable, but he wasn't pushing for any.

He looked forward to reuniting her with Joanne, an occurrence that was far and few between nowadays. The last thing he wanted was for her to bolt from him in fear.

"Almost there," he said.

They passed through a few more patches of trees, climbing down an incline toward the road. Just as they came around another boulder, Creek grew still, his tail curling between his legs. He let out a soft growl.

Raven motioned for Lara to stay still. Had some thieves found his Jeep? He had taken every precaution, but the vehicle wasn't invisible.

Slowly, he slipped his rifle from his back and drew it up to his shoulder. Then he peeked around the boulder, peering through his scope.

Moonlight glinted off the bits of glass and metal showing through the branches and netting he'd draped over his Jeep.

Sure enough, he heard footsteps in the pine needles and gravel. He sucked in a breath and pressed himself tight against the rock.

The crunching continued, and he drew his aim toward the source of the sound as a shape stalked out of the obsidian darkness, growling.

Creek, who was somewhere in the forest behind Raven and Lara, growled back.

Raven aimed his rifle at the wolf, his heart pounding. He could practically see the ripple of its muscles as it stalked forward, its fur undulating gently with each precise movement.

Two more wolves curled down the road, baring their fangs.

Raven kept his rifle on the lead wolf, the biggest of the trio. Lara stayed calm as he jerked his chin for her to get behind with Creek.

The beast in front of them froze.

"Brother Wolf, I don't want to harm you, but I won't let you hurt my dog," he said.

Creek trotted up behind Raven as the wolves studied them.

"Go, get out of here," he said, jerking his rifle barrel.

After just a couple seconds, the lead wolf turned and casually walked into the woods. The others bolted after it, disappearing into the brush.

"They're after Creek," Raven said.

"No," Lara replied. "They're protecting us. If they wanted to kill your dog, they would have."

Raven kept silent as they continued to the Jeep, watching the forest for the creatures.

He peeled off the branches and netting, then opened the passenger door. Creek hopped in, sneaking to the back seat, safe now.

Raven motioned for Lara to get into the passenger seat. She hesitated, looking at him suspiciously.

"It's okay," Raven said. "I'm taking you home."

She finally climbed inside. When he hopped in, he noticed she had left muddy prints on the floor. The grime coating her clothes smeared across her seat. She tossed her dirty gear into the footwell.

Raven cringed, wanting to tell her to be careful, but decided against it.

"What?" she asked.

Raven forced a smile as he inserted the key in the ignition. "Nothing."

The engine started with a low growl. He pulled onto the highway, watching for hostiles. Sometimes the most dangerous moments getting into and out of the Badlands was driving down these open roads.

Lara seemed to know that from experience. She stared out the windows, looking even more shaken up than before.

Whatever she had seen out here had left some permanent mental scars.

Raven took the Jeep out onto the asphalt. They started the long drive out of the mountains.

For the first fifteen minutes, they sat in silence. Although he wanted to ask her questions, he still feared he would upset her.

Finally, after another thirty minutes passed, he decided to break the silence.

"Can I ask why you and your father never made it back to Estes Park?" Raven tried. "You said he got sick. Was that it?"

Lara was quiet for a moment.

"If you don't want to—" he started.

"I just never talked to anyone about this." She shook her head. "It's... It's..."

Raven thought he'd pushed his luck. She let out a quiet sob.

"We didn't know what happened in those first days. The explosion in the sky. Our cellphones stopped working. Our car wouldn't start... and then... then when we were prepared to start heading back, the wildfires were everywhere."

"I remember those fires. Those first few days were just chaos."

"We were cut off from everything."

Lara shivered, and Raven knew it wasn't from the cold night air.

"After a few weeks, we found some people we thought would help us. A group of men that... they had guns," she continued. "They took everything from us. Everything."

She pressed her hands to her eyes.

Raven didn't push it. He wasn't quite sure what she meant.

She looked out the window, brushing away a tear.

"We came across a dead deer," Lara started again. "It looked like it had broken its ankle. That's how I got the stuff to make my bow, and when we ate it... well, it wasn't any good. It made my dad violently ill. I tried everything my mom taught me, but he was sick for weeks. Dysentery, I guess. He wanted me to go back to Estes Park alone. But I knew if I left him, he would die."

"Is that how...?" Raven let his words trail off.

"No, eventually, he got better, but he was still so weak." The words were coming out a mile a minute now. Like she'd been storing all this up and just waiting for an emotional release. "It took months before he could even walk a mile without collapsing. We wanted to try hiking out to see if there was anything left beyond the mountains. I don't really even know how much time passed."

She started to cry, sniffling.

"No, you did everything you could," Raven said. "Nothing you could have done would have saved him."

She shook. Not in sadness but anger this time. Raven could see her fists balled up, her tears tracing over her wrinkled nose.

They took a curve in the road, quiet for a few moments. He kept his headlights off, still using the moon to guide their way. The rumble of the engine would be loud enough to attract any attention nearby, but the lights would be a dead giveaway.

"My dad thought it was better if we stayed put for a few months anyway." She spoke more calmly now. "He always said the best thing you could do when you were lost was stay put. That you were more likely to be found, and he started to get stronger. He told me that if all the rumors we'd heard were true, if civilization really did collapse, the most dangerous place we could be was back near the cities and towns. He wanted to protect me, and he said the wilderness was where he could do that. I think by then, he'd just given up on us ever trying to make it to Estes Park."

She slammed a fist against the door.

"But he was wrong! Some men found us when we were out hunting again," she said. "He got shot trying to protect me. I got away, but I couldn't... he couldn't..."

She broke down again, crying, her face in her palms.

"I got away, and when I came back, he was dead," she whispered.

"I'm so sorry," Raven said.

"You said other people came to look for us."

"Yeah, your grandma sent them."

"Well, if they actually made it here when she sent them, he would still be alive, and I wouldn't be—"

She suddenly stopped.

Raven glanced over to find her staring at the side mirror.

"I think... I think someone's following us," she said quietly.

Raven glanced in the rearview mirror.

Sure enough, moonlight reflected off the windshield of another vehicle, far behind them. He couldn't quite make out whether it was a truck or SUV, especially since they seemed to be a good two hundred or so yards back with their headlights off.

"Hold on," he said.

The engine roared louder as he pressed the pedal to the floor, accelerating down Trough Road. He could barely see the road ahead, but he kept his headlights off. The abandoned vehicles left on the mountain roads had mostly been pushed off to the side of the road over the past two years, giving him a clean route. His heart thudded in his chest with every speeding curve, and his palms grew sweaty on the wheel. Creek whined in the backseat.

The vehicle behind him turned on their brights. The light glared into his rearview mirror and temporarily blinded him. He pushed up the rearview mirror, blinking as his eyes adjusted. Besides the danger of running into an abandoned vehicle, the roads had gone into disrepair. Potholes and cracks pocked the asphalt.

Now that their pursuers had spotted him, there was no point in *not* using his own headlights to see better. He flicked them on.

They took another sharp turn down Trough Road around San Toy Mountain. Soon enough, they would hit Highway 9 and he would be able to rocket away.

The vehicle accelerated after them.

Raven took out his Sig Sauer from his holster, placing it on the console between him and Lara.

"Can you shoot?" he asked.

"Of course," she said. "My dad taught me. He took me target shooting, hunting, and—"

"Got it," he said, concentrating on the road.

The more important question might've been if he trusted her to shoot.

"I'm going to try to outrun them," he said. "Just stay down."

Trees and rocks flashed by as he pressed the pedal to the floor. Still, the vehicle behind them kept up. He curved hard around another bend in the road, inertia threatening to tip the Jeep. Rubber squealed against asphalt. His heart thundered.

"Son of a..." Raven said.

The road straightened, and he took a ramp onto the highway.

A sudden crack and boom filled the vehicle. It took a second to realize a bullet had pierced the rear windshield. More rounds lanced into the metal, pinging and clanging as they punched into the Jeep.

A few bullets seared past Raven and speared through the front windshield.

"Keep down!" Raven said.

But instead of listening, Lara already had the passenger window rolled down. She scooped up the Sig Sauer and started firing back at their pursuers.

"Lara, careful!" he yelled over the blasts of gunfire.

She didn't hear him or ignored him as she kept firing.

Suddenly, the vehicle chasing them swerved back and forth before jerking hard to the left. It slammed into the guardrail and flipped. Sparks flew as the roof scraped over concrete, wheels spinning, and headlights spearing off into the darkness.

"Holy shit," Raven mumbled.

He couldn't believe the girl had hit the driver.

She was back inside now.

"Sorry about your Jeep," Lara said.

"Glass and leather can be patched up," he said. "Patching up a person isn't so easy. You okay?"

She nodded.

"Now I know how you survived out there." Raven was hardly able to believe what had just happened. "Thanks... you are a heck of a shot."

For the first time, she actually cracked a genuine smile.

———

Lindsey sat at her desk in the office at Fort Golden, stirring sugar into her coffee. It was only nine in the morning, but this was her second cup. From the stack of reports sitting on her desk, she was probably going to need a third.

Maybe with some whiskey this time.

She had become an LEO to protect and serve the public, not to sign and send an endless stream of documents. Everyone told her being an LEO would be demanding. But no one told incoming cadets the sheer mountain of paperwork they had to climb—especially when they took leadership positions.

One document this morning had piqued her interest. It was a wire from the official Steel Runners' Union. She didn't usually get memos or letters from the Union. At least, not when things were going smoothly.

Lindsey took a deep breath and stared at it, knowing whatever it said wasn't good.

She opened it and read it quickly.

Apparently, an incoming Angel Line train had been hit by a surprise attack in Iowa.

Of all places, Iowa?

The Midwest had largely been free from train attacks.

Not this week, apparently.

Four Steel Runners had died, and another thirteen were injured. From the report, they would have to disembark at Denver for medical treatment. If the injured couldn't continue their journey, that meant potentially seventeen less Steel Runners to protect the train through the most dangerous part of its travel: the Rocky Mountains.

At the end of the wire, the Steel Runners' Union was requesting help from the Colorado Rangers. They wanted additional protection to ensure the train made it safely across the border to Utah, where the train could travel in relative safety again.

Most importantly, the Union had received a radio call from their Iron Lead, a man named Calvin Jackson.

Calvin hypothesized the attack in Iowa was meant to soften up the Steel Runners' numbers. He feared that this might precede a much larger attack in the Badlands.

Steel Runners didn't usually ask for help. So if they were requesting aid now, that meant either they were hurting or they were actually frightened. Problem was, Lindsey didn't have a ton of muscle to spare.

She considered her options, deciding the right thing to do was answer the call for help.

She read the request slower this time.

On top of reinforcements, they had asked for scouts to check the tracks for IEDs or ambush sites.

Lindsey placed the wire down on her desk.

What they really needed was Raven Spears.

While she hadn't called on his help in months, now might finally be the time. He knew the mountains—and most importantly, the current threats lurking in those mountains—better than anyone.

Someone knocked on her door.

"Come in," she said, looking up from the papers scattered over her desk.

Palmer strode inside, aviators on top of his shaved head. He pulled his sleeves up over the patriotic ink on his arms. That meant he was nervous.

"Mornin', ma'am," he said.

"Morning," she replied. "I'm guessing you didn't come by for an early gossip session. You heard about the attack on the Angel Line too?"

He sat and leaned back in the chair in front of her desk, folding his arms behind his head. "Sure as hell did. You think these assholes are people from our neck of the woods leaking out?"

"Wish I knew, but I can't imagine you're wrong." She pulled out a printout on her desk. "I need you to see if we can scrounge up any available contract Steel Runners in town. The incoming line took some casualties, and they'll need reinforcements."

"Okay."

"Once they get to Denver, they're going to have to take out a few cars damaged by fire too. We're going to need a medical team standing by. As the Steel Runners get treated and we work on the train, that'll be our chance to scout the tracks and figure out some better defensive measures."

"You know who's good at scouting out those mountains."

"You don't need to say it," Lindsey said.

"Your old boyfriend, Crow."

"My old boyfriend? What are we, in middle school?"

He pulled his hands away from his head. "Sorry, ma'am."

"Relax. And his name is Raven. Don't let him hear you screw that up. Alright, *Pamela?*"

Palmer straightened in his chair with a smirk. "Knew it was some kind of bird, sorry."

She looked back down at her desk and the piles of paperwork.

"I'm also going to need you to help me with the Foreign Advisory Council," she said. "I want them to deploy some of their peacekeeping troops in a convoy to watch out for the Angel Line."

"How do you expect me to do that? They seem happy to hide in their outposts."

"I've already asked and explained how important that cargo is; your job is to make sure everyone understands the security will be top-notch and there is little threat to their people."

Palmer scratched at his chin.

"We have to make sure no one is hurt, or those peace-keepers will be going right back into their safe outposts."

"Understood. I will make sure security is top-notch."

"Good, is there something else?" she asked. "You seem worried."

"I'm sure it's nothing, but I was doing my daily rounds at

the clinics. You know, checking to see if any Badlanders wandered in with gunshot wounds or something so we could question them."

That was yet another report Lindsey usually had to review. Intel they squeezed out of the outlaws who were so desperate they came to the Front Range for medical treatment.

"Yeah, and?" She picked up her coffee.

Palmer leaned forward, growing stern. "Sure enough, a couple sick people wandered in from the New Frontier. Very sick people."

"Sick with what?" Lindsey set her coffee back down without drinking any.

"Don't know."

They'd had their fair share of health scares during the recovery. Cholera and typhoid had run rampant through the population, especially when the country was having a hard time supplying people with fresh, clean water and reliable power.

In much of Colorado, they *still* didn't have reliable power, and the water supply wasn't what it was prior to the Collapse. So, if another disease outbreak threatened to take her state, she wanted to stay ahead of it.

She looked through the pile of papers but didn't find any reports. "I've got nothing on this at all."

"I'm sure you'll be hearing something soon," Palmer said. "The doctors were all concerned. I even saw one wearing a hazmat suit."

She stood and started heading toward the door. "If the docs are concerned, I don't want to wait. Let's go see now."

Palmer stood and pulled on his sleeves again.

Now she knew what had him so nervous.

They were in her dusty white Ford Bronco headed toward the Golden clinic in just under five minutes.

Public health issues weren't actually under the umbrella of the Colorado Rangers Sheriff's office, but Lindsey liked to stay involved in anything that might affect the security of her state. Much to the annoyance of the clinic's doctors and other government workers within her reach, that meant she liked regular reports from them.

"I sure hope this isn't cholera," Palmer said. "We haven't had an outbreak in months."

"That's why this worries me, but it was just a matter of time," Lindsey said.

"Yeah, until we get the power restored, clean water, and hospitals set up again in the New Frontier, all these diseases that keep popping up are like a cancer that keeps eating us up from the inside."

Lindsey agreed with a nod.

Hopefully, what Palmer had seen was nothing more than a couple bad cases of dysentery or some lingering radiation poisoning. Maybe that was why the doctors hadn't said anything to her yet.

She pulled up outside the small medical facility. Upon entering the lobby, a young nurse greeted her from behind an intake desk. She recognized the nurse, Mary, from her relatively frequent visits to the clinic.

"I'm looking for Doctor Divekar," she said. The staff didn't seem to be panicking or setting up any kind of isolation unit. Maybe it was Palmer that had overreacted.

"Of course, follow me."

Mary led Lindsey and Palmer through the hall until they reached the doctor.

"Doctor Divekar, Sheriff Plymouth is here to see you," Mary said, before disappearing back down the hall.

A shorter woman in a white coat looked up at Lindsey. She had dark black hair tied up behind her head and deep brown eyes set behind round, perennially cheerful features that belied her usually sour mood. "Sheriff Plymouth, I wasn't expecting you."

"I know. Sorry to drop in, but Palmer said he was by earlier and you had some sick patients come in from the New Frontier."

At that, Divekar nodded. "We do... did..."

"Did?"

"I'm working on a report that aligns with our protocols."

"Screw protocols. If these people are already dead, I need to know why and what we're dealing with."

Divekar sighed. "Follow me."

She led Lindsey and Palmer back between the quiet corridors of the clinic toward a back room.

"We got two more patients in since Palmer was here, apparently," Divekar explained. "They had the same symptoms, and we immediately put them in the isolation ward."

She gestured toward a clear glass partition separating a patient room from the corridor. Signs at the closed door reminded the medical staff to use personal protective equipment when checking on the patients.

Lindsey looked past the glass to see two men. Each had skin wrinkled by sun exposure and long, tangled beards. Normally, she expected the men's skin to be leathery and tanned from spending all their time in the mountains.

But these guys looked as pale as the sheets draping their bodies. Sweat poured over their foreheads. A nurse in a full body gown, face shield, and mask appeared to be checking their vitals.

"They drove in about an hour ago," Divekar said. "Well,

one of them did. The other was already passed out in the passenger seat."

Lindsey stepped up for a better look.

"Both have fevers charting anywhere between 102 to 105. Lymph nodes are swollen. A lot of coughing and mucus drainage from both. One of the guys has lesions that may or may not be related to his illness. Either way, they're not responding to any medicine yet."

"Do you know what it is?"

"Not yet. Power's been too unreliable lately for some of our testing here, even with the generators, so we sent our labs down to Denver for processing from the first two victims."

"No guesses?" Lindsey asked. "A sudden onset illness like this worries me, especially with your nurse in a bunny suit."

"We're not taking any chances. Everyone that treated the first patients without proper PPE is currently in quarantine and being observed."

"Any symptoms yet?"

"Not that I've heard, Sheriff."

Lindsey turned from the window. "You still haven't answered my first question."

"I don't like to make guesses, but if you insist, it could be anything from an unknown viral infection to an influenza variant or even Rocky Mountain spotted fever. We've been trying to treat for bacterial diseases too, like pneumonia, diphtheria, or even Legionnaire's disease, but the patients aren't responding to broad-spectrum antibiotics. Right now, we're just shooting in the dark."

"I see," Lindsey said. She let out a sigh. "Thank you, Doctor. Please, let me know when you do get the lab results back."

"I will."

Divekar stepped away, but Lindsey remained at the

window, watching the nurse work on the patients. Her heart thumped, thinking about one of her Rangers being on the other side of this glass.

"We better get back," Lindsey said. She walked with Palmer back to their Bronco.

"That shit looks pretty bad," he said once they were inside.

Lindsey stared out the windshield at the mountain peaks, growing more concerned by the minute.

Her job was about to get a hell of a lot harder.

First, she had to convince Raven to come down to help her secure the Angel Line route through Colorado and assist the Steel Runners. Second, if these sick men were wandering in here, that meant there could be plenty more out there spreading whatever it was they had contracted.

"When we get back, I want you to make sure we've got a meeting set up with Calvin Jackson, the Iron Lead, as soon as he gets to Denver," Lindsey said. "I'm going north to find Raven."

"Why not just try and get him on the radio?"

"Because I don't want to give him a chance to say no."

6

WITH THE EARLY MORNING SUN AT HIS BACK, RAVEN walked up to the two-story house nestled between the trees in Estes Park with Lara. Creek stayed in the Jeep, sleeping peacefully.

After Raven had taken the initial payment from Joanne Lithgow, he was all but certain he would return here alone, covered in mud, and without a shred of evidence to tell the woman what had happened to her son and granddaughter.

Now, striding up the sidewalk beside him was living proof that he'd succeeded.

He turned to Lara. She ran a hand through her matted, wild hair. The dirt on her face was even more apparent in the daylight.

She was quiet again. While she was tall for sixteen, she slouched, looking like she wanted to disappear.

"Go ahead," Raven said,

"I'm just scared to tell her about... about my dad."

"Don't worry. She's going to be overjoyed just to have you back."

Raven stayed back while Lara sucked in a breath and

went to knock on the door. Two raps later, and a voice called out.

"I'm coming!"

The door whipped open.

Joanne looked first at Raven, a sorrowful expression—the same he'd seen yesterday—painted across her features. From the dark bags under her eyes, it looked like she hadn't been able to sleep.

Her gaze traced from Raven over to Lara.

"Lara, is it really you?"

Tears sprang from Joanne's wrinkle-lined eyes. She walked out and wrapped her thin arms around her grand-daughter.

"Oh, my God. Oh, my God. Sweet Jesus, thank you!" Joanne said.

"I'm sorry, Grandma," Lara began, choking up. "I couldn't... I couldn't save Dad."

"Hush, child... Hush." Joanne held the embrace as she sobbed.

She finally pulled back and looked to Raven. He smiled, a real smile, not one of those forced grins that were habit for him.

"I can't believe it," Joanne said. "Praise the Lord, and thank you, Raven. You're a godsend. A miracle worker."

"My pleasure, ma'am," he replied.

Raven stepped back again as Lara and Joanne continued to embrace.

He felt himself giving in to the moment too.

After all the pain he'd delivered to people for the past couple years, the feeling of joy wasn't one he expected to experience.

When they finally parted, Joanne went over to Raven and reached out for a hug. He gladly accepted. She was strong for a little old lady.

"Wow." She pulled away. "What an amazing gift you've brought me. Come. Let's get you paid up right away."

Raven definitely could use it. Especially with the damage to the Jeep. Fixing those windows would cost a pretty penny. Right now, though, his heart was full. Lara would need her grandmother's care—and they could both no doubt use the money—to ensure she had everything she required to first heal then flourish again.

Joanne certainly didn't come off as wealthy. Those other so-called trackers had swindled enough from her.

"Finding Lara and bringing her home is payment enough," Raven quickly said.

Joanne looked visibly stunned. She held Raven's gaze, then glanced at Lara again. Her mouth moved, but no words came out as if she was struggling to find a way to thank Raven.

Finally, she softly said, "Please, there must be something I can do."

"Take care of Lara," he said. Then he turned and glanced down at the girl. "And you take care of your grandmother."

"I will," Lara said.

Raven nodded. "If you ever need me, you know where to find me."

He started to leave, but Joanne called out, "Wait, really, is there anything I can do? Are you hungry?"

"Honestly, I'm exhausted, ma'am." Raven looked down at his clothes. "And I need a bath and a change."

Lara grinned through her joyful tears. "Me too."

"Maybe we can have dinner sometime," Raven suggested.

"You are more than welcome here any night," Joanne said.

Raven started to leave again but stopped.

"Lara, if you ever want to learn about your Sioux heritage, well, I'm happy to share about that half of myself with you."

He almost couldn't believe he was making the offer. Maybe he was letting the emotions get to him. Then he thought about Lara's dad. How he'd been sick. "Same with my sister, Sandra, too. She's a nurse in town. You might want to drop by the clinic just to have her make sure you're healthy, okay?"

"I will," Lara said. "Thank you."

Raven finally went back to his Jeep. Creek sat upright in the front passenger seat, but then curled back up.

Raven turned on the engine and pulled away, waving out one of his busted windows. Lara and Joanne stayed on the porch, waving as he left.

Seeing these two together had tugged at his heart. He figured he should visit his sister and niece, then clean up at their house.

Since his sister worked all kinds of shifts, she wasn't there to let him into her house, so he used the key she'd given him. It was almost seven in the morning. He didn't want to wake Allie, his eight-year-old niece, so he went to the living room to rest on the couch.

One of Sandra's elderly neighbors, a man named Elmer, was sitting in a recliner, a shotgun propped next to his armchair, also snoozing.

Raven cleared his throat.

Elmer fumbled for the shotgun.

"It's me. Raven."

Blinking, Elmer focused his old brown eyes on Raven. He relaxed back onto the chair.

"Ah, morning, Raven," he said. "I guess I fell asleep."

Raven chuckled. "Guard duty is tough."

Elmer laughed back. He was a gentle, kind man, but Raven knew if shit ever went down, the older man would rip people limb from limb to protect his sister and niece.

"Have a good morning," Elmer said. "I'm gonna go home."

"Thanks for everything you do."

"It's an honor, Raven."

After Elmer left, Raven took a shower, then changed into an extra set of clothes he had upstairs. When he finished, he returned to the living room and sat on the couch.

He put a fresh bandage on his neck before lying down.

The windows were open, letting in the crisp mountain breeze.

While he tried to get some shuteye, the excitement from all that had just happened kept him awake. Creek seemed to have more luck. The dog had stayed upstairs, drifting off at his favorite spot in front of Allie's door.

Raven waited a half hour or so before deciding he was too restless to fit in a nap. Instead, he made coffee and eggs with toast while he waited for his sister to return and for Allie to wake. About halfway through, he heard pounding footsteps come down the steps.

Allie bounded in with Creek at her heels, his tail whipping madly. Her dark hair and tanned skin matched her mother's. Every day, she seemed to look more and more like Sandra.

"Uncle Raven!" She ran toward him.

He gave her a hug and then went back to the gas stove.

"Did you make me some eggs?" Allie asked.

"Nope, I ate all of 'em."

She let out a huff. "Seriously?"

"I'm jokin', kiddo," he said. "How do you want them this morning?"

"Scrambled, please."

"You got it."

He set about cracking eggs and mixing them, then listening to them pop as he poured them into the hot skillet.

"Think I should make some for your mom too?" he asked, looking up at an analog clock on the wall.

"Yeah! She's supposed to be back before I go to school."

"School? It's summer! You don't get summer break?" He added a bit of black pepper to the eggs. Not too much. Everything they had was rationed and precious.

"No, the teachers say we already missed too many days. We have to catch up, I think. Plus, Mom says it helps keep the kids out of trouble."

"But you wouldn't cause any trouble, would you?"

"Not like you used to."

"What's that mean?" Raven asked.

Allie laughed. "You were a troublemaker. Mom told me *all* about it."

The front door to the house opened, and another set of plodding footsteps entered the kitchen.

"Look who it is." Sandra gave him a sly grin. "The troublemaker."

Raven laughed as he plated the eggs.

His sister set her bag down, still dressed in scrubs from her nightshift at the Estes Park clinic. Dark bags hung under her brown eyes, and her black hair was slightly disheveled. Creek trotted over and nudged up against her leg.

"Oh, good, you made coffee," she said.

He handed her a mug.

"Thanks, so what's the occasion and—" She paused, staring at his neck. "Holy... what happened to your neck?"

Raven reached up to the fresh bandage. "Just got back from a mission where the person I was looking for almost killed me."

"Raven!"

"Don't worry. She's okay, and so am I."

"Glad you're fine," Allie said, leaning her head on his shoulder.

For a second, Raven relished the moment. He was sober over two years now and had his family around him. Family that had at one point lost faith in him. Faith he had finally earned back.

"Your luck is going to run out, Sam," Sandra said.

He knew when she called him by his birthname he was in for it.

"I'm really tired, sis..."

"So am I," Sandra growled. "And I don't have much mental space to be worrying about you."

She was right to be worried.

He was lucky to be alive, and luck was a finite resource.

"Look, it's actually a cool story," Raven said. "Have a seat. I'll tell you."

Sandra reluctantly sat with Allie. As they ate, he told them how he had found Lara and brought her home.

"And get this, she has Sioux blood," Raven said. "I told her you and I would be happy to talk to her about, you know, us. She seemed like she could use some friends to help ease her back into this world."

"Sure," Sandra said.

Allie finished her eggs and left to get ready for school, leaving Raven with his sister. Sandra seemed distracted, her eyes glued out the kitchen windows.

"Something else wrong?" Raven asked.

Sandra took another drink of coffee. "We had three new patients from the Badlands come into the clinic yesterday."

"That's not unusual," Raven said.

"These men were all sick. Like nothing we've seen before. We couldn't get them stable. One died before I got off shift."

Raven raised a brow.

"I heard there were cases like this in the Golden clinic too," she continued. "Same with another clinic on the Front Range. All over the past week."

"Cholera again?"

Sandra sighed. "I don't think so. It's not just bullets out there, Sam. Disease is still a major threat."

"Don't worry," he said. "I do my best to stay *away* from people. That includes the sick."

"Yeah, I know."

"Should I be worried about *you* catching whatever this is?"

"I'm taking precautions," Sandra said. "We all are. Everyone's using personal protective equipment again. Masks, gloves, face shields, you name it."

Allie bolted back down the stairs. "I'm ready."

"Good, Raven is going to walk you to school," Sandra said.

"Can Creek come too?" Allie asked.

"He'd be delighted," Raven said.

He took his plate of mostly eaten eggs and slid them onto the ground. Creek wolfed them down in seconds.

"Let's go, kiddo." Raven headed to the front door.

"Wait," Sandra said.

She walked over, a rueful look on her face.

"I'm sorry for being harsh, Raven," Sandra said. "I miss you and worry about you all the time."

"I know. I do the same, but we're strong, and we'll get through anything."

He kissed her on the forehead and then went outside.

Allie followed him onto the porch with Creek. Just as they started down the stairs, a dusty Ford Bronco rolled up the gravel driveway.

He knew that vehicle well.

"Ah, shit," Raven whispered.

"Good timing!" Lindsey Plymouth called as she stepped out of the vehicle.

Bad timing, he thought.

"Hi, Allie," Lindsey said. "How are you doing?"

"Fine," Allie said sheepishly.

"Allie, go play with Creek," Raven said. "I'll be over in a few minutes."

"Okay, but I'm gonna be late if we—"

"I'll drive you."

"Okay."

Allie scampered off with Creek while Raven walked over to the Bronco.

"Lindsey, how you doing?" Raven asked.

"Fine. You look surprisingly good."

"Got my beauty sleep."

Lindsey smiled but didn't hold it for long. Raven knew then she wasn't here to rekindle what they used to have.

"I dropped by your place just a few minutes ago," she said. "Since you weren't there, I figured I'd find you here."

"What happened?"

"A lot. I need your help."

She reached out but stopped short of touching him.

"I got a job," she continued, "and I need someone I can trust. I know things didn't end well for us, but I'm asking because I got nowhere else to turn."

"What's the job?"

Lindsey raised a hand at a window in the cabin where Sandra stood watching. Sandra didn't wave back, but Raven did see her nod before vanishing inside.

"I got to take Allie to school," Raven said. "How about we talk after that?"

Lindsey hesitated, as if she couldn't wait, but finally nodded.

"Okay, but how about I drive?" she asked. "Your Jeep looks worse for wear."

"Yeah..."

After last night, Lindsey wasn't wrong. He didn't have any other work lined up, and after ditching the second half of his payment from Joanne, he'd need money to fix his Jeep.

"Fine," he said. "Let's get going."

———

It was midafternoon when the Angel Line finally made it to Union Station, deep in the heart of half-destroyed Denver. Calvin was in the SR Supply Car watching over some of the injured he, Mouse, Anna, and Travis had transported to the bunks.

Redbeard was lying in Calvin's bunk. The man continued to cough, and the blistering burns over his arms and face had grown more scarlet. They required fresh bandages every couple hours, and they were starting to run out. A middle-aged Steel Runner named Jennifer, with burns running down her arms, was in Mouse's bunk. Travis and Anna had given their bunks up for two more injured Steel Runners who had third-degree burns.

Another Steel Runner, Maggie Olsen, the one Calvin thought he'd saved, had succumbed to her injuries just before entering Denver, after Calvin called in his report to the Union.

She had been a single mother of two, living outside Philly. From what Calvin knew, the woman relied on her neighbors to take care of the kids when she was running steel. Now those kids would be staying with their neighbors permanently.

That meant a total of five Steel Runners had died thanks to those monsters in Iowa. Last Calvin counted, there were another thirteen with injuries, ranging from minor burns and lacerations to smoke inhalation. Six were in such bad shape, they wouldn't be continuing the journey.

After the attack, there had been nowhere they could stop. No safe zone. Calvin feared the attackers would come after them if they paused to treat the injured.

So his best bet to save the Steel Runners had been to get them to Denver, where they would have better access to medical facilities.

As soon as the brakes squealed to a stop and the train jolted into the station, Calvin began barking orders.

"Travis, Anna, help Jennifer off," he said. "Mouse, take Redbeard."

"You got it, Boss," Mouse said. He slipped one big arm around Redbeard's shoulder. Redbeard's eyes seemed glassy, and part of his beard was singed off. "Careful now, buddy."

The older man groaned as he came off the train.

Calvin stepped onto the chaotic loading platform. Medics with Red Cross armbands stood at the edge of the loading platform with gurneys. But there was also work to be done.

Yard workers lined up carts to take off cargo and resupply the train.

"Over here!" Calvin yelled. "I need two gurneys on the Supply Car." Then he pointed to another car. "The rest of you, get your asses down to SR Car 20!"

The medics sprang into action, winding between the other workers and crates lined up on the loading platform. Mouse and the others were already helping their charges walk toward a triage area set up on the end of the loading platform.

"Hurry, hurry," Calvin said, motioning the first paramedics into SR Supply Car. He led them in and showed them two other Steel Runners, who were still groaning in pain in the bunks. Both were covered in gauze that had once again soaked through with blood and pus.

The paramedics began to load Randall Briggs, one of the badly injured Runners, onto a rolling gurney a bit too hard. Randall let out a cry of pain.

"Careful with him," Calvin barked.

Two more paramedics loaded the other Steel Runner, Peter. Calvin grimaced when he saw the expression of pain on his bandaged face.

"Just hold on, brother," Calvin said.

"What about my family?" Peter asked. "They... they..."

"Don't you worry about them," Calvin said. "I'll make sure Sheila and your kids get your check. Bonus too. I'll promise her you're making it home soon. You got that, Peter?"

Peter managed a weak nod as Calvin paused on the loading platform. The rest of the paramedics had already loaded up the other car of injured Runners.

"Need any more help?" Mouse asked, jogging back over to him.

Anna and Travis joined them.

"Yeah." Calvin signaled to another group of paramedics with gurneys and began marching with them toward SR Car 40. On his way, he passed by the Steel Runner car where Redbeard and his group had been. The steel plates on the side of the car were stained with black soot.

"If I was faster, maybe I could've saved them," he muttered.

"I never saw anyone run faster," Mouse said.

"Wasn't fast enough."

When they made it to SR Car 40, Calvin opened the door. The stench of death rolled out. Anna turned and vomited over the concrete. Travis pulled his shirt up over his nose and mouth, his scarred face going pale.

Calvin pushed past the terrible odor inside.

All five of the deceased Steel Runners were lying in bunks, covered in white sheets. The sheets were stained with blood. It physically pained Calvin to see them.

He wanted to curse and scream.

But there was a lesson he'd learned as an officer in the Navy SEALs.

A harsh one.

Any good officer had to suppress their pain when faced with tragedy, because they didn't have the time or luxury of a breakdown. They had to be strong for the others relying on their support and leadership. They had to be the team's anchor, the one preventing everyone else from being blown away in the storm of disaster.

Sometimes it made good officers seem like callous dicks, but Calvin knew the truth. Those officers were just trying to complete the mission. And at night, when they weren't in front of their men, the horror of all they endured came crashing down on them.

"We need to get these bodies to a morgue," Calvin said to the others.

"Sir, we can handle it," one of the paramedics said.

"No, these are my people."

He and the other three Steel Runners helped load the gurneys with the deceased. Then they pushed them all the way back to the triage area. Calvin was sweating by the time they got to the ambulances waiting off the loading dock.

"Make sure you take good care of these people," Calvin ordered. "They deserve honorable burials."

One of the paramedics nodded.

Calvin watched all five bodies until they were loaded into the ambulances. He said a mental prayer, not usually his thing, but for the believers of the group.

"Rest in peace, brothers and sisters," Calvin said aloud.

He turned to Mouse, who had his head bowed.

"Mouse, make sure wires are sent to all their families," Calvin said. "I don't want the Union to hesitate on giving their loved ones their last paychecks and family survivor benefits."

"Consider it done," Mouse said.

"Travis, Anna, if Mouse needs help making calls—"

"We'll take care of it," Anna said. "No problem."

"Good," Calvin said. "I'd do it myself, but I got to go meet with the transit officials now. Sooner we can get this train moving, the sooner the rest of the Steel Runners get to go home."

Calvin strode out and away from Union Station. Each street to the east seemed to be filled with collapsed buildings. Rubble filled the roadways, and half-buried vehicles stuck out under piles of concrete scree.

The sound of hammers, drills, and other power tools echoed as he approached his destination—the scaffold-covered Colorado State Capitol building.

Calvin made his way past a pair of security guards, showing his SR badge. He asked for directions to the office he was looking for and then jogged the rest of the way.

He combed a finger through his hair. Dirt and ash came away on his hand. Nothing he could do about his appearance now. He opened the door and stepped into a small lobby with a reception desk and two chairs.

The door to the connecting conference room was open.

"Hello?" he called out.

"Come in," responded a female voice.

Calvin walked into a large office with wood-paneled walls that gave the room a dark, oppressive appearance. A massive mahogany table surrounded by a menagerie of leather chairs was centered in the room.

A thin but muscular woman sat at the table. She had red hair and a slight smirk on her face that seemed permanent. Her tan uniform revealed she was a member of the Colorado Rangers. Next to the five-pointed gold sheriff star, the nametape above her chest pocket read: PLYMOUTH.

Beside her stood a man who looked to be of Native American descent. A black ponytail trailed down the back of his neck. He wore jeans, hiking boots, and a plaid shirt that made him look more like a backwoods hiker than a government official.

Neither were the usual transit authority representatives.

"Damn, you look like you just went through hell," said the man.

Calvin didn't reply.

"I'm Sheriff Lindsey Plymouth with the Colorado Rangers, and this is Raven Spears," said the woman. "I got the Steel Runner Union's wire about Iowa, and we want to express our condolences for your losses. Please, have a seat."

Calvin eyed the chair, not really wanting to sit, but deciding to anyway.

"I've done what I can to organize some assistance with the limited time we've had," Lindsey said. "Unfortunately, I'm not sure it will be everything you might need."

Calvin almost started to get out of his chair. He should have known this was a waste of time.

"I'm used to not getting what we need," he said.

"Wait." Lindsey motioned for him to stay. "Resources are strained here, sure. However, my deputy recruited a few local contract Steel Runners for you. They should be on the way down to your train now."

"How many?"

"Four."

"Four? I am down almost twenty with the injured included."

"Yes, but that's not all we're offering."

"And how much are these four going to cost? I know it's not easy finding people to run steel..."

"Don't worry about the cost. We will take care of it."

Calvin reared back some. "No way this is free."

"The sheriff isn't a liar, pal," Raven said.

"Yeah, well, you'll have to excuse me if I'm a little leery when someone tells me they're going to help me for free." Calvin borrowed a quote from his mother. "Ain't nothing for free in this world."

"You've got that right," Lindsey said. "This is my territory, and I can't afford to have another disaster. Helping you is helping people that need those supplies you're transporting. Helping you deliver them is the right thing to do."

Calvin wasn't sure he believed her, but he figured he'd at least hear her out. "So what else is it that you're offering?"

Lindsey jerked her chin at Raven. "My colleague here is an expert tracker working in the New Frontier for the past two years. Before that, he was a Recon Marine."

"You may know the mountains, but I know the rails," Calvin said. "If you're going to help me, I got to know you're going to listen to me."

"Goes both ways," Raven replied. "I'll provide you maps with areas I scouted."

He went and grabbed a map, unraveling it on the table with various locations circled. Calvin got up for a better look.

"I believe these are the most vulnerable points for the train, places snipers might set up, or places armed convoys might attack," Raven said.

"I'll have scouts in the mountains, Raven being one of them," Lindsey added.

Calvin nodded. "Good start."

"That's not all. I'm going to organize a convoy to escort the train. We'll follow you on I-70 to provide fire support."

Calvin looked up, brows raised.

"Really, there's no catch," Lindsey said as if she could read his mind. "This is an opportunity for me to find the people responsible for an earlier supply depot attack in Eagle."

"I heard you took out those raiders."

"Not all of them," Lindsey said. "There are more out there."

Calvin shook his head. "Maybe the same people that attacked us in Iowa?"

"Maybe... and working together. We'll figure it out."

"I'm beginning to like you, Sheriff." Calvin flashed a rare half-grin.

"Glad to hear it," Lindsey replied. "I'm also one of those lucky LEOs that has been assigned a Foreign Advisory Council. Most of the time, they're a royal pain in the ass, but we need them and sometimes they pull through."

"Oh?" Calvin said.

"I've convinced a couple of them to provide armed assistance for the Angel Line."

"You're kidding," Calvin said. "We got your Rangers and some military people coming with us? This has to be an Angel Line first."

"Like I always say, your success is our success. Everything has a domino effect out here, and our foreign allies understand that, thanks to some recent hard talks we've had behind closed doors."

She leaned forward and slid another piece of paper over

to Calvin. "One last thing, here's the new departure time and schedule for your train. I've personally adjusted it."

Calvin picked up the paper and examined the schedule. "This has us getting into Salt Lake City almost a day earlier than expected. We barely have time for repairs and taking care of my injured Runners. We can't make a change like that without the Steel Runner Union's consent."

"We can and we will," Lindsey said. "The only people that have any idea what we've done with the schedule will be a few Rangers, the FAC, and those of us in this room. I don't even want you to tell your Runners until last minute. The less eyes on this schedule, the less chance we have of leaks."

Calvin couldn't argue with her logic. "I'll agree so long as it saves my people's lives."

"That's the goal, but there's one last thing."

He put the schedule down.

"We've had a few incidents of an unidentified disease spreading in the New Frontier," she said.

"Disease is always spreading through the New Frontier."

"This seems particularly deadly, and it's spreading more rapidly than usual," Raven said.

"Good thing we're going to be on the train," Calvin said. "Got enough ways for my people to die that I don't need one more to worry about."

7

RAVEN WASN'T SURE WHAT TO THINK OF HIS NEW mission, but it was a good change from heading into the New Frontier to search for people.

He drove down I-70 under a brilliant moon that looked so large, it seemed like it might crash right into the Earth. It gave Raven enough light that he could turn his headlights off and avoid the clusters of rusting and abandoned vehicles along the road. Creek sat alert in the passenger seat.

Running parallel to the route the Angel Line would take, he had already personally surveyed Vail and Wolcott well before the train took off from Denver. Those were both places where bandits had attempted attacks before. He had found no sign of recent human activity, though, much less a waiting ambush party.

He picked up his radio. "All teams, Recon Alpha here. Anyone got eyes?"

"Recon Alpha, Recon Bravo here," the first of twelve Ranger teams called back. "No evidence of hostiles in Sector One."

Team by team, the reports came back the same. None of them found evidence of IEDs or spotted any ambushes.

Lindsey's efforts to expedite the train schedule and send it into the mountains unannounced might actually have paid off. He thought of her as he drove, remembering how it felt once again to be next to her. There was no denying he had feelings for her and probably always would.

But it was too complicated with their jobs.

A sign for Glenwood Springs ahead reminded him of how difficult her role as sheriff was now. Just days earlier, she had led her Rangers and the Royal Marines up there to track those responsible for the Eagle supply depot attack.

He felt guilty for not being up there to help and was grateful they had come back without any injuries or fatalities.

Raven decided to turn off to investigate the area himself to see if they had missed anything. Not that he didn't trust Lindsey's people. He just figured he knew these mountains better.

On his approach to the once bustling tourist town, he eased off the gas but didn't kill the engine, just in case someone was watching. The parking lot of the Glenwood Hot Springs resort where the shootout occurred wasn't far.

He tucked the Jeep into the former hotel's enclosed garage, then ducked out of the vehicle. Creek padded obediently behind him.

Carrying his crossbow, Raven advanced toward the abandoned town that was set in Sector Seven. His pack and M4 were slung over his back, ready in case he needed more firepower as he treaded across the site of the shootout.

Spent brass bullet casings littered the pebbles and ash surrounding the hotel. He strode through the debris, careful with every step. Bending down, he checked the blood stains from where Lindsey's three prisoners were killed by snipers.

Raven looked around at the surrounding mountains. He

hoped to figure out where he would set up shop if he was a scout or group of raiders waiting to ambush the train.

There appeared to be two good locations. One was a peak just north of and above the hotel; the other was a mountain that rose above the train tracks on the southern side of the river, opposite this one.

Raven started back through the hotel with Creek trotting ahead. They passed a few other buildings that were little more than brick walls and charred support beams.

From there, they climbed up the steep mountainside. Branches from the dry honey locust and hackberry trees snagged at his jacket. The constant buzz of insects droned on despite the relatively cool night air.

Just as he neared a crest nearly a thousand feet above Glenwood Springs, he heard a familiar sound.

A single howl pierced the night.

Were these the same wolves he encountered with Lara?

She'd thought they were protecting her. Maybe that was true. As far as he knew, they might be looking out for him too.

Or maybe they were like Iktomi, the trickster?

According to lore, Iktomi had taken the form of a wolf when the Earth was newly formed. She traveled beneath the planet to find humans dwelling in a subterranean world and promised them that the surface of the world was full of food, green grass, and blue skies.

But when the humans left their protected subterranean villages, Iktomi led them to a world where food was scarce, the weather was inhospitable, and many people died.

Was this wolf leading Raven into a false sense of security like Iktomi had done?

He tried to shake the thought, to tell himself he was being superstitious. Maybe it was his exhaustion. Maybe it was the eerie size of the moon looking down on him. That feeling of foreboding dread would not go away.

Chances were good the wolves were just stalking Creek, after people had driven the rest of their prey out of the area.

He kept his eyes on his dog as they approached a plateau just under the peaks of the forested mountains overlooking the town. The fur along Creek's back stood on end and his tail curled beneath his legs.

They had made it to the Glenwood Caverns Adventure Park. The amusement park had fallen into disrepair. The giant swing tilted over the canyon. It had a massive yellow arm that riders would once strap into. Now that arm hung precariously over the edge as if it might snap off at any moment.

The funicular lines had failed at some point, collapsing to the mountain's slope. Moonlight glimmered off a trail of cars and cables leading back down to Glenwood Springs.

A rollercoaster looked like a skeletal metal serpent coiled atop the mountain peak, silent and foreboding. Nearby was an overlook that provided a perfect view over the entire town and the surrounding canyon.

Great place for a sniper or scout.

Creek stuck his nose into the air, sniffing.

Raven cradled his crossbow and searched the other rides and food stands as they snuck through the amusement park.

He listened for the snap of twigs or the crunch of boots on dirt and gravel, but heard nothing besides the wind whispering softly through the trees and the click and hum of the insects.

He searched the remains of the rides and the few SUVs left to rust within the park. But he found no sign anyone had been using them as shelter.

Scouring the amusement park, he headed toward one of the main attractions: King's Row Cave. A perfect hideout.

Sure enough, at the cavern entrance, he spotted a pickup truck. It was relatively clean. No rust. Fully inflated tires and the windshield wasn't covered in dust.

A wolf howled in the distance. Four more wolves answered in succession. Their howls came from every direction at once.

Another warning?

Raven began to wonder if maybe the snipers that killed the prisoners and fired on the Rangers were still up here.

No way... Pretty brazen, if they are, he thought.

Raven switched to his rifle and crept to the cavern entrance with Creek behind him. Together, they delved into the dark recesses of the cave. The moonlight didn't make it far. He could only see the silhouette of the teethlike stalactites and stalagmites alongside the smooth walking path. The steady drip of water into a pool echoed from deeper in the darkness.

If ever there was a place to hide out around Glenwood Springs, this would be it.

For a few minutes, he crouched quietly in the dark, listening intently for signs of life. Creek sat dutifully next to him. The tension radiating off his canine partner was nearly palpable.

His dog clearly sensed something in this cavern.

Raven withdrew a tactical LED flashlight from his utility belt, secured a red filter, and set it on low. The flashlight gave off a meager pane of red light.

Sure, it would be noticeable, but it was a hell of lot less noticeable than shining a bright white light through the pitch-black like a lighthouse.

He aimed the red light over the cavern floor while still

holding his rifle. It gave off just enough illumination for him to see several yards ahead.

Creek helped guide Raven between the columns of rock. As they rounded a bend, the red light reflected off a pool of clear water.

Raven halted at the sight of three men lying in sleeping bags, all out cold. Next to them were rifles and hiking packs.

He slowly swung his light up to see if it caught any other interlopers waiting in the shadows to attack. Surely, they had someone on sentry to watch their backs.

After a few moments of listening, Raven heard nothing.

He traced his light over a forest of stalactites and stalagmites. Water glistened on smooth limestone, and bulbous rock formations grew from the cavern wall like tumors.

He didn't see anyone else.

Raven carefully walked over to the sleeping men, his rifle aimed at the closest guy. The man was sleeping on his side, facing away from Raven.

One of these men might be the sniper that executed the raiders Lindsey had captured. If so, that meant they were extremely valuable.

Raven would give them one chance to surrender and bring them in to the Rangers.

If they fought back, then he would take a page out of Lindsey's book and bring them in full of holes.

With his boot, he nudged the first man's back.

"Don't reach for your gun or you're dead," Raven said.

The man didn't move. Nor did the other two.

Raven nudged the same guy a little harder.

Still, the man didn't wake up.

A chill tore through Raven. It wasn't because of the cave's cold, damp air.

He used his boot to push the guy onto his spine so his eyes were aimed at the ceiling.

"Holy fu—" Raven said, barely stopping himself.

Blank eyes looked up at him, glassy orbs frozen in death. Knobby lesions covered his pale skin, and his cracked dry lips were peeled back like he'd died moaning in agony.

Raven moved on to the other two, finding each face just as gruesome.

He heard Lindsey's warning in his mind. Sandra's too.

These men had probably died from the same mysterious disease that had stricken the patients now entering the Front Range clinics.

Raven held his breath and slowly backed away with Creek.

He led his dog out of that cavern, hoping that neither he nor Creek would be the next victims of the microscopic murderer that killed these men.

———

Lindsey rode in one of the backseats of an armored personnel carrier along Interstate 70, racing along the highway with Blair. Palmer sat in the front passenger seat by another Colorado Ranger who was driving.

One other member of the Foreign Advisory Council had come along in another APC full of his own troops, Lieutenant Tiankai. He was toward the end of the eight-vehicle convoy. Even though the rest of the FAC wasn't here, they'd actually come through.

The convoy was filled with squads of armed forces from Canada, Mexico, UK, and China, along with a contingent of UN peacekeepers.

If a single person was killed, it could mean the end of

support from the FAC. But a successful night with the Angel Line getting through the mountains could also mean more support.

It was a gamble, and while Lindsey normally hated taking a risk, she had no choice.

She took in the view, feeling confident with the support she had managed to wrangle.

Atop each APC, soldiers manned machine guns. A Humvee in front of the convoy served as a scout. Lindsey hoped this would provide an extra layer of protection for the Angel Line train running parallel with them. Even if Raven and the Ranger scouts missed an ambush, she hoped this show of force would dissuade any would-be raiders.

The Steel Runners on top of the trains were alert, eyeing their surroundings. Each poked above their nests with rifles aimed toward the mountains. The machine gunners on the top of a few armored SR cars swiveled back and forth.

Tonight, she vowed they would get this train safely out of Colorado.

"Guardian One, Recon Alpha, do you read?" a voice crackled over the radio.

It was Raven. He sounded worried, which was unlike him.

"Recon Alpha, Guardian One here," Lindsey said. "I read."

"I've located three dead men in Sector Seven." It took Lindsey just a moment to register that Raven was talking about Glenwood Springs.

He had warned her before that this was one of the mostly likely places for an ambush. It sounded like he'd been right after all.

"Pretty sure one might have been the sniper that took out your prisoners from the other day at the hotel," he said.

Lindsey's mind flashed back to the way those mysterious gunmen had massacred the people she'd tried to take in as prisoners. "Assassinated?"

"Not by bullets. That disease you keep talking about killed 'em."

"Oh, shit," she said.

Blair glanced over at her with a skeptical look.

She ignored him. "Recon Alpha, I'm going to patch in the medical team. Hold on."

It took just a moment before Doctor Divekar answered. "Medical here. Casualties?"

"No, no casualties," Lindsey replied. She wanted to add, *yet*, but stopped herself, praying Raven wasn't about to become one. "I've got Recon Alpha here. He found some deceased hostiles with signs of infection in Sector Seven."

"Sector Seven, Sector Seven... Oh. Oh. Okay. Can he describe the symptoms?" Divekar asked.

Raven's voice piped in over the channel. "I saw three men with cracked lips and pale skin. They had lesions all over their faces and, from what I could see, their hands. I didn't exactly stick around to examine them."

"Good," Divekar replied. "I mean, good that you didn't stick around."

There was a pause.

"How do you feel?" she asked.

"Like normal," Raven replied. "I think."

"Could he be infected?" Lindsey asked.

"From what we've recorded, all cases within the hospital were spread from live hosts," Divekar said. "No one has caught this disease, whatever it is, from a corpse. Well, I mean, one person did. One of my nurses. She came into contact with one of those lesions, though. Rav... I mean, Recon Alpha, did you touch one of those lesions?"

"Hard negative," Raven called back.

Lindsey wanted to breathe a sigh of relief.

"From what little we've discovered, this disease seems to spread from person to person via bodily fluids or respiratory droplets," Divekar continued. "You're probably much safer encountering a diseased corpse than a live person hacking up a lung."

"Probably isn't exactly reassuring, Doc," Raven replied.

"Probably is all I can offer. We still don't have lab results back. At least, nothing concrete. From our initial tests, we think its bacterial, but like I said, it's like nothing we're used to seeing and antibiotics aren't working."

"Damn," Lindsey said. "Recon Alpha, did you finish clearing Sector Seven?"

"Affirmative," Raven replied.

"Then you better head back home," she said. "Get yourself quarantined. Watch for symptoms."

"That would be wise," Divekar said. "Every case we've seen, symptoms appear in less than twelve hours. So if you aren't coughing, sneezing, or have a fever by then, you're probably fine."

"I still got a job to finish," Raven said.

"Recon Alpha, this isn't a discussion," Lindsey said. "Get your ass back home and isolate yourself. Your only job right now is making sure you aren't sick. You've done enough already."

There was a long pause, then, "Fine, Guardian One, Recon Alpha out."

Lindsey swallowed hard.

She wanted to believe that Divekar was right about how this was spread. But there were still so many unknowns. Hell, they didn't even know what this thing was yet.

"You have a personal relationship with this bloke Raven?" Blair asked.

It seemed to be as much of a statement as a question. His placid expression irked her. She couldn't tell if he was merely curious or judging her.

"Professional only," Lindsey said.

"I see." Blair was about as expressive as a statue, his mustache twitching only slightly. "I recall, at the beginning of my deployment working with you, it was more personal."

"For shit's sake, you've worked with me for nearly two years," she said. "I'm not going to risk the security of Colorado over one man, if that's what you're implying. You know that."

Blair held up his hands defensively. "Fair enough, Sheriff. I just wanted to be sure we don't make any hasty decisions based off him being potentially ill. But as you Americans like to say, you're the boss."

"I'm not in the habit of making hasty decisions, regardless of who they involve," Lindsey said.

Alongside the highway, the train rushed over its tracks next to the Eagle River.

"We're headed toward Eagle now." Lindsey changed the subject. "Then it'll be Gypsum, which is just twenty-five miles from Glenwood Springs."

"The scouts already searched Gypsum thoroughly," Palmer reported. "It should be a clean ride onward."

"I hope you're right."

Sweat beaded down Blair's brow. He wiped at it with a white handkerchief he kept in his pocket.

"Raven hasn't let me down before," she said. "All the security precautions we've taken... even if a group of ambushers evaded our teams—"

"Which is possible," Blair said. "The mountains are rather large."

"Yes, but they won't expect this escort convoy. If they see us, they'll have second thoughts."

"Perhaps, but when hunger dominates men's thoughts, logic is nothing but a whisper at the back of their minds compared to the shouts of desperation."

"Poetic," Palmer said.

"Fact," Blair replied.

The Royal Marine had a good point.

Lindsey used her binoculars to survey the rolling hills and mountains. She spotted a trailer park alongside the rails. Plastic bags and tarps fluttered on the breeze. Discarded clothes and torn open luggage bags had been left in front of the trailers.

They came around a curve in the mountain. Through the front windshield of the APCs, Lindsey watched the Angel Line machine gunners swivel in their turrets, aiming their weapons toward the tree-covered crests.

The train chugged alongside them, just across the river. Every Steel Runner nestled on top of the train cars mirrored the movements of the machine gunners.

Their gazes and guns were aimed at the rocks and trees looming along the mountainside.

Lindsey scanned the slopes for movement, reminding herself to breathe. She couldn't help but think what her old mentor Marcus Colton would tell her now.

After they had worked together for a few years, he admitted that when he had hired her, he wasn't sure how long she would last. She was fiery and outspoken. Maybe a touch sarcastic. She knew how to work hard and play harder. But he worried she didn't take the job as seriously as some of the other detectives.

He said his opinion of her had changed dramatically since

then, especially after those first few days when the United States seemed to have turned into one big dumpster fire.

She figured she had some idea of what he would say in this moment: *You can handle anything. Whatever it is, you can handle it.*

Or maybe something along the lines of never underestimating the enemy. Because as soon as you did, you'd get your ass whooped.

He wasn't as poetic as Blair, but Colton was often right.

"Sierra Romeo One, Guardian One," Lindsey said into her radio. "You got a SITREP?

"Lookin' good out here, Guardian One," Calvin replied in his deep voice. "Updates from the Recon teams?"

"So far, so good. Recon Alpha is returning to roost."

"Returning? Already?"

"He may have come into contact with that disease, but he also found three hostiles. All dead in Sector Seven."

"Guess we know that way is clear."

"Copy that." Lindsey set her radio down and looked up at the moon, the pale light glistening off the leaves of the trees rushing by.

"The night's far from over," Palmer said. He cradled his rifle in the front passenger seat.

They were almost halfway out of the Rockies. And just beyond the Rockies was Utah. Even with Raven taken out of the mix, she was more certain than ever they were going to deliver these Steel Runners to safety.

Maybe their luck would hold for once.

Or maybe, there was something insidious waiting ahead.

She stiffened at the thought and kept focused, ready for anything.

Whatever it was, she could handle it.

8

ONE OF THE FIRST RULES CALVIN HAD LEARNED AS A
SEAL was that when shit hit the fan, you didn't have anyone
to rely on except yourself and your swim buddies.

Right now, his swim buddies were Steel Runners, and
they were stretched out between the train's one hundred ten
cars. They were no doubt drained from the Iowa ambush both
mentally and physically. Morale after an attack was never
good, especially one that claimed the lives of your comrades.

And truth was, the Steel Runners weren't SEALs. Not
even close.

Sure, a few were former military, but they weren't trained
for the type of attack they were hit with in Iowa or what might
be waiting along the tracks in the Rockies.

That meant Calvin and Mouse had a harder job. He was
hoping the extra help they were getting from Sheriff
Plymouth and her tracker friend Raven would help, but
Raven had just been pulled off the field.

The mountains rushed by as the train barreled through
the darkness.

"Anyone see anything?" Calvin asked.

"Negative," Mouse replied.

"Nope," came the reply from Travis. He was posted at the other corner of the nest with Anna.

Calvin checked in with the sheriff on the radio.

"Still clear," she reported back.

"I don't like this," Mouse said. "Reminds me of the HVT escort outside of Bagram."

Calvin thought back to that terrible day.

They had made it only a dozen klicks outside the base when everything had gone to shit. An IED had taken out the lead Humvee. RPG fire then slammed into their positions. Small arms fire came from every direction.

Calvin had just managed to get his team into gear to extract the two survivors of the lead Humvee before a mortar round turned the vehicle into scrap metal. Their five-vehicle convoy limped back to base, two vehicles and four men short.

"They kept telling us it was clear then too," Mouse said. "And as much as I'm grateful for the help of the sheriff and her Rangers, they aren't even military."

"Only thing we can do is stay vigilant."

Mouse gave Calvin a nod as the train's wheels squealed, going around a curve.

Picking up the map the sheriff had provided, Calvin identified the area where Raven just located the dead sniper and his pals. According to the map, they were about to hit a series of potential ambush sites that Raven had marked.

Lindsey had vouched for Raven and her scout teams, but the mountains were vast. To truly clear the Rockies, it would take days, if not weeks. And what if someone was tracking the trackers?

There were far too many variables on this run.

If Calvin had learned one thing, the fewer uncontrolled variables affecting a mission, the better.

"If something's gonna happen, it could be up here," Calvin said. "Stay alert."

"Copy that," Anna said.

Calvin picked up his radio again. "All Sierra Romeos, this is Sierra Romeo One. Be advised, we are about to enter territory with three confirmed deceased hostiles, but more might be out there."

A flurry of "copies" came back from each of the Steel Runner teams. As the train went around another bend, Calvin got a good look at all the gun barrels poking out of the SR car nests.

The burning cars and odor of death lingered on his mind. He pictured Redbeard lurching out of the smoke-filled car, and the charcoaled bodies of Sean and Otto. Then he imagined Maggie, dying in her bunk because they couldn't get her to Denver in time.

They couldn't afford another attack.

Calvin crossed over to Anna and Travis.

"Got anything?" he asked.

They both shook their heads.

Calvin pushed down on Travis's White Sox hat. "Stay lower, my man. Christ. You want to give a sniper an easy target?"

"Sorry," Travis said.

He ducked down some.

Calvin dragged a couple spare ammo crates closer to the duo.

"Damn, guys, you want these things closer to you than your jockstrap," Mouse said.

"Man, you got a thing for jockstraps?" Travis asked. "You sure as hell talk about them a lot."

"What I do in my free time is my own business." Mouse gave him a ridiculous wink.

A gust of wind slammed into the exposed nest, nearly taking Travis's hat. He reached up as it lifted off his head.

"Shit!" he called out.

Mouse turned and caught it before it could fly out of the car.

"Damn, thanks, man," Travis said.

"Focus," Calvin said.

The men turned back to their positions, keeping a watchful eye over a ridgeline with plenty of boulders and trees to hide behind.

"You know how we used to poke fun at the pilots who always had those lucky socks or keychains or shirts or whatever?" Mouse asked.

"Yeah," Calvin said.

"Maybe it isn't such a bad idea. Maybe I should get a hat like Travis's." Then he grinned. "Or maybe a lucky jockstrap?"

"You're too much, bro," Travis said. "And by the way, if this hat was so lucky, I would never lose at cards, right?"

"We don't need luck." Calvin grinned. "We're Navy SEALs. We make our own luck."

"You're Navy SEALs." Anna sighed. "The rest of us are just mortals."

———

Raven drove down I-70 with Creek, trying to keep calm.

Divekar had assured him he was *most likely* okay. Most likely didn't mean definitely, though.

"It's gonna be okay, boy." He gave Creek a pat.

The dog actually didn't seem to have a worry in the world right now. He was curled up in the passenger seat.

Raven focused on the road, feeling guilty for having to

head home and quarantine when he should have been out tracking.

He picked up his radio, anxious for an update.

"Recon Alpha here, all teams report in," Raven said.

He was heading in the direction the train was coming from. Judging by the train's last location, he'd intercept the convoy in less than an hour.

"Recon Bravo, here. No contacts."

"Recon Charlie, Sector Four is still clear."

All the teams quickly reported in.

Except for one.

"Recon Delta, report," Raven said.

Silence reigned over the channel.

"Son of a bitch," he whispered.

Recon Delta was in charge of Sector Six.

The Angel Line was headed for Sector Six right now. And suddenly, those two scouts were dark?

Raven felt his heartbeat quicken. Sure, it could be a coincidence. But the chances of all this lining up?

No way.

"Guardian One, Recon Alpha," he said into the radio.

"Copy Recon Alpha," she replied. "You should be focusing on getting back to—"

"Can you get ahold of Recon Delta?" he interrupted.

"Standby."

Raven waited, pressing on the accelerator harder. He was just a couple minutes outside Sector Six, which bordered Glenwood Springs.

"No contact," Lindsey reported a couple minutes later. There was a tremor in her voice. "Delta is dark."

"Shit," Raven said. "I've got to investigate."

The line was silent for a second. "Recon Alpha, you may

be infected. You need to quarantine. I don't... I don't want to lose anyone else out there."

"No one is closer to Sector Six. I can check it out right now."

"You hardly have time," Lindsey continued. Her voice shook slightly. He could tell she was upset about the missing Rangers. But she was trying to hold it together. "We'll be there soon. Maybe forty minutes. More if we slow a bit."

"All the more reason for me to investigate."

"You're not getting what I'm saying," Lindsey said. "We can send more scouts. We'll slow the train. Buy time. I don't want anyone else getting taken out, if this is true."

"If these two scouts *were* killed, that means there are hostiles in the area," Raven said. "Someone has to get there before the train does. Even if you do slow, none of the other Rangers can make it in time."

"We don't even know where to begin looking," Lindsey said. "The closest team in the mountains is a good fifty minutes from Cinnamon Creek."

Raven racked his brain for a moment for a solution. All these coincidences were adding up, making him piece together a puzzle that he didn't like.

If there were people out there that had taken out two scouts, that meant they had something else planned.

He wasn't sure if he wanted to tell Lindsey what he now suspected.

Whoever was in Sector Six must have had advanced warning about the train, and the scouts.

Was it possible there was a mole in the Rangers that Lindsey didn't know about? Someone feeding these outlaws intel?

He couldn't just ask her now. It wasn't the time.

The wind rushed in through the open windows of the Jeep. His heart was pounding faster than the Jeep's wheels were spinning. That wasn't totally unusual in situations like this, but he feared maybe it was the virus. Maybe he was infected.

Raven shook away the fear for his life to the side.

He focused on what he had to do. But there was so much ground to cover. How could he alone find the hostiles the other scouts had missed?

The only chance to rout out any trouble before the train arrived was to put himself into the mind of his enemy.

If he was a raider, knew the escort convoy was with the train, and still planned to attack... he would want the train at its most vulnerable location.

Which meant he would want to attack when the escort convoy couldn't provide fire support. It hit him then.

"Lindsey, they're going to attack near Cinnamon Creek," he said finally.

"While the convoy is stuck in the Hanging Lake Tunnel," she whispered over the line to him, like she didn't want anyone else to hear.

Good. She had come to the same conclusion.

The creek flowed under the rails at that point. It was safely hidden behind a bend in the canyon. No one entering the Hanging Lake tunnel could see any attackers waiting at the creek.

The spot would be enough to hide a group of men with RPGs, an IED under the rails, or any other number of heavy weapons. A well-placed explosive there could derail the train far from the escort convoy's reach. Whatever men were waiting in the forest would finish off any Steel Runners and have time to raid the train.

"There's no road for you to follow the train tracks there,"

Raven said. "You won't be able to get off the interstate until you reach the other side of the tunnel either."

"We can have the train brake before we get there, but it's going to take a good mile or two for them to slow," Lindsey said. "As soon as they stop, if there is an attack force out there, they'll descend on us. It'll turn into a bloody battle. Imagine if the train had stopped somewhere in Iowa..."

"Don't tell them to stop yet." Raven pushed the pedal all the way to the floor. "A stopped train is a dead train, and we want to avoid a firefight at all costs. Most importantly, if whoever is out there figures out we know what they're up to, they'll probably run and just set the trap elsewhere. We might not get another chance to stop them."

"What are you planning to do?"

"I'll tell you when I know."

The Jeep raced down the empty highway, dodging between abandoned cars left to rust.

"Be careful," Lindsey said over the line.

He didn't have time to reply.

After another curve, he went down an offramp, bouncing over cracked and buckled chunks of neglected asphalt. Ahead was the tree-lined parking lot and rest area at the trailhead to Hanging Lake.

Sure enough, two black GM SUVs were parked there near the Colorado River.

Neither had been there before when he passed a couple hours ago.

"I got you now," Raven whispered.

Creek was sitting straight up in his seat, panting, trying to look out the side window. As soon as Raven reached the edge of the parking lot, he braked hard and threw the vehicle into park.

He grabbed his M4 and cleared the area, seeing no sentries in his first sweep. With his crossbow slung over his back and both hatchets hooked to his utility belt, he set off with his dog to hunt.

Raven paused a moment behind the wall of trees lining the Colorado. Then he took out his binoculars and scoped out the terrain. Creek came up by his side.

Sure enough, when Raven zoomed in, he saw movement near the rails. From the pale moonlight, he could just make out the dark shapes of maybe two men near the short drainage pipes that sent Cinnamon Creek into the Colorado. He could just barely see them ducking behind the drainage pipes, their heads bobbing as they worked on something near the rails.

His suspicions were right. Time to let the Steel Runners know what they were about to run into.

"Sierra Romeo One, Recon Alpha here. What's the train's ETA to Hanging Lake?" he asked.

"Thirty minutes now," Calvin replied. "Guardian One apprised me of the situation. We've slowed the train as much as we can without opening ourselves up to an assault. We still have twenty minutes before we need to order the train to brake. What's going on?"

"I've got eyes on two contacts near Cinnamon Creek," Raven replied. "Get your Runners ready if shit goes down, but don't brake unless I tell you. I'll deal with these guys."

There was a moment of hesitation.

"Two against one, plus maybe more," Calvin replied. "Bad odds, man."

"Not when they don't see me."

Raven switched the channel to a private line to Lindsey, telling her what he'd told Calvin.

"No way, Sam, you—" she started to say.

"Lindsey, we don't have much else of a choice. Too many lives are on the line tonight."

He shut off the channel. She was too far away to help anyway, and he wasn't in the mood to argue. He needed to use the precious time to figure out a plan on how to take down these two hostiles.

The best he could come up with was crossing the Colorado River and flanking them.

Raven looked at Creek. The dog wagged his tail, and they were off. A few minutes later, they found a narrow crossing. The water was still deep in the middle, forcing Raven to wade out. He winced as the frigid water came up to his balls.

Keeping his rifle above his head, he waded to the other side with Creek swimming by him. When they got there, the Akita shook the water from his fur.

Together, they stalked through the woods. The ambushers would be expecting their quarry to come straight at them on the rail tracks.

Unfortunately for them, they didn't know Raven Spears had figured out their ploy.

He headed up the slope with Creek, so they could come back down to attack the enemy on their southern flank. It was probably the last place they would expect to be hit.

The pair crept through the verdant forest as quietly as possible, using the cover of the towering fir, spruce, and cedar trees.

Raven and Creek made it up the side of the mountain, then trekked eastward just a couple minutes before coming back down. Lifting his M4 and aiming back down the mountain, the scope revealed both men near the drainage pipe.

Even through the dark, he could see them setting something up near the rails. An IED no doubt.

Scanning between the trees, Raven looked for more crushed leaves and footprints with the help of the meager moonlight.

"Shit..." he muttered.

He saw two more men guarding the pair by the rails. Now that he had a closer view, he could see each was armed with a rifle and wore what appeared to be hunting camo.

Maybe these guys had more reinforcements waiting in the mountains somewhere. Those men were probably hiding to avoid the Ranger scouts that had been combing through Sector Six.

If that IED derailed the train, the four men here would call in backup to help slaughter the Steel Runners and escape with the cargo.

Raven couldn't stop them all, but he could take a few down and maybe derail their plan, forcing them to flee. It was either that or have the train brake and become easy targets for any other reinforcements out there. Doing so would be a massacre, even if the Steel Runners were ultimately victorious.

He considered his options, thinking about radioing Lindsey, but there wasn't anything she could do. This was on him.

Stay low, stay silent, and take them down one by one, Raven thought. He let his M4 fall on its strap again and readied his crossbow instead.

At a hand signal from Raven, Creek ran to the foliage and ducked under the leaves.

Then Raven crept silently through the forest until he was about ten yards away from the nearest guard. He centered his crossbow on the guy. The man was currently turned in the opposite direction with his rifle.

Raven held his breath, then pulled the trigger.

The arrow lanced through the back of his target's throat. The man fell to his knees as Raven came around with a hatchet in one hand.

His eyes flitted up to Raven, bulging over his bulbous

nose. He choked out something as Raven brought the hatchet down with a heavy thwack to the skull.

The noise was enough to grab the attention of the other guard.

He had been made, but there was still time to silence the other asshole if he was fast enough.

9

RAVEN PITCHED HIS OTHER HATCHET AT THE OTHER guard. The blade whistled through the tree branches, but the man dodged it. With a *thunk*, the hatchet cracked right into a tree trunk.

The guard raised his rifle toward Raven.

A whistle from Raven sent Creek launching out of his position. With a vicious growl, the dog leapt and latched onto the guard's neck. The man let out a booming shot that seared past Raven as Creek tore into flesh and muscle.

By the time Raven was there to help, the dog had ripped the guy's throat out. Blood streamed out, soiling the ground.

Raven unslung his rifle and brought it up, looking around for reinforcements. The shot the guy had managed to get off meant the time for sneaking and surprise was over.

But Raven didn't much care now. He was on the warpath.

"Fifteen minutes, Recon Alpha," Calvin's voice came over the comms. "We need to make a call whether this train stops or not. My men are ready for a prolonged engagement, if that's what it comes to."

"Not yet," he said.

Raven ran down the slope, keeping hidden while searching for the other two men fifty yards down the mountain. From behind a tree, he saw them. They hid behind the train tracks, crouching behind the berm where the rails were. Neither were firing yet.

Another couple bursts from his M4 would finish the job.

But he also had a chance to figure out who they were. Lindsey would want to talk to these men. They were worth more alive than dead.

Still, he wasn't about to risk them shooting his ass by calling out from his position.

No, he had to do something to disable them that wasn't putting bullets into their bodies.

Raven looked down to his flash grenades on his vest. They would have to do.

He moved into a new position, then threw one of the grenades. It went off with a deafening pop and blinding flash of light.

Cries rang out.

Raven fired around the men before yelling, "Drop your weapons!"

The stunned raiders did as ordered.

"Smart. Now step away from your rifles, and throw out your sidearms," he called out. "Nice and easy."

Again, they complied, tossing their pistols to the ground.

"We just need this medicine, man," one of the men said, blinking. He spoke in a loud voice, apparently still struggling with his damaged hearing. "You don't understand... They promised they'd help us if we just—"

"Shut the fuck up!" The other guy shot his comrade a glare. "They'll kill us if you say another word!"

Were these guys talking about the same disease that sent

all those mountain dwellers from the Badlands into the Front Range clinics?

Last he'd heard, neither Divekar nor anyone else back on the Front Range knew shit about a cure. Especially not a cure being shipped via the Angel Lines. These guys must be mistaken.

Still, this talk of someone killing them... like the people in Glenwood Springs...

"Hands up and step over here," Raven said.

They continued to follow his instructions.

"Are there any others out there?" he asked.

Raven glanced around, looking for Creek or signs of another attacker. But as soon as Raven took his eyes off his captives, the one that had yelled at his comrade reached for something at his hip.

"No!" Raven shouted.

By the time he looked back, the guy had drawn another pistol.

Damn it.

Raven unleashed a burst into his chest. As the gunman fell forward toward the train tracks, the other man dove for his pistol, then started to bring it up toward Raven.

Another squeeze of the M4's trigger sent a three-round burst punching into the man's chest and shoulder. He dropped his pistol, his hand reaching for the bullet wounds. He made it a few steps before collapsing into the grass.

Raven looked around the slope, searching between the trees. He didn't hear any other boots crunching over the rock or through the leaves. No movement either.

Creek was looking around too, but didn't seem to have any scent.

Satisfied, Raven pulled out his radio.

"Guardian One and Sierra Romeo One, Recon Alpha," he

said. "Sector Six is clear. I repeat, Sector Six is clear of hostiles."

"Copy that," Lindsey replied. He could practically hear the relief in her voice. "IEDs?"

"Taking care of that right now."

He raced down the hill toward the two new corpses. He wasn't an expert at defusing bombs, but it was easy enough to remove the unsecured plastic explosives on the sides of the rails. He retreated back up the slope and placed them on the ground far enough away they couldn't hurt the train even if they did explode.

A pit formed at the bottom of his stomach when he examined the IEDs.

From his time as a Recon Marine, he knew exactly what these were.

C4 plastic explosives.

Exceedingly stable, it wouldn't go off if a few stray bullets hit it or even if it was tossed in a fire. The only thing that would really make it explode was a detonator or intense pressure wave.

Which meant when he withdrew the detonator and fuse from the molded plastic explosives, he should be safe.

"Guardian One, Sierra Romeo One, these guys had C4," he reported. "It's no longer a threat, though. Tracks are clean."

"C4? You sure?" Lindsey called back.

"Does a bear shit in the woods?"

"How would they have gotten ahold of something like that? Or if they didn't get it intact, how would they have had the supplies to make it?"

"I'd ask them, but they're all dead."

"Secure the area, but see if you can find any clues," Lindsey said. "I'm going to make sure my escort gets the train safely to the Colorado border. I'm sending scouts to your position to take over the search. You get home and quarantine as soon they relieve you. Got it?"

"Understood," Raven said.

While he left the first two dead guards where they lay up the slope, he treaded back down toward the two bodies lying around the track and dragged both away. Didn't need them to get diced up by the train if Lindsey wanted to examine them.

The two men wore a mishmash of camouflage clothes and jeans. They had combat boots that looked like they'd come from an army surplus store. Each carried an AK-47, just like the men that Lindsey had taken out in Glenwood Springs.

Otherwise, they looked like nearly every other asshole out here.

Which begged the question: who was giving these guys C4 and AK-47s? And most importantly, *why*?

Lindsey was going to have her work cut out for her.

Raven continued searching for clues until the train slowed down on its approach to the Hanging Lake area. It rumbled past cautiously. No explosions went off. No one else tried to attack it.

He spotted Calvin atop the SR supply car. The man waved at Raven as he went by.

"Thanks, Recon Alpha," he called over the radio as he passed. "Next time I see you, drinks are on me."

Raven watched the train wind by. Men and women filled the nests atop the cars. Men and women that had potentially been saved by disarming the C4 and taking down the four hostiles. Knowing he'd made a difference gave Raven a small bit of satisfaction, like back when he'd been in the Marines.

He'd made a difference, and for tonight, that was all that mattered. He just prayed this small difference was enough.

———

Lindsey was still riding in the APC with Palmer in the front passenger seat and Blair beside her. Their convoy drove on the interstate parallel to the Angel Line train. Seeing the train intact gave her a sense of pride.

After Raven took down those hostiles, they made it past Glenwood Springs without further incident. Her security plan had worked and they had kept all the peacekeeping soldiers out of harm's way in their efforts to protect the train.

Not everything was going to plan, though.

She prayed Raven wasn't sick and tried to suppress her worry for his well-being. It wasn't just him on her mind. Two Rangers, Luke Ferris and Mark Cranston, had gone dark on the radio. She had deployed a team to look for them in Sector Six. It wasn't long before she got a SITREP from the search party over the comms.

"Recon Echo here. No more living contacts," a Ranger replied. "We found all four hostiles Recon Alpha dispatched."

"What about Recon Delta?" Lindsey asked.

"We found both of them too," the Ranger said. There was a short pause. "KIA, ma'am."

Lindsey closed her eyes for a moment. She had hoped the two men were somehow still alive. News of the deaths sent an icy stab of regret through her. She thought of them both as the convoy continued down the interstate.

Ferris had just gotten engaged to his high school sweetheart. Lindsey was supposed to attend their wedding in Fort Collins. Cranston was a forty-year-old father of two girls. He'd told Lindsey before he was glad to be working for her because his daughters had an inspirational role model to look up to.

And now both were gone.

There would be no wedding, and Cranston's girls would grow up without the father they deserved.

Lindsey clenched her jaw to hold back the emotion roiling inside her. She would be sure to visit both families when they returned to Golden to personally express her condolences.

"Damn," Palmer said. "Both good men. I'm gonna miss 'em. At least Raven took care of their killers, although part of me wishes it was me that did it."

"I'm sorry for your loss," Blair offered. "Hopefully, we can figure out where these people got their C_4 and their weapons."

"Maybe they made the C_4," Palmer offered.

"Then where did they get the components to synthesize it?" Lindsey asked. "Someone's supplying these people materials and weapons."

She twisted her watch to check the time. Already an hour-and-a-half had passed since Raven had taken out the team setting up that IED.

"Recon Charlie and Echo, have you found any trails leading out of the ambush site?" she asked over the radio.

"Negative, ma'am," another Ranger reported. "They covered their tracks."

"Understood," she said. "Keep looking. We'll escort the Angel Line across the border into Utah, then when we turn around, we'll come back to rendezvous with all Recon Scout teams."

"Yes, ma'am," the Ranger called back.

It wasn't much longer until they made it to the edge of Colorado where the tree-covered mountains gave way to a desert landscape. The sun was just beginning to rise behind them, making the barren rock and stark canyon walls shine an almost golden hue.

"Sierra Romeo One, Guardian One," she called over the channel to Calvin. "How are you all holding up?"

"We're alive and well, thanks to your team," Calvin replied. "I owe you one."

"You owe me nothing," she said. "Glad we could get you through the mountains. I'm going to call my counterparts in Utah to let them know to expect you in Salt Lake City by late this afternoon."

"Great work, Sheriff," Calvin replied. "Thanks again."

"Smooth rails," she said.

"Thank you, and back at you, whatever the equivalent of that is in your world."

"Good luck works just fine."

"Then stay safe and good luck."

Red sunlight glared off the bulky armor panels down the sides of the lengthy train. Billows of sand kicked up around it as it tore along the rails toward spires of crimson rock.

Lindsey picked up her radio for another call. "Utah Scouts Command, Colorado Rangers Sheriff here. How do you copy?"

"Loud and clear, Sheriff," a woman, the Utah Scouts comms officer on duty, chimed in.

"Angel Line is exiting Colorado territory and headed your way."

"Copy that. Train status?"

"We diverted an attack, but the train is otherwise untouched. No casualties."

"Thank you, Sheriff. We'll send out our scout and escort team immediately to welcome the train in. Should be free and clear from here on out."

"Copy, and Godspeed to your scouts." Lindsey breathed a sigh of relief as she watched the train head west.

She called the lead car of the convoy and told them to turn around. They would be heading back toward Fort Golden.

"Ferris and Cranston didn't die for nothing," Palmer said with a sigh. "The supplies on that train will save a lot of lives."

"When we get back, I want you to start preparing a ceremony to honor those men," Lindsey said.

"Yes, ma'am. Of course."

"Those men made a noble sacrifice," Blair said. "I have to say, I'm impressed that your largely civilian force pulled this off. I'll be sure to let my higher-ups know. They'll appreciate hearing that their money and supplies flowing into Colorado's security are working."

Lindsey nodded.

There was someone else who Lindsey figured would want updates on all that had happened. On their way back toward Glenwood Springs to pick up their scout teams, Lindsey placed an encrypted call to Secretary Charlize Montgomery.

"Sheriff, how is everything?" Charlize asked.

"Good. The Angel Line made it through the mountains unscathed after we thwarted an attack thanks to the FAC peacekeeping teams and Raven."

"He's a valuable asset. Always was. And I'm glad to hear you got the FAC to help with troops. Good to hear no one was hurt."

"None of their people were hurt, I made sure of that, but I lost two of my Rangers."

"I'm very sorry to hear that."

"Thank you." Lindsey paused a moment. "After what happened to the Steel Runners in Iowa, and now this, it makes me nervous there are some dangerous forces behind these attacks."

"I agree, but I trust you to figure out who they are. If you need my help, I'll do what I can."

"We're doing the best we can with what we've got," Lindsey said. "But it's hard enough to keep our borders safe with less manpower. In the past, I was worried about illegal firearms, and the criminal activities going on in the New Frontier, but now it seems something more sinister is going on. Have you heard anything else since our last call?"

Charlize let out an audible sigh over the line.

"Keep this between us," she said.

"Okay," Lindsey replied.

"I've seen reports that foreign interests are still trying to use our weaknesses against us. President Diego is doing all he can to keep us safe. As you know, Lindsey, this is an election year. We are so close to recovery in multiple sectors of the country, but it's taking all our manpower to secure them against the violence from our own people."

She sighed.

"There are plenty of people who hate what America stands for and would like nothing better than to see us completely crumble," Charlize said. "Sometimes I feel like the dam is so cracked, it's just a matter of time before it breaks again."

"I can relate."

"I know, and I'm sorry we can't do more right now, but you've done a fine job getting your FAC to work for you. Well done."

"Thank you, Madame Secretary."

"Keep me updated and I will do the same."

After the call ended, they continued on toward Glenwood Springs. Not only did they pick up the scout teams, but they also recovered the bodies of the two Rangers, Ferris and Cranston. Lindsey oversaw the men being loaded into the convoy vehicles along with all the weapons and supplies her Rangers had found on the bandits that Raven had killed.

Right before they were ready to load up into the vehicles

to leave, Blair stopped in front of the APC he'd taken with Palmer and Lindsey.

"I'm going to go ride with Tiankai," he said.

"Why's that?" Lindsey asked.

"You know I'm on your side, Sheriff," he said. "Sometimes I fear the other FAC members are not as enthusiastic to support your efforts. I'd like to gauge Tiankai's response to tonight's events and see if I can't cajole him into getting his government to give a little more to your cause. Would that be a problem?"

"Not in the slightest," Lindsey said. "I appreciate it."

"My pleasure." Blair marched off to the last APC where Tiankai and a couple of his men lingered outside.

She waved Palmer into the lead Humvee in the column. After everything that had happened, she needed to speak with him in private.

They slipped into the backseat, past a Ranger manning the mounted machine gun. The driver gave them a nod, and they took off back for the mountains.

"I hope Blair can help talk some sense into Tiankai," Palmer said. "All this diplomacy stuff is a pain in the ass."

"I don't love it either," Lindsey said. "The thing is, we've got to be adaptable if we want to defeat evil. And rest assured, evil exists in these mountains. We have to do everything in our power to stop it, even if that means learning about evil things as despicable as diplomacy and politics."

"I'm just glad you're the one in charge and not me," Palmer said.

"Listen, Palmer." She leaned closer to him. "Getting more support from the FAC isn't all that's on my mind. I also want you to keep your eyes and ears open. Today was too much of a coincidence. Somehow these raiders were ready for our adjusted train schedule. They tracked down and killed our scouts too. They knew we were coming."

"You smell a rat?"

Lindsey looked around and shrugged. "We might have a traitor in our midst."

"One of us, though?" he asked. "A fellow Ranger?"

"Could be, but if I had to guess, it's someone related to our Foreign Advisory Council."

"Blair? Tiankai? Martinez or one of the others?"

"Them, or someone who works with them. All I'm saying is that I want you to report anything or *anyone* suspicious."

"I'm on it, ma'am."

Lindsey stared off at the mountains in the golden morning light.

Was it really possible? Could one of their foreign allies, that was supposed to be helping her country defend their supply lines, really be trying to sabotage them instead?

10

THE EARLY MORNING UTAH SUN BEAT DOWN ON CALVIN.
Sweat trickled down the back of his neck in long rivulets. The
train roared over the sand-covered rails, sending up billows of
grit, a massive cloud of yellow rising behind them as they
churned past giant columns and walls of red rock.

Mouse sat beside him in the SR Supply Car nest, cradling
his rifle. Anna and Travis were both getting some well-
deserved sleep belowdecks. Now that they were out of
Colorado, and it was daytime, Calvin had the Steel Runners
resume their normal watch shifts so they could finally rest up.

He lifted a radio to his lips. "Sierra Romeo One from
Angel Line calling for Utah Scouts Command. How do you
copy?"

Static came over the line for a second. "Sierra Romeo
One, Utah Scouts Command. I read you five by five. Over."

"Sierra Romeo One reporting Echo Tango Alpha to Sierra
Lima Charlie by 1600 hours."

"Utah Scouts Command roger. Scouts confirmed clear
transit to Sierra Lima Charlie. Patrols are moving to watch
your six. Smooth rails, Sierra Romeo."

"Thanks, Utah Scouts Command. Out."

Calvin put the radio down, then turned to Mouse. "If all goes well, we'll be unloaded in Salt Lake City by nightfall."

"Hell yeah, Boss," Mouse said, gazing at the sheer rock walls on either side of them. "Sooner we're off this ride, the better. I'm starting to bake up here."

"There will be cold beer waiting for us too."

"Oh man, you're making me thirsty." Mouse adjusted his back against the nest wall. "We'll have to raise a glass or ten to our fallen brothers and sisters."

"No doubt, brother. No doubt."

It wasn't the first time, and Calvin knew it wouldn't be the last.

He used binos to scope out their surroundings again. Everything was so dry. So desolate.

"Did you ever imagine a pair of SEALs on a train in the middle of the desert?" he asked Mouse, then let out a low laugh. "Definitely not where I thought I'd be serving when I joined up."

"Guess it's not so different than Iraq."

Calvin shrugged. "Yup. It's hot. It's sandy. Constantly scratching at my eyes to get the grit out, and we got assholes trying to bomb us with IEDs."

"Only difference is we're on a train with a metric shit-ton of armor."

"Minor difference. Plus, none of those huge fucking camel spiders."

"So, what do you say? Wanna get wasted when we get to Salt Lake City? I mean, really shitfaced. Forget-the-world shitfaced."

"I'd love to, but I've got work to do."

"Work? Train will be in the station. What you got to..." Mouse let his words trail off.

All the good humor they'd shared evaporated as quickly as a puddle out here. He seemed to pick up on exactly what Calvin was thinking.

"I want to make sure all the paperwork goes through," Calvin said. "That the Union gets the payments to their families as soon as they possibly can... and I've got to make those calls."

"I understand," Mouse said.

'Those calls' referred to the calls to the family, next of kin, or other emergency contacts of the Steel Runners whose lives had been lost or who had been too injured to continue running steel. The Union would send the families letters and wires too, of course.

Most Steel Runner team leads left it at that.

But that kind of silence from the Iron Lead, the person responsible for all these lives, didn't sit well with Calvin.

Calvin lowered his binos. "At least the Rangers pulled through for us in Colorado. I'm going to put in a word with the Union to see if we can get that kind of support every time an Angel Line runs through the New Frontier. We'd save a lot more lives."

"Yeah, I'm sure if you mention how much money it'll save by preventing stolen cargo, they'll jump right on it."

"Hopefully."

Against the streamers of white clouds drifting in the blue sky, Calvin noticed a pair of vultures circling above the rocks. Those birds wouldn't be getting a meal from him or his crew today at least.

The hatch to the deck suddenly opened, and Travis poked his scarred face out. "Man, did we end up in the devil's armpit while I was sleeping?"

That drew a laugh from both Calvin and Mouse.

Travis got out of the hatch and knelt near one of the nest walls, adjusting his White Sox cap. "Did I mention my ba—"

"I've heard enough about balls from Mouse, brother," Calvin said.

"The big guy's stealing my material again." Travis scratched at one of the long scars down his face. He suddenly stopped and sighed, pointing at the scars. "I ever tell you where I got these?"

Calvin shook his head. Mouse shot the guy a confused look.

"I know this sounds random, but I promise I got a point," Travis said. "Back in the early days of the Collapse, I was just trying to survive in North Carolina. Charlotte, to be exact. Things were going to shit. Looters and gangs and just panicked people everywhere. Me and my buddy, Paul, God rest his soul, were trying to scavenge enough food and water to stay alive."

"I heard Charlotte was rough," Mouse said.

"Understatement. It was its own little slice of hell." Travis started to choke up a bit before he continued. "Paul and I were trying to make our way through Belmont, a neighborhood just northeast of downtown. We were going to see if we could get safely to a friend's place. The guy was a prepper. We thought if we could just make it to his house..."

Again, Travis paused, eyes falling to the deck of the car.

"Let's just say we weren't the only ones with the bright idea of visiting him. Problem was that the other people who got to him first weren't really friends of his. His house had been looted, his guns were gone, his food ransacked, and the only things left... These four asshole guys with rifles."

Travis swallowed hard.

"They tried to rob us," he continued. "But, me and Paul, we didn't have shit. So instead, these twisted fucks tortured us. Tied us up and tortured us, trying to get us to admit we had some hidden stash of weapons or food like our friend."

Travis shuddered. The train thumped over the rails for a few long moments.

"I still remember when they slit Paul's throat," he said. "I'm not too much of a man to admit I cried. I mean, I bawled like a fricking baby. His screams were terrible. Then they came for me."

Travis shuddered.

"At that moment, I thought it was all over," he continued. "I didn't beg God to save me, because I knew even He couldn't save me from those monsters."

"But you're here today," Calvin said.

"I am," he said. "Because some of the UN peacekeepers that had *just* been dispatched to help bring Charlotte back under control had heard Paul's scream. They busted in. Saved my sorry ass."

He took off his White Sox cap, brushing off some of the dust from the bill, before placing it back on his head.

"I got to say, I thought that day, America was dead," he continued. "We were an occupied land barely kept under control by a bunch of people who shouldn't be policing our streets."

Travis's chest swelled and he locked eyes with Calvin.

"Still, I made a promise to myself," he said. "I'd never served before. Never done much for our country besides keep a few casinos in business, so I said, first chance I get to do something to help rebuild, I'm going to take it."

"And you joined up with the Steel Runners," Mouse said.

Travis nodded. "Never looked back. After last night, after the way the Rangers worked with us, even after Iowa, I see America getting back on her feet. Sure, it's going to take a while, but we're getting there. That convoy had some foreigners, but it was Americans that stopped the IEDs. Americans that stopped that ambush. We're doing it. We're finally doing it. Best of all, as a Steel Runner, I get to be part of it."

Travis pointed at his scars again.

"These scars remind me of what was taken from America. But they're also a reminder that we won't forget, and we *will* heal."

Calvin gave the man a grin. "I couldn't be more honored to have you serving with us, Travis. You and the rest of the Steel Runners."

As Calvin looked back out over the desert, he had a feeling Travis was right. America was clawing her way back from destruction. It would take a lot of hard work. A lot of sacrifice.

But with men and women like his Steel Runners working to make it happen, she would make it there.

He was sure of it.

———

Raven sat in the chair on his porch. He closed his eyes, enjoying the warmth of the morning sun. He couldn't help but feel lucky to be alive today. Right now, he was glad to be relaxing, especially after the tense moments had just endured.

A wet nose pressed up against one of his palms, followed by a whine. Creek sat on his hindlegs. There was still blood in his fur around his maw.

His tail whipped, happily.

"It's a good day, buddy," Raven said. "We're alive, and we got the train to Utah."

Raven leaned back and sighed.

It had been well over twelve hours since he first discovered those dead men in the cave. He had called Sandra on his way back to Estes Park, explaining what had happened. She made him promise to let her know if he felt anything that *might* be a symptom.

So far, he hadn't had to make that call.

In fact, he was pretty sure he had only good news to report.

He went back into his kitchen and picked up his radio, using the channel he used to speak with Sandra.

"Sis, you there?" he tried.

He waited a beat. Nothing.

"Sandra, Raven here. You know, the brother you were all worried about last night."

Another couple seconds passed.

"Raven, what's wrong?" Sandra asked. She sounded slightly breathless, like she'd run to pick up the radio.

"Nothing, besides being bored," Raven said.

"No fever?"

"I even used the thermometer you dropped off. Nothing."

"No coughs? No headaches? No stuffed nose? No sneezing?"

"Nope, nope, nopity nope."

"Oh, thank God," Sandra said. "The patients we've had at the clinic... they... they aren't doing so well, Raven. I don't want to see you in here, okay?"

"Are you being careful?" he asked. "You're the one around all those sick people that are actually alive. Doctor Divekar thinks only the living can spread this, right?"

"Don't worry about me, okay? Look, I've got to go. But I'll talk to you later."

"Love you, sis."

"Love you too, Sam."

Raven set the radio down and gave Creek a good scratch behind the ears.

"I'll be back soon, boy," he said.

Getting up, Raven grabbed his pack.

While it seemed like he might not need modern medicine for his body, he decided to use a traditional remedy to heal his mind for all the death over the past few days.

With his pack slung over a shoulder, he trekked to his sweat lodge on the eastern side of his cabin. Willow branches formed a curved structure over which he'd laid a tarpaulin. Just outside the door, he had built up cedar logs.

Creek watched him start the fire. They both stood by and watched the flames lap at the wood for a few minutes. Below the logs, were a pile of smooth stones.

He took off his shirt, and wearing just his shorts, he used a pair of metal tongs to pick up several of the stones. Then he ducked low to enter the sweat lodge. He placed the rocks in a pile. Then he used a ladle to scoop water from a bucket by the entrance and poured it over the hot stones. The water sizzled. Steam filled the lodge in a gray haze, the warmth funneling into his nose and down into his lungs.

He breathed in deep, then sat down on a small log, bowing his head and soaking up the steam. Almost immediately, he could feel the sweat budding across his back and face, dripping down his flesh.

Maybe if Sandra and Divekar were wrong and he was in fact infected, the heat would help burn out the disease. He soaked in the atmosphere in quiet solitude.

Every part of the lodge had its purpose. The heat and steam functioned as a kind of artificial fever, helping the body do the work of burning out a virus or bacteria. The willow scaffolds also could be used medicinally as an analgesic. Burning cedar was thought to purify the space.

Whether it worked or not, it gave Raven time to think. To reflect on his life. To reflect on death.

He poured another ladle full of water on the stones. Water simmered against the rock, bubbling and popping.

While he'd spent the last two years on tracking missions into the New Frontier, the past several days had been filled with death. He thought about the souls he'd separated from bodies. Wondered where the place would be after death. Whether Heaven and Hell really existed—and if he had to do some thinking about where he might belong.

Even if others thought he'd killed out of necessity, some days he questioned if taking so many lives really could be justified.

It hurt him to his core, even if these men were evil, that he'd taken them from parents or children, wives or siblings.

And then he got to thinking what these men had said about the medicine. How they just wanted medicine. As if that was why they were attacking the train.

But someone had also supplied them those weapons. Could that be the same *someone* that had supplied AK-47s to the men in Glenwood Springs? Maybe even the same men who sniped those prisoners of Lindsey's? And had they even recruited or been related to the three guys he found in the caverns above Glenwood Springs?

Shit. Those guys had been sick too. They might have needed this medicine the ambushers were talking about.

It made him wonder if this mythical medicine or whatever the hell these guys were after had somehow been used to convince others to ambush the trains.

Maybe he was getting paranoid. His thoughts were quickly devolving into a conspiracy.

Lindsey was better equipped to deal with all this, and he'd already told her everything he knew and thought so far.

The crunch of twigs and gravel snapped him from his trance.

Had Sandra come to check on him?

His mind whirled back to the ambushers. They had evaded the Rangers—and if there was a traitor following Lindsey's every move, maybe that traitor had sent someone to kill Raven in revenge.

He reached instinctively for a weapon, but he had nothing in here.

Raven rushed over to the door, peeling it back and looking for the hatchet propped up near the logs by the fire.

That would have to do.

He poked his head outside.

Creek was quiet. The dog had been running around outside just minutes ago.

Had he somehow missed this intruder?

That wasn't like Creek at all.

Which brought only dark thoughts to Raven's mind.

He snatched the hatchet and crept quietly to the side of the cabin. Holding his breath, he quietly peered around the side to see who had invaded his property.

"Good boy!" a girl's voice called.

Raven couldn't believe it. He dropped the hatchet and moved around to the front of the cabin.

There, standing on the porch with Creek wagging his tail and circling her, was Lara.

The teenager had a big Tupperware bowl cradled under one arm. She was petting Creek with her free hand.

When she saw Raven, her face blanched.

"I'm... Mr. Spears..."

"Sorry, I was..." He gestured to the side of the house. "I was in the sweat lodge."

"It's okay, I'm just dropping this off." She set the big 2-liter bowl down on the porch. "I heard your sister was worried you might get sick, so I made some *Wahonpi* soup."

That was a Sioux recipe.

"You talked to my sister?"

Lara stepped off the porch and started to walk closer to Raven. "Yeah, I saw Sandra—"

He held out his hand to stop her. "Look, I don't think I'm sick, but if I am, I don't want to give it to you."

"You look fine to me, but okay," she said. Then she pointed at the soup back on his porch again. A sad look crossed her face. "We didn't have any bison, so I had to use beef. The carrot and potatoes are all grown at my grandmother's place too. My mom used to make it for me when I wasn't feeling great, so I hope it helps you like it did me."

"Thanks. Back to my sister."

"My grandma brought me to the clinic to get checked out after you dropped me off. I met your sister there. She invited me over for a meal. She said if I needed some more friends in the area, she would be happy to help."

"Oh, I see."

"She was very nice. Allie is too." Lara forced a slight smile. "Allie wants me to show her how to make a bow."

"I bet Sandra loved that."

"She didn't seem to mind too much." Lara paused briefly, then glanced away. "Anyway, I just wanted to say thank you for helping me again."

Raven crossed his arms over his chest. He expected Lara to start the long trek back to Joanne's place, but instead, she shuffled her feet, looking down at the ground.

"Something else on your mind?" Raven asked.

She let out a long sigh. "I wanted to ask if you could teach me more about our ancestors. Could you, please, Mr. Spears?"

"Raven," he said again.

"Sorry. Raven."

"What do you want to know?"

Her voice hitched up slightly. Raven thought he actually saw a bit of joy behind her wary expression. "I want to know the legends and history and how to track like you do."

"Now's not a good time, but soon, okay?"

"Okay. Thanks, Raven."

She started to walk away, giving room for Raven to get to his porch. He looked down at the Tupperware bowl, feeling guilty all of a sudden.

He whistled and when Lara turned, he said, "You want to hear a story?"

Raven could see her features brighten.

"It's not Sioux, but do you want to hear about where disease and medicine come from?" he asked.

"Yeah."

Lara jogged over but stopped when Raven held up a hand.

She nodded, staying a healthy distance away from him, wrapping her thin arms over her sweatshirt. "This is from your Cherokee side?"

"Yeah," he said. Then he began to tell her. "There was a time before civilization, well before the Collapse, before history books were ever written. Back then, all the animals could talk, from the trout in the river to the ants crawling through the dirt to the bears scrounging through the foliage. Animals and people lived together in harmony."

"Must have been nice," Lara said almost dreamily.

Raven dipped his chin. "Of course, as you know, people started to settle down and create towns and villages and settlements that spread over the Earth like wildfire."

He paused and looked around at the trees.

"People then invented weapons the animals couldn't defend themselves against. Our bows, spears, fishing hooks, knives, and blowguns were used to slaughter animals.

"Smaller creatures, like bugs, didn't stand a chance either. They were stepped on and smashed."

Lara seemed to sulk in despair. Creek settled at her feet as if to comfort her.

"The animals realized they needed to protect themselves and met in a council," Raven continued. "Almost immediately, the bears agreed to go to war with the humans. They figured they should arm themselves with bows and arrows like the humans had. They cut down locust trees to make bows."

Raven went silent for a second.

"But then they realized that they needed to make the strings," he said. "The bears knew humans made those strings from animal entrails. One bear sacrificed himself so the others could harvest his entrails to create a string."

Lara reared back some. "Wow."

"The bears constructed their bows and arrows thanks to their selfless brother," Raven said. "But when the first bear drew back the bowstring to fire it, his claw cut right through the string. He tried again and again. Even when his claw didn't harm the string, it got in the way when he tried to fire the arrows. As a result, the arrows never flew straight.

"Another bear suggested cutting their claws so they could fire an arrow. The chief of the bears said that wouldn't work. They needed their claws to climb trees and hunt. They would starve without the claws nature had given them."

A look of concern crossed Lara's face.

"The deer met to come up with a better alternative," Raven said. "They suggested that if a human hunter didn't pardon themselves after he killed a deer, they would inflict the hunter with rheumatism so it would be too painful for him to hunt again. It's only if the human asks for forgiveness that the hunter can avoid painful joints that would keep him bedridden."

Raven took a moment, thinking about the animal's lives he'd taken to survive. He had spent much of his time in the sweat lodge thinking of human lives, but he often made a habit of thanking animals he hunted for their sacrifice.

"The fish and reptiles liked this idea too," he went on. "They decided that humans who didn't ask for forgiveness for killing their kind should dream about snakes blowing foul breath into their faces or about eating raw and rotten fish. Those disgusting thoughts would plague the humans' waking hours, making them lose their appetites and grow sick until they starved to death."

"I'd say the humans in this story deserved it," Lara said.

"The animals certainly thought so too," Raven said. "Each species created new ideas for diseases. They hoped that these diseases would tear through the humans that took them for granted and didn't ask for forgiveness, killing them so the animals could once again live in peace."

"How would people have survived against all these diseases?" Lara said. "If every animal conspired against humanity, it seems like we shouldn't even be here today."

"Exactly. Man would be extinct today if it weren't for the plants. They felt this punishment was too evil. All the shrubs, herbs, trees, grass, and mosses agreed that they would offer the cures to the ailments animals had invented. They allowed men to extract medicine from them."

When Raven finished, he thought he saw a slight smile form across Lara's lips.

"Thanks for sharing that with me, Mr..., uh, Raven," she said. "It might not mean much to you, but I appreciate it."

"Anytime."

Lara looked longingly up at the ponderosa pine branches swaying overhead. "Maybe the plant spirits can tell us how to heal whatever sickness is spreading through the New Frontier."

Raven wasn't so sure.

He didn't tell Lara what he was thinking, but whatever was striking people down out there was worse than anything he had seen in his days as a Marine or during the aftermath of the Collapse.

Whatever this was, it was going to take more than some soup to cure.

11

CALVIN STOOD IN HIS NEST ATOP THE SR SUPPLY CAR. The sun was beginning its afternoon dive toward the horizon. A harsh wind blew grit all around them, dyeing the sky a yellow hue. Canyon walls had given way to distant plateaus of red and gold rock, barely visible, thanks to the haze.

He brushed some of the sand from his wiry hair, but he knew it was a losing battle. The grit got everywhere, on his clothes, inside his clothes, sometimes inside his body.

To make matters worse, his old injuries were acting up again.

Some of that was probably due to his nerves finally getting to him.

Every jostling movement of the train bumping over the rails sent them chattering with electricity. It felt like a thousand knives were being swiveled around inside his back and down his leg.

"You okay, Boss?" Mouse asked, settling in beside him. Anna and Travis, seated at the opposite end of the nest, glanced in his direction.

"The sand is annoying me, my back hurts, and..." Calvin laughed. "And now I sound like a feeble old man."

"I got some ibuprofen inside the car," Anna offered. "I can get it before our shift's up, if that's cool."

"Nah, I'm good. Thanks, though."

Mouse clapped a hand on Calvin's shoulder. Maybe a little too strongly.

"Pardon me for being blunt, you look like absolute shit. I mean," he said. "I've *taken* shits that look better than you. Maybe you should go snag some sleep before we're relieved."

Calvin shrugged it off. "I'd rather stay here like I'm supposed to for the next hour."

"But we're through the hard shit. Why not take a rest? You earned it, Boss. I don't think you've slept more than two hours during a single stretch of this trip. Plus, you better be well-rested when you come down to visit the kids."

"Again, with the guilt trip," Calvin said. He tried to readjust to find a more comfortable position. But there wasn't a position more comfortable than "hurts like all nine circles of hell" or "feels like a sword plunging through the spine."

"I'm not tired," he said. "Honestly, who could sleep in this heat anyways?"

"Fine. Have it your way," Mouse said.

They returned to their posts, watching the sandy terrain rush by. Calvin found himself drifting off into a trance, his mind wandering to the dead. People he had cared about that never made it home.

From Afghanistan, to Iraq, to Iowa...

He tried not to give in to the despair, but truth be told, he was exhausted. Both his mind and his body.

An hour later, their relief showed up. They'd doubled the usual shift to four people after their close call in the Rockies. After signing off on the switch, Calvin headed down to the

SR supply car. The car was furnished with bunks and a corner-table bolted to the deck. Travis pulled the poker chips and cards out of a cubby.

"Anyone want to play some cards?" he asked. "We're pretty much at home plate, which means we got money waiting."

"You anxious to lose it?" Anna smirked. "Okay, I'm in."

Travis looked to Mouse. "Come on, big guy, you said you could take me, right?"

"I was gonna snag some sleep," Mouse replied.

"You can sleep when the trip is over," Travis said. "You worried I'm gonna beat you?"

Mouse grunted and walked over to the table. "Deal me in, shithead."

Everyone looked to Calvin. He stood by the open window, watching the distant mounds of sand.

"Come on, Boss, you got nothin' to worry about now," Mouse said. "I still think you should get some rest, though."

"Yeah," Travis said.

"I told ya', I ain't tired," Calvin replied. He finally relaxed and joined his comrades. Maybe cards were exactly what he needed to get his mind off everyone they had lost.

"Hell yeah, we got a game," Anna said.

"Okay, boys and girls, the game is Texas Hold 'em," Travis said. "You all know how to play?"

"Yes, sir," Mouse replied.

Calvin nodded. He was a bigger fan of Seven Card Stud and Omaha, but Hold 'em was what the young guys were all playing these days.

Travis distributed the chips. Each of them sitting with about two weeks' pay in front of them. Calvin had no plans of putting that much into action.

Mouse dealt out two cards to each of them. For the first few hands, Calvin tossed them away. All garbage. He picked up two Jacks about thirty minutes in and raised the bet. Travis called, and the board came in. Ten, Nine, Two, a rainbow of different suits.

Calvin bet the pot, and after a few seconds of thinking, Travis folded.

"Next time," he said.

After scooping the pot, Calvin sat the next hand out and went to the window. He used his radio to call in SITREPs. Each one came back clear.

"See? Nothing to worry about," Mouse said.

Still, Calvin stayed at the window. By the time he turned, Mouse and Travis were in the biggest pot of the session.

With all five of the community cards down, Travis shoved his entire remaining stack into the middle and stared at Mouse.

"All of it," Travis said. "And my bonus."

"You're betting your bonus before we're even there?" Mouse asked.

"I got the best hand," Travis said.

Mouse eyed him. "Not better than mine."

Calvin squinted at the community cards, seeing two Aces, a Six, a Five, and a King.

"Then call my bet, and let the cards talk," Travis said.

Calvin turned away from his team and back to the window, watching the desert.

The pot was two weeks' worth of pay, plus the bonus, and Calvin had a feeling Maureen was going to be pretty pissed at Mouse if he lost it. But Mouse wasn't the type to back down.

Chances were good they both had good hands, and this was going to come down to whichever man was luckier.

"I call this and lose, Maureen will have my balls," Mouse said.

Calvin chuckled. "You said she already does."

"This is different," Mouse replied seriously.

He reached for his chips with one hand and started to push them into the middle but then used his other hand to toss his cards away.

"I fold," he said. "Had trip Aces with a lousy kicker. Guess you had a better hand."

Travis leaned back in his seat, let out a sigh, then stood and threw his cards over, face-up. A Seven and a Two.

The worst hand in poker.

Mouse got up, studied the cards like he couldn't believe it, and then shook his head. "You lyin' son of a bitch!"

"Hey, man, this game rewards the better liar!" Travis scooped the chips over. "I ain't used to winning!" He held up his Sox hat. "I am the champion! Yeeeee-haw, baby!"

Anna chuckled, but Mouse just kept shaking his head in disbelief.

Just as Calvin was beginning to walk back to the table, an explosion shook the train, followed by a deafening boom that sounded like the sky itself was splitting in two.

Heart racing, Calvin looked to the window to see shapes emerge from camouflage netting and ditches dug alongside the tracks.

"Get down!" Calvin cried to the other three Steel Runners.

Another tremendous blast roared from the tracks behind them.

Calvin quickly climbed up into the nest to see what was happening. The four Steel Runners there were all hunched down.

"The hell is—"

Before Calvin could finish his sentence, a high-pitched

squeal and the shriek of protesting metal erupted from the train engine.

The locomotive careened off the tracks in a violent spray of fire and sparks. Flames vented high into the sky as another explosion tore through the engine, metal shrapnel flying. The heat of the blast seared over Calvin's skin.

An icy rush of adrenaline barreled through his veins. He grabbed the side of the Steel Runner nest to hang on, every wild vibration shaking through his arms.

As the train engine hit the sand alongside the rails, it dragged the SR Supply Car and other carriages after it. Each one let out a horrifying crashing cry as the wheels separated from the gnarled track.

More roaring fire ripped up from other cars carrying ammunition or fuel, each one detonating with monstrous blasts that sucked the air from his lungs. Their car and the burning locomotive plowed through the grit.

"Hold on!" Calvin yelled, straining to be heard over the madness.

When the car hit a massive bump, he lost his grip and fell back down the ladder into the car.

Mouse had his thick fingers wrapped around a post next to their bunks. His rifle was strapped over his back, eyes narrowed against the intense light of the building flames outside. He gave Calvin a brief glance.

It wasn't anger or fear. More like grim acceptance. Mouse's face was solid as stone.

Anna was screaming, holding on to a pole beside Travis, whose face was etched in terror.

Then their car, dragged by the locomotive, finally flipped on its side.

Calvin could barely tell what was going on as all of them went tumbling inside the car.

Metal exploded into bent shards as part of the roof peeled away. Sand plumed around them, shooting in through broken side windows. Smoke and grit swirled into the car like demonic desert spirits until the car ground to a halt.

Pushing himself up, Calvin went to one of the hatches. Those hatches were now like windows in the sideways car. He saw other burning cars scattered in the sand.

Flashes of the Black Hawk crash that ended his SEAL career popped through his mind. Only this was even more terrifying.

"Get to the hatches!" he called to Anna, Mouse, and Travis. "Watch for hostiles!"

His ears were ringing, and he could barely hear his own voice.

Calvin reached for his radio, finding it had been smashed in the crash.

"Son of a..." He turned toward where the cook's station was at the rear of the Supply Car. "Zach, you okay?"

"I'm... I'm alive..." the man called back from under the jumble of pots and pans that had fallen around him.

Calvin pressed his rifle to his shoulder. "I need you to get to the SR radio near the back of this car. Call Utah Scouts Command. Tell them what's happening!"

"Yes, sir," Zach said, pushing himself up from the debris. Part of the roof near that side had also peeled away, forcing Zach to claw his way through piles of sand that had been pushed in.

Even as the dust began to settle, all Calvin could make out through the hatches and destroyed roof were the scattered train cars. Chunks of metal debris stuck up like tombstones between broken crates and barrels.

Then human shapes began to coalesce through the haze.

At first, Calvin thought they might be Steel Runners.

Then he saw people wearing gas masks and desert camouflage hazard suits. They were carrying AK-47s. Something his people definitely weren't equipped with.

"We got three contacts straight ahead," Calvin said.

He immediately opened fire. The enemies dropped to their knees, finding shelter behind the wreckage scattered about the sand.

Return fire smacked against the car. Each hit rang through the metal, but the armor, damaged as it was from the crash, deflected most of the small arms fire.

Mouse's rifle chattered beside him. One of the attackers flipped backward, blood spraying from a hole in his broken gas mask.

Anna and Travis were fighting back to the left, neither cowering, both right up against a hatch with rifles blazing.

Calvin thought they might have a chance until he saw flames licking up from a car nearby. He could just barely see it from his vantage, but the fire suddenly billowed out with a puff of black smoke.

The neighboring car had been a tanker. Maybe it was filled with fuel or some kind of chemical.

Calvin watched in horror as something in the adjacent car detonated. Flames lashed at their car.

"Down!" he shouted.

Everything seemed to happen in slow motion after the words left his mouth. More of the car's roof peeled away from the intense explosion. The wall of heat slammed into them, blowing through the opening.

Another explosion went off, hammering the car, the pressure wave tossing the car and its contents. He flew out and into the sand against another carriage. He saw Anna, Travis, and Mouse thrown by the explosion in different directions. The cook's station in the rear of the car was completely gone, replaced by a ball of black smoke and metal debris.

Calvin tried to scrabble for his rifle to fight back the hostiles, but he realized his rifle had been torn from his grip. He tried to mouth the names of his friends. *Anna. Travis. Mouse.*

But nothing came out.

Before he could search for them, another thundering explosion rattled the desert. Sand blasted across his face, burying him, and barely saving him from a tidal wave of fire that blasted overhead.

———

Lindsey wasted no time when she returned to the Front Range. The first thing she did was stop by to see the families of Ferris and Cranston, relaying the news to Ferris' fiancée and Cranston's daughters. Being the messenger was difficult, but Lindsey remained strong when delivering the tragic news.

She reassured the families she would do everything she could to support them in the difficult days ahead.

After leaving the Cranston house, she linked back up with Deputy Palmer and drove straight to Doctor Divekar's clinic. Her next task was to see if Divekar had finally figured out what was going on.

Last time she had been to the clinic, it seemed relatively normal.

Not now.

Clear plastic sheets partitioned off the lobby. Everyone beyond those sheets wore face shields, bunny suits, and other protective gear.

An exhausted nurse shuffled toward them from the other side of the sheets. "Sheriff, can I help you?"

"We're supposed to see Doctor Divekar," Lindsey said.

"Get gowned up, then come find me." The nurse pointed to a table covered in bottles of sanitizer, gloves, and masks.

Lindsey and Palmer did as instructed and returned to the partition. The nurse was still on the other side, scanning some charts on a clipboard.

She pulled back the plastic sheet.

"Is it... safe?" Palmer asked.

"Safe enough if you follow precautions," the nurse said. "All the patients in the ICU are in another isolated area. We're just trying to be extra careful in the non-ICU portions."

They wound past other medical personnel in full gowns, gloves, and face-shields. All the patients in this non-ICU ward seemed to be either behind closed doors or in their own plastic partitioned areas.

"Doctor Divekar always says it's better to be overprepared and look paranoid than to underprepare for a contagion," the nurse added. "Hence all of this."

The nurse waved her hand at the plastic sheets.

That wasn't so different than what Lindsey had said to Palmer about her preparations for the Angel Line. And her efforts had paid off. She prayed Divekar's would as well.

"There she is." The nurse pointed to yet another gowned individual talking to people at a nurses' station.

Lindsey wasn't sure how the nurse knew who Divekar was under all the PPE, but sure enough, when the nurse called Divekar's name, she recognized those tired nut-brown eyes behind the face-shield.

"Sheriff Plymouth!" Divekar called. She hustled over to Lindsey.

"What's the status on those patients with the unidentified disease?" Lindsey asked.

"I'm not going to be able to show you them," Divekar said. "Not now."

"I can see the precautions you're taking."

"Exactly." Divekar took a tablet from the nurses' station. "We've isolated everyone we suspect has the disease. With the rate it's spreading, we're calling it Wild Fire until we identify what it really is."

Wild Fire. It unfortunately seemed an apt name.

Divekar tapped on her tablet. Images of patients showed on the screen.

"I prepared this for you." She handed the tablet to Lindsey so she and Palmer could see it better. Inflamed flesh and lesions marred the bodies of each patient.

"Ho-ly shit," Palmer said.

Lindsey shared the sentiment.

"How many are sick?" Lindsey asked.

"We're up to thirty-two now," Divekar said. "Some show symptoms like this. Others are just respiratory. It seems like it's manifesting differently in every patient."

"I get that the lab results aren't back or conclusive, but you've got to have some idea what it is."

"I mean, given it's bacterial, I'd say the plague now, but it doesn't match the profile of any cases of plague in Colorado's history. Plus, it looks way worse. Whatever this is, it's *new*."

Lindsey's stomach turned. "Has it reached our community yet? Or are all these coming from the mountains?"

"Most are from the mountains," Divekar said. "Those that it spread to here were some of the first nurses and medics to treat our patients. They didn't use masks or PPE. A couple patients who were in the same room also passed Wild Fire to each other. Otherwise, using our precautions, we've managed to stop the spread between people at the clinic. So far, no one in the local community has come in."

"How are the other Front Range clinics doing?" Lindsey asked.

"We have scattered reports of Wild Fire in several of them," Divekar said.

"I assume you already told them how to protect against it."

"I've shared everything we're doing."

"Good, good," Lindsey said. She handed the tablet back to Divekar. "And my scout—"

"Raven Spears, yes," Divekar said. "His sister, Sandra, is a nurse at an Estes Park clinic, I believe."

"That's right."

"I talked with her earlier. She's headed up to Raven's house to make sure he's okay. If he doesn't show any symptoms by now, then I'd say he's clear."

"You're sure?" Lindsey asked.

Divekar didn't seem to be sure.

"Until I get an accurate antigen or DNA test back, I can't tell you anything one hundred percent," she explained. "So far, we just don't have a match from any of the pathology labs we've run. For all we know, the entire Front Range is infected and we're all carriers. But from what I've seen so far, that's not how I suspect this disease works. I'm holding on to that hope. Our biggest threat is containing Wild Fire to the New Frontier, where it's coming from."

"How do you expect to do that?" Palmer asked.

"That's the million-dollar question," Divekar said. "A lot of these people have no idea Wild Fire is even a thing. Some of our incoming patients say they got sick from their friends and family, who are still out there, so the numbers we're seeing in the clinics are probably just the tip of the iceberg."

"Damn," Lindsey said. This was getting worse by the minute. "We have to prepare for an influx of patients coming down on us like an avalanche."

Divekar turned toward her staff. "You can see we're already at our limits as it is. Anything you can do to help, I'd appreciate."

"I'll talk to Governor Anders. We'll see what the National Guard can wrangle up to help you." Lindsey looked to Palmer. "In the meantime, we're going to need to lock down our borders. I want our Rangers, allies, and everyone else watching the New Frontier to intercept any of these diseased outlaws before they spread Wild Fire to our people."

"You got it, ma'am," Palmer replied.

"Anything else I should know?" Lindsey asked Divekar.

"You've got everything covered so far," Divekar said. "I just hope it's enough."

After a short decon spray down and handwash, Lindsey was back in the Humvee with Palmer on their way to Fort Golden. She placed requests for aid with Governor Anders and began taking notes on a report for the FAC. Maybe she could recruit additional manpower and medical supplies through them.

Her sat phone rang.

"Sheriff Plymouth," she answered.

A worried male voice replied. "Sheriff, this is John Slinde with the Utah Scouts Command."

Lindsey checked her watch. Travel through the desert could be slow at times with the state of the rails and the caution trains had to take to avoid ambushers. The Angel Line train should be just a few hours outside Salt Lake City now, but they definitely wouldn't have arrived yet.

Which meant this call couldn't be anything good.

"What's going on, Commander Slinde?" Lindsey asked.

"The Angel Line was attacked."

It took Lindsey a second to register those words.

"No, no, we got it through the Rockies," she said. "It can't..."

"We had scouts positioned to watch over it on the last stretch in Utah. We thought everything was clear. But some-one... someone took out our scouts and then... We lost contact with the train. It hasn't reached any scheduled points past Arches National Park."

Lindsey didn't respond for a moment, the shock getting the best of her.

"Sheriff?" Slinde asked.

"Sorry, I just can't believe it. Are your teams en route to search the tracks?"

"I'm afraid that's why I'm calling," John said. "Our scouts are already stretched thin, and the three I lost were some of my best. Salt Lake City barely has enough manpower to keep our city safe. We just can't afford to lose any more trying to find out what happened to the Angel Line. In fact, we *needed* that line. It had ammunition for us. Medical supplies. Foreign aid we desperately need."

"You're asking me for help," Lindsey said.

Palmer shot her a suspicious glance.

"I am," John replied.

Lindsey took a moment to think. Utah was far less popu-lated than Colorado. They'd lost more of their population than Colorado had during the Collapse too. It didn't help that the city was firmly embedded in the middle of the New Fron-tier either, even if it wasn't the most dangerous area.

Salt Lake City was now a shadow of its former self. The Utah government had barely retained control. Even though Utah was generally safer than the Rocky Mountains, its isola-tion meant any threat could lead to its downfall.

A threat like whatever was brewing in the New Frontier. She had to find whoever was responsible for these dogged attacks on the Angel Line and the raid on her supply depot in Eagle. And she had to find out fast before they lost any more people or essential provisions.

There was a good chance the people responsible for the attack in Utah were connected to the earlier attack in Colorado. That meant they were also connected to whoever might be a traitor within her own operations. The web of treachery was getting wider and wider.

And with Wild Fire spreading, she felt like her entire world was crashing down around her.

"Sheriff?" Slinde said again.

"Yes, I'll round up my people, and deploy them ASAP, but chances are good by the time we get there, these attackers will probably be long gone with whatever supplies they wanted."

"Anything we can scavenge will be useful. Everything helps nowadays." John paused a second. "Really, we're absolutely desperate here, Sheriff, and we know you have some of the best trackers in the region."

"We'll do our best."

"Thank you, Sheriff."

She ended the call with him after getting the last known coordinates of the Angel Line.

"Palmer, as soon as we get to Fort Golden, I'll assemble a team to head out to the Angel Line," she said.

"I'll get ready to—"

"You're not going," she said. "I need you here to work on reinforcing our checkpoints and border security. Keep an eye on the FAC too."

"Who are you taking with you then?" he asked.

The Humvee rumbled down the streets of Golden, passing by restaurants and bars that were still boarded up.

"If Raven's sister confirms he's clear to go, I'm going to

bring him and a couple of our best scouts," she said. "There's one more thing I want you to do when I'm gone."

"Ma'am?"

"Have our Investigations team uncover everything they can related to the Angel Line. I've never seen so much effort put into taking down one train. I want to know about the shipping manifests, who contracted cargo, everything."

"I can handle that." Palmer jotted the orders down in a small notepad.

Lindsey eyed the pad. "I don't want *anyone* outside Investigations to know what you find. Just me. Got it?"

"Yes, ma'am." Palmer slipped the notepad into his chest pocket.

The Humvee passed through the gates of Fort Golden. She pulled up to the side of their offices and Palmer hopped out.

"Be careful out there," he said. "I'll hold down the fort while you're gone."

Lindsey nodded. "Good luck, and stay in touch."

"You got it, Sheriff."

He patted the truck and she pulled away.

They were going to need more than luck with Wild Fire spreading and dangerous forces operating beyond their borders.

She couldn't help but feel everything she had worked to protect was about to collapse.

12

CALVIN WOKE TO THE RATTLE OF GUNFIRE.

He blinked through blurred vision. Light pierced his retinas, igniting a fire behind his eyes, and he closed them again.

Pain throbbed through every part of his body, hammering him worst beneath his skull, as the acrid smell of smoke filled his nostrils.

His mouth was dry, his tongue sticking to the roof.

Where the hell was he?

Sand poured off his head as he tried to stand. He was buried in the grit. He started to struggle free, reaching for his rifle. Then he remembered he'd lost it somehow.

Instead, he pushed his hand into the sand toward his hip. Right where he had his pistol holstered. At least he had one weapon.

He couldn't remember what had happened or why he was lying down in this grit. He took in a deep breath that carried a storm of smells: death, charred skin, blood. It mixed with the pungent odor of spilled diesel fuel.

Despite the agony from light tearing through his optic nerves, he forced his eyes open.

Bits of paper and ash floated everywhere between bright orange embers. Black smoke pumped into the sky, fed by crackling fires. Broken train cars had torn huge gouges in the earth surrounding him. A whole line of them walled him in to his right. To his left, other cars had buckled, spread out. The rails that he could see looked like they'd been hit by explosives in several places, which must have caused the separation of these cars.

He couldn't see much else past them, but columns of black smoke climbed into the air, evidence that this crash was a jumbled mess stretching for hundreds of yards.

He blinked again as his vision returned.

Nearby was a singed White Sox cap with dried blood stains. He reached for it, dragging it toward him.

No, no, no.

Awful memories started to flood back right as crunching sounded between a couple of yells past another fallen boxcar.

Two men wearing black fatigues, rifles strapped over their shoulders were carrying some small crates away from a sideways train car. Each crate had a blue-and-white triangular logo with Siegler Pharm in big black letters. They disappeared around a car, following another pair of men dragging a barrel with the same logo.

The wind scraped over Calvin as he dragged himself around a shrub for a better view. Other metal barrels with different labels and logos had fallen from a car and broken open. They leaked dark viscous fluids into the sand. A body was sprawled between steel pipes and panels that had come loose from one of the toppled train cars.

A sinking feeling enveloped him when he recognized the halo of brown hair around a blood-caked skull.

It was a thirty-year-old woman named Lauren. She had

been running steel to support her husband, who'd been disabled in the initial Collapse.

He crawled toward her, unable to gather the strength to pull himself to his feet. She was lying flat beneath a crate.

"Lauren..." He reached toward her arm, trying to pick up her hand.

There was no pulse.

"God, no..."

He craned his head, seeing Travis next, his body pinned under the panel of another car.

Calvin began to crawl in that direction to help when he saw there would be no helping his friend. Travis was dead, his head crushed.

Still gripping the White Sox hat, Calvin squeezed it hard, recalling the final moments of the poker game. Travis had danced around the table, thrilled to have finally won, only to have those winnings, and his life, ripped away.

Calvin took in the gruesome scene, searching for Mouse.

Coughs racked up through his throat, but he held his hand over his mouth to keep from drawing attention to his location.

Groans and screams came from other parts of the train wreckage. Some called for help, others shrieked in unbridled agony.

A gunshot rang out, silencing one of them.

Calvin tensed.

These raiders were executing the surviving Steel Runners.

You have to do something!

"Help..." He heard a voice near another sand drift pressed up against a fallen train car.

He rushed over to the voice as fast as he could. Buried in the sand, her head just visible, was Anna.

"Anna," he whispered as he began to free her from the grit.

Another gunshot rang out, distracting him.

"Calvin," Anna groaned.

"Are you injured?" he asked.

She winced. "My head, I think, and my arm hurts really bad."

"Which one?"

"My right..."

He moved over to that side and slowly unburied her right arm. Bone from a fracture stuck out of the skin.

"Okay," he said, fighting back his own worry. "You're okay."

She looked down and groaned.

"Look at me, Anna," he said. "You're going to be okay."

Using his knife, he cut off a piece of canvas tarp over one of the nearby crates. He fashioned it into a quick bandage and sling for her. She yelled in pain when he tightened it over her wound.

Calvin turned in anticipation with his pistol drawn, but her scream didn't seem to attract any attention. He returned his attention to Anna.

"I want you to stay hidden," he said. "Let's get you into cover."

"I'll fight. I can..." Her eyes seemed glassy.

She was clearly in shock, and with her injury, there was no way she could do much to help.

"No, we need to get you inside one of the train cars. Go hide."

Then he remembered what Raven had told him about the ambushers near Hanging Lake. They had been asking about medicine.

"Whatever you do, don't hide near the medical supplies. You got it?" he asked.

She nodded slowly as he helped her to her feet. Another gunshot cracked, followed by a scream.

"Go, Anna," Calvin said.

She lurched around the other side of the car.

Calvin wiped the sand off his watch. It had been at least an hour since the train derailed. If Zach had gotten the radio call off, Utah Scouts Command would have already deployed armed men to see what had happened to the train.

Unless they too had already been killed.

Then the Steel Runners would be on their own.

As the ringing faded in his ears, he heard the low rumble of idling truck engines. Indistinct voices shouted.

A pickup truck suddenly powered through the smoke, winding between a couple of train cars. Barrels and crates were secured to the back, all with the Siegler Pharm logo. Smoke quickly swallowed the truck as it accelerated away.

Calvin heard someone banging on the side of a train car. Then he heard the whine of a drill biting into metal.

With smoke still grating at his eyes and throat, he fought back a coughing fit, resuming his search for Mouse, other survivors, and a better weapon.

He walked at a hunch through the dust and grit, gripping his pistol. Thick smoke drifted away from the destruction. He brought his bandana up over his face, but still coughed.

Each cough sent a jolt of pain down his injured back. When he started to move again, his entire body fought back. The pain was intense. Normally, he could handle the mental anguish, but that didn't mean his body would respond.

Another two gunshots cracked deeper within the train wreckage.

The sounds forced him to hurry, but again his body gave out. He collapsed in the sand.

He thought back to his days in SEAL training, when he had to do the fifty-meter underwater swim.

Fifty meters didn't sound like a lot.

Until you realized you couldn't push off from the wall and had to do it all in one breath. If you came up too early, that was it for your SEAL career. You were immediately kicked out of the program.

Most guys made it out of the water, their eyes glazed over or wide with panic, gulping down air, straining to stay upright on their hands and knees. One man passed out when he hit the end of the swim, his hand touching the side just in time for the instructors to pull his unconscious body out.

After the instructors dragged him out and checked his pulse, the first thing he said was: "Did I make it?"

Mouse was one of those guys that kept cool under pressure. He swam the full fifty at an even pace without a breath. Popped right up and out of the water at the end like he'd enjoyed the swim.

When it was Calvin's turn, Mouse clapped him on the shoulder and said, "It's just a mind game, Boss."

That was all this was now too.

A mind game.

Now he had to convince his body to respond.

You're stronger than this, he thought. *You've been through way worse!*

Calvin pushed himself back toward another busted car. He walked at a hunch, coughing in the smoke, and doing his best to stick to the shadows of the train cars. Where were the rest of his people?

Every step sent agonizing pain up and down his spine, but

his legs were finally working. He took a step, then another, then two more.

Mouse's words rang through his head: *It's just a mind game.*

He bent down when he saw a rifle protruding from the sand. Grabbing it, he checked to find half a magazine. He palmed it back in and raised the weapon at two figures around the next car.

"Thank God," Calvin said when he saw two more Steel Runners. Jaron Thomas and Kelly Hart, both in their early twenties, limped toward him as he lowered his rifle.

They were struggling to stay upright, leaning against each other, looking lost. Calvin gave them directions to meet up with Anna, and they took off. He encountered another three Runners, one who could barely walk, and told them where to go too.

Another burst of gunfire went off in the distance, followed by a plea. "No, please, no, NO!"

Calvin thought he recognized the voice of Zach, the cook.

The man's screams were quickly quieted by another blast. Calvin shuddered. He had to find Mouse.

With the rifle shouldered, he stumbled around another overturned train car, following the snaking line of broken cars. The noxious odor of oil and smoke made him dizzy. More viscous black liquid dripped from a punctured steel barrel in the sand.

Definitely oil or fuel of some kind, judging by the odor.

As it poured over the ground, some of it pooled and then sank into the sand. Small streams of the black liquid rolled toward the adjacent car that was still burning.

Calvin hurried around the car dripping oil, fighting the dizziness and pain.

He suddenly stopped at the sight of a hulking man

surrounded by broken metal barrels and slabs of armor that had peeled off a train car.

"Mouse," Calvin said.

He leaned down to his brother, finding he was pinned under an armor sheet. His M4 was on the ground next to him, just out of his reach.

Mouse looked at Calvin with eyes completely red from burst blood vessels.

"Boss..." Mouse said. He tried to move, but Calvin put a hand on his chest.

"Stay calm, and watch my back," Calvin said. "I'm going to get you out of here."

Calvin handed the M4 to Mouse.

Shouts burst somewhere beyond the screen of smoke surrounding them as Calvin turned to look for a way to lift the panel. The oil continued to trickle toward the fire.

"Hold on," Calvin said as he started to try and free his friend.

"No," Mouse protested. "You got to get out of here."

Calvin ignored him as he shoveled the sand around his legs. More sand kept spilling back in every time Calvin thought he'd made progress. He watched the leaking oil, seeing it inch closer and closer to the fire. Embers from the flames landed on some of the dry bushes nearby, igniting them like torches.

All it took was for one ember to hit the oil, and then Calvin and Mouse would both be burned alive.

"Get your ass out of here, Boss," Mouse said.

Calvin dug harder, faster, his back screaming at him to stop,

A gunshot cracked beyond the line of cars crumpled around them. Another Steel Runner executed.

"You got to get out—" Mouse coughed and spat out bloody saliva.

Calvin dug more frantically now. The fire spread to more of the withered plants. Each one sparked to life with a ferocious claw of flames.

A burst of gunfire rang out. This time, the shots sounded even closer.

Calvin thought he saw silhouettes coming toward them in the smoke.

"Go, please, Boss, please." A tear ran down Mouse's cheek, carving through some of the soot. "Tell my kids I—"

Calvin looked up as Mouse aimed his rifle at someone walking through the smoke. The person stalking toward them was just barely visible, tendrils of smoke wrapping around them in a shroud.

As the figure got closer, Calvin saw it was a man wearing a desert camouflage protective suit and gas mask, just like he had seen before. The man carried a rifle. Clearly some kind of AK-variant. Blood spatter covered the man's chest.

The man was definitely no Steel Runner. He carried himself with the confident, smooth movements of a Special Forces operator. With his boot, he pushed aside a few planks from a broken crate. He appeared to be looking for something.

As the man drew closer to Calvin and Mouse, he raised his rifle.

A shot boomed, echoing between the train cars.

The man slumped to the ground. His weapon clattered next to him with a puff of dust.

Mouse had hit the man square in the chest.

Three more raiders in full battle gear with gas masks rushed through the smoke, falling into firing positions near their downed comrade.

"Run," Mouse said to Calvin. "You have to live. My kids, Cal. They will need you."

Calvin unslung his rifle and prepared to fire over the wall of bent metal giving them some protection. It was clear these guys hadn't seen them yet, but it was just a matter of seconds, and with Mouse only halfway unburied, there was only one option—fight.

Things weren't like they had been in BUD/S.

There was no way to save his best friend, nothing he could do but choose to die beside him or run away to save his own ass.

To Calvin, there was only one acceptable option. He fired calculated shots at the three men right as a poof of embers drifted around the oil.

The hiss of fire erupted across the oil trail.

Calvin realized it wasn't a mind game any longer.

A wave of fire expanded over the sand.

The raiders twisted to flee.

As soon as the flames hit the first leaking barrel, it exploded with a deafening boom. The other barrels went off with it. Flames rushed outward like a diabolical creature erupting from the bowels of hell. The three men dove away from the inferno.

Calvin was blown back, thrown inside another busted train car. His body slammed into wooden crates already half broken by the crash. Boards cracked and splintered around him.

Torn bags of grain spilled out from on top of the crates and poured over him, half-burying him in seed. He could barely see, blinking past the resurgent pain. But through the broken hole which he'd been thrown, he caught a glimpse of where Mouse had been pinned.

All that was left were chunks of twisted metal and a

blackened crater. A cloud of dark smoke poured up into the sky.

Calvin didn't see any evidence of Mouse, nor the men that had attacked them.

He blinked, trying to fight past the pain tugging him toward unconsciousness. But he'd lost the mind game when he lost his brother.

If death had come to take him, Calvin would welcome it with open arms.

———

Raven finished up his soup and licked the bowl clean. Creek did the same on the porch floor.

"Pretty good stuff, huh?" he said.

Raven stood and stretched his arms, looking out over the trees and the adjacent clearing near his cabin. Just beyond, a stream burbled over smooth black rocks that caught the morning sunlight.

The whole world could go to hell, and Raven would be perfectly content to spend his life on this piece of land. Especially with Sandra and Allie close to him.

Just as he was starting to relax, a car engine rumbled in the distance.

"Speaking of," Raven said.

He stood and started walking down the porch as Sandra pulled the car to a stop on his drive. She got out with a mask, face shield, and blue nitrile gloves on.

"Hey, sis, you sure this is okay?" he said.

"You feeling all right?"

"Like an eagle soaring over the Rockies."

She tossed him a surgical mask, and he put it on. "We're

not *exactly* sure how this bug is spreading between people, but we're pretty sure it's airborne."

Creek rushed out to meet Sandra, wagging his tail and whining. She gave him a pat as she approached Raven.

"You still have that thermometer I dropped off?" she asked.

Raven nodded and took it from his front pants pocket. "Ready like you said."

"Stick that under your mask. Take your temp."

Raven did exactly as she said.

When it beeped, he looked down to the reading.

"Well?" she asked.

"Still no fever," he said.

"Good. From what I can tell, you're fine."

"How sure are you?"

"So far, myself and the whole staff have been okay with proper safety gear. A few patients who were in the clinic for other reasons caught the disease. They didn't have any personal protective gear. We think they came into direct contact with the infected patients."

"Damn. I really wish you could take time off until this passes, but I already know what you're going to say."

"Yeah, same thing I say to you, that you ignore."

"Somebody has to do our jobs," Raven said.

"Yup, and this is going to get worse. We need people to take care of the sick. It's not just bad people from the Frontier at risk of getting it. It's people in our communities."

Creek returned to Raven and curled up near his feet.

"Are they thinking about closing down the school?"

"There's been talk of it, but Allie's there now. They're watching for infections in the local community before doing anything drastic."

"I'm actually taking a break now that I helped Lindsey get

that last train through the mountains. I'm not planning on anything anytime soon." He jerked his chin to the cabin. "If you think I'm not sick, that girl, Lara, made some Wahonpi soup and dropped it by earlier today. I've got a lot if you're interested."

Sandra hesitated.

"Come on," he said.

She peeled off her protective gear and put it into a sack, depositing it all inside her car. Once inside, Raven served her a bowl of the soup at his kitchen table, and Creek joined them.

"Kind of reminds me of when Grandma made it," she said. "Lara knows what she's doing."

"I know," Raven said. "I feel bad for her, though. Absent from the community for two years. Now that she's back, everything she once knew is gone, except for her grandmother."

"Tough for a young woman her age." Sandra spooned some more soup into her mouth. "When she came by and talked to me, she seemed like a smart girl. I was thinking of getting her hired on as a nurse's assistant. I mean, she doesn't have the official training for it... but I think I could get her up to speed. Sixteen is the minimum age for it, and God knows we need the help."

"Now's a pretty dangerous time, but she's a strong girl."

"And with the influx of patients, our clinic manager is getting desperate, hiring just about anyone off the street. For all I know, we could start using Lara's help tomorrow."

"She would probably like having something to do, to keep her mind off everything. You know what they say about idle minds and hands."

"They cause trouble, like when we grew up on the rez, huh?"

For a moment, their conversation turned back toward life on South Dakota's Rosebud Indian Reservation. Most of their time there had been spent in poverty. Their education had been less than desirable. Raven had managed to escape by joining the Marines, while Sandra had pursued a vocation in nursing that offered her a new life. But she had married a man with a drinking problem that eventually turned to violence.

Raven recalled going to rescue Allie from his house in Loveland not long after the power went off. They hadn't seen that asshole since.

"Always looking out for me," Sandra said.

"You got my back too."

"Always."

Raven smiled contently. It had been so long since he and his sister had just sat down and talked. He realized he missed this time with her.

He was about to tell her as much when a distant thumping caught his ear.

Creek shot up from where he was lying by the table, ears perked.

"You hear that?" Raven asked.

Sandra narrowed her eyes, brow scrunching together like she was trying to figure out what he was hearing. "Is that a helicopter?"

Raven stood from the table.

They abandoned their soup and stood out on the front porch with Creek. The thumping of the chopper grew louder.

Raven expected the bird to blast past them into the mountains, but the noise got closer until it was almost on top of them. Soon enough, between the trees came the familiar silhouette of a black Bell 407GX Helicopter, a staple of law enforcement agencies.

It started to descend toward his driveway.

"You expecting someone?" Sandra yelled.

"No!" Raven shouted.

If someone was using a helicopter to come out here, it had to be extremely important. The fuel was too important for anything short of an emergency.

He shielded his eyes against the sun as the chopper lowered into the clearing.

Creek's fur shook in the rotor wash.

As soon as the helicopter touched down, Lindsey Plymouth stepped out of the passenger cabin, holding her wide-brimmed sheriff's hat.

"Raven!" she called, jogging over to him. Behind her, Raven spotted two other men in the leather bucket seats in the chopper's passenger hold.

"What's going on?" he yelled.

"You sick?" Lindsey called back.

"No, I'm fine!"

He motioned for Lindsey to follow him to the porch where they could talk without shouting. Sandra stood there looking down as Raven approached with the sheriff.

"What's this all about?" Sandra asked.

"The Angel Line got hit bad." Lindsey said. "It completely derailed. We're still trying to figure out what happened. I need help tracking down who did it immediately before they can escape."

Now the visit made sense. Raven massaged his temple, trying to understand how this could have happened. "Why didn't you call?"

"You weren't answering your radio," Lindsey said.

Of course. He'd had it off because he wasn't looking to do another job.

Sandra looked at Raven with concern. "My brother's still recovering from his last mission."

Lindsey nodded. "I understand, but we need him."

Raven could see the two women sizing each other up, like always.

Dammit, I just wanted a peaceful day.

But there would be no peace in the Frontier today, not with the Angel Line destroyed. And Raven could tell Lindsey needed his help bad. She wouldn't have come to him if she wasn't desperate.

"What do I need?" he asked.

"Sam," Sandra said.

"Remember our talk about our jobs? You got yours, sis, and I got mine. Without us, good people are going to die."

Sandra sighed, glared at Lindsey, then stepped away.

"Be prepared to be out there for a couple days," Lindsey said.

Five minutes later, Raven returned from his cabin with Creek. Lindsey was back on the bird and Sandra was still on the porch.

His sister grabbed his sleeve. "Raven, I got a bad feeling about this."

"It'll be okay," he replied.

Sandra gave him a hug, pulling him in tight.

"Be careful at the clinic," he said.

"Be careful in the Badlands."

13

LINDSEY CHECKED HER WATCH AS THE HELICOPTER TOOK to the sky. Their flight out to Utah would be just under a couple hours. They soared high above the tree-covered mountains, and over the snow-capped peaks of Rocky Mountain National Park. Sunlight glistened off the alpine lakes and rivers winding between the trees.

It was beautiful up here, but Lindsey felt dread rising in her chest. She glanced over at Raven settled into one of the four black bucket seats. He was across from her with Creek at his boots. She handed him a headset, and Raven placed it over his long hair.

Besides him, she had brought two of her most trusted and talented Rangers. Both wore the standard khaki fatigues of the Colorado Rangers, helmets, and body armor. They each carried suppressed M4s for this mission.

"This is Larry Yoon," she said, indicating a shorter man with a thin black mustache. His arms were roped with thick muscle, and he had a bulldog face.

He gave Raven a sly grin that Lindsey only recognized

because she was used to seeing it. Most people would have considered it a scowl.

"And Juan Molina," Lindsey said.

Molina was younger than Yoon, but his youthful face didn't make him seem any less formidable. He had a goatee that bristled when he eyed Raven.

"Good to meet you," Molina said, stretching out a hand to Raven.

Raven shook it. "You guys too."

Then he looked over at Lindsey.

"You're coming with?" he asked.

"At least for the start."

"Got to say I'm a little surprised you aren't back at Fort Golden."

"I wanted to help," she said. "Plus, we want our best trackers on the job. You're one of them."

"What's that have to do with you coming?"

"I needed you on this job. If I didn't come personally to ask you, would you have gone?"

Raven didn't answer her. He didn't need to.

She could see the look in his eyes, and she had seen his sister's expression when the chopper landed at his cabin.

Coming to him in person, he couldn't so easily turn her down. Maybe she was taking advantage of their relationship, and that certainly wasn't fair. But fair didn't matter in the New Frontier. Fair wasn't part of the vocabulary in the Wild West. There was only victory or failure.

She had a job to protect the people of Colorado, to find the people responsible for the Angel Line attack, and she needed Raven to help her accomplish this mission.

"Okay, here's what I've pieced together," Lindsey said. "The Angel Line was attacked well outside of Salt Lake City, though we're not exactly sure of the location. We have only a rough idea based on their route and the time they went dark.

"We do know the Utah Scouts had a small group watching for the train's arrival. However, their team has also gone dark. They're assumed to be either captured or KIA. My counterpart in Salt Lake City has insisted they won't spare any more men until the area is deemed safe."

Lindsey took a deep breath.

"Like I mentioned, Raven, the train has almost certainly completely derailed. There might be dozens of casualties. Maybe more. Either way, the raiders responsible must be prepared and extremely well-armed."

Lindsey ran a hand through her hair. Raven had never seen her so exhausted and stressed.

"Unfortunately, no one has heard from Iron Lead Calvin Jackson or any other Runner in the past couple hours," she continued.

"Jesus Christ," Raven said. "All that work to get them through Colorado... then they get hit in *Utah?*"

"We had no indication there were groups powerful enough to pull this off in Utah," Lindsey said. "Utah Scouts Command wasn't expecting it either. Which is why it's so important we find whoever is responsible."

"Are we headed straight to the train?" Raven asked.

"We are," Lindsey said. "We have a rough idea of where it might have been derailed, based on its route, and the time, it went dark."

The chopper banked as it soared above the mountains, going lower over the other side of one of the snowcaps.

"There were eighty-one Steel Runners aboard and another fifteen crew members," Lindsey said. "We don't know what their condition will be. I've already got my Rangers and even the Utah Scouts Command organizing armed medical evac convoys that will be ready to go once we confirm the area is now clear from the sky. They'll be about two hours behind us, by land. Chances are good whoever is responsible for this smash and grab will be long gone by the time we get there, but we're going in prepared for hostiles."

"And if they are gone, my task is to track them down," Raven said.

"Yes, if we're lucky, there will be a trail to follow."

"And if we're not, no trail and a bunch of armed scavengers," Molina said.

Yoon nodded. "Might be some desperate people trying to salvage whatever's left at the trains. They might just be people looking for a quick bite to eat—or they might be dangerous. No way of knowing until we get closer, and we have to be ready to put down any threat."

"What are you saying?" Raven asked. "Shoot anyone down there?"

That stung. Lindsey knew Raven didn't fully buy her aggressive efforts to put down the resistance in the Colorado Rockies. In fact, they'd disagreed so much about her tactics, it had caused the rift that still lay wide between them.

"We're not firing on anyone unless we confirm they're dangerous," she said.

"Unlikely that we find any friendlies," Molina added.

"Hope for the best, but prepare for the worst," Yoon said.

"I trust your judgment, Sam," Lindsey said. "You might not be a Ranger, but you have my permission to defend yourself, that train, and any survivors."

"Understood," Raven said.

The rest of the flight went by relatively smoothly as the greens and grays of the Rockies gave way to the golds and reds of Western Colorado, then Utah. Rocky outcroppings and plateaus rose above the sands.

It didn't take long to see plumes of black smoke drifting up from the desert.

"There it is," Lindsey said. Then to the primary pilot, "Bring us in to make a recon sweep before we head down."

"Copy that," the primary pilot said.

The chopper closed in to the crash site, then banked to give Lindsey and the Rangers a view of the destruction. Giant columns of smoke made it difficult to see much. Between those snaking pillars of haze, Lindsey could make out the derailed frames of train cars snarled and coiled in the sand. She took out a pair of binos to survey the wreckage.

Fires still blazed between several of the cars. She identified multiple bodies sprawled throughout the scene of the wrecks. Most of which she assumed were dead.

Vultures circled in the sky, but many were already on the ground, feasting on the dead.

"My God," Lindsey whispered.

Molina performed the sign of the cross over his chest.

The chopper swooped a little lower, just enough that some of the smaller birds flapped away from the gruesome scene. Most of the vultures weren't deterred and continued to rip pieces away from the corpses.

"Anyone got eyes on potential hostiles?" Lindsey asked.

"Nothing." Molina leaned out of his seat and stared out the window.

"Negative on my side," Yoon said.

"Look there." Raven pointed out the window.

Lindsey followed his finger. He had spotted several tire tracks. Even from above, they appeared particularly wide and deep, the shadows from the afternoon sun revealing their paths.

"Some big trucks came through there," Lindsey said, "but I don't see any vehicles like that now."

"Stole the goods and ran," Yoon said.

Molina scanned the horizon with his binos. "I got nothing here."

"You see anything?" Lindsey asked the pilots.

Both shook their heads.

Raven pointed out a few smaller tracks too. "Looks like passenger vehicles too. Maybe SUVs, pickups, Jeeps."

Lindsey followed the tracks with her eyes into the smoke and wreckage. The tire tracks led right to the middle of the smoke.

"Wait a second," Lindsey said. "I think I see something."

"Movement?" Molina asked.

"No, but past the smoke, it looks like there's an SUV still parked between the wrecked train cars. Black. Maybe a Ford?"

"Could be opportunistic scavengers," Yoon said.

"I got eyes at three o'clock," reported one of the pilots. "Looks like a second SUV. A Chevy Tahoe."

"I still don't see any contacts," Lindsey said. "Maybe they took casualties."

"Maybe," Raven said.

Lindsey had the pilots perform another sweep to see if they could flush out any enemy combatants.

Nothing moved.

"All right, looks clear," she said. "Put us down on the northeast side of the wreck,"

She fastened the strap on her helmet and charged her rifle.

The chopper started to lower toward the desert. Rotor wash kicked up a cloud of dust that rolled over the wreckage. Smoke was blown back from the crumpled train cars.

Enough cleared that Lindsey could see the black Ford Explorer and the Tahoe they had spotted. They were only about ten yards from the ground when she saw something move near the SUVs.

"Potential contacts," Lindsey said.

"Steel Runners?" Raven asked.

Lindsey searched the ground, hoping some of them were alive. She saw movement again, dashing through the plumes of smoke.

Raising her binos, she zoomed in when she saw the glint of sun on the barrel of a rifle aimed right at them.

"Pull up!" she shouted.

The pilot cranked the chopper hard to its left. The heavy tap of bullets smacked against the light armor of the chopper.

"Guess we know they ain't friendly," Raven said.

Raven looked out of the chopper's window as Creek pressed against his legs. All the smoke and fire curling up around the maze of sideways, derailed cars was making it hard to see the shapes flitting between.

But his eyes were honed from years of tracking the most minute clues in the mountains. He did his best to study the shifting sands and smoke, identifying where the bandit had fired from.

They were far from the only dangers, though.

Several of the derailed cars were tankers. They had armor, but if the fires and crash had weakened their integrity, there was no telling what vile gases or liquids they might release. Anything from combustible fuel to toxic vapors.

"Seems like they were just trying to scare us off with a warning." Raven turned back from the window. "How many we got down there?"

"I only saw one hostile," Lindsey said.

Yoon shrugged. "I didn't see anyone else."

"Me neither," Molina replied.

Raven didn't get a good look at all.

Lindsey thought of Calvin. He was a good man, and she hoped he had made it. She took in a deep breath.

"What do you want me to do?" asked one of the pilots.

Raven looked to Lindsey as she considered their options.

"We got one hostile, maybe more," she said. "And we don't know where they are."

Yoon shook his helmet. "Risky, if you ask me."

"I don't like it," Molina said. "Maybe we should wait for backup."

Lindsey checked with Raven.

"We fly around, and we waste fuel and risk getting shot down," Raven said. "I'd rather be on the ground, personally, especially if we still got Steel Runners that need our help." He paused. "I mean, if you're asking me and all."

Lindsey seemed to think on it again, then agreed. "Drop us off, then set down somewhere safe north of the wreck."

The pilots nodded and banked over to the eastern side of the wreck, far away from where they had been shot.

"Molina and I will take the eastern approach," Lindsey said. "Raven and Yoon, curl around south to take the western. We got all kinds of fumes down there, so I want you all to take one of these." Lindsey handed out gas masks hanging from the bulkhead. "This should help against Wild Fire exposures too. Let's meet at the center of the wrecked boxcars where we saw those SUVs. I want to surround and trap whoever took a shot at us. Use extreme caution. Shoot first, ask questions later. I'd rather we all stay alive and help any Steel Runners, than try to take one person prisoner if it's too big of a risk."

"Agreed." Raven strapped on his gas mask.

The chopper lowered toward the desert floor just beside

the burning train engine. Black smoke was dispelled by the rotor wash, and yellow grit kicked up in a fierce cloud. The skids of the helicopter hit the ground with a jolt.

"Raven, Yoon, go first!" Lindsey said, her voice slightly muffled through the gas mask.

Raven jumped out at a hunch, and Creek leaped into the sand beside him. Yoon barreled out right after. They pushed through the black columns of smoke around a toppled cargo car before Lindsey and Molina made their exit.

Two bodies were crushed and twisted beneath the mangled steel. Something moved in Raven's gut, but he suppressed it.

The chopper was soaring above them again, its rotors helping to push back some of the black, oily smoke from the raging fires devouring what remained of the cargo.

"Recon Team, Condor One," the primary pilot of the chopper called on the comms. The bird was already rising above the wreckage again, heading north a safe distance. "Looks like two men, both with rifles."

"They might be trying to run," Raven replied. "We can't let them escape."

He pressed himself against the torn metal side of a cargo car. Yoon was watching his back as Creek prowled low to the ground between them.

Raven checked the other side of the car, seeing it was clear and signaling for Yoon to follow. They quickly made their way toward the Ford Explorer and the Chevy Tahoe. The Tahoe had a couple boxes of food Raven could see through the open doors. Through the windows of the Explorer, Raven noticed stacks of ammo boxes and more food that must have been scavenged from the train wreck.

One man was on the ground working on patching a tire.

The other guy, dressed in camouflage, stood guard with an AK-47, aiming it in the opposite direction.

Raven considered telling him to lower the rifle. He hated shooting a man in the back, but after what he had seen out here, this person didn't deserve mercy.

Two trigger pulls was all it took. Blood spurted out of the openings in his back as the man crashed face-first into the ground.

The man changing the tire whirled right into Yoon's gunfire. The bullets ripped into his faded leather jacket and grimy jeans as he cried out.

The passenger door of the truck suddenly opened, and gunfire forced Yoon and Raven to the ground. Creek scrambled for cover, yelping.

"We got a third!" Raven shouted.

The gunman took off running into the smoke.

Raven checked on Creek and Yoon. Both were okay.

"On me," Raven said.

He rushed past the Explorer and into an area of sand where bodies of more Steel Runners and train crew members were sprawled between sheets of metal and broken crates.

The heat from the fires raging nearby sweltered over Raven's skin. He passed a massive, blackened crater filled with gnarled pieces of metal and charred wood. Something else had exploded here before they had arrived.

That made their mission all the more urgent.

Stop this man, save anyone they could, and get out of here before more explosions ripped through the crash site.

Raven and Creek ran side by side with Yoon covering them. They cleared another train car, and on the other side, Raven saw the fleeing outlaw. The guy ran with a backpack bouncing against his back, stuffed to the brim. No doubt with things he'd stolen from the boxcars and dead Steel Runners.

In his hand, he carried a revolver, which didn't look so menacing at this range.

"Stop!" Raven bellowed, bringing his own weapon to bear. Maybe bringing this guy in wasn't a bad idea.

Yoon knelt beside him, sighting up the runner.

The man took one look at Raven but kept going.

"Stop!" Raven tried again. "Or you're—"

A gunshot cracked over the sand.

The scavenger let out a screech, which was quickly cut off by another gunshot. He fell to the sand, and his backpack ripped open, spilling canned goods and magazines of ammunition into the grit.

Raven glanced toward another train car across from the small clearing. Lindsey stood with her rifle still shouldered and aimed at the guy she had shot. He lay in the sand, limbs still.

With a hand signal, she ordered Molina to approach.

Raven, Creek, and Yoon advanced toward them.

"We could've questioned that guy," Raven said when he got close to Lindsey.

She nudged the dead man over with one of her boots. "I had the same thought until he aimed that revolver at me."

Raven suddenly felt guilty for not taking the shot when he could have. What if this asshole had managed to shoot Lindsey?

Raven quickly began to search the scattered footprints and tire tracks. A hot wind blew through the smoke and fire, covering some of the prints with sand.

"This guy wasn't part of the initial attackers," Lindsey said. "Just a scavenger, but steer clear of these guys. For all we know, they're sick, like those men Raven found in Glenwood Springs."

Molina and Yoon provided security while Lindsey called to the pilots.

"Condor One, can you do another sweep to make sure the sector is clear?"

"On it," replied the primary pilot.

Raven and Creek continued their search until the bird flew overhead, circling several times like one of the vultures.

"Recon Team, Condor One here," the primary pilot said. "Sector seems clear."

"Copy," Lindsey said. "We're going to start looking for survivors and any clues to the people responsible for this attack."

She twisted her wrist to check her watch. "It's still going to be two hours before our closest support convoy reaches us. Let's move out."

Not a minute after the group began to move, a massive roar tore through the air from deeper within the wreckage. Fire clawed at the sky, followed by ballooning black smoke.

"Shit, what was that?" Yoon asked.

"I don't know, but this site is far from safe. We've got to move fast," Lindsey said. "Raven, Yoon, you head back toward the western side of the wreckage. We'll take the eastern."

The group parted ways. Raven took point and headed out in the direction from which they'd come in order to make a more thorough sweep. He did his best to guide them around the thick smoke and spreading fires, but it was almost impossible to avoid.

For the first twenty minutes, they found little more than ruined cargo and corpses.

The bodies of the train's crew were everywhere.

"Shit, look at this guy," Yoon said, pointing to a Steel Runner.

Raven crouched to examine the bullet hole in the middle of his forehead. "He was executed..."

That sent a shudder down Raven's spine. They searched other bodies, hoping at least one was alive.

The existential terror of all these lives wiped out in a horrific attack would haunt Raven later. He shifted past the dead, many of whom looked to have been killed in cold blood.

Creek sniffed at the air, his nose twitching with every grating odor. Raven could only imagine what the mix of death and fire smelled like to the poor canine.

Even the dog seemed to be getting depressed by the horrifying scene.

Car by twisted car, he and Yoon cleared a few more train carriages near the blackened crater they had passed earlier. Creek pressed his nose to the sand, sniffing wildly, tail between his legs.

Suddenly, the dog froze, his eyes lifting toward a broken train car straight ahead. Creek let out a soft growl, his tail standing up straight.

"You got something, boy?" Raven asked.

Before he could get another word out, Creek barreled straight at the broken train car, climbing up a pile of sand and grain spilling from the car. The dog disappeared through a massive tear in its side.

"Creek!" Raven called.

He and Yoon started toward the upended freight car.

Raven thought he heard noises from inside.

Rustling, then coughing.

A person.

Creek emerged from the car, his paws sliding on the piles of seed. The dog's tail wagged as Raven drew closer with his rifle up. He swept it over the interior of the broken carriage.

"Is someone in there?" Raven asked.

A figure emerged from the shadows of the grain car, limping, blood covering his clothes and carrying a pistol in one hand. Raven centered his rifle at the shadowed face of a man.

Creek suddenly growled as the guy raised his pistol. The dog took the guy down before Raven could get a shot.

14

Ferocious growling was all Calvin could hear as a dog ripped at his sleeve.

His pounding head made everything worse. He'd hardly been able to see the dog inside the train car when it had approached.

And after hearing the helicopter, Calvin wasn't sure if it was a friendly, or another raider here to finish him off. These guys were wearing gas masks, though. Just like the monsters that had massacred his people.

He tried to fight off the dog as it tore another hole in his jacket arm, teeth dragging across his skin.

A whistle suddenly made it all stop.

The dog let go, and Calvin thrashed at the air. Two figures stepped toward him, brandishing rifles. They raised their weapon.

"Just finish it!" Calvin shouted, starting to push up toward his feet, raising his pistol. "Finish it! FINISH—"

Someone tackled him.

Calvin thrashed against the man, but then someone else pressed their body against him.

"Calvin! It's us!"

Calvin recognized the voice, though he couldn't quite place it. His head still pounded with the fury of a thousand elephants stomping his skull.

"Easy, Calvin, easy," came the familiar voice. The two men that had tackled him started to back away.

Calvin squinted, trying to make out the face of the guy with the dog. It was hard to tell with the man wearing a gas mask... but he thought he recognized the long dark hair trailing from under the guy's helmet.

Could it be?

"Raven?" Calvin asked.

"Yeah," Raven said, letting his rifle fall on his sling. "Sorry about Creek. He thought you were one of the scavengers that tried to kill us when you raised a gun." He motioned at the other man. "This is Yoon. A Ranger. We came to help."

Calvin groaned, then began coughing again. The air was acrid with smoke and fumes. Raven handed him a handkerchief. He took it.

"We'll get you a gas mask, if you can just hang on," Raven said.

It wasn't much, but the handkerchief helped filter out some of the garbage in the air.

"I... I thought... I thought *you* guys were the raiders, with those gas masks," Calvin said.

"We didn't see any guys with gas masks." Raven shook his head. "Look, we're going to get you out of here. Just relax. We got a chopper close to the wreckage."

Raven put his radio up to the gas mask.

"Recon Alpha, Recon Bravo here," Raven said. "I found Calvin Jackson. He's alive."

Calvin pushed himself up to his feet, but he felt dizzy. Yoon caught him before he fell.

"What about the rest of my team?" he asked. "What about Mouse?"

He tried to say more, but he started coughing. It felt like glass was scraping up from his throat. "He's taken in a lot of this smoke and the fumes," Yoon said. "We need to move him."

Calvin could see better now, the haze of confusion lifting. Despite his blurred vision, he could see Raven's tawny features and Yoon's serious face through their masks.

"You okay to get up?" Raven asked.

Calvin nodded.

The two men helped him out into the sun, away from the toppled train cars and the drifting smoke. Still, Calvin continued to heave and paw at his swollen eyes. They burned something mighty. When they were safely away from the wreckage, his vision finally cleared enough. What he saw seemed straight out of Dante's nine circles.

"Mouse," Calvin whispered.

Between flickering fires were bodies strewn between broken crates and toppled steel barrels. The slopes of distant mountains rose behind the columns of smoke.

Raven offered Calvin a canteen. He waved it away, but Raven insisted.

"You need water," he said.

Calvin took it, and after the water hit his throat, he began gulping greedily, some sluicing down his vest as he took in the scene.

Raven stared at Calvin, probably surprised to see him alive, but also with eyes full of sympathy. Calvin knew both looks well.

It was painted on the face of every nurse and doctor when he'd been sent from Afghanistan back to Germany for emergency surgery after his Black Hawk accident. He saw it on the face of his physical rehab therapists when he was struggling to learn to walk again, even when they tried to encourage him. Then on the faces of civilians when they saw him on his worst days, when he was limping through a grocery store or when he was at the VA to get checked out.

"Tell me," Calvin snapped.

"Right now, you're it," Raven said. "I'm so sorry, man. We're still looking, but—"

"That can't be possible." Calvin pushed himself upright. "I found three others..."

His words trailed when he remembered none of them were armed. If the raiders had found them, it would have been a slaughter.

Calvin marched past Raven and Yoon, doing his best to stand up straight. The smoke continued to surround him, making him cough.

"What are you doing?" Yoon asked. "You probably got a concussion."

"I don't give a fuck," Calvin said. "I sent three of my own to find cover during the attack. I have to find them."

"We're gonna keep looking," Raven said. "We've got more search and rescue teams coming too."

"And all the while, the monsters who did this are getting away," Calvin said.

"They won't get far," Raven said. "I'll find them."

"*We'll* find them," Calvin said.

Calvin wasn't sure he would make it out of here standing, let alone chase down the people responsible. Raven had to know the same thing. The tracker gave him an encouraging nod nonetheless.

Crunching footsteps sounded before Sheriff Lindsey Plymouth came running around a burning train carriage, wearing a gas mask. She lifted it up over her face.

"Calvin, holy shit," Lindsey called. "Thank God, you're alive."

"God ain't got nothin' to do with it." Calvin spat bloody saliva on the ground. "You find anyone else?"

"We did," Lindsey said. "I found a whole car full of survivors. They were hiding from us, until I called out that I was with the Rangers. A woman named Anna—"

"Anna! She made it?" Calvin asked, renewed hope exploding in his chest.

"Yes," Lindsey said. "Twenty-five others too. Molina is escorting them a safe distance away from the trains. Quite a few are hurt, but—"

"How soon until your medics get out here?" Calvin asked. "Hell, why aren't they here already?"

"We could only get one helo. We got here as soon as we could."

"Not soon enough. If we only got twenty-five left, that means we lost nearly seventy people. Maybe there are still more in the wreckage. We got to keep looking."

"Calvin, please, hold on," Raven said.

"I can't hold on!" he snarled. "I'm not fucking around here."

"Man, I know this shit is hard, but you can't go back in there. Those fumes, those gases; it'll knock you out again."

"Then give me one of your masks," Calvin said.

"That won't make a difference," Lindsey said. "We searched all the areas we could and evacuated those Steel Runners, but we don't have the right equipment for the more damaged cars that are still on fire. We need to wait for the rescue teams now."

Calvin started to turn toward the cars, picturing his friends burning inside. But he knew if anyone else was out there, they were already dead. If not from the fire, then from the fumes and smoke.

A flare of hot anger burned in him, but he let out a long breath. He looked at Raven, Yoon, and Lindsey in turn. They had all risked their necks to come help in an incredibly dangerous situation. He was hurting right now, speaking out of a place of anger.

Because even though they had saved some, they hadn't saved Mouse. *He* hadn't saved Mouse. But there were twenty-six other Steel Runners still alive, and the rescue teams could take better care of them than Calvin.

His job was to find those responsible for the death and misery all around him.

"We'll get the survivors out of here," Lindsey said.

Calvin held her gaze. He could see she was being honest. "Okay, but what about the people that did this? We can't afford to stand around any longer."

Lindsey looked around for a moment.

"Okay, here's what I'm thinking," she said. "After Molina finds a safe place for the survivors to wait for the rescue teams, Raven, you take Yoon and Molina in that Tahoe we found. It's got gas, and the tires are good."

"Are you going to send more reinforcements?" Calvin asked. "Three men against those people that attacked us doesn't seem like an even match."

"Right now, we may have a mole in our ranks," Lindsey said. "If I send too many more people, I risk that mole finding out. Then the chances we find our culprits are nil. We need this to be a covert mission. The fewer people combing the desert, the better."

"We'll work faster too," Raven said.

"I expect you will," Lindsey continued. "You radio me as soon as you find anything out. I'll have people standing by to meet you - wherever that may be - to nab these pieces of shit. In the meantime, I'll stay here with the chopper to keep an eye on things. As soon as the first rescue team gets here, I'll take off back for the Front Range with Calvin and the other survivors."

"No," Calvin said.

"What?" Lindsey asked.

"I know you'll take care of the dead and the injured," he said, "but I need to take care of the bastards that killed my people."

"You've probably have a concussion, and that arm... You look like hell and—"

"I've been through worse, and as long as I can shoot, I'll be fine." He flexed his arm. The skin was torn and bleeding, but he could move it just fine. He looked at Raven. "I won't slow you down, I promise."

Raven hesitated, but then shrugged.

"You sure about this?" Lindsey asked Calvin.

"Positive," Calvin said. "You take care of my people. I'm going with Raven and your Rangers. You said you need people you can trust, I'm one of them."

"Okay," Lindsey said. "I'll get you a gas mask from the chopper too. Don't know what you guys are going to run into out there. But before you go, is there anything you can tell me about the people that attacked you?"

Calvin again was bombarded with a flood of ugly memories. He pictured what the raiders looked like, dressed in their full battle gear, almost like Special Forces. After explaining that, he recalled something else and shared it with the sheriff.

"They seemed to be taking out some specific cargo from the wreckage," he said. "A bunch of crates and steel barrels."

"Anything distinguishing about them?" she asked.

"A few had Siegler Pharmaceuticals written on them. That mean anything to you?"

"Not yet," Lindsey said. "But I have a feeling it will very soon."

———

Lindsey peered out of the window of the main cabin as the helicopter soared above I-70, winding between the mountains toward Golden. It had only been a little over an hour and a half since the backup rescue team had finally arrived at the site of the Angel Line wreckage.

The Utah Scouts Command were scavenging what they could from the Angel Line wreck with the help of the Rangers. But that wasn't the only problem she faced.

She had to control the rush of Wild Fire patients coming into the clinics.

"Take me closer to the interstate," Lindsey said to the primary pilot. "I want to see how our border control is looking."

"Yes, ma'am," he replied.

The chopper soared lower toward a stretch of highway between Georgetown and Idaho Springs. A crystalline river ran alongside the interstate, frothy white waves crashing and swirling around rocks.

Between the evergreen-filled mountainsides were lengths of newly installed barbed wire fences and barricades demarcating the New Frontier.

Four Colorado Ranger SUVs were parked at a border gate on the main highway. Fresh sandbag barriers had also been set up, with six armed Rangers positioned behind them. A few people were on the New Frontier side of the gate, waiting to get into her side of Colorado. Guards appeared to be talking to them, along with a medic in a white uniform.

Palmer had executed her plans perfectly.

"Thanks," Lindsey said to the pilot. "Everything's looking good. Let's get to Golden."

As the chopper banked around the mountains, she took out her sat phone, hooking it up to her headset.

She dialed Palmer, and he picked up almost immediately.

"Sheriff, glad to hear from you," he said. "What did you find?"

"Nothing good. It was a massacre." She told him as much as she could, including about the survivors.

"I'm sorry, Sheriff."

"Me too..."

"But I am glad to hear we got some men and women returning."

"The day's still young." She changed the subject, not a single second to waste. "I want Investigations to look into a specific company in the manifests and contracts. Siegler Pharmaceuticals. Find out what you can about it. Who they are. What they shipped on that train. Iron Lead Calvin Jackson said the people who sabotaged the train were stealing Siegler Pharm property. I don't know if they took anything else, but I do want to know why they'd be interested in Siegler."

"Count on me, ma'am."

"Which brings me to another thing. I saw the border control reinforcements are in place."

"As much as they can be, ma'am. The mountains are as porous as an old sponge, though. I'm afraid we can't cover every entry and exit."

"How many people have been through so far?" Lindsey said.

"We've got about one hundred people requesting safe

asylum," Palmer said. "We've also got quarantine tents set up at each border gate, so the docs can keep an eye on people coming and going. All that gives us a total of nine secured gates with lockdown and quarantine operations. We got more popping up on some of the lesser used roads too, just to cover all our bases."

They passed over Idaho Springs. What once had been a bustling little tourist town was mostly abandoned. Only a few vehicles were left parked in front of the houses, and trash was carried by the wind down the picturesque but abandoned Miner Street.

"You have the latest numbers on the Wild Fire cases back home?" she asked.

"Divekar submitted a report about an hour ago. She said we were looking at fifty patients in the clinics now. Probably more, but they're having trouble confirming diagnoses still. She mentioned a few new groups had just made it to their clinics after passing through our checkpoints, so I don't know how accurate the latest numbers really are. Anyways, the docs keep throwing around suspected diseases like plagues and whooping cough and other bacterial things."

Lindsey was silent for a moment. "Did she mention anything about a working treatment?"

"Not to me," Palmer said. "She's still waiting on the labs in Denver to identify something that will work, but even they're not having any luck."

That gave Lindsey an idea. "I want to get as much attention on this as we can. Palmer, get the FAC loaded up and send them to the UCHealth Labs at Cherry Creek. Make sure Divekar comes with."

That was where Divekar's samples were being analyzed.

"Change of plans," Lindsey called to the pilot. "We're headed to UCHealth at Cherry Creek."

Not long after, the chopper was swooping past downtown Denver. Scaffolds covered many of the buildings. While a few had toppled, most of the rubble had been cleared. The streets were filled with construction crews, many of which were aid workers from their foreign allies.

Southeast past downtown, they descended toward Cherry Creek. The once-ritzy neighborhood was still mostly intact. Shops and restaurants and even the mall had been spared the worst of Denver's destruction, though many of the businesses inside had since died.

One building was still bustling with activity. The UCHealth Medical Center. Patients, doctors, and other employees flowed into and out of the building. The bird landed on a helipad atop the sheer-glass five-story building.

Lindsey opened the side door and ran at a hunch under the rotor wash to the rooftop door.

From there, she made her way down the stairs to the building's lobby, bypassing the floors with the labs and clinics. The lobby was alive with patients checking in at desks, nurses triaging, and staff asking every visitor to don PPE.

That included Lindsey.

She put on a mask, gloves, and paper gown as she counted a good ten or so patients waiting in the green chairs near the entrance.

Nurses whisked some of those patients down the halls or up elevators. Doctors conferred behind clear plastic partitions that separated some of the corridors from the lobby.

It took another fifteen minutes before Palmer and the available FAC members arrived from Golden.

The deputy came in with Divekar through the main doors. Martinez and Uwase followed. The last person in the group was Blair.

As soon as they entered, a pair of nurses descended on them, providing masks, gloves, and gowns.

The group circled around Lindsey.

"Glad you all could join so quickly," she said. "Things have taken a turn for the worse. Before I get into things, I want to know how your people are doing. Anyone have service men or women experiencing any sickness?"

"Everyone's still healthy from my side," Martinez said.

"The Marines are doing well," Blair said.

"Uwase?" Lindsey asked, looking at the man.

"Oh, no, the UN workers appear to be okay," Uwase said. He sounded like he was distracted.

"You're the only one who brought their family here," Lindsey said. "Tell me, are they doing all right with everything going on?"

Uwase smiled. It looked forced. Like maybe he was regretting bringing them. "Agathe and Emmanuel are still healthy." Then his smile faded, like he was ready to change the subject. "But what about the train? What happened?"

Lindsey nodded. "Many of the Steel Runners were wiped out. As we speak, Utah Scouts and Colorado Rangers are holding security as teams salvage what they can from the wreck. So far, we've only confirmed twenty-seven survivors, including Iron Lead Calvin Jackson."

Martinez shook his head sadly. "It is an unexpected tragedy."

Is it, though?

She still suspected someone—maybe one of the FAC members, maybe a Ranger—had helped relay the critical information that led to that successful attack.

The fact that Tiankai wasn't here made her suspicious.

But for now, she had to focus on the task at hand:

convincing the FAC that they needed more help preparing for the coming health crisis.

"You all should already know that over fifty people are infected with what we're calling Wild Fire," Lindsey said. "I'm going to have Doctor Divekar brief us all on our current progress. Hopefully, as a group, we can come up with new ways to support her efforts."

"Sheriff, things are already worse," Doctor Divekar said. "Before I left the clinic, we got more patients in from the mountains. Militiamen, survivalists, and even a family. And... and some of our own from the patrol groups on the Front Range."

"How many?" Lindsey asked.

"Sixty-two infected now. That includes a handful of US military personnel."

"My God," Lindsey said. The numbers rose every time she spoke to Divekar.

"We still don't know what this thing is?" Blair asked.

"I'm a doctor, not an epidemiologist, and we don't have resources like we did before the Collapse," Divekar said. "However, we do have the few scientists at our disposal working 24/7 to figure this out. Follow me."

"Hold on," Uwase said. "Is this really safe? All these suits, these precautions..."

"We aren't going into any of the isolation wards," Divekar said. "We're just headed to the corridors outside the labs."

Divekar took them through a hall behind the check-in desk. The corridor was empty except for a few lone carts with different glassware and boxes of lab supplies.

"This is where we're trying to isolate and sequence the pathogen," Divekar said.

An expansive window revealed a laboratory. Three

researchers worked at the lab benches. Each wore a face shield, goggles, gloves, and a gown over their lab coats.

Microscopes and glassware covered the lab benches. There were other pieces of buzzing equipment and machinery that Lindsey didn't recognize.

Two scientists huddled around one piece of equipment slightly bigger than a PC, staring at a monitor with a bunch of arcing lines.

"We're trying to genetically sequence samples we've obtained from the patients," Divekar said. "Mucus, blood, everything."

"Why's that?" Blair asked.

"We're still trying to track down the genetic material from bacteria we think might be responsible for Wild Fire," Divekar said. "Our hope is that we can sequence enough genetic data to isolate anything that *doesn't* match the genetic material we *expect* to find in humans. It's a tedious process. So far, the material we *have* matches nothing in our databases."

"This doesn't sound easy," Blair said.

"It isn't," Divekar said. "These are the only three scientists we have on staff capable of running these experiments."

"You need more scientists, then," Uwase said. "I can talk to the UN officials. Perhaps we can bring in more over the next week."

"It's not just scientists we need," Divekar said. "It's everything. Most labs in the area were ransacked during the Collapse. We simply haven't been able to prioritize their repairs."

"You need more lab space too?" Blair asked.

"I do."

"Is it even possible to build labs overnight?" Martinez asked.

"Trust me," Uwase said, "the UN has dealt with

epidemics before. We can bring people and supplies together in a matter of weeks to construct field labs."

"This could work," Martinez said. "I'll see what we can do too."

Lindsey was glad to see how quickly they had agreed to cooperate.

Unfortunately, Divekar didn't seem convinced. "A matter of weeks is too long. With the lack of personnel, lab space, and supplies, it'll take months just to figure out exactly what this disease is, much less how to cure it," Divekar said.

This disease, the train sabotage; it was all happening so quickly. Lindsey feared all the progress they'd made over the past two years looked like it might all come toppling down in the next couple weeks.

"To make matters worse, the supplies you see in this corridor are all we've got left for our experiments." Divekar indicated the carts they'd passed by. "Most of the PPE our scientists need are being used in the clinics too. Plus, we need more basic things like cell media, pipettes, cuvettes, centrifuge tubes, and more."

"The UN can provide these things with a little time," Uwase said.

"We could use all the help we can get," replied the doctor.

Lindsey looked to the others. She didn't want to play hard ball and hoped bringing them here would get them all to commit. But some of them still looked uncertain.

"We don't want this thing to spread outside of the Frontier," Lindsey said. "God forbid it starts moving across the country and beyond."

Divekar nodded. "Even with travel at only a fraction of what it once was, this thing could find itself spreading to all corners of the globe if we're not careful."

"I'm certain the UK can ship *something* over," Blair said.

"It'll take some calls, but perhaps in a few days, I can secure some of the scientific aid you need."

Martinez gave a stern nod. "Mexico will send supplies."

"Thank you," Lindsey said.

"Yes, thank you," Divekar said. "I just hope it's not too late…"

Lindsey nodded. "Doctor Divekar, you're trying to paddle upstream. I get it."

She thought for just a moment. There was one person she and Raven had helped in the past. Someone who might be able to pull the strings to get Divekar the help she needed much faster than the FAC could.

"I'm going to put in a call with the Secretary of Defense. Maybe she can pull some personnel from USAMRIID to help, although I doubt President Diego will authorize that as much as he wants to isolate the New Frontier."

"Does the president understand what happens if this disease spreads beyond the borders?" Divekar asked. "Because that is how I would pitch your offer for help."

When Lindsey was back outside, she took a deep breath of air and called the Secretary of Defense.

"Madame Secretary," Lindsey said. "I'm sorry to bother you again, but I've got another problem. This time, President Diego can't ignore it."

She explained everything she knew so far.

"Just what we need," Charlize said.

"I know it's an election year, and all that, but—" Lindsey started to say.

"If this thing is as bad as it sounds, there won't be an election," Charlize said. "I'll talk to the president. We'll get you the help you need before it's too late."

15

THE SUN BLAZED ACROSS THE ARID LANDSCAPE. EVERY craggy rock formation and grain of sand looked like it might burn Raven if he touched it. The sporadic tire tracks in the sand and the crushed dry foliage left behind by their enemy was easy enough to follow. Assuming, of course, they were following the right enemy.

However, the trail wouldn't last long.

They'd been driving through the desert, taking a tediously slow path, trying to track their target for the past several hours. The farther they went, the more the winds had covered up the tire tracks. Raven had to keep his eyes open for foliage that had been freshly smashed to keep them on the right path.

He sat in the front passenger seat of the Chevy Tahoe with Creek between his legs. Molina drove and Yoon was still in the back seat with Calvin. The man was already looking better after having had his fill of water, electrolytes, and nutrition. Bandages wrapped around his arm, too, where Creek had bit him, but Calvin looked as ready as anyone else in the vehicle.

The trail Raven directed them to follow took them into Arches National Park.

Large red rock formations curved around them. Imposing mountains with lingering snowcaps guarded the eastern horizon.

The constant slopes of the park made following the tracks even more difficult.

"Stay to the left of their trail," Raven said to Molina. "Stick closer to the shadows of the rocks. It'll give us a better chance at finding cover if we do have to get out and fight."

Molina turned the wheel.

The SUV kicked up a rooster tail of dirt and dust that Raven feared might give their position away. Tracking their enemy stealthily out here was far more difficult than in the forested mountains of Colorado. They didn't have the benefit of thick forests to help conceal them.

They drove for a couple of long, bumpy hours down stretches of desert.

"If we don't find these people soon, we're going to need to turn back and hit the highway to resupply," Molina said. "We don't have the fuel to keep this up."

"It'll be too late by then," Calvin said. "We'll lose our advantage and the trail. I'll get out and walk if I have to."

"No one's walking," Raven replied. "More help will come; we're just getting a head start."

He turned to look Calvin in the eye. "Don't worry. We're going to find the people that did this. It's just a matter of time."

Calvin winced as he nodded. He was in rough shape, partly due to Creek, but it wasn't his physical wounds that worried Raven. The mental agony of what Calvin had endured with losing his people could cause him to do something irrational, like get out and walk.

Raven wasn't the type to run from a fight either, but he had learned from making irrational decisions in the past.

As they came around a curve in the tall mesas and rocky pillars, Raven surveyed the top of the towering formations.

Raven went to pull out his binos when he saw a glint of light. "I got eyes on something."

"What? Where?" Molina asked.

"Up on top of that mesa." Raven pointed toward a plateau of red rock.

"I don't see anything," Molina said.

Raven scoped the edge of the plateau covered in dried brush, gangly trees, and boulders. But he didn't see any people.

"Maybe it was just an animal," Yoon offered.

"Animals don't glint in the sun," Raven said. "Pull off over there."

Molina put them under a rocky overhang.

"I'm going to check it out," Raven said, pulling on his gas mask again. "You guys continue driving. Just in case someone's up there, I want you to distract them. I'll let you know if I spot anyone."

"If no one is up there, then we're wasting more time and gas," Molina said.

"Yeah, but if someone is, we might not make it another two minutes if they open fire. Besides, if I can capture someone, then we have a better chance of figuring out who hit the train."

"You're sure you saw something?" Yoon asked.

"Raven helped get the Angel Line through the Rockies," Calvin said. "We need to trust him now."

Raven looked back, somewhat surprised that it was Calvin speaking. They exchanged a nod, and Raven opened the door. Creek tried to follow. "No, boy."

The dog wouldn't be able to climb the sheer rock walls if that was what it came to.

"Watch Creek for me," Raven said.

"You got it," Molina replied.

Raven shut the door and ran hard, using the cover of the arches and pillars of rock. Grit blew against his mask as he neared his target. He approached it from the western side, away from where the Tahoe had been headed.

"Start drawing closer to the mesa now," Raven called over the radio. "Try to stay close to the boulders and arches for cover, just in case someone starts shooting."

"We're on it," Molina said.

The growl of the V8 engine echoed off the rock walls of the mesa.

The last stretch to the mesa was open ground. Raven scoped the plateau once more. Again, he saw nothing, but he had a gut feeling since seeing that flicker of metal.

He sprinted hard for the far side of the mesa. When he got there, he glanced up, still seeing no one.

But this time, he saw tracks leading around the mesa. They appeared to slowly be filling with sand from the wind. If they had gotten here only an hour or so later, the trail might have been completely gone.

Satisfied, he started climbing up the rocky wall. There was a slight slope on the bottom half, allowing him to scrabble up it. But after fifty feet up, the slope turned into a vertical wall.

Raven reached for a handhold and used his legs to push himself up. Foot by painful foot, he probed the loose rock and dirt for steady purchase. Each time the gravel and rocks loosened slightly, threatening to send him tumbling back to the earth.

The falling rock and dust could also attract the eyes of his enemy.

A quick glance at the ground, now nearly seventy feet below, made his stomach lurch.

Come on, Raven.

He was named after a bird, for God's sake.

Heights should be no problem.

After a few more death-defying yards, he flung himself over the edge. Raven took a moment to recover his breath. He found shelter behind a boulder draped in a desiccated plant with gnarled roots. A hot wind blew in his face as he curled around the rock with his rifle at the ready.

Crouched just near the precipice were three men. His instincts had been right after all.

One man was serving as a spotter, a pair of binoculars in his hand and an AK-variant strapped over his back. The other two were on their bellies in sandy brown and yellow camo, barely peering beyond the edge with their weapons poking out of a tangle of dried plants.

Raven was too close to use the radio and warn the Rangers and Calvin, but he wasn't going to let these guys get off a single shot.

Boulder by boulder, he advanced toward the gunmen. He reached another rocky outcropping and ducked behind it. It was close enough he could hear the three men talking.

"They stopped," the spotter said.

"Want me to take them out?" asked the sniper. "They're just within range. It'll be an easy shot."

"We're just supposed to be lookout until we get orders to take 'em down," the spotter said.

"Fuck that," the other sniper said. "We take them out now, then we can get off this rock and head back home."

"No man, orders are orders," the first sniper said. "These

people are supposed to be valuable. Ted, why don't you go to the other side of the mesa? Make sure these guys don't got anyone else with 'em trying to get around us. If they do, we'll call up the rest of the team. That's *all* we're supposed to do."

Footsteps crunched in Raven's direction. As soon as Ted made it past the rock Raven was hiding behind, Ted would see him.

He had only a few seconds to take down Ted, then turn his rifle on those other two men to try taking them alive. He had plenty of questions, and these men might have some answers.

Here we go.

Ted moved past the rock, cradling his weapon with a leather cowboy hat pulled low over his brow, a dingy plaid shirt, and blue jeans. The wannabe cowboy started to stride past, and Raven raised his rifle. Ted suddenly froze, doing a double take. He looked as if he had seen a ghost, his mouth wide open, eyes laser-focused on Raven.

One squeeze of the trigger sent a bullet piercing into the man's forehead. The gunshot boomed across the mesa.

As Ted's body crumpled into the dusty ground, Raven swung around the boulder and sighted up the sniper that had been talking about shooting his team.

"Freeze, and I won't shoot!" he called.

The man twisted toward Raven, bearing his rifle.

But Raven had the drop on him.

Bullets riddled the side of the camouflaged sniper and snapped into the sand around him, sending up puffs of dust. The second sniper took off, sprinting for cover. Raven fired, but the rounds ricocheted harmlessly off the rocks, chips flying.

The sniper had disappeared behind another boulder.

"Give up now, and we'll let you live," the sniper called

from behind the boulder. "You ain't getting out of here alive otherwise."

Raven said nothing, creeping closer to the boulder. He knew the man was bluffing. There was no one else up here.

"Cavalry is already on the way," said the sniper. "Soon as they get here, don't matter if I'm alive or not. Because they'll kill you too."

That was the last thing Raven needed, this bastard sending a warning to his whole team.

He rushed around the far side of the boulder. To his luck, the man had anticipated Raven coming from the other, far side.

Raven let his M4 fall on its strap and barreled into the guy, letting out a war cry as he knocked him to the ground. The sniper's head cracked against the rock. His gun flew into the dirt.

Grunting, the man turned to his side and reached for it, but Raven already had a hatchet out. He flipped the guy back over and pressed the blade to the sniper's neck.

Frightened eyes squinted at Raven. Realization seemed to pass over them.

"You damn injun," he hissed from his back. "I heard about you."

Raven made sure the guy was pinned down good, pressing a knee into his sternum. "If you heard of me, then you heard what I do to people like you."

He dug his knee in deeper and pressed the blade of his hatchet until it split skin.

All the man's aggression melted away as quickly as a snowman in the Utah desert.

"No, please," the man said, his fierce façade suddenly breaking. "Ain't nothing personal, okay?"

"What's your name?"

"Jeff," he said. "Jeff Calloway of the Mountain Brigade. We were told to watch out for you, understand?"

"Not sure I do. Help me understand, and maybe there's a chance for you to get off this mesa," Raven said. He leaned down closer. "One move, and you'll meet your friends in hell."

"Okay, okay."

This man was leaking like an old bucket shot full of holes. He seemed eager to save his own hide.

"Who hit the train, and where are they now?" Raven asked. "You got one chance to answer."

"I, uh..."

Raven's chest swelled. "Spit it out."

"If I do, they'll kill me."

Raven bent down in the raider's face.

"If you don't," he growled menacingly, "then *I'll* kill you."

———

"They're landing now, ma'am," Palmer said, poking his head into Lindsey's office at Fort Golden. She had just been examining the troop allotments for each border control site along the New Frontier.

But this was even more dire.

"Let's go see them." Lindsey stood from her desk and grabbed her hat hanging near the doorway.

They hurried down the hall, moving past other Rangers and office workers at Fort Golden.

"Secretary Montgomery sure works fast, doesn't she?" Palmer said.

They turned a corner, dodging past a man pushing a mail-cart. "I suppose President Diego realized there are some things you can't ignore."

"No shit. Sixty-some people already... I mean, crap, Sheriff, it's turning into an epidemic."

"Divekar tells me it *is* an epidemic."

They hurried outside. It was early evening, and the sun was still bright in the sky. She had to shield her eyes with a hand when she reached Fort Golden's helipad.

"You see them?" she asked Palmer.

He twisted on his heels, searching the sky. "There." He pointed at a black speck in the distance slowly growing larger. "That must be them."

The speck soon morphed into the silhouette of a CH-47 Chinook.

"Boy, they're really sending in the big guns," Palmer said with a whistle.

"Big problems call for big guns," Lindsey replied.

It was another thing Marcus Colton liked to say. At the time, she'd thought it was a bit too *simple* of a saying.

But hell, he had a point.

She just hoped the guns Charlize had sent were big enough.

A Humvee rolled up beside them as they waited, and Doctor Divekar got out. Her eyelids seemed to droop, and her hair was in disarray. She was clearly exhausted.

"Thanks for joining us," Lindsey said.

The Chinook came in low over Fort Golden.

Soldiers at the watchtowers and along the walls shielded their eyes as its two huge rotors kicked up a rolling cloud of dust.

The wheels of the chopper hit the helipad with a jolt, and the bird came to rest, its engines winding down. Before the blades even stopped, the rear ramp of the helicopter lowered to the tarmac.

As soon as it did, men and women in Army service

uniforms filed off the plane. Some wheeled carts filled with pallets of equipment; others carried metal cases or computer bags.

While all these people were members of the US Army, they weren't here to fight with guns and bullets. Instead, they came armed with laboratory equipment and supplies.

These were the scientists and technicians from USAM-RIID, the US Army Medical Research Institute of Infectious Diseases. The best and brightest of America.

A few transport trucks idled beside the helicopter tarmac, their diesel engines rumbling. Lindsey motioned for the USAMRIID service members to start loading their supplies in those trucks. The vehicles would take the cargo to the Red Rocks Medical Center, where she had instructed the staff to set up space for USAMRIID in the facility's clinical laboratories.

Within the horde of newcomers, Lindsey spotted a man with wispy blond hair and thick-framed black glasses. He stood slightly shorter than most of the others around him, but he walked around with his chest puffed out like he already owned all of Fort Golden.

Lindsey strode toward him, Divekar following. When he caught her eye, he stepped her direction and held out a hand.

"Doctor David Wheeler," he said. "You must be Sheriff Lindsey Plymouth."

"Yes, I... We are grateful you're here." She gripped his hand and shook it. "This is Doctor Divekar."

"Welcome to the New Frontier," the doctor said.

"It's a different world out here." Wheeler adjusted his glasses. "Can't say I'm happy to be here to solve this little disease problem, but we have to keep it from becoming a bigger one, now, don't we?"

Lindsey didn't know this guy well yet, but based off that

statement, there was a pretty good chance she wasn't going to like him.

Palmer gave her a side glance, confirming he too wasn't an instant fan.

"Follow me, Doctor." Lindsey gestured toward a Humvee. "We'll brief you on the way."

She walked to the vehicle that would take them to the Medical Center. She got into the front passenger seat. Divekar, Palmer, and Wheeler hopped into the back, and the driver, another Colorado Ranger, took them through the gates of Fort Golden.

They started down West 6th Avenue toward the Red Rocks Medical Center, the shadows of the foothills stretching over them. Most of the construction efforts to restore the houses and apartment buildings alongside the road had stopped for the day, making the town look eerily empty.

"Your clinicians' reports call this disease Wild Fire," Wheeler said.

"It's spread faster than anything we've dealt with so far," Divekar added.

"I thought you might be exaggerating the threat initially, but now I fear they are right. It really is spreading like wild-fire, which means if we fail, thousands, maybe hundreds of thousands of lives, will be lost. Since I've been airborne, any progress on identifying the disease?"

"It's bacteria unlike anything in our local databases." Divekar shook her head. "We're at a complete standstill. I was hoping you would have access to better information."

"I see." Wheeler paused, scratching at his chin. "Then our people will immediately begin working to determine what the disease actually is."

"How long will that take?" Palmer asked.

"That depends."

"Can you give us any kind of timeline for when we might get some answers?" Lindsey asked.

"We must first perform an exhaustive battery of tests for all known pathogens," Wheeler said. "I wish this was like the good old days when someone could just overnight some samples to my lab in Maryland, and I could work with them at home. But even the mail services I once trusted have become too unreliable and slow. If you've got as dangerous of a pathogen on your hands as this Wild Fire, the last thing I want to do is try shipping it across the country."

"Of course," Divekar said, "which is why I'm glad you're setting up your labs here. I'm looking for quick results and quick answers."

"Quick is a subjective term. The genetic sequencing of this virus or bacteria could be done relatively quickly *if* it's similar to something we've seen before."

Divekar shook her head. "Which we don't think it is."

"I know you don't think so, but I want to run all our tests before we make that conclusion. Assuming you all are correct, though, we'll need to analyze the Wild Fire pathogen gene by gene, base pair by base pair. Do you have any idea what the mode of transmission is?"

"From our experience, we believe it's airborne," Divekar said. "We're judging that based purely on the few transmissions we believe took place in our clinics. So far, we believe we've quarantined all individuals in our community that have Wild Fire."

"I see." Wheeler took a second. "Of course, I can't expect clinicians to be epidemiologists. For all we know, you could have asymptomatic people spreading it already throughout eastern Colorado. Or maybe the disease vector is a flea or a parasite we haven't yet identified. Quarantining these patients might prove to be useless if we don't know that it will actually stop the disease spread. At least, it seems you're putting Colorado on lockdown already."

Lindsey nodded. "We've put stringent quarantine requirements in place to control our borders. For the most part, we're not letting anyone through, but the borders aren't exactly impenetrable."

"You're trying to do exactly what you need to do, Sheriff." Wheeler adjusted his glasses. "I also want to be careful about train shipments. We don't want to send an entire train full of infected people out to the West Coast or this localized epidemic could turn into a pandemic extremely quickly. We must contain this."

"Well, we won't be sending out any shipments any time soon," Lindsey said. "I'm assuming you've been briefed on the Angel Line attack last night. The line is being repaired and resecured as we speak."

Wheeler's eyes widened in shock. "Cease all those efforts and, if those men have come into contact with *anyone* in the Frontier, quarantine those people immediately."

"What? They aren't done. That is a lifeline to communities beyond the New Frontier."

"And like I said, those tracks could also spell doom for those communities if it enables the spread of Wild Fire."

Lindsey understood what he was saying, but shut the rails down?

"This comes from the top," Wheeler said. "We must make sure this is contained."

"So what do we do about the people we already have across the boundaries?" Lindsey asked. She stared out at the mountains, thinking about Raven. "They're behind enemy lines, and they're going to need our help."

"We pray we can identify what this disease is, what's causing it, and that we can stop it," Wheeler said. "Otherwise, every person you send into the mountains might as well be dead."

"Holy crap," Palmer said.

The Humvee started to pull into the parking lot of the Red Rocks Medical Center. A couple of the transport trucks had just arrived. Already the USAMRIID personnel were unloading equipment and carting it into the three-story building.

"Since I have teams in the field, is there anything else we can do to help you figure out what's causing this disease?" Lindsey asked.

The Humvee pulled into a parking spot. Wheeler was about to open his door but paused.

"There is. To truly stop this disease, we need to find the disease reservoir and control it. For example, during the latest Ebola outbreak in Liberia, destroying the suspected reservoir hosts of the virus—bats or primates—might've prevented the outbreak in the first place. USAMRIID is going to be sending out some of our own experienced teams. But if you still have teams in the field, any information they uncover could be vital. Maybe your team can help with that."

"Maybe," Lindsey said.

Raven was used to tracking ruthless killers. Of course, all his previous targets had been humans, not a microscopic virus.

Either way, she needed to warn her team in the field. She picked up her radio and placed a call to Raven and the Rangers.

16

"MOLINA, WE'RE CLEAR," RAVEN TRANSMITTED OVER THE
radio. "Meet me at the north side of the mesa. I got a hostage."
"On our way," Molina replied. "We just got an update
from Lindsey you're going to want to hear about too."
"Looking forward to it. Right after we have a talk with our
new friend."
Raven used the path the hostile snipers had originally
traveled to get back down. He kept his gun pointed at Jeff, the
surviving sniper.
At the bottom of the mesa, the Tahoe waited. Yoon
opened the rear passenger door and got out.
"I got some ropes from the back of the truck," Yoon said,
holding them up. "Let's hogtie this asshole."
Yoon started tying up Jeff's hands.
Calvin got out to help, and Creek leapt out after. The dog
started growling as soon as he saw Jeff.
"Are you part of the trash that attacked the train?" Calvin
asked.
Jeff hesitated.
"Answer me!" Calvin shouted.

"Don't shoot me," the man whimpered.

Calvin lowered his rifle, lip raised in a snarl. "Answer."

"I was there, but I wasn't part of the attack—"

Before he could finish, Calvin barreled into him, knocking him to the ground in a puff of dust. Raven should have seen this coming. He rushed over to help Yoon and Molina pull Calvin off the only living soul they knew of with knowledge of the train attack.

Jeff screamed as Calvin punched and beat him.

"Stop!" Raven yelled. "Get off him, Calvin! We need intel!"

It took all three of the men to pull Calvin off Jeff. And then it took all three to hold him back from leaping back down on the sniper again.

"Please, I didn't want to do it," Jeff cried. "They made us."

"Don't bullshit us," Raven said. "Tell us everything you know."

Calvin tried to break free, but Raven put a hand on his chest. "Calm the fuck down! You want to find out who killed your Steel Runners or not?"

Calvin grunted and then backed away, wiping snot and blood off his face.

He stood there, chest heaving as Yoon and Molina made sure he didn't try anything. After a few seconds, he seemed to simmer down some, and Raven crouched down in front of Jeff.

"Talk," he said. "Or I will let my buddy have at you again."

Creek growled from a few feet away.

Raven tied up Jeff and then made him sit inside the trunk of the Tahoe, worried that some sniper might be out here that didn't want him to talk.

"Watch for hostiles," he said to Yoon and Molina.

The Rangers walked off to hold security while Raven and Calvin stayed with Jeff.

"Look, we were told you all were coming to kill us," Jeff said. "We set up here for self-defense purposes. Honest."

"Self-defense?" Calvin asked. He took another limping step toward Jeff. "Was it self-defense when you murdered a train full of people too?"

"I didn't murder anyone," Jeff said.

Raven thought back to how Jeff's comrade was ready to open fire on their Tahoe and wasn't sure he believed the sniper.

"You certainly seemed ready to on that mesa."

"No, we only wanted to defend ourselves. I swear. The train... it's a different story."

Raven narrowed his eyes. "Then explain what happened and do it fast."

"I wasn't part of the group that attacked the train," Jeff said. "I mean, I was with the group that came afterward, but we were just cleanup. Honest."

"What group are you talking about?" Raven asked.

"How do I explain this?" Jeff asked, as if an answer was waiting for him in the sky.

"Try," Calvin grunted.

"I'm part of the Mountain Brigade," Jeff explained. "We don't want nothing but to be left alone, but our people were dying and we needed help."

"So you attack a train and murder us?" Calvin asked.

"I promise you, that's not what we're doing out here," he said. "We just want the freedom to build our sovereign town in peace."

"You're in the United States of America." Calvin limped closer. "I bled for this country. You don't get to decide to make your own little fantasyland in it."

Jeff started to shake. "Ever since the EMP, you think our government has been—"

"We aren't here to debate your dumb conspiracy theories," Raven said.

"Okay, okay," Jeff said. "A couple weeks ago, a few people in our town started getting sick. Just a couple at first. It started spreading, okay? Almost every person who has gotten sick has died. Men. Women. Children. Old. Young. Didn't matter."

For the first time, Raven had a hard time controlling his expression. All he could think about was Sandra and Allie and the patients showing up at the Front Range clinics.

"What kind of symptoms?" he asked.

Jeff told them all about the lesions and vomiting and trouble breathing. How some of the healthy Mountain Brigadiers, including him, had left as fast as they could when they realized their home was dying. They hoped to provide help to the families and friends who stayed back while they tried to find food and medical assistance.

"Not long ago, a few of our people even went over the boundaries into East Colorado to get treatment," Jeff said. "None of 'em came back. We tried reaching out to other communities, but no one wanted to help us either."

"What's this have to do with you guys derailing our train and killing our people?" Calvin asked.

"A few days ago, some guys came to where me and a bunch of other Brigadiers were camping and hunting."

"Guys?" Raven asked. "What kind of guys?"

"They were real military-like. Camo and black fatigues, masks, military-grade weapons. Called themselves the Reapers Militia. They gave us an encrypted radio, the same one they used to call our home base and tell us you were coming this way."

Raven narrowed his eyes.

"They told us that they could get our people medicine if we helped them," Jeff explained. "We just had to wait and follow their instructions."

"You really just make a deal like that with some militia you didn't even know," Calvin said.

"We didn't have much of a choice. It was either that or let our people die. We weren't the only ones either."

"What do you mean?" Raven asked.

"There are other groups out here that were working with them for the same reason we were," Jeff said. "I heard about some guys near Glenwood Springs, for instance. I think the Reapers got some people to attack Eagle, Colorado. Then there were some other men that were supposed to hit the train when it was back in Colorado last night. The Reapers told us they fucked up, and that's why they made us go with them here in Utah."

Raven couldn't believe it. His and Lindsey's suspicions were right. There was a party responsible for coordinating all these smaller militias and groups. Some insidious organization that had the power to convince all these outlaws to work for them. And someone in Colorado was feeding them intel.

"Did the Reapers tell you what this disease is?" Raven asked.

"No."

"How do you know they even have a cure?"

The man made a half-shrug—or at least the best he could while tied up in the SUV. "We didn't. But you got to understand how desperate we are. I got a kid and wife back at our town that got sick. I need to help them."

Raven was losing his patience. "You made a mistake, buddy."

"We didn't have much of a choice," Jeff said. "So when the Reapers told us to meet them near some coordinates with the weapons they gave us, we did. They said we'd need to be ready to defend ourselves. We didn't know until we arrived and saw them setting up explosives on the train track what they wanted to do. They were the ones that blew up the train. Then they made us help them load their supplies onto their trucks."

"Why the hell did they want your help?" Raven asked.

"When we showed up with thirty of our guys, they only had about ten of theirs. They made us do all the heavy lifting, loading their trucks and stuff. Guess it would've taken them way too long if they were doing it alone."

Raven might be able to buy that answer, but he was still skeptical.

"What kind of cargo?" Raven asked.

"I have no idea," Jeff said. "Honest. Just a bunch of heavy metal cylinders and big crates."

"The Siegler crap," Calvin said. "Can you tell us anything about these Reapers? What did they look like? Where did they come from?"

"They were all in protective gear with gas masks," Jeff said. "I didn't see their faces. Only a couple of them would even talk to us."

"We didn't see any bodies with that sort of gear," Raven said. "But you saw guys with gas masks, right, Calvin?"

"I did," Calvin said. "Shot one of them dead."

"Did you see them removing the bodies?" Raven asked Jeff.

"Yeah, they took all their dead with them." Jeff shook his head. "I think there were four of their guys that got killed. It didn't look to me like they expected those casualties."

Raven scratched at his chin. "You said you had thirty people with you. Where are the rest?"

"We got another five guys camped out nearby, waiting for

my team to return," Jeff said. "The others all took off south. Most are now off searching for medical help from other frontier groups."

"I thought the Reapers were going to help you," Calvin said.

Jeff shook his head. "So far, they haven't given us anything, and we're running out of time."

"They lied to you," Calvin growled, "and you helped them kill my Steel Runners. All for nothing."

"We didn't kill no one. You got to believe me. The Reapers told us they'd kill us and our families if we didn't do what they said."

"We're supposed to believe they really told you we were coming to kill you, too," Calvin said, "but they didn't want you to kill us."

"Orders were to keep you alive," Jeff said. "I guess they wanted us to capture you and bring you in for questioning or something. I'm not quite sure."

"They have scouts following us or something?" Raven asked. He started to get paranoid, looking around the desert, wondering who else was following them.

"I have no idea. I swear on my mother's soul, I have no idea."

"Then tell me this," Raven said. "Where the hell is this Reapers Militia? And where's your Mountain Brigade territory, or whatever the hell it is you people call home?"

"I don't know where the Reapers are, but like I said, we got a few guys camped out nearby. They might be able to help. And if not, our governor back in town is the one who spoke to the Reapers the most."

"I don't believe a word this piece of shit says," Calvin said.

Raven wasn't sure he did either. But Jeff was their only lead.

"I swear, I can get you a meeting with our governor," Jeff said.

Raven considered it.

"Where's this group camped?" Raven asked.

"Just a few miles from here," Jeff said.

"You said five guys?" Calvin asked.

"Yes."

"How many vehicles?"

"Two trucks."

"If we're going to make it to this guy's town and talk to his governor, we need the gas anyway," Raven said to Calvin.

"That we do," Calvin replied. He moved right up to Jeff.

"If you betray us, you're getting a bullet straight to the gut," Calvin said. "Not the head, not the chest. The gut. You know why?"

Jeff shook his head.

"That's the most painful place I can shoot you," he said. "Your bile will mix with your blood, and while you're slowly bleeding out, you'll feel agony unlike anything you can imagine."

Jeff gulped.

"Good," Raven said. "It's settled then. You take us to your governor, and my friend shoots you in the gut if you screw us."

———

After a twenty-minute drive, Calvin found himself staring down the scope of the M40A6 sniper rifle Raven had taken from one of the dead Brigadiers. He was prone next to one of the towering red rock arch formations in Arches National Park, Creek waiting patiently beside him.

They had sent a brief message to Lindsey apprising her of everything they'd found out. They'd also thought about asking her for backup. But truth was, they didn't have time to wait.

These Brigadiers might slip out of their grip if they didn't do something immediately.

Jeff had led the group right to the Brigadier camp as promised. Boulders and dried plants surrounded the meager camp where five men sat next to a pair of lean-to tents they'd set up by a dead tree.

Calvin resisted the urge to open fire on all of these wannabee militia soldiers.

Clenching his jaw, he tried to focus down the sights. It didn't help that he could feel Travis's White Sox hat that he'd stuffed in his jacket's chest pocket. The hat was a constant reminder of all that he had lost.

Mouse, Travis, all those other Runners.

He was happy that Anna and the other survivors had made it back to Golden, Colorado. But he worried, based on what Lindsey had told them, that none of them were out of danger now. Even if the Brigadiers and Reapers hadn't killed his people, it sounded like the Wild Fire might.

The wind tugged on Calvin slightly, coming in gentle gusts. He knew exactly how to adjust his aim to put a 7.62 mm round straight through the skull of each man he saw around the campsite fifty yards away, even though they'd all crouched behind the rocks and boulders, no doubt hearing the Tahoe's approach.

He traced his scope over each of the five men.

They wore a ragtag mix of clothes, ranging from black biker vests to camo jackets. Most wore their hair long and ratty, just like their beards.

One guy had the gall to pin *medals* to his jacket. They were all in the wrong place. No doubt the guy had a bad case of stolen valor. Wanted to be military so bad, he probably scoured estate sales and thrift stores for old medals that some poor veteran lost or whose family had to sell to make ends meet.

If Calvin had to drop these guys, that man would be his first target.

Zooming out, he watched Raven, wearing a gas mask, march Jeff toward the encampment using the shelter of the boulders. Yoon and Molina kept back behind cover.

While Yoon had untied Jeff's leg restraints, the man's wrists were still secured behind his back. Their hope was that Raven could get the Brigadiers to lay down their weapons and surrender.

If the men resisted, though, Yoon, Molina, Raven, and Calvin were ready to do battle. Calvin hoped it didn't come to that.

If even one of them got hurt or killed out here, their chances of getting out of the Badlands dropped faster than a drunk trying to sandboard down the side of a mesa.

Raven used Jeff as a human shield, approaching the five Brigadiers with a message to drop their weapons.

The Brigadiers started shouting as they knelt or lay prone in firing positions. Calvin couldn't hear them clearly, but none put down their rifles.

Raven backed away from Jeff slightly with his M4 aimed at the guy's back. Jeff stood stock-still.

One of the Brigadiers started yelling something at Raven again.

More shouting followed.

Raven raised his radio.

"Calvin, green light," he said over the channel.

With pleasure.

Calvin squeezed the trigger.

A 7.62 mm round punched straight out the barrel of the sniper rifle and slammed home.

Mr. Stolen Valor's face was erased instantly, blood and gore spraying across the Brigadier next to him wearing a leather vest. The man in the vest started to stand, letting go of his rifle. He wiped at the blood and bits of bone fragments on his vest, raising his hands shakily in the air.

The other three men started to push themselves up to their knees too. But they didn't abandon their weapons.

Maybe they were planning on standing first before they made a show of tossing down their weapons. Maybe they were still in shock, not really thinking about what they were doing.

But Calvin wasn't taking chances.

He moved his crosshairs over another man. Squeezed the trigger, the rifle shuddering against his shoulder.

The man's chest caved in where the round smashed through ribs and organs, and the Brigadier crumpled.

The other two gunmen opened fire, rounds spraying from their rifles. The man in the vest bent back down to retrieve his rifle. Gunshots boomed back in response from Yoon and Molina.

Calvin wasn't sure what was going on with the other two Rangers or Raven. He focused down his scope and moved his aim just slightly. His sights fell right on the chest of a third man who was dropping to his knees and trying to get a bead on Raven.

Not today.

The man fell backward when a bullet exploded through his chest.

Calvin roved his aim toward another target, but the man tumbled backward before he could open fire. He'd been shot by either the Rangers or Raven.

A burst of gunfire erupted from the last Brigadier. The

man was backpedaling toward one of the vehicles. He nearly reached it when Calvin put a bullet through his head.

The round punched cleanly through and into the GMC Sierra behind him.

"All clear," Calvin said over the comms.

He lowered his scope. Raven was standing over Jeff with his M4 sweeping over the camp.

Calvin checked on Yoon. He was kneeling on the ground near a large rock. On the other side, sprawled in the brush, was Molina.

"Help!" Yoon yelled.

Calvin slung the sniper rifle over his back and sprinted at the downed Ranger with Creek. Yoon was trying desperately to press his hands over Molina's neck. Blood pumped up between his fingers.

Yoon grimaced. "Come on, bro. Stay with me."

Calvin reached into one of his vest pockets for gauze and hemostatic gel and gave it to Yoon. He knew it was useless, but Calvin couldn't just watch this man die, doing nothing while Molina bled out.

The Ranger's skin was turning whiter by the moment. He tried to open his lips to say something, but only blood dribbled out.

"Fuck, fuck, fuck," Yoon said. "Stay with me, buddy."

Molina's eyes started to glaze over, his chest finally going still. His hand fell into the blood-soaked sand.

Creek let out a soft whine.

Raven mouthed a silent prayer, placing a hand on Molina's chest.

Yoon wiped at his eyes. "I've known this guy since the start of the Collapse. Since we both joined up as Rangers. I never..."

The man never finished his thoughts. He didn't need to.

After having just lost Mouse, Calvin knew the storm raging in Yoon's head.

Calvin felt nothing but anger. Another needless death. He wanted to scream and curse at the heavens.

He looked up to see Raven stalking toward Jeff, shaking with rage. His fists were clenched by his side.

"That didn't go very well, Jeff," Raven said menacingly. "This next part better go right."

"You killed all of them," Jeff said, voice trembling. "Some of those guys were my friends."

"I had friends too," Calvin snarled. "But the Reapers didn't give us a chance to put our weapons down before killing us. Raven extended that offer to your buddies."

Calvin had to remind himself that they stilled needed Jeff. He wanted so badly to put a bullet in the man's head.

"A lot of our people were killed without even a gun in their hands. Your Reaper friends executed them in cold blood. So don't you dare act like those assholes deserved better."

For several long moments, not a sound came from Jeff. The man looked down at the grains of sand rustling by in the soft breeze. Everyone seemed too lost in their own thoughts and emotions.

Yoon finally turned back to the others, his posture rigid and tone serious. "Let's get the gas."

Raven stayed with Creek and Jeff. The Brigadier was in a trance, staring at the dead.

Moving quickly, Yoon and Calvin collected fuel from the other vehicles. When they were done, Calvin and Yoon retrieved a tarpaulin from the camp and secured it over Molina's body with several heavy rocks.

"Raven, can you mark on our maps where this is?" Calvin asked. "I want to make sure someone comes back for him when this is all through."

"You got it," Raven said.

They piled back into the Tahoe and stuffed Jeff in the backseat. As he took the driver's seat, Raven handed Calvin the sat phone. "Call Sheriff Plymouth. Give her an update."

Lindsey picked up almost immediately. "I got your message from earlier about the Reapers. What's going on now?"

Calvin told her everything that had happened since they'd last spoken to her.

"So Molina's... God, I'm sorry," Lindsey said.

There was a pause.

"I have some bad news..." she said. "We've got people from USAMRIID here, and they are shutting down the border, which means no one is going in or out without USAMRIID authorization."

Raven exchanged a glance with Calvin.

"Wait, we're trapped?" Yoon asked. "And we aren't getting help?"

"I know it's a lot to ask, but you're the only ones that can find out who these Reapers are right now," Lindsey said. "Look, I've got another favor to ask. USAMRIID is sending out a few of their field teams to see if they can find the source of the Wild Fire. Thing is, there are only a handful of them. If you see or hear anything about Wild Fire, please let us know. So stay in touch and be careful. We're counting on you."

Calvin hung up, feeling worse than before he'd called the sheriff. "As Mouse would've said, this is a shit sandwich."

"I've been in worse situations." Raven seemed to tighten his grip on the wheel.

"You're kidding," Yoon said. "We just lost Molina and now this."

"At least right now, we got a prisoner who can help us find out the truth about the Reapers."

"Just the three of us?"

Calvin glanced back. The man looked broken mentally. Much like Calvin felt.

"When I was in the Marines, my squad got sent to North Korea," Raven said. "A senator pulled some strings, and we went in to extract his daughter and her friend from a prison camp near the DMZ."

Yoon let out a knowing sigh.

"We didn't all make it out, but we brought them home," Raven said. "The odds may be stacked against us, but we got more than you think, Yoon. We got each other, and a lot of people counting on us, which means we can't fail."

"Okay," Yoon said after a pause. "I'm with you wherever this trail leads."

17

LINDSEY STOOD IN FRONT OF THE FAC IN THE WAR ROOM at Fort Golden. The concrete walls were covered by satellite images, topographical maps, and other bird's eye views of Colorado and the Rocky Mountains. But it was one particular map the members of the Council studied.

"You can see here where our Rangers found the wreckage of the Angel Line train," Lindsey said, pointing to an X on a map of Utah. She traced her finger south toward Arches National Park. "This is approximately where our trackers and Calvin Jackson encountered the Brigadiers, a group trying to stake out some kind of apparent sovereign nation. They allegedly have been working with the group responsible for the Angel Line attack, an organization known as the Reapers Militia."

"Where are your trackers headed now?" Martinez asked.

Lindsey wasn't sure what to tell her FAC yet. She had debated with Palmer how best to approach the situation, given the suspected leak.

"I'm not sure," she said. It wasn't a complete lie. "I just

know they're in the Badlands, far from our help, unfortunately."

Blair's brows scrunched together like he didn't believe her. And why should he?

She had never been a "wait-and-see" type of woman. Blair knew that by now. He might have assumed she had deployed additional Rangers.

Lindsey had considered doing exactly that but feared if Doctor Wheeler and his teams found out, they would pull some of their support or stop working with her altogether. She couldn't take that risk. She had to trust Raven would get the job done on his own.

She couldn't think of a better person for it, that was for sure.

"What exactly is your team doing out there?" Piard said.

"Like I said, I'll inform you all as soon as—" Lindsey started to say.

The door of the conference room swung open. Dr. Wheeler barreled in, white coat flapping behind him and a laptop under one arm. Palmer followed him inside.

"I'm sorry, Sheriff," said the deputy. "I told the doc you were in a meeting, but he insisted he had to see you. Now, Doctor Wheeler, you see she's busy. Let's give her a minute, okay?"

"We don't have a minute." Wheeler looked right at Lindsey, but didn't bother apologizing to anyone for interrupting. "I need to talk to you, Sheriff. Alone."

"What she hears, we hear," Uwase said. "This affects our families. Our friends. Our colleagues."

"Yes, we deserve to know what we're facing," Piard said. "If you indeed know anything new."

Martinez looked at Lindsey for her reaction. A test, she realized.

"If you want an audience, we'll discuss with an audience." Wheeler's face grew red behind his glasses. "Your call, Sheriff."

He deposited his laptop on the table, sat between Blair and Uwase, and popped his computer open. "So?"

All eyes turned to the sheriff.

"Yeah, go ahead and spill it, Doctor," Lindsey said.

"What I'm about to tell you is classified and stays inside this room," Wheeler said. "Do you all understand?"

A chorus of acknowledgments came from around the room.

Wheeler spun his laptop around.

"I can say with almost one hundred percent certainty that Wild Fire is caused by a plague bacterium," he reported.

"Pardon, but did you actually say this really is the bloody *plague*?" Blair asked. "I didn't think the plague was *this* bad."

"The plague?" Martinez forced a laugh loud enough Lindsey winced. "I like a good mezcal, but this guy must like a nice drink more than me."

"I'm not drunk, if that's what you're implying," Wheeler said, peering over his glasses. He pointed at his computer screen. "You can look at the results yourself."

"Please, ignore Martinez," Piard said. "Continue."

"Yes, Doctor," Uwase said. "I can call the WHO too. We've dealt with localized plague cases before." His eyes narrowed over his round nose. "We understand the plague is a very real threat, and we do not take it lightly."

"Where to begin, where to begin..." Wheeler glanced down at his laptop like it held all the answers. "The plague *is* endemic to North America. It's caused by bacteria, *Yersinia pestis*. The bacteria's life cycle involves both fleas and rodents. You may know this from the infamous Black Death from the

Middle Ages, but I promise you, the plague has never really gone away since. I'll show you."

He picked up his laptop and plugged it in to the projector. It shone a map of the United States on the wall. Clusters of red dots showed across the western half of the United States, particularly concentrated where Utah, Colorado, Arizona, and New Mexico met.

"These are recorded cases of the plague in the United States," Wheeler said. "All of these occurred *before* the Collapse."

Those cases were frighteningly close to where Raven and Calvin were now.

"The good news is that your medical teams have acted appropriately to limit their exposure to the plague," Wheeler said. "Doctor Divekar and her staff are correct in their assumptions that Wild Fire is infectious via respiratory droplets. Typically, infectious droplets are only caused when an individual's plague is pneumonic, not bubonic or septicemic."

"Could you explain what this means?" Tiankai said.

"Yes, of course," Wheeler said. He clicked a button on his computer.

An image of a person's hip appeared. A lump protruded where their leg met their abdomen. The bump was tipped with a red and white lesion.

"Bubonic plague like this affects the lymph nodes," Wheeler explained. "From here, it can spread to other parts of the body."

He tapped on another key. This time, an image of a person with blackened fingers appeared. Lindsey narrowed her eyes at the disgusting images.

"This is septicemic plague," Wheeler explained. "The plague has spread to the skin and possibly other tissues, necrotizing them. Believe it or not, these are not the most serious forms of plague."

"It gets worse?" Blair asked.

"Yes, pneumonic plague, the kind that may spread through respiratory droplets, transmits directly between people. It can cause respiratory failure, leading to death. What we're seeing in the clinic is a plague that rapidly infects people and shows all three of these clinical forms at once."

"Okay," Lindsey said. "We know what it is. How do we stop it?"

"Normally, common antibiotics can stop the plague. The antibiotics in your clinics *should* be more than adequate."

"I'm sensing a 'but,'" Lindsey said.

Wheeler inhaled sharply. "None of the antibiotics we have seem to have much effect."

"*Merde*, you are telling me the cures that should be working aren't?" Piard asked.

"I can't say with absolute certainty yet," Wheeler replied. "We've only just begun a new round of experimental treatment regimens. But your clinicians told me they tried everything they had on other patients already. Doctor Divekar said, in fact, the first four patients she had underwent direct IV administration of a powerful course of antibiotics."

"How are those patients doing?" Blair asked.

"Dead. All of them," Wheeler said. "So far, nothing has worked, but now that we know it's plague, we can be more diligent and laser-focused on the specific antibiotic courses these patients undergo."

"So there's hope," Uwase said.

"Hope is nothing but an analgesic to distract us from the pain of reality," Wheeler said. "I do not want to tell you there is any hope. I'll tell you, instead, if—that's a big if—we find our cure."

"Do we need to worry about it spreading across the country?" Palmer asked.

Wheeler faced the deputy, and then returned his gaze to Lindsey.

"Of course we do," Wheeler said. "That is why we must be diligent about keeping the New Frontier locked down. After all, it's not just the United States at stake here if it becomes a full-blown pandemic."

The Council members exchanged worried glances, no doubt thinking about this spreading to their home countries.

"I do have a theory why this plague is so resistant to antibiotics," Wheeler said.

All eyes flitted back to the doctor.

"What?" Lindsey asked.

"Back at USAMRIID, we have a genomic database of every infectious disease we've ever encountered. Each pathogenic virus, bacteria, or fungus we can get our hands on is genetically sequenced, so we always have a genomic reference when dealing with cases like this. Partly, that makes it easier to track diseases, contain them, and treat them."

Lindsey's heart picked up a beat. She was no stranger to USAMRIID's origins dealing with biological weapons, and she feared where Wheeler was going with this.

"We also use this to track when new variants of a disease pop up," he continued. "For example, the Wild Fire plague that we have isolated and characterized from all your patients is unlike anything that we've ever recorded in the United States. For that matter, it's unlike any variant of the plague we've discovered in the world."

"What are you saying, Doctor?" Blair asked.

"I don't yet have definitive proof, but I don't think this plague is a natural variant. I believe it was engineered."

For the first time in Lindsey's two years of working with the FAC, the group was stunned into silence.

———

The extra gasoline they salvaged from the Brigadier campsite was enough to get Raven, Calvin, and Yoon down to La Sal, Utah, the small town where Jeff claimed the Mountain Brigade had established their enclave.

Night was quickly falling over the barren landscape.

Toward the north, the mountain range morphed into ominous dark silhouettes. The closer they got to the rocky peaks, the more the sandy landscape was replaced by patches of trees and dry grass.

They drove past a few lonely houses that sat dark and vacant in enormous acreages. Raven guessed they used to be small ranches or farms. Most had broken windows, and the wire fences demarcating their properties had been torn down.

At the end of a long road, Raven could just make out a cluster of buildings surrounded by a fence consisting of patchwork chain-link pieces and wooden planks. Dark smoke billowed up from inside the compound.

"What's burning?" Calvin asked.

"That's the Free Town of the Mountain Brigade," Jeff said. "Something's not right."

"It's not just a signal fire, warning about our arrival, or some kind of campfire?" Raven asked.

"No," Jeff said. "Not that big."

Raven could see the defensive wall as they closed in. Even calling it a wall was generous. Most of it looked flimsy, thrown together haphazardly. Two empty watchtowers stood sentinel over a gate that was cracked open.

"Looks like maybe someone broke in before us," Yoon said.

Raven started to slow the SUV before they got too close.

"Anyone got eyes on hostiles?" Raven asked.

"None that I can see," Yoon said.

"Same," Calvin said.

"Jeff, what are the defenses usually like here?" Raven asked.

"We always got at least two guys in each watchtower," Jeff replied. "Usually, there are two guys just beyond the gate too."

"No one today. You know why?" Raven asked. He worried that the five guys at the camp they'd just killed had warned the rest of the Mountain Brigade. Worse, maybe the Reapers were out there, tracking them, setting up a trap.

"No idea," Jeff said. "All I can think of is what I told you before. The governor sent part of the Brigade down south to look for medical help immediately after the attack when the Reapers still hadn't given us the meds they promised."

"That doesn't explain the fire, though," Calvin said.

"No, and I hadn't heard anything about this either," Jeff said.

"Calvin, Yoon," Raven said. "Get out and scope the area. Make sure we don't have any tails. Put on gas masks. If people are sick here, I don't want us catching anything. We'll meet up by the gate."

"You got it," Calvin said. After slipping on a gas mask, he took off from the vehicle with Yoon, the two of them using the cover of dried-out trees and rocks to get closer to the gate.

Raven slowly approached the gates, ready to take cover if anyone ambushed them.

"I don't know what's going on," Jeff said. "How would I have told them?"

Raven waited several minutes until Calvin called back over their radio.

"Area looks clear," Calvin said. "I found a bunch of footprints headed out and away from the town, but no people anywhere."

"Copy that," Raven replied.

He parked the Tahoe, donned his own mask, and yanked Jeff out of the seat.

"Let's go, buddy," he said.

They exited the Tahoe. Creek followed close behind Raven, and they met Calvin and Yoon just outside the gate.

A cool evening wind blew toward them, carrying with it tumbleweed and silence.

"Something's definitely wrong." Jeff walked ahead of Yoon. "My family... Oh, God, what do you think happened? What's going on?"

Right when they got to the gate, the howl of a wolf cut through the unsettling quiet. Creek immediately went low and started growling.

Raven wondered again if this was the work of Iktomi. Had the trickster dragged them all the way to this Brigadiers' hideout to lure him into disaster? Or was this simply a warning from yet another pack of wolves?

Iktomi, if it is you, leave us. Wolves, if you are nothing but animals, I have no quarrel with you.

"You go first, Jeff," Raven said, crouching near the wooden planks of the fence.

"Go on," Yoon hissed at the Brigadier.

Nervous sweat beaded down the man's wrinkled, leathery forehead despite the cool breeze. He nudged through the gate with his shoulder.

"Call your people," Raven said. "Let them know we're not

here to kill them. I really don't want another firefight if anyone's left."

"We got a passcode for that." Jeff's voice shook.

"Do it then," Calvin said, voice slightly muffled by his mask.

"Brigadiers, freedom calls!" he cried out, voice cracking.

Raven roved his rifle along the watchtowers just to make sure Jeff wasn't lying and had actually let out a warning.

No one popped up.

"Freedom calls!" Jeff yelled again.

The man stood in the middle of the road outside the gate, calling the passcode over and over. He started to walk through the narrow crack between the open gates, briefly disappearing out of Raven's sight.

"Hold on, Jeff!" Raven hissed.

"Hello? Anyone—?" Jeff suddenly started to back up toward the crack in the gate.

From where Raven was situated, he couldn't see what had frightened Jeff. He moved through the gate with the others for a better vantage when a flash of gray and black lunged at the Brigadier.

"Help me!" the man said, falling to his back.

Creek went wild, barking and growling, all the fur on his back standing straight. He put himself between Raven and the large gray wolf that sank its teeth into Jeff's arm. It pulled on Jeff's jacket sleeve.

Instead of risking a shot that would kill Jeff, Raven ran at the animal and slammed his body into its ribs. His shoulder hit the mass of wiry fur and muscle with a crack. The wolf yelped and tumbled off into the dusty road.

"Yoon, guard Jeff!" Raven shouted. He didn't look back to see if the Ranger had followed his order.

The wolf scrambled back to its feet. Its lips curled back,

revealing a mouthful of curved teeth. Bloody saliva dripped from its fangs, the beast's nose wrinkling into a fearsome snarl. Its fur was patchy, lesions bumping up out of its skin. Ribs pushed up between those patchy portions. The poor animal was clearly starving and diseased.

"Back!" Raven said to the wolf, holding his ground.

Creek growled and snapped. He let out a series of vicious barks.

"Back!" Raven yelled again. He let his rifle hang from the strap and spread his arms wide to look bigger. Then he let out a roar that summoned the animal inside him, willing himself to be louder and more frightening than the wolf.

Wolves shouldn't be a threat to humans. Only if they were desperate or diseased, which this one seemed to be both. The sick animal looked like it had been caught by surprise too, scared by Jeff's sudden entrance into the town. All it was doing was defending itself and perhaps its pack. And for all he knew, maybe the wolf had Wild Fire too.

Raven roared again.

The wolf's ears went flat against the back of its head, its tail curling between its legs. In that moment, when its yellow eyes caught Raven's, he sensed a brotherhood. A realization that the wolf understood Raven didn't want to kill it. That he wanted to spare the poor, sick animal if he could help it.

Slowly, the wolf took a step backward, its eyes still on Raven.

Yes, Raven thought, *go in peace.*

But before the wolf took another step, a gunshot boomed across the road.

The wolf lurched. It took a couple unsteady steps before crashing into the asphalt. Blood poured from a wound in its chest, clinging to its matted fur.

As the wolf took its final belabored breath, the beast

looked up at Raven with its tongue hanging from his mouth. Its eyes no longer carried the undercurrent of understanding, but rather the hot hatred of betrayal.

I'm sorry, Raven thought.

Howls wailed up from elsewhere in La Sal. The patter of padded feet over rock and cement echoed between the meager concrete and wooden buildings lining the street inside the Mountain Brigade complex.

A few wolves shot out of the town through a half-open gate that Raven could see partway up the mountain slope to their north nearly two hundred yards away.

He turned to see Calvin holding his M4, still aiming at the downed wolf. "Why did you do that?"

"I saved your life," Calvin said, lowering the weapon.

"You did no such thing," Raven snapped.

Just beyond Calvin, Yoon was bent over Jeff. The man was writhing on the ground, holding his arm and moaning. The Ranger, despite his hatred for Jeff and his people, was already applying antibiotic ointment and gauze to the bleeding wounds on the Brigadier's bicep.

"The wolf was going to leave," said Raven.

"You don't know that." Calvin towered over him.

"I do know that," Raven said. "We didn't need to kill the animal."

"It's a fucking animal, and it attacked Jeff, who you claim we need so badly," Calvin said.

Raven's fingers curled into fists. On another day, maybe in the past, he would have taken his frustration out on Calvin. But right now, he needed to focus his anger and his energy on finding the Mountain Brigade's governor and the Reapers.

"Get him up," Raven said, "but don't stick too close to him. That wolf looked sick, which means Jeff might be too."

Yoon prodded Jeff with his rifle.

Jeff got to his feet shakily. "God, I hope I'm not sick. No, no, no."

Raven thought back to the legend he told Lara. It was this kind of disrespect that had inspired the animals to call their Councils and create disease in the first place.

Perhaps the bandits and outlaws of the Badlands had been as careless with animal life as Calvin just now.

Maybe it was mankind's fault that the Wild Fire was spreading.

And if it was, Raven couldn't say he blamed the animals.

18

CALVIN FOLLOWED RAVEN AND CREEK BETWEEN THE dilapidated homes of La Sal. Jeff hobbled along after them, with Yoon prodding him along. They'd been in the small town for only a matter of minutes and already Calvin had seen more destruction than he'd expected. If it weren't for his gas mask, he was certain he'd catch the odor of burnt plastic and wood drifting in every gust.

Most of the houses were mobile homes and RVs that had been set up along the street. About half of them were little more than blackened skeletons and ash blowing on the wind. Others still smoldered, small fires licking up around chunks of walls or furniture, embers glowing in piles of ash.

"Oh, no," Jeff said. "This can't be real. Who would do this?"

"The Reapers?" Calvin offered.

Jeff had no answer.

After passing about twenty homes, many burned, there was a warehouse at the eastern end. The warehouse was the first in a line of concrete and wood buildings with labels like "La Sal Post Office," "General Store," and "Town Hall." The roofs of each were blackened, smoke drifting up from inside them.

The squat building with "Town Hall" painted across the top had concertina wire lining a waist-high wall of corrugated steel on top. A couple of mounted machine guns lay unmanned on their posts.

If someone had raided this place, it was odd they left the weapons behind. And it was also odd that anyone fleeing would leave them behind if they abandoned this place.

So far, to their surprise, they hadn't seen any people, dead or alive, to help them figure out what had happened.

"Who could have done this?" Jeff sobbed again. "My wife. My kid. Where'd they go?"

Calvin turned back to Jeff. "See. Your 'allies' turned on you. You can't trust people who raid trains and attack innocent people."

Beads of sweat rolled down the Brigadier's face, and his lips trembled.

"It was either the Reapers or someone else came and robbed this place while you and your militia of dumbasses were busy helping the Reapers rob a train," Yoon said.

"Based off how some of these buildings are still smoldering, I'm guessing it happened either last night or early this morning," Raven said.

"Why would the Reapers kill us?" Jeff asked. "We did everything they asked."

"To keep you quiet obviously," Raven said. "Your folks wouldn't be the first group of the Reapers' 'friends' to be treated like this."

Raven explained what had happened at Glenwood Springs.

Calvin racked his brain as he tried to understand what was happening.

"If the governor stayed here, where would he have been during an attack?" he asked.

"Governor McGregor spent all his time in town hall or..." Jeff jerked his chin toward a trailer home near the northeast corner of the compound.

Raven took them to the town hall first.

A single pair of windows lined the front façade, each covered in steel bars, with black soot staining outward.

A steel bar had been used to keep the heavy wooden doors shut.

Raven removed it, then signaled for Calvin to open the doors as Yoon covered them.

Calvin pulled them open.

The single-room concrete building was filled with mounds of white and black ash. Several embers still glowed in a pile of collapsed wood from the rafters in the center.

Behind them, Jeff vomited over the ground. He collapsed and started sobbing, tears mixing with the sweat on his cheeks.

"Where's my family?" Jeff asked. "Please, where did they go? Do you think they're hurt? Did they burn them?"

Calvin backed away from the town hall.

"We have to keep looking," he muttered.

As Jeff wallowed in a mixture of grief and agony, Calvin, Yoon, and Raven checked the other couple buildings nearby. They were left mostly untouched and abandoned.

"Looks like we lost our lead," Calvin said. "That's probably exactly what these Reaper people Jeff was talking about wanted, huh? Cover their tracks by murdering everyone who might snitch."

Raven's expression was stoic, stern. "No witnesses. Which ain't good for us if the Reapers are following."

He turned to scan the streets.

"Stay alert," Calvin said.

"Jeff said a bunch of his people were infected too," Yoon said. "Maybe burning this place was to contain the disease."

"Possibly." Raven let out a sigh. "But then, where did the people go?"

"We still got McGregor's house to check out," Calvin said. "Maybe we can find some clues there."

"Or that encrypted radio to the Reapers Jeff was talking about," Raven said.

They trudged between the trampled dry grass toward the trailer home. Jeff followed them with his head hung low, whimpering with vomit clinging to his beard.

A wooden trellis covered up the bottom of McGregor's house where it stood on its one-and-a-half-foot tall concrete posts. Attached to the house was a diesel generator.

The door swung on its hinges in the wind and the wood near the lock was cracked.

Calvin's hope of finding McGregor was quickly dwindling.

Raven led them into a living room with a ragged couch and matching armchair. There was a refrigerator with a missing door. It appeared to serve as a pantry, canned goods lining the shelves.

Their footsteps made the floor creak as they looked around.

Muddy footprints tracked over clothes and papers were strewn across the floor. Creek sniffed around, shoving his nose through the garbage. Then the dog went still and started whining, pawing at a shirt and camo jacket.

"What is it, boy?" Raven asked.

He picked up the clothes and threw them onto the couch to get a better look at what had attracted Creek's attention.

Dark stains marked the light-blue carpet where the clothes had been.

"Blood," Raven said simply.

"I'll check out the rest of the place," Calvin said.

Signaling for Yoon to follow, he crept down the narrow hallway toward the bathroom while Raven examined the bloodstain.

Yoon checked the hall closet. "Nothing."

"Bathroom's clear too," Calvin said.

They cleared the bathroom, then moved back out to the living room where Raven was pawing through the papers.

"This is all trash." Raven pushed a few of the papers toward Calvin and Yoon. "Looks like all anti-government manifestos. Nothing about the train attack or Wild Fire or the Reapers."

Creek whined while sniffing at the blood.

"What's got him so worked up?" Yoon asked.

"The blood," Raven said. "He's probably got McGregor's scent in his nose now, and—" Raven stopped, then stooped beside Creek again. "Hold on a second."

He pulled at the stained carpet.

To Calvin's surprise, it came up with ease.

"Of course," Raven said. "A guy that leads a dangerous cult at the edge of the desert is going to have multiple getaway routes. Maybe..."

As he flipped up the carpet, he revealed a wooden trapdoor.

Raven lifted it. "This leads right to the space under the house."

Calvin heard the crack of wood.

"I see him!" Raven was looking through the trapdoor. "The coward was hiding! Get back here!"

Calvin bounded outside first, ignoring the pain in his leg. He and Yoon got a head start, Raven and Creek behind them.

A chunk of the wooden trellis under the home had been torn away.

Jeff was no longer seated outside where they had left him either. Instead, he was lumbering away from the trailer home, his hands still secured behind his back.

Running away alongside Jeff was another man in a blood-stained white t-shirt and camouflage pants. The man was leaning on Jeff as he ran. He had a bloody bandage wrapped around his leg.

Calvin raised his M4. "Stop or I'll shoot!"

Neither of the men even looked back.

Calvin slung his M4 over his back with a curse. As much as he wanted to blow these bastards away, they needed answers, not more corpses.

He ran at a lurch. Pain coursed up Calvin's leg and back, but he gritted his jaw against it, focusing on the rage building inside him. His anger fueled him, and he caught up with the slow-moving pair.

Raven and Creek were just behind them.

Yoon took Jeff down and Calvin slammed into the man he presumed to be McGregor. They went down hard on a gravel road.

Calvin cranked his head back to miss a blow. He slammed a fist into the man's head. With his other hand, he pushed a fist into the bandage.

McGregor let out an agonized howl.

Jeff tried to headbutt Yoon, but the Ranger moved, and then clocked their prisoner right in his temple, knocking him on his back. Creek growled at Jeff, baring his fangs, and Raven put a boot on Jeff's chest.

With McGregor writhing in pain, Calvin dug his knee

into his sternum. Then he took out his pistol and aimed it at the governor's face.

"Move again and I'll put a bullet in your brain," Calvin said.

Next to McGregor, Jeff was sprawled on the ground with Yoon on top of him. Raven stood above them both with Creek by his side, growling.

"You McGregor?" Calvin asked.

The man's eyes narrowed, his big chest rising and falling. Calvin pressed his pistol into the side of the man's head.

"Don't make me ask again," he said.

Finally, McGregor nodded. "Yes. Who the hell are you?"

"Where are the Reapers?" Calvin asked, ignoring him.

"I don't know—"

Calvin pressed the barrel against the governor's lips, prying them open, and forcing the barrel inside.

McGregor writhed, his mouth opening and closing like a fish trying to breathe on land.

"Tell me where the fuck they are!" Calvin yelled.

He pulled the barrel out to let the prisoner talk.

"I... I don't know," McGregor said.

"Those motherfuckers killed your people and burned them like they did mine," Calvin said. "All you got to do is tell me where they are, and we'll track the Reapers down and rip them to pieces."

Yoon pointed to Jeff. "He said you have an encrypted radio to contact the Reapers. We need it."

"Nah, it's broken now," McGregor said.

"The Reapers broke their own radio?" Calvin asked.

McGregor let out a rough laugh. "You think the Reapers did *this?*"

"If they didn't, who did?" Raven asked.

The governor's swollen eyes flitted over to the tracker.

"Why don't you ask your friends from Navajo Nation, you redskin?" McGregor said with a scowl. "They came here, torched everything, and broke that radio so we couldn't even call for help."

While security lights glowed along the walls and buildings of Fort Golden, most of the neighborhoods and communities spread in the foothills were still dark. Here and there, Lindsey could see the flicker of a kerosene lamp, but most everyone was fast asleep.

Even as the first bright stars speckled the night sky, Lindsey's shift wasn't over.

Truthfully, it never was.

But especially now.

On the one hand, she was dealing with what could be an engineered virus spreading like its namesake through the Badlands. On the other, Raven was out looking for the shadowy forces that had attacked the Angel Line, and he was now trapped out there.

She couldn't help but wonder if the Reapers he tracked had something to do with Wild Fire. Especially with all the groups they had seemed to have enlisted with promises for a cure to the pathogen. Raven's latest report had her thinking she was missing a key piece to this puzzle. A clue as to who their real enemy was. She had to figure out what was going on before it was too late.

She strode toward her Ford Bronco, ready to take a ride to visit some people she hoped could help. Palmer followed, carrying a box of papers and reports submitted from Investigations.

As Lindsey rounded the vehicle toward the driver's side,

she heard the distinct crunch of gravel behind her. She turned, her hand instinctively sliding down her side toward her holstered pistol.

"Sorry to sneak up on you," Lieutenant Blair said. "I see you are fully alert at this hour."

"Old habits die hard," she replied.

Palmer and Blair exchanged a nod.

"I need to have a word with the sheriff, if you please, Deputy," Blair said.

"Everything good?" Palmer asked.

"It's all right, Palmer," Lindsey said.

Palmer ducked into the vehicle and closed the door.

"Something wrong?" Lindsey asked Blair as they took a few steps away from the Bronco.

"I could ask you the same question."

"You're going to have to be clearer than that."

"Sheriff, I have worked with you for the better part of two years," Blair said.

"I realize that, and I'm extraordinarily thankful."

"I'm afraid it doesn't appear that way at this point," he said. "I understand the threat of the Wild Fire plague, especially after what Doctor Wheeler said about it potentially being a bioweapon..."

"But?"

"But I don't believe you are being completely upfront with me or the Council on everything you are doing to combat the disease. Or if you are, then you aren't doing enough."

"Enough? What do you want me to do?"

"Send more people out there to figure out where it came from. Right now, you have a single Ranger with your tracker friend, Raven, and they're hunting for the raiders of the Angel Line alone, correct?"

"Look, I understand your concern, and if it were up to me,

I would send out more people, but Doctor Wheeler and USAMRIID have forbidden it. They've got their teams out there seeking answers too, and I'm not anxious to send more of my people to their death thanks to what could be an engineered disease. My Rangers simply don't have the training to deal with such a contagious, deadly disease."

"My Royal Marines do. And while you've been asked to hold back your people, I have not."

Lindsey lifted a brow. She wanted to trust him and deploy some of his troops, but right now, her gut told her someone was leaking info to their enemy. Someone, perhaps, on the Council.

"I'll talk to Doctor Wheeler," she said. "Okay?"

Blair looked like he was about to protest again, but Lindsey got into the Bronco. She nodded at Blair before they drove away.

"Guy's awfully nosy," Palmer said.

"He's got a right to be," Lindsey said. "As much as I believe him, I hate to say it, but I have no idea if one of his Marines is slipping info to someone, accidentally or otherwise. Maybe someone's spying on *him* for all we know."

"I get it, ma'am."

They started out of Fort Golden and up Interstate 36, skirting under the dark mountains. Besides a few scattered security forces, the highway was nearly empty. While Lindsey had plenty on her plate, there was one thing she had to do first. She could not bear for Molina's wife to hear about his sacrifice from anyone but her first. So right now, she was headed with Palmer up to the Estes Park clinic where Victoria Molina worked as a nurse.

"What's the latest from Investigations?" Lindsey asked.

Palmer shuffled through some papers. He clicked on the

ceiling light to get a better look. "They pored over the shipping manifests like you asked."

"Siegler Pharmaceuticals?"

"Yes, ma'am," Palmer said. "We didn't have access to all the resources we needed, so we had to get the Feds involved."

"FBI?"

"We couldn't do it on our own."

"I understand. What did they find?"

"Well, apparently, Siegler Pharmaceuticals doesn't really exist."

"What do you mean?" Lindsey asked.

"They're just a shell company in Germany. You look under that shell, you find another based out of Turkey, then Saudi Arabia, then who the hell knows. As the Feds call it, it's a Byzantine labyrinth, ma'am."

"They have no idea who owns Siegler?"

"Nope."

"Do we know what was in that shipment?"

"Supposed to be generic medical supplies," Palmer said. "Everything from antibiotics to gauze to water treatment chemicals. Nothing suspicious."

"Which is why it's even more suspicious," Lindsey said. "No one needs a shell company to transport common medical products. The manifest was forged—or else they used those items to smuggle something through."

"Feds' thoughts exactly, and before you ask, no, none of us have any idea *what* it could have been."

"Figured."

The fact that the shell companies were foreign only reaffirmed Lindsey's suspicions that someone with international connections was playing games in the New Frontier. Which led her right back to the FAC.

They finally pulled off Interstate 36 and headed into Estes Park. Many of the streetlights no longer worked. Sporadic lanterns glowed from inside some of the storefronts and homes.

She took the Bronco up Prospect Avenue to the Estes Park Health Clinic.

They pulled into the parking lot and got out. A group of nearly thirty or so people clamored at the entrance to the Emergency Room.

"What's going on?" Palmer asked.

"Your guess is as good as mine," Lindsey replied.

She took them around the side of the building to a secondary entrance. Two men in security uniforms were guarding it.

"Hold up right there," one said, stepping forward. "Main entrance is—"

"Colorado Rangers." Lindsey revealed her badge. "Sheriff Plymouth here to see Victoria Molina."

The first security guard glanced at her badge, then waved her into the building. They were immediately met by a nurse. He was a middled-aged man in personal protective gear who offered them gowns, masks, and gloves. By now, Lindsey and Palmer both knew the routine and changed quickly.

"I'm looking for Sandra Spears," Lindsey said.

"Sheriff Plymouth, right?" the nurse queried.

Lindsey nodded.

"Great. Name's Bobby. Follow me."

He started down another corridor. Lindsey could hear voices demanding treatment or help from another hall connecting to the emergency room.

"What's going on?" Lindsey asked.

"Word has spread faster than the Wild Fire," Bobby replied. "Everyone thinks they and their family might have it."

"How many are actually sick?" Lindsey said.

He ushered them down another busy hall filled with nurses and doctors rushing between rooms.

"From what we can tell, none of the Estes Park citizens," Bobby said. "But the more they congregate, the more they force themselves into the emergency room, the bigger the risk of coming in contact with the couple dozen patients who are sick."

"Couple dozen here already?" Lindsey asked.

Bobby let out a sigh. "Our numbers have rocketed. Border security brought in another batch of sick people trying to drive over from the New Frontier just a couple hours ago."

"Is security sufficient to keep things under control?"

"I'm just a nurse, so I'm not really qualified to say."

"I don't care about qualifications. What's your unbiased opinion?"

Bobby let out a sigh. "Ma'am, you know those cartoons where a character is trying to plug a dam with their fingers? Then the dam bursts anyway?"

Lindsey nodded.

"I get the feeling we're just at the point where all our collective fingers are plugging holes and we don't have any more free fingers left."

"'Bout to burst then," Palmer added.

"Yes, sir."

Just as they rounded another corner, another woman in PPE turned her direction. Sandra Spears. A thinner, smaller young woman followed her.

Sandra strode down the corridor. "Lindsey."

Even in that one word, Lindsey could feel the woman's exhaustion, and see the worry cross her face.

"Why did you come all the way up here?" Sandra asked. "Is Raven..."

"Raven's okay," Lindsey said. "I spoke to him not long ago. It's Juan Molina, unfortunately."

Lindsey tensed up, trying to hold back her own emotion.

"Oh, no, I'm so sorry. Vicky is such a nice woman, and they've got two sons. Oh, God. Poor Vicky." Sandra turned her eyes away for just a moment. "We'll look out for her. As soon as you get done talking to her, I'll check on her."

"Thank you, Sandra. I'd appreciate that." Lindsey looked down at the younger woman beside her. "You must be Lara Lithgow."

"Yes," the younger woman said. "I'm training to be a nurse's assistant."

"Raven told me a bit about you. Pretty remarkable what you went through. Are you okay to be working here?"

"Yes," Lara said.

"We need all the help we can get, and sixteen is the cutoff for nurses' assistants now," Sandra explained.

"I had to do something to help," Lara said. "I couldn't stand by while so many people are suffering."

"I'm sure the people here appreciate that." Lindsey nodded. "Thanks again. And, Sandra, I'll do my best to keep you updated on Raven."

"Thank you, be safe," Sandra replied.

"You too."

Lindsey and Palmer followed Bobby again. He motioned down the corridor to a woman standing next to the nurses' station, examining a clipboard.

As soon as they started toward her, the nurse turned around. Her blue eyes caught Lindsey's behind her face-shield, and for a fleeting moment, Lindsey saw recognition in the woman's gaze. She put a glove up to her mask.

"Sheriff, don't tell me... Juan... is he..." Vicky started.

"Vicky, I'm so, so sorry," Lindsey said. Even in their PPE,

she embraced the woman. "Juan was a good man. One of my best."

"No..." Vicky sobbed. "He can't be gone..."

Her words trailed off as she cried into Lindsey's shoulder. Footsteps sounded behind her as Sandra came around to comfort Vicky too.

"I promise you, we won't forget Juan," Lindsey said. "He's done so much for this state. So much for this country. I just wanted to be the first to tell you how much he meant to us. To the Rangers."

Vicky said nothing as tears spilled behind her clear plastic visor. Sandra ushered the woman out of the corridor, with Lara at her heels, hopefully to find a breakroom where they could be in private.

Lindsey heaved a long sigh and turned back to Palmer, trying to hold back tears of her own.

"I can't keep doing this. We can't keep losing people," she said. "We have to stop the Wild Fire... the Reapers... stop ALL of it!"

Lindsey dropped her voice to a whisper.

"We have to stop it before there isn't anyone left."

19

Only a couple hours after leaving La Sal, white stars studded the night sky. The landscape was so dark, Raven could see nothing except the road in front of them. The Chevy Tahoe's headlights glared over the highway, the only manmade light for miles.

They had left Jeff and McGregor behind. The two men would be nothing but a mission risk. Both had potentially been exposed to Wild Fire, and neither would be helpful if they got into another firefight.

With their gas masks in their laps, Calvin and Yoon had been quiet most of the ride.

They were both broken shells of their former selves, with Calvin full of rage and Yoon grieving over his friend Molina.

Raven's grandfather had once told him that a man who made decisions from a place of anger was not a man at all, lower than an animal.

Anger corrupted a man's spirit.

He only hoped he could keep the man from following that path. Maybe Yoon could be Raven's backup, a counter to Calvin's anger. But Yoon was obviously struggling.

"Vicky worried this would happen," Yoon said. "Molina always told me how much she begged him to stop working for the Rangers. She wanted him to find a job back in Golden. Something safe, so he could see his boys more."

"I'm sorry." Raven didn't know what else to say.

All he could do was keep Calvin's rage in check and try to encourage Yoon to keep strong.

"I still don't like that we left Jeff and McGregor tied up back at their crappy fort," Calvin said. "I ain't got no crystal ball, but I see them worming their way free and trying to start some other militia. We should've taken care of that problem before it starts."

"Sometimes you have to let one venomous snake go to find the nest of vipers," Raven said.

Calvin was quiet for a while.

Raven took that moment to use their sat phone to call Lindsey, as he headed down the dusty road toward Navajo Nation.

She answered after only a couple rings. "Sheriff Plymouth here."

"Lindsey, it's Raven."

"Raven. I just saw your sister."

"She okay?"

"She's hanging in there. Working with Lara Lithgow at the clinic right now. I'm glad they are there to help Vicky Molina."

"Is she..."

"In shock."

"Understandable... I'm sorry, damn."

"Not to change the subject, but I take it you got something for me?"

"We got a new lead." He told her about McGregor and the Mountain Brigade, along with giving her the coordinates to the compound so she or maybe the USAMRIID teams out in the New Frontier could take in Jeff and McGregor for further questioning later. "McGregor said that the Navajo Nation is responsible for burning their people."

"Why?"

After capturing him, Raven, Calvin, and Yoon had questioned McGregor for several excruciating minutes, so he had some idea. "McGregor seemed to think it was because the Brigadiers were working with the Reapers, but I'm not one hundred percent confident."

"Does he know who the Reapers really are?" Lindsey asked.

"Doesn't seem that way. He doesn't really know much about them. Mostly McGregor just told us about their run-ins with Navajo Nation. These Navajo guys came up to the Mountain Brigade's Fort demanding they stop roaming around, spreading the disease. They traded some words, and the whole thing turned into a battle. McGregor claims the Navajo men rounded everyone up, then told them to leave the area. Get the hell out of Dodge, so to speak."

"You believe him?" Lindsey asked.

"Yeah, I threatened to bring him to the reservation to let them finish what they started," Raven said. "I've never seen a man more scared in my life."

"This doesn't sound like something the Navajo Nation would condone."

"I know. Something's not right. McGregor might've left out some details, but he was certain the Nation knows more about the Reapers than he did."

"Okay, is there anything at all I can do?" Lindsey asked.

"More manpower?"

"Wheeler *still* thinks it's suicide, at least until his field teams figure out where Wild Fire is popping up from."

"Fine then. I'm headed south. We're not far from the Navajo Nation, and I need to set up a meeting with someone who can represent them. I want to get the story straight about the Reapers and the Brigadiers. I planned on showing up on my own, but if you can help pull some strings to get them talking, it might make things easier."

"I'll see what I can do."

The Navajo Nation was one of the rare enclaves in the Badlands that had done a decent job establishing their own security forces and weathering the storm after the Collapse.

Of course, Raven knew from personal experience, that those who grew up on the reservations understood what it was like to survive in the face of overwhelming adversity.

"Raven," Lindsey said, "before you go, there's been a new development."

"You want to apologize for how things went down last year?" Raven asked. "That's great to hear."

He chuckled, but then grew serious when Calvin glanced over at him.

"Raven, cut the shit," Lindsey replied. The tone in her voice conveyed that none of his usual humor could make her feel any better. "Things are getting worse. More people are getting sick, and we identified why."

She told him about Doctor Wheeler's findings regarding the Wild Fire.

A chill traced Raven's spine. "Engineered?"

Creek looked up at Raven from where he was camped out on a seat. The dog seemed to sense his fear.

"The disease reservoir USAMRIID's teams are looking for might not be a nest of wild animals," Lindsey continued. "I'm worried that all this recent Reapers activity and Wild Fire are intimately connected. So like I said before, I need you to keep an ear out if you hear anything from the Nation or anyone else out there."

"Train ambushes, engineered plague, and wild militias," Raven said. "What else can you throw at us? Because this hasn't been hard enough."

"And I think things are going to get a lot worse before they get better."

Raven could hear Lindsey sigh. He felt bad about being so flippant with her. He couldn't imagine the stress she must be under, especially after having to break the news to Molina's wife about his death.

"Get back safely, Raven. I don't want to lose anyone else. Tell your team to be careful too. Okay?"

"Yeah, will do."

They continued south on the slim chance that Lindsey could use the government's tenuous relationship with Navajo Nation to help set up their meeting.

Creek snoozed in the back seat. Yoon also seemed to have succumbed to his exhaustion, judging by his closed eyes.

Raven thought Calvin might've been sleeping too until the SEAL spoke up. "So you were in North Korea?"

"Yeah..."

"Those evil fucks changed everything. Destroyed our world in one devastating night."

Raven simply nodded.

The retired SEAL straightened in his seat. Even with only the pale moonlight bleeding into the SUV, Raven noticed a grimace cross the man's face.

"You okay?" Raven asked.

"My back's hurting again." He took a drink of water. "It ain't from the train wreck. I was in a Black Hawk crash. Afghanistan. We were after an HVT on a midnight direct action mission. Didn't even make it to the DZ. The bird went belly-side up, smearing two of my brothers across the rock and dirt. I got caught up in the wreck. Went through six surgeries with the VA before they told me I'd never walk normal again."

"Damn."

"When I close my eyes, sometimes I still hear the scraping metal and the cries of my brothers. It never goes away. Each night's the same. Now I got another nightmare to relive every fucking night. This time, the one that took my best friend."

"I'm sorry," Raven said. "I've lost a lot of my brothers and sisters. It never gets easier. You just keep shedding more of the shell around your heart until it's nothing but a raw yolk."

He thought back to watching his buddy, Billy Franks, take that sniper bullet. Then losing Marcus Colton. The guy had been a mentor to Lindsey, and a close friend to Raven.

He decided to tell Calvin both stories.

Calvin shook his head when he was finished. "You and I are more alike than I thought, man."

"Yeah, I guess so. At least some of your people made it back. That's got to count for something."

"Maybe, but you know the worst part for me?" Calvin didn't give Raven a chance to answer. "When it's your fault when shit goes bad. On the helicopter, I wasn't piloting the thing. It wasn't my fault it got hit. Nothing I could do. But the train, I keep thinking I could've done something more. Unlike the chopper, I was the one responsible for protecting the train, and I couldn't even save Mouse, for God's sake."

"That's where I've changed," Raven said. He turned the wheel slightly, following a long curve in the highway. "I've stopped blaming myself and instead focus on what I can do."

"What do you mean?"

"I used to dwell on what I could have done to save Billy or Colton. Like all the time. It never stopped. Then I started to realize if I had done things differently, well, maybe the girls we went to North Korea to rescue would have died instead of Billy. Or maybe after the Collapse, with all the shit going on, I would have lost Lindsey instead of Colton. Maybe even both of them." Raven shook his head. "Things happen the way they're supposed to, I think, and all we can do is fight to our last breath to try and keep people alive. When they die, it's not because of our failures."

Calvin was quiet a moment, probably considering what Raven had said.

"I spent too many nights and days drinking away my dread," Raven went on. "No more, man, no fucking more. Colton was a lawman. I didn't much care for guys like him back then, but he earned my respect. I even considered him a friend. When he died, he left behind a wife, Kelly, and a daughter, Risa. I try to do my best to help them when I can, because that is one thing I can do now."

"My best bud, Mouse left behind a family too. They're the type of people that will drop everything if you say you need help. I mean, I don't know many folks who will actually come help load the truck when you got to move. But Mouse would be there an hour early and bring donuts. Same with his lady. And now... I don't know how I'm going to tell her what happened."

"There's not a worse feeling in the world, brother, but all you can do is be there for them when you get back."

"There's one other thing I can do," Calvin said.

Raven looked over.

"I can make sure every Reaper is buried six feet under—or better yet, wolf food."

"I get that, but just don't do anything rash."

Calvin was quiet for another long moment. "I'm sorry for killing that wolf. Maybe I should have let it go. I just thought it was diseased and better off dead."

"Maybe so. That's not for me to say, but you don't owe me an apology. If you feel bad, apologize to the wolf."

For a second, Raven thought Calvin was going to tell him to shove it. But the SEAL merely nodded and closed his eyes, mumbling something to himself.

He hoped the wolf's spirit heard Calvin. Because humans didn't need any more sicknesses sprouting from the animal world.

If what Lindsey had said was true, humans were perfectly good at inventing their own.

For a solid hour, they sat in silence until the sat phone rang.

Raven answered it. "Go ahead."

"I just got word from President Tso of the Navajo Nation," Lindsey said. "Took a lot of convincing, but he agreed to have some of his people in the area meet you."

"He say anything?"

"We didn't go over details. I'll leave that up to your discretion, Raven. But please, make sure you don't say anything offensive, or do anything stupid."

"I can't make that promise."

"Raven."

"Sorry, I promise that I will do my best."

"Be careful."

"Yup."

He set the phone down and sighed. Then he rapped on the back of Calvin's seat a few times to stir Yoon, who sat up slowly and yawned.

"Ok, fellas. Hope everyone got some shut-eye," Raven said. "Because I have a feeling we're about to cross over into some dangerous territory."

When they finally arrived on the outskirts of Montezuma Creek, spotlights lanced through the windshield. The bright white lights nearly blinded Calvin as he held up a hand to shield his eyes.

"What a welcome," he muttered.

"They didn't survive out here by being stupid," Raven said. "Just being cautious."

"You better hope so," Yoon said.

Creek began barking at the silhouettes backlit by the spotlights as they surrounded the vehicle. Eight or nine men, all with rifles shouldered.

Raven opened his door, shielding his eyes.

"Relax," he called out. "We're friends."

A low voice responded, belonging to a man stepping toward Raven, silhouetted by a spotlight. "No one is a friend until they prove it."

The man that spoke snapped his fingers and the spotlights blinked off. He was clearly the leader. It took Calvin's eyes a moment to adjust. He focused on the tall guy with broad shoulders, and muscles pushing against a tan T-shirt. He had dark black hair draping over his shoulders, and brown eyes that looked nearly black, especially now.

"Sheriff Plymouth said you would be expecting us," Raven said.

Calvin opened the door and began to step out of the Tahoe. Weapons clicked and raised toward him.

"I'm Eddy Nez," the man in the tan shirt said.

"I'm Raven Spears, this is Larry Yoon, and Calvin Jackson," Raven said.

"I know who you are," Eddy replied. "Leave your weapons in the truck."

Calvin didn't like the idea of following these guys anywhere unarmed and looked to Raven.

"You come at the orders of a sheriff with the Colorado Rangers," Eddy said. Then he glared at Raven. "You of all people should know why I might not trust their word."

Yoon muttered something under his breath.

"Leave your weapons behind," Raven said.

"You serious?" Yoon asked.

"Do it," Calvin said.

They took out their pistols, and knives, leaving everything with their rifles in the car.

"The dog stays too."

"What?" Raven asked.

"Those are my terms," Eddy replied. "Either listen or drive back the way you came."

This time, Raven muttered something under his breath. He leaned down to Creek and told him to stay put. The dog let out a long whine.

"All right," Eddy said. "Come with me."

Calvin, Raven, and Yoon followed the heavily armed group of Navajo warriors toward a squat white building. The sign had been removed, but Calvin could still make out the ghostly shadows of where letters had been removed from the wall. It appeared to have once said, *Welcome. Church of Christ Meets Here.*

"A church?" Yoon asked.

"That was one of the Mormons' churches before they ran off after the Great Reversal," Eddy replied.

Great Reversal? Calvin made a mental note of the term. He assumed it was the Navajo Nation's term for the Collapse.

Five of the Navajo men followed them into the abandoned church. The rest stayed outside, guarding the SUV and the street.

Inside, folding chairs were scattered around a few flimsy tables. A lone lectern gathering dust stood at the front of the narrow building. Kerosene lanterns hanging off support columns and sitting on tables gave off flickering yellow light and an oily smell.

"Have a seat," Eddy said, his voice deep and throaty.

Calvin didn't like the idea of letting his guard down by sitting, but out of respect, he lowered himself gently into the seat like an old arthritic man in his nineties.

Better to let these guys think he was weak and wounded. Let them underestimate him. He really wasn't liking the vibe they were putting off. Felt like the tension at a bar right before a fight broke out.

Calvin nodded at the other Navajo men. "Who are your friends?"

"Not your concern; you speak to me," Eddy replied.

"That's how it's going to be, huh?" Calvin asked.

This whole setup felt like trying to arrange teatime with a rabid coyote. He supposed he should play it cooler.

"My friend's had a hell of a day," Raven explained. "You know that attack on the train our sheriff told you about?"

"I'm aware," Eddy said.

"That's why I'm here," Calvin said. "To find the people responsible."

"You're here because you want *our help.*"

Raven glanced at Calvin.

"Yeah, I'm sorry," he said in his most convincing tone. "I need your help finding the group responsible for killing my people."

"What are you offering?" Eddy asked.

"Offering?" Calvin asked. "I doubt you want a rogue paramilitary group out there. You helping us, helps you."

"The Rattlesnakes have protected these borders since the Great Reversal. We don't need your help. We're aware of this paramilitary group and any threat they pose."

Rattlesnakes. Calvin made another mental note. He hadn't heard of the group.

"You know where the Reapers Militia is, then?" Calvin asked.

"I do," Eddy said. "But it will cost you."

"Cost us?" Heat rose in Calvin's face. "We're doing you a favor, pal. I'll get rid of this threat. All I need to know is where they make their bed at night."

Eddy laughed, along with the rest of his men.

"One man," he said. "One man thinks he can take out the Reapers."

"More than one," Raven said.

"Why do you work with them?" Eddy asked. His face concentrated into a stern mask of anger. "You betray your people."

"I do what I think is right," Raven said. "And who are you to judge me? After what you did at La Sal."

Eddy rose from his seat, quaking in anger. "They came down here, demanding we help them and their sick people. They said they'd kill us all if we didn't open our clinic to them." McGregor sure as hell hadn't mentioned that. "Their visit spread that disease to my people. We had to protect ourselves. Governor McGregor betrayed us, and his people paid the price. We had to burn their town and run them off so they wouldn't bother us again."

Calvin didn't know much about the Navajo Nation, but what he saw at La Sal told him they didn't deal with enemies kindly.

"I have a way to help you," Raven said.

Eddy stepped forward and lifted his chin.

"You have that disease here, don't you?" Raven asked.

"Four patients now. Do you have a cure?" Eddy asked.

Raven shrugged.

Eddy leaned forward over the table. "A cure is the price of the information you have come here for."

"Give us the intel, and we will make sure you get the cure," Raven said.

Calvin kept his gaze ahead, knowing damn well they didn't have a cure yet.

Eddy laughed. "I don't trust you, or your government."

He stood and snorted.

"Just because you and I share a similar past doesn't mean you have a heart or spirit like mine, Raven," Eddy growled. "You are every bit their puppet as these men."

Yoon fidgeted and Calvin grew tense watching Eddy pace frantically back and forth.

"My scouts have every one of those survivalist strongholds mapped out, including the Reapers," Eddy said. "They even had the nerve to try getting *my* people to work for them."

"Did they promise a cure?" Yoon asked.

"They did," Eddy said. "Just like you are now. You and them aren't so different."

"Eddy, if you give us the location of the Reapers, it will cost you nothing," Raven said. "If you don't ...."

Eddy gave him a diabolical grin, his teeth reflecting the light of the kerosene lamp at their table. "Are you about to threaten me?"

"I just want us to all stay friends," Raven said. "Allies, if you will."

"I'm starting to wonder if President Tso knows about what happened at La Sal," Calvin said.

Eddy's gaze flitted from Raven to Calvin. "What the Rattlesnakes do is none of the president's business. They don't have us on a leash like beaten dogs. Not like you three. We do things no one else is willing to do to protect our people, because if we don't do it, no one will."

Calvin could see then that Eddy was drunk on his own power. The Rattlesnakes weren't the noble protectors of the Navajo Nation that Eddy thought they were. This man was forming his own budding terrorist organization.

Worse, it also meant that President Tso's promise of Raven, Yoon, and Calvin's safety didn't mean much, which was no fault of Tso's.

"Tie these men up," Eddy said to his guards. "I don't want them blabbing their heads off to anyone and interfering with our mission."

Calvin stood, ready to fight. But before he could even make it a step, one of the guards aimed his rifle straight at his face. The other guards leveled their rifles at Raven and Yoon.

There was no chance to defend themselves.

Calvin froze, anger heating his chest.

"You'll regret this," Raven said.

Eddy laughed. "I'm pretty sure it's the three of you that'll regret coming here and making threats."

"We'll see about that," Calvin said.

20

AFTER THE TRIP BACK FROM ESTES PARK, A CHILLY night blanketed Golden. Lindsey felt exhausted.

As much as she wanted to sleep, she couldn't.

After all, plagues didn't sleep either. Someone had to burn the midnight oil to keep her people safe.

Which meant after dropping Palmer back off at Fort Golden, her next stop was the Red Rocks Medical Center where Doctor Wheeler was running his labs.

She left her Bronco in the parking lot and passed the security guards outside with a flash of her badge. Wheeler had quickly evolved this community health center into a full-blown biohazard facility.

While the main corridor allowed easy access between the improvised labs, other offshoot hallways were blocked with clear plastic partitions. The whole place had been set up for maximum safety, complete with inflatable ventilation ducts, fans pushing in clean air, and sterilization antechambers full of fresh PPE, decon showers, and chemicals Lindsey didn't recognize.

Behind those partitions, there were researchers wearing

big, bulky biohazard suits. They looked a little like earthborn astronauts cautiously moving around lab equipment.

Lindsey took the stairs up to the third floor. USAMRIID men and women in civilian and military service uniforms filed through the halls. She made it past them into what had once been a breakroom with views of several different medical labs.

This was where Wheeler had set up his so-called command information center. The long table at the center of the room was filled with stacks of papers. Ten men and women were at laptops hooked up to servers that the USAM-RIID personnel had brought in. The room was hot from all the buzzing computer activity.

At the head of the table were Doctors Wheeler and Divekar, pointing at a laptop screen and talking.

Engrossed in their work, neither doctor noticed her until she strode right up.

"Oh, Sheriff Plymouth," Wheeler said.

"What's the status of things here?" she asked.

"We're up to one hundred ten people with confirmed cases of Wild Fire," Divekar said.

"One hundred... Damn," Lindsey said.

"There are probably far more than that," Wheeler said with a sigh. "You see, we don't have a rapid way to confirm these cases. Now that we've sequenced the genomic data of the Wild Fire bacteria, we can test lab specimens via PCR to identify if patients do indeed have Wild Fire. The only problem is, because this is so new for us, the tests take a while."

"Do you have estimates on how many people out there might have Wild Fire?"

Divekar folded her arms over her chest. "Last I checked, the Front Range clinics had nearly two hundred people in the ICUs with symptoms consistent with Wild Fire. We hit sixty-seven deaths just ten minutes ago that we think are related to Wild Fire infections."

Lindsey was taken aback. The growth in numbers was staggering. It would only get worse until they identified a cure.

"What's the situation on finding a treatment?" Lindsey asked.

Wheeler motioned for her to follow him to one of the big windows. He gestured toward a group of four researchers using built-in gloves to deposit different liquids into plastic culture dishes behind enclosed stainless steel flow hoods.

"We're running through a second series of high-throughput antibiotic resistance tests now," he said. "These experiments are directly challenging the Wild Fire bacteria with all the antibiotics we have on hand."

Then he pointed to the breakroom full of people working on computers.

"Since we now have the genomic data on Wild Fire, we're also doing bioinformatics and protein modeling experiments to simulate the likely composition of the cellular wall."

"In layman's terms?" Lindsey asked.

"Basically, we're doing everything we can to understand this bacterium, inside and out. We're using the most advanced, well-understood computational and experimental models."

"I assume we're still waiting on results from the first set of experiments to determine if any antibiotics on hand are effective since this is the *second* set."

Wheeler was quiet for a moment. His eyes shot back toward the laboratory as if the answer was somewhere inside.

"Doctor?" Lindsey tried.

Wheeler didn't turn back to face her. "Well, you're right that we ran the first complete series of antibiotic experiments.

We tested every antibiotic on hand, and others that USAM-RIID brought. But we are no longer waiting on those results. We got them back. Nothing worked."

"No," Lindsey said. "That has to be a mistake. There must be a way to stop it."

"I hoped so too," Wheeler said. "Maybe we missed something or made an error. That's the purpose of these second series. After all, we're using test samples straight from patients, so we may have inadvertently introduced variables that negatively affected our tests. Either way, these are some of the most talented scientific minds at USAMRIID. We will figure out something. We just need time."

"Time..." Lindsey looked back to Divekar, who appeared exhausted almost beyond recognition.

"Aren't there alternatives you can try?" Lindsey asked.

"Sure, there are millions of different substances and chemicals in this world that we can try," Wheeler said. "However, we're limited by our computational power and experimental output. We have to start with the most obvious candidates, then work our way outward. So, unless one of our field teams comes across some clue in the New Frontier—the reservoir for instance—we're shooting in the dark."

"By then, it might already be too late," Divekar said. "Our clinics and hospitals will be overrun."

After more discussion on the science of the matter and thanking everyone for their time, Lindsey left with a heavy weight in her gut. While she knew how to fight outlaws with guns and bullets, this microscopic enemy was far more difficult to defeat. She was glad to have Wheeler and Divekar on the job.

Unfortunately, it wasn't just the disease that remained a mystery. She still had the matter of the traitor in her midst. She wanted to curse at all their bad luck, but she remembered something her former mentor, Colton, had told her during the Collapse.

When multiple threats are closing in, you have to deal with them differently. Approach each one with a plan, eliminate that threat, and then move on, one at a time.

Lindsey had a plan to do just that, starting with the Reapers.

On her way to Fort Golden, she called Palmer and requested he meet her outside their building.

He was waiting outside the front doors when she got there with two coffees. She put the Bronco in park, left the engine running, and waved him inside.

"Coffee, you are a blessing," Lindsey said.

"That's what the ladies always tell me." He slumped into the seat beside her.

Lindsey took one of the coffees. "I'm half tempted to fire you for comparing me to one of your *ladies.*"

"Ah, ma'am, you know I don't mean no offense," Palmer said, face growing red. "I don't even really, well, you know, with the ladies and—"

"You're too easy, Palmer."

The man let out a short laugh, then tipped his cowboy hat. "That's another thing they always tell me."

"Now you're pressing your luck." Lindsey took another sip of coffee, then opened the console between their seats.

She took out a stack of envelopes from the open console. Each manila envelope was labeled for a different member of the Foreign Advisory Council. She'd prepared them earlier, in the solitude of her Bronco to prevent prying eyes.

"I want to provide Raven and the team a little assistance," Lindsey said. While that was true, the next part wasn't. She hoped Palmer couldn't tell she was telling a lie. "I'm scheduling an airdrop for a resupply. I also plan to send in an armed squad of Rangers. I want the FAC to know so we can organize a *second* resupply and potentially more manpower from them."

"I thought we were forbidden from sending people out by Wheeler until his teams figured out where the disease was coming from."

"The situation's more desperate now."

Palmer's head bobbed. "I understand, ma'am."

There was more she wanted to say, but she held back. The plan she'd concocted relied on him not knowing. She felt bad deceiving him, but he would forgive her when he learned why.

"I want you to hand deliver these to each member of the FAC," Lindsey said.

"Yes, ma'am."

"I mean directly too. Not to their secretaries or assistants or anyone else. It's for their eyes only. You make sure to tell them that. Absolutely no one else sees what's in these envelopes. I don't even want them talking to each other about them. We can't risk this information falling into anyone else's hands."

"Understood. I'll get right on it."

As soon as Palmer slipped out of the car, Lindsey picked up her phone and dialed the Secretary of Defense. It only took a few rings before the stern voice of the most powerful woman in America answered.

"Secretary, Lindsey Plymouth here."

"Ah, Sheriff, how are things going?"

"Not well."

Lindsey explained what was going on with Wild Fire, most of which the Secretary already knew from the USAM-RIID staff.

"I need another favor, Madame Secretary," Lindsey said.

"Speak."

"I'm going to need to get access to five drones. Five drones we can take over the New Frontier."

"That's a lot to ask for, Sheriff. I already sent you half of USAMRIID."

"I know, but if this works, I could stop a potentially devastating situation that threatens to infect the whole country."

The Secretary was silent for a moment.

"If you want these drones, I need to know what for," Charlize finally said.

———

Raven was seated on the floor of the church next to Calvin and Yoon. The three of them had their hands tied with ropes behind their backs and were pressed up against the back wall of the building.

About twelve feet away, Eddy was still at the table. Raven eyed the weapons. There was an axe strapped to his belt, and he also wore a holstered pistol. His rifle was on the table. The guard looking at the map with Eddy had a slung rifle.

Another guard stood beside Calvin and Yoon, watching over the prisoners with another rifle. Meager light flickered from the kerosene lanterns hanging off the support columns.

"We move north," Eddy said, tracing his finger along the map. "Maybe we take more land. We run into trouble, we can use those three as bargaining points with the US government."

He used a thumb to indicate Calvin, Yoon, and Raven.

Raven didn't like that he might become a pawn for whatever nefarious purposes Eddy had in mind. But fortunately, he didn't plan on being a prisoner of the Rattlesnakes for much longer. If Eddy wanted to rant about his plan aloud, Raven would gladly accept the intel.

As Eddy ran his mouth, Raven worked a hand free from the ropes binding his wrists. He gave Calvin a slight nod when their guard turned away a moment, then scooted toward the Steel Runner.

With one hand hidden behind them, he worked at Calvin's ropes, until Calvin could take over. When he was free, they waited for their chance.

Right now, there was just the two guards and Eddy.

The closest guard glanced over at Raven, Calvin, and Yoon again. Raven kept his wrists behind his back, doing his best to pretend to still be tied up.

The guard rotated back to looking out a window.

Raven gave a subtle nod to Calvin.

The Steel Runner lunged up, slamming a fist right into the guard's chin. At the same time, Raven surged toward the now-dazed guard and wrenched away his rifle, immediately turning it on Eddy and the second guard.

That guard began swinging his rifle around. Raven barely had time to aim, firing a burst that stitched into the man's chest.

As he fell backward, Eddy went for the rifle, but Raven fired in his direction. Eddy gave up on the rifle and flipped the table for cover.

"Get Yoon loose!" Raven yelled to Calvin.

He started advancing toward the table, firing several shots. But Raven couldn't see if he'd hit Eddy or not. He kept firing, knowing that Eddy still had a pistol.

"Eddy, give up!" Raven said.

Outside, voices clamored in response to the gunfire. People shouted just outside the front of the church.

They might only have seconds to escape, but Raven didn't

want Eddy shooting him in the back. He fired into the table again, prompting a cry of agony.

Suddenly, Eddy bounded up from around the other side of the table with his pistol in one hand and axe in the other. Raven tried to readjust his aim, but Eddy slashed his axe right into Raven's rifle barrel and fired at Raven's head.

The bullet narrowly missed, and the loud crack made Raven wince. Out of desperation, he swung the rifle at Eddy's hand, knocking the pistol away.

"I'm going to rip you apart!" Eddy shouted.

He swung the axe at Raven before he could fire his rifle, forcing Raven to duck. Then he had to parry another blow with his rifle, holding it up in both hands. The blade nearly hit one of his fingers, forcing him to lose his grip on the stock.

He tried to back away from Eddy, but slipped on blood from the dead guard and fell to his back.

A crash of glass sounded over the ringing in his ear. A window behind them had broken. Was that Yoon?

Raven didn't have time to confirm anything. The Rattlesnake leader lifted the axe again, grinning as he prepared to swing it down on Raven. A chair suddenly crashed into Eddy.

From the corner of his eye, Raven saw that Calvin had thrown it.

The Steel Runner barreled toward Eddy, yelling. He ducked low to tackle the man. Before he could, Eddy grabbed Calvin by the neck and flung him sideways into the table.

Eddy was a monster, a beast with unholy strength.

He snorted and came down hard with the axe again. Raven had only enough time to bring up the rifle, firing a blast that lanced into the ceiling and a support column. One of the lanterns fell to the ground, cracking.

Eddy shouldered the barrel away from Raven. Then he

headbutted Raven in the face, knocking him back to the ground.

As Eddy cranked back the axe again, Raven snatched the cracked kerosene lantern to his right. He swung it hard at his enemy's face as the axe whooshed down again.

Glass shattered in a dazzling spray of oil and fire. Eddy swatted at the flames dancing on his skin, screaming an agonizing cry. Raven picked up his rifle and aimed it at his foe, but the burning Rattlesnake leader ran and jumped through a window, breaking right through the glass.

At the same time, more glass broke from the front of the church. Gunfire peppered through the windows, forcing Raven down.

"This way!" Yoon yelled.

Raven twisted to see the Ranger hunched just beneath a broken window.

Calvin rounded past the table where Eddy had thrown him. His lip was busted open and bleeding. In his hands, he had the rifle from the other guard Raven had killed. He shot off a blast of covering fire toward the front window as he and Raven sprinted to join Yoon.

Raven thought about recovering Eddy's pistol, but another volley of incoming fire tore into the church. More windows shattered. Splinters of wood flew from each round punching through the walls as bullets lanced into folding chairs and tore up tables.

They needed to run. Now.

Yoon climbed through the broken window first, followed by Calvin, then Raven.

"I'll kill you!" Eddy screamed in the distance. "I'll skin you all alive!"

His enraged voice pierced the night.

Raven kept running without looking back.

Only once they were behind a trailer home about two hundred yards away from the church did the trio pause.

"We got to get the hell out of here," Calvin said.

"Back to the Tahoe?" Yoon asked.

Raven thought on it, but he wasn't sure that was where Creek would still be.

"I have to find Creek," Raven said.

Yoon looked like he was about to argue, but the barking of search dogs filled the neighborhood. Kerosene and battery-powered lamps flicked on in some of the trailer home windows.

The gunfire in front of the church had finally quieted.

"They know we're not there," Calvin whispered. "We got to move, so what's your plan, Raven?"

"Head back to the Tahoe and see if Creek is still there," he said. "If not, I'll stay behind and find him, and you guys get the hell out of here."

"Let's cross that bridge if Creek isn't there," Calvin said.

Raven nodded.

He got up and snuck into the darkness with their only rifle. Indistinct shouting exploded from the distant church as Raven and the others sprinted toward the eastern edge of Montezuma Creek. They then looped back around into the main street through town.

Rust-pocked cars and trailer homes provided cover as they advanced. From a new vantage behind a burned SUV, Raven faced back down the street toward the medical facility and church.

The Tahoe was still there, guarded by two men, but he didn't see Creek. Raven's heart quickened with fear. He couldn't lose his best bud.

He continued to scan the area, seeing only the two guards.

Most of the other Rattlesnakes appeared to be looking for him and his team.

"I'm going to take those two out. As soon as I do, you guys run to the Tahoe. I'll keep searching for Creek."

"Wait, look," Yoon said. He pointed at the back of the Tahoe where a furry face suddenly emerged in the back window.

"Creek." Raven breathed a sigh of relief.

"Kill these motherfuckers, and let's go before it's too late," Calvin said.

"With pleasure," Raven said. He lined up his sights on one man standing near the front of the Tahoe and fired. Bullets cracked into his chest, dropping him to the road.

The other guard took cover as Raven ran along the road to a new spot behind a minivan with no tires propped up on cement blocks.

The guy near the vehicle was aiming at the spot where Raven had been a couple seconds ago.

Good.

Raven opened fire again. Bullets slammed into the final guard's head.

Yoon and Calvin were with him a moment later, all of them running toward the Tahoe. Muzzle flashes suddenly lit up the end of the street like fireflies.

"Down!" Raven yelled.

He stared in horror as a posse of soldiers - six or seven strong - ran toward them. Raven went up and fired a covering burst. That bought them a few seconds to continue to the Tahoe. He fired another blast on the way, but that was the last of the ammo.

Yoon got in the driver's side door, ducking as bullets shattered the window.

"Go!" Raven screamed.

The engine roared, and he put the vehicle into reverse as Raven jumped in the back, shielding Creek. More bullets peppered the Tahoe, punching the side without mercy.

Raven looked up to see Eddy's men flanking them.

"Behind us!" he shouted.

Yoon put on the brakes, the vehicle jolting to a stop. They all ducked as more gunfire smacked into the vehicle. Creek barked as Raven covered the dog.

"GO!" Calvin shouted.

Yoon yanked the wheel hard so they tore off the road and into a field. Bullets chased them as they bobbed up and down in their desperate escape.

"I got a flat tire," Yoon said.

"Fuckin A, keep going man, we have to keep going!" Calvin shouted. "Shit, all our gear is still here!"

He grabbed one of the rifles they'd left in the car and leaned out the window, letting loose another covering blast.

Raven gripped Creek tight, fearing the vehicle would stall and they'd be riddled by a flurry of gunfire. But Yoon kept driving, even with the flat.

He turned off the headlights to help disguise their escape. Raven finally looked up, seeing a bright moon guiding them through the desert.

Finally, after another thirty minutes, the tire gave, and they were forced to stop behind an abandoned trailer. Calvin and Yoon hopped out while Raven held security. The Ranger and Steel Runner changed the tire with a spare as fast as possible.

Just as they began to get the bolts on, Raven saw headlights in the distance.

"Hurry," he said.

They finished as the vehicles closed in, the headlights dancing over the dry terrain.

The Tahoe sped away, heading down a dirt road intersecting with the main highway.

"I can't believe we made it," Raven said.

After all, they'd escaped with their lives—and Creek's.

"We're not safe yet, and we still don't have a lead," Calvin said. "We trusted our lives to those traitors, and for what?"

"Maybe for this," Yoon said. He reached into his jacket and pulled out a folded, bloodstained piece of paper.

Raven took it and unfolded it. "This is Eddy's map."

"I took it when you two were busy getting your asses kicked," Yoon said.

"Holy shit, brother," Raven said. "You know, I underestimated you."

"Me too," Calvin said.

Raven held up the map to study it in the moonlight. He spotted where Eddy believed the Reapers Militia was.

"Someone got the sat phone?" Raven asked.

"Still got it." Yoon passed it back to Raven.

"I'm calling Lindsey," Raven said. "She needs to know everything that just happened—and where we're going now."

"Which is where?" Yoon asked.

Raven, Yoon, and Calvin's careers serving their countries may have changed drastically since they'd first enlisted in the armed forces. But they were still going to do what they did best: fulfill their oath to defend the United States.

"Moab," Raven said. "Home of the Pueblos, and now, apparently, the Reapers."

21

"THANKS FOR THE UPDATE, RAVEN, I'M GLAD YOU'RE okay," Lindsey said. "Hopefully, this map is right, and these Reapers are actually in Moab. You find out where they are, and I'll wrangle up some backup right now to bring them in. I'm going to tell Tso about the Rattlesnakes too."

"Good," Raven replied. "He needs to know what kind of wolves he's got roaming around."

Lindsey clicked off the satellite phone. She was shocked to hear what had gone down in Montezuma Creek, but also hopeful now that Raven had a lead on the Reapers.

They still didn't know who might be feeding the enemy intel from her FAC—but she was about to find out.

Lindsey parked her Bronco atop Lookout Mountain, a once popular tourist site where Buffalo Bill's grave and his eponymous museum were. It used to be a favorite spot for her to take out-of-town guests, allowing both views of the mountains to the west and Golden and Denver to the east. The sprawling vistas of the contrasting Great Plains and Rocky Mountains never failed to impress visitors.

But she wasn't here to sightsee. This spot, devoid of visitors, was the perfect place to get away from the chaos at Fort Golden.

Most importantly, she was far from the spies she hoped to expose.

Only one person had been invited to join her. From the grind of rubber tires over asphalt, she could hear that he was arriving now.

Palmer's lifted Ford F-250 came around the bend up to the parking lot. He parked the truck next to her Bronco and turned off the gurgling V-8.

She got out an encrypted Toughbook laptop. The computer had a secured satellite-internet connection.

"Sheriff." Palmer tipped his cowboy hat at her.

She nodded back and took him over to a bench.

As he sat, he asked, "You going to tell me everything that's going on now?"

"We're about to find out if that experiment I had you run earlier this morning worked," Lindsey said.

"Didn't quite realize I was running an experiment."

"That was the point." Lindsey powered up the Toughbook.

She used a specially encrypted line that connected her to a government office in New York City.

A live video stream appeared on her monitor.

On the other end was a woman with well-toned muscles pushing slightly against her white blouse. She had a slightly crooked nose and puffy ears, which Lindsey guessed may have been due to martial arts. Her square jaw looked like it could absorb a punch or two.

It had to be Aditi Rajawat, the Under Secretary of Defense for Intelligence & Security.

"Hi," Lindsey said. "Sheriff Plymouth and Deputy Palmer here."

"Nice to meet you," Rajawat said. "Secretary Montgomery wanted me to personally walk you through this morning's surveillance, given the drones belong to my department."

"Thank you. We're anxious to see what we can dig up."

"We're minutes away from go-time. I'm going to start streaming the drone feeds to your computer the moment we're in the appropriate area of operation."

"Excellent, I'll standby," Lindsey said. She turned to Palmer. "Each of those envelopes you passed out contained different locations for that supposed resupply and reinforcement drop."

"Supposed?" Palmer asked. "So it's not real, ma'am?"

"Nope. But the FAC and the Reapers don't know that. Everyone in the FAC got different intel. We're going to scan the locations I gave them. If anyone is the spy, I'm expecting they'll have sent a welcome party—or at least a scout—to greet our pretend Rangers."

"Impressive."

"Drones are ready," Rajawat said.

Five boxes popped up on the laptop screen. A cool wind blew, and Lindsey shivered. She steeled herself for the moment of truth.

"I know this is probably an expensive operation," Lindsey said. "We appreciate this help more than you know. If I'm right, this will pay off in huge dividends, and we'll be able to root out some nasty rot in Colorado that could threaten the rest of the country."

"Then let's hope you're right, Sheriff," Rajawat said.

Each of the boxes on the screen showed expansive natural landscapes. Some displayed mountaintops filled with craggy rocks and lingering snowpack. Others revealed empty stretches of desert where only a few stubborn plants and scattered rocks remained. The images slowly morphed as the drones flew above the terrain.

"Any theory on who our leaker might be?" Lindsey asked as she watched the changing landscapes.

"Hard to say," Rajawat said. "My first guess would be the Chinese."

"You distrust them?"

"I certainly wouldn't share my email password with them, and I'd be surprised if they hadn't already tried to crack it," Rajawat said. "They have helped immensely since the Collapse. But as you know, there are different factions with different priorities. I'm not sure they all have America's best interests in mind."

"No shit," Palmer whispered.

"Keep your friends close and your enemies closer," Lindsey said.

"That's basically how Jiu Jitsu works." Rajawat smirked, answering Lindsey's earlier suspicions. "I hold my enemies close enough until they tap out or pass out."

"Then let's do the same today."

Rajawat tapped a button on her end. The first of the six boxes expanded to take up the whole screen. Palmer leaned in closer to the display.

"Drone One is approaching site designation Test Alpha," Rajawat said. "Test Alpha is the UK. I wouldn't suspect them, but I want to be thorough."

The drone swept over a stretch of desert interspersed with dried riverbeds and boulders. Besides a few scraggly plants, the drone's camera didn't reveal any other living thing.

"Empty," Rajawat said. "I'm going to do a thermal scan just to make sure."

She pressed another key on her laptop. The image changed, piping in an infrared view of the desert.

While much of the landscape was bathed in sun-drenched heat, Lindsey didn't see the telltale white forms of people trying to hide in the area.

"Unless things change, I'm calling that good," Rajawat said. "Bravo's next. This will be Canada."

Lindsey never really suspected Blair of being a traitor, but was glad to have that in stone now.

Another image of a mountainous slope showed from a different drone. This time a handful of trees stood against a windswept incline covered in wildflowers.

Piard definitely didn't strike Lindsey as a spy.

Then again, the best spies probably wouldn't.

"Landscape looks..." Rajawat paused. "Hold on, let's zoom in right there."

She indicated a spot next to some trees. A stream ran next to the swaying pines.

"I see movement," Rajawat said.

Lindsey saw it too. Like the shadows were morphing. The trees were blocking whoever or whatever it was.

"Don't tell me the Canadian representative is our snitch," Lindsey said. "I don't want to believe it. That just doesn't make any sense."

"Switching to infrared now."

The heat signature of the culprit suddenly become strikingly apparent.

Lindsey breathed a sigh of relief. "That's a moose. Never been happier to see one."

Rajawat scanned the rest of the area to ensure they hadn't missed anything else. "Looks like we're clear. Don't worry too much. We're bound to come across some false positives since we're predominantly using thermal tracking. We've got a lot of animals out there we may inadvertently identify."

Next came Test Charlie. This location had been given to

the United Nations representative, Uwase. A scan of an alpine meadow next to a pristine lake revealed nothing but wildflowers and trees.

"Clear," Rajawat confirmed.

Delta followed. Tiankai and the Chinese.

Lindsey held her breath as they scanned an area filled with arches of red rock and dried streambeds. Plenty of places to lay an ambush.

She wondered if Rajawat was right. If the Chinese had played a long con after all or if Tiankai was pulling strings from some rogue faction that wanted to see America collapse, again.

Many in the US government had protested allowing any Chinese military aid into the country. They feared turning into a bad version of the movie *Red Dawn*. It turned out the Chinese benefited far more from helping restore the grid than it would have by taking it down.

"I think I've got movement," Rajawat said.

She switched to infrared.

The unmistakable form of a person appeared between the brush and rocks, crouched as if aiming a rifle.

"Are you seeing what I am?" Lindsey asked. "We have a hostile contact."

"This is definitely a contact, but I can't say if it's hostile," Rajawat said.

They watched the person for several minutes.

"Would they really just send one scout to intercept a resupply and reinforcement attempt?" Lindsey asked.

"Hard to say," Rajawat said. "After all, each drone is surveying an area nearly twenty square miles. We don't know anything about who the contact is yet. It's possible we're picking up a bystander."

"Or maybe they have their own Raven Spears," Palmer said quietly.

The gunman on screen stalked toward a clutch of trees closer to a flowing stream.

Then another shape popped into view.

"Second contact," Rajawat reported. "Wait a minute... this is..."

The rifleman noticed the second contact too. He appeared to freeze. The rifle bucked slightly, the only sign that he had fired.

Their second contact dropped. It was then that Lindsey could see the four thin legs and stocky body of a mule deer.

"Our contact is a hunter," Rajawat said.

Lindsey breathed a long sigh of relief. "So the Chinese aren't our enemy."

"Seems that way," Rajawat said. "Let's move to Test Echo."

"Mexico," Lindsey said. "This'll be the location I gave Martinez."

The next overhead view of the mountainous terrain came into focus. Trees and rocks popped up around a stream rushing down the mountainside in a spray of white rapids.

Nothing appeared on the screen. No sign of movement. No heat signatures.

"This is disconcerting," Lindsey said. "Maybe we've been looking at the wrong people for leaks. Maybe it's someone inside my office."

She hated to believe it.

Palmer shifted uneasily next to her. "I don't like that idea."

"It wouldn't be the first time our country's been double-crossed by one of our own," Rajawat said. "Then again, maybe the leaker didn't take the bait."

"Maybe," Lindsey agreed. She was feeling deflated, worried that the mole was still out there, unidentified. "Either way, I still want to do a flyover around Moab. Even if we can't find out who is selling us out, we can at least provide Raven some intel."

"Sure. We'll switch to that drone now."

Of course, even if they saw people in Moab, it wasn't definitive proof they were the culprits.

Raven could've been fed false intel. The only way to truly know was by having him infiltrate the site himself and find evidence.

"Here's Moab," Rajawat said.

Surrounded by craggy red rocks, the relatively green town of Moab sprouted from the desert with the Colorado River flowing past. Trees grew in lush patches near creeks and streams.

Hundreds of cars were still parked in the streets between stores, inns, and restaurants.

Lindsey had expected to see someone, anyone wandering around town. Plenty of structures still looked habitable, even if there was no power.

But no one was walking down the road. Not a man or woman or child in one of the town's parks. Not a single person outside, or inside the old tourist shops, grocery stores, or restaurants.

"It's a ghost town," Lindsey said.

Before she could spend too long considering what that meant about Raven's intel, Rajawat pressed a finger to her ear. She appeared to be listening to an incoming message.

Her eyelids seemed to peel back, her lips parting slightly. "Lindsey, I just heard something from one of the drone pilots. They found new heat signatures. We got contacts at one of the target sites."

Rajawat switched the view on the laptop away from the empty streets of Moab to a different view. One they'd already looked at.

Sixteen white shapes popped up on the infrared. All sixteen were lying prone. They definitely weren't hunters. They appeared ready to execute an ambush.

She could hardly believe it.

The honey trap she'd laid *had* worked.

Now that they had identified the leaker, the realization of their betrayal hit like a hammer blow to the chest.

She wanted to curse and throw the Toughbook off the side of the mountain.

"This is Test Site Charlie," she said to Palmer, hardly able to believe what she was seeing. "We need to call Raven. Uwase, the United Nations rep, is feeding someone intel. Question is: who?"

———

Raven stashed the sat phone in his pack as he hiked beside Creek, Yoon, and Calvin. They'd left their Tahoe farther south off the side of Highway 191. All three wore gas masks now. They had no idea what to expect when they entered Moab, but they weren't taking any chances if Wild Fire had reached the town.

"Lindsey told me it was the UN representative," Raven said.

Even saying it aloud, he could hardly believe it.

This was worse than he could have imagined. Who would the United Nations Representative be feeding information to? And most importantly, why?

"This is fucked," Raven said.

"It's bad, but we don't know the full truth yet," Calvin said.

He limped alongside Raven with his M4 cradled. Creek walked beside them, his one good eye glued to the trail ahead. Yoon held rearguard with his own M4, eying every rock and patch of brush suspiciously.

"Drone surveillance didn't reveal anyone there, even though sixteen Reapers showed up at Lindsey's test site," Raven said. "We might be SOL."

The team continued their trek toward the outskirts of the city.

"It still pisses me off, though," Raven suddenly huffed.

"What's that?" Calvin asked.

"I just think President Diego should've sent more reinforcements out here a long time ago to find and clean up the Badlands. It's because of his stubbornness and political bullshit that we're going through this mess right now."

"I agree," Yoon said.

"You guys aren't fans?" Calvin asked.

"Not a huge fan of career politicians for starters," Raven said. "I'm also not a fan of career politicians that write off a huge chunk of their constituents, which has been what the Diego Administration has done out here all along."

"I despise politics, always did, but I got to give credit where it's due," Calvin said. "The rest of the country was in terrible shape after the Collapse, and much of it has come back to life, thanks partly to POTUS and the Secretary of Defense."

"I get that, but Diego has left us out to dry here with minimal support," Raven said.

Calvin shook his head. "Look, man, I've seen shit all across the country. It ain't pretty and everyone is saying the same thing about lack of support."

"Well, I guess you need to see more of the New Frontier, then maybe you will see how bad things are for us," Raven said.

"Politics doesn't matter much right now," Yoon said. "What matters is finding the Reapers."

Quiet again, they made their way under the shadow of a rock wall running parallel to the highway. Plenty of abandoned vehicles, homes, and gas stations provided sporadic cover, along with occasional patches of juniper and cottonwood trees.

Strands of pinyons had also given them shelter and shadow that spared them from the late afternoon sun. Finally, the sun began to set, allowing them to infiltrate closer to Moab in the dark.

The men began the climb up another rocky slope. A tumbleweed bounced lazily past as if even it was exhausted by the relentless heat. They paused at a crest in the rocky landscape. Creek nudged up in front of Raven's feet.

From this vantage, they could see Moab in the dying panes of orange sunlight. The sunset made the whole desert look like it was on fire.

Raven figured that was a fitting metaphor for all the shit they'd seen. As far as he was concerned, the desert—and the Badlands—really were on fire.

"So far, I don't see anything out there," Yoon whispered.

"Think we've been given bad intel?" Calvin adjusted his gas mask and used a hand to wipe the streaming sweat from his forehead.

"Maybe, maybe not," Raven said. "We're going to proceed like the Reapers are hiding out there. If they are really some foreign paramilitary operation, then they might know how to disappear. A drone could easily miss them from above."

Raven took out a pair of binoculars from his pack and

knelt. Sweeping the binos over the town, he looked for any sign people had been there recently. All he saw were more empty streets and storefronts. Many houses had busted windows, and the few stores he could see into clearly had been ransacked. Nothing but toppled shelves and trash were left inside.

"See anything?" Calvin asked.

Raven was about to tell him no.

The whole landscape was eerily silent.

No people. No singing birds. No grazing beasts. Not even a lone coyote.

Which surprised him.

This area should be rife with wildlife.

After all, the shelter offered by the buildings and trees in town would be welcome relief for any animal escaping the heat. Plus, the river and the creeks would be a natural congregating spot.

He couldn't help but think of the legend he had told Lara. Why would all the animals have abandoned this place? The only reason he could think of was because humans had been stomping around and perhaps even killing them off.

Even the hungriest of wolves learned to avoid places where humans frequented. The deer and coyotes, too, didn't like places where humans traipsed around with weapons, ready to kill them for food or sport.

Animals were often smarter than people gave them credit for. Raven had seen it in the Rockies all the time.

The same group of deer that would brazenly approach friendly hikers would scatter when they saw a hunter brandishing a gun. These animals didn't need their legendary Councils tell them to run from humans with weapons.

Was that why this place was so quiet?

"Something's off," Raven said. "I think someone is hiding

out there. That's why you don't see any evidence of animals. We just need to find out where in town these people are hiding."

"Well, if you're talking about hiding paramilitary operations and vehicles and all that shit, I'd start looking wherever they got truck depots, warehouses, and storage facilities, right?" Calvin asked.

"Right. Smart thinking."

"I didn't eat crayons like you as a kid," Calvin said.

"I still eat crayons." Raven chuckled.

"'Course you do," Calvin said. "All the other guys in the Navy gave Marines shit, calling 'em crayon-eaters. Why am I not surprised?"

"You can both eat crayons later," Yoon said. "Let's get down there and look."

"Patience." Raven held up a hand. "We don't want to run straight in there."

For a few more moments, Raven scanned Moab. He searched for any sign of movement. Even just footprints to prove people were there.

All the while, night settled over the town with its suffocating darkness.

Any chance Raven had of spotting someone from a distance was going to disappear. His only hope was that someone would turn on some lamps or lanterns.

"Still nothing?" Calvin asked after a long pause.

Raven lowered his binos. Even with the moonlight, it was quickly growing too difficult to see. "Maybe the Reapers knew we were coming and took off..." Goosebumps spread down his skin. "Especially if they've been tracking our movements and someone's been giving them intel..."

"Wait," Yoon said. "I think I see something."

"Where?" Raven asked.

"On the road." Yoon pointed. "Doesn't that look like sand?"

Raven looked at what he had missed, confirming Yoon was correct.

"If those were *old* tire tracks, the wind would've scattered those tracks long ago," he said. "That's our trail."

"Let's go," Calvin said.

"Wait." Raven held the man back. "All we need to do is get down there, confirm the Reapers are here, then get out. No need for heroics or a firefight."

Calvin stared hard at Raven "You telling me I can't shoot these assholes if they are down there? After what they did to Mouse and my Steel Runners?"

"Sheriff Plymouth just wants us to confirm the location because we might only have one shot. If we spook them and they run, then we have to start from square one. Lindsey's going to send reinforcements to help us bring these guys in."

Calvin's nostrils flared, and Raven noticed his fingers tighten around his rifle. Creek looked between Calvin and Raven as if he could sense the tension.

"Our goal is to stop these people," Raven said. "If that means we wait for reinforcements, then so be it. Once we have the Reapers cornered, you can do whatever you want with them after, okay?"

Calvin looked back toward Moab. "Fine."

Raven worried the temptation of vengeance would be too much for Calvin. Revenge could sometimes be as powerful as any narcotic, driving men to do wild, illogical things. Like run into a town of hostiles in a quixotic attempt to shoot up a paramilitary group all by yourself.

"Calvin, I'm serious," Raven said. "I don't go out into the field much with others. I find it hard to rely on them, and when I do..." Raven had to fight back the emotion. "When I do, they usually end up six feet under. So, please, man, I want you and Yoon to prove me wrong tonight. We're not just a former Marine, ex-SEAL, and retired National Guardsman. We're a team, let's act like it."

"Yeah, no Army of One tonight," Yoon said. "I've got your backs; just tell me what to do, and I'll do it."

"I got this, trust me," Calvin said.

Trust me.

The words harkened back to a conversation Raven had once with Major Nathan Sardetti. The two of them had been surrounded by an encroaching forest fire near the beginning of the Collapse. Those flames had nearly killed them when Nathan had said to Raven, "Just trust me."

And because Raven did trust him, Nathan helped guide them out of that near-death experience.

Nathan had even become a close friend and ally afterward.

Of course, that trust did nothing to later prevent Nathan's death. Just like Marcus Colton. Just like Billy Franks.

This mission had to be different.

22

WHILE IT WAS NEARLY MIDNIGHT, THE MOON HUNG bright in the sky, making the terrain around Moab glow with an almost silver sheen. That was good and bad for Calvin and team. It meant they could get a decent view of their surroundings, but also that any enemies tracking them could see just as easily.

He prowled along the sidewalk beside Highway 191, breathing plastic-smelling air through his gas mask. Yoon followed, watching his back. They were careful not to crunch over the pebbles of glass or gravel strewn over the cracked concrete.

Across the street, traveling in parallel with them were Raven and Creek. The dog sniffed at the sidewalk, his nose pausing at empty glass bottles or piles of trash that had been left to rot and dry out long ago.

All down the road, abandoned cars covered in dust sat on rotted, deflated tires. They passed by a diner with white-and-red paint. A sign reading "EAT" with a big red arrow hung over a neon OPEN light that probably hadn't tasted electricity in two years.

Smaller taverns and souvenir shops lined the road, each dripping in that Old West Americana décor that once captivated tourists.

The tire tracks Yoon had spotted took them down the main drag through Moab and then detoured down another road. This tree-lined street was cleared. The abandoned vehicles were all plowed to the side.

This wasn't an accident; this was by design.

Calvin's body might have been wrecked, but his mind was still that of a Navy SEAL. All those alarms built into him from years of training and direct-action missions overseas were ringing and booming like fireworks on the Fourth of July.

Raven seemed to realize something was up too, and flashed hand signals to continue along the tracks. They led to the Moab Valley District Fire Station through one of the big doors where the fire engines would normally be. Two flagpoles stood outside, one bare, the other displaying a ragged American flag.

Beyond the flag poles was a parking lot blocked by the neighboring buildings and broken-down vehicles. Calvin couldn't quite see in from his vantage point.

He signaled to Raven that he and Yoon were going to advance. Raven gestured back that he would provide cover.

Calvin and Yoon snuck past a minivan and a box truck to the edge of the parking lot. As soon as they were past, Calvin gestured for Yoon to pause again. He held two fingers to his eyes, then to the sight in front of them.

This was why the drones had been unable to see anything suspicious.

Half the parking lot was covered with a solar panel-topped roof to protect cars and soak in the desert sun.

Wires ran from the solar panels into the fire station and a rundown inn next door.

"Someone is using that solar power," he whispered to Yoon.

The Ranger nodded.

They moved for a better view, seeing aerial surveillance had also missed the tarps covering the forms of crates and the dozens upon dozens of steel barrels on pallets next to a pair of big box trucks under the roof.

Calvin tensed up when he saw one of those tarps was fluttering in the wind, revealing the blue-and-white Siegler Pharm logo on the barrels.

Five men examined the crates and rifled through their contents. All the crates he could see were marked with the blue-and-white Siegler logo too.

Shit.

Had the Reapers orchestrated the shipment from this medical company? Was Siegler a front for them to smuggle whatever the hell was in these barrels and crates into the Badlands?

Calvin whispered to Yoon, "All those supplies came from the Angel Line."

Raven crept over to their location with Creek by his side.

"You see anyone?" Calvin asked.

"Negative," Raven replied.

"This enough to call in reinforcements?" Yoon asked.

Calvin surveyed the supplies. "That should be enough evidence right there."

"Yeah, but we need locations on the Reapers," Raven said.

"Okay, then, let's sniff these evil bastards out."

He understood why Lindsey and the Rangers needed to be cautious. It wasn't just the threat of spooking their targets. They also had to send personnel into a disease-stricken area. The risk had to be worth it.

"You two check out the fire station," Raven said. "I'm

going to try and get a better vantage in the hotel down the street with Creek. Maybe find a rooftop or something."

Calvin and Yoon took off at a hunch, their rifles shouldered and sweeping the buildings.

A cool wind cut through the parking lot as Calvin led them toward the fire station. The torn American flag flapped noisily, clinking on the metal ties holding it to the line.

There weren't many windows on the front of the fire station. The few that were there were nothing but hazy glass blocks.

No way to see through.

Calvin slunk along the wall to the eastern side with Yoon right behind.

A set of doors next to a picnic table were just a few yards away. They passed the doors and headed toward three big windows on the side of the building.

As they drew near the windows, Calvin heard voices. He held up a fist, and Yoon froze.

The voices were nearly indecipherable, but the language was all too clear.

Farsi.

These men were Iranian.

But it still didn't make sense why the UN Rep, a man from Rwanda for God's sake, would be working with these guys.

Calvin felt his heart began to climb in his throat. If all their intel was correct, these had to be the Reapers, but none of this was making sense.

He risked peeking through the nearest window at the men that had killed Mouse, and most everyone Calvin gave a damn about.

While the window itself was open, presumably to let in the breeze, a dark black curtain hung over it.

No wonder the drones hadn't seen any lights from the buildings.

The Reapers had thoroughly camouflaged the inside too.

Maybe Lindsey would be more willing to send in those promised reinforcements now that Calvin and Yoon had heard Iranian voices.

Any personnel sent to Moab would be going in blind, though. No idea how many hostiles they might face. No idea how well-armed they were.

In every battle Calvin had fought overseas, they rarely went in without some idea of what awaited them.

Rough numbers, possible weapons.

Intel was the oxygen they breathed to survive risky ops.

If a bunch of other men were going to come storming into Utah on his account, he wanted to prepare them as best he could.

Yoon covered him as he continued toward the next window. The voices were growing louder. He heard at least three distinct voices, all male. They didn't seem worried about keeping their voices down, which told him they probably didn't realize a pair of intruders were in their midst.

While he wasn't about to risk breaking radio silence to tell Raven what he was hearing, he did open the channel so the tracker could at least listen in.

He maneuvered under the windows when the crack of a door opening and closing forced him against the wall.

Calvin tightened his grip on his rifle and held his breath, doing his best to blend into the shadows. Yoon pressed himself flat against the wall not far away.

Back near the door came the brief flicker of a lighter.

A man with a square jaw held a cigarette in his lips, his face pale in the moonlight. The lighter illuminated the front of his black fatigues when it sparked to life again, catching on his cigarette.

If Calvin could see this guy, then it was possible he could see Calvin and Yoon. Slowly, Calvin tried to back away, Yoon creeping his direction.

The door swung open again, more light flooding through.

Two more men came out, exchanging words in brash voices. One man with a mustache gestured wildly at the guy with the cigarette like he was pissed about something. He kept one foot on the door to keep it open.

The smoker pointed at the mustached man with the end of his cigarette.

In a flurry of motions Calvin could hardly see, the smoker had his cigarette smacked away. It sailed through the air toward their location.

As Calvin watched in what seemed like slow motion, a bucket of adrenaline dumped through his vessels. The moment seemed to stretch into its own purgatory.

These guys were seconds from seeing him and Yoon.

He could shoot at these men and start a gunfight, maybe taking them all down. But that would alert their comrades inside and give them a chance to escape.

Second option was to turn and run this instant, and hope that he and Yoon could get away and disappear into the darkness without getting a bullet in their backs.

All those calculations ran in a fraction of a second beneath his consciousness.

Just like when he'd been overseas.

Calvin really only had one choice when the cigarette hit the ground and the smoker looked in their direction.

Aiming his rifle, Calvin fired a burst of rounds right into the face of his target. The man with the mustache reached for his hip only to have a flurry of rounds stitch into his side and chest.

The third guy managed to jump through the open door.

Calvin and Yoon backpedaled away as voices shouted from inside the fire station. More voices called out from the motel next door. Bootsteps pounded over concrete, and Calvin heard the unmistakable sound of clicking weapons ready for action.

A dozen silhouettes poured out of the motel, filling the street in front of the fire station, blocking any chance of escape that direction.

Return fire blazed, bullets zipping toward them. Somehow, Calvin and Yoon made it to the back of the parking lot with the covered supplies.

Rounds pinged hollowly against the barrels. Sparks flew where they skimmed off the metal. Others lanced into the barrels or crates.

He lurched toward the shelter behind the barrels farthest from the station. Yoon was behind him.

Other voices barked out orders in Farsi. The firing suddenly stopped. More bootsteps crunched over the parking lot.

The radio Calvin carried crackled to life, Raven breaking the silence.

"Stay down until I tell you," he said. "I'll provide covering fire."

Calvin glanced around the crates, seeing a dozen plus figures surrounding them. There was no way he and Yoon were getting out of here even if Raven took a few down.

"Shit, shit, shit," Yoon said.

"Don't give up your position," Calvin said into his radio. "Call Lindsey. Tell her the Reapers are Iranians. Now. Finish what we started."

He looked to Yoon.

"I won't let them take me alive," Calvin said. "I'll try and cover you."

Yoon stared at him a moment, but then shook his head. "I'm not running."

"We kill as many as we can," Calvin said.

Yoon nodded.

They both got up and fired at two Reapers approaching from the fire station. The two Reapers collapsed.

Panicked and enraged shouts followed, along with gunfire that slammed into the jungle of crates and barrels. Calvin leaned around the other side to see how many men were coming from the motel into the parking lot.

He sighted up another four in that direction.

Yoon popped up again, firing three shots, and then ducked back down. They moved to another position, and this time, Calvin fired at the Reapers coming from the motel.

More gunfire slammed into their position, forcing them down.

Yoon got up again to fire when his head flicked back. Blood and bone sprayed up in a mist from his forehead. Calvin caught him as he slumped down.

The Ranger's lifeless eyes stared up as blood pumped from the gunshot wounds in the center of his face and forehead.

"Damn it," Calvin said.

Footsteps and hushed voices came from all directions. He set Yoon down and picked up his rifle, raising them both.

Sweat dripped down his brow, stinging his eyes as he waited, trying to control his wild heart as the Reapers drew closer, their boots rapping the parking lot.

He readied his rifles.

Then the footsteps suddenly stopped. No one appeared

in front of him like he'd expected. He started to peer out from the right side of the barrel, catching movement, ready to fire.

The clank of metal erupted against asphalt. He knew that sound and closed his eyes in preparation of the flash grenade. The explosion of pyrotechnic chemicals burst, blinding him temporarily, and making his ears ring to the point he couldn't hear anything.

The pain forced him to lower his rifles.

Sharp pain flared in his skull, but that was nothing compared to whatever hit him in the head. He crumpled to the ground, the world fading away.

His last thought was that Raven was still out there. That he could get the intel to Sheriff Plymouth.

But in the end, Calvin Jackson had failed Mouse, Travis, and the Angel Line.

———

Lindsey held the ringing satellite phone to her ear as she prepared to walk into the main offices at Fort Golden. She was headed to the emergency FAC meeting she had called. One that would set off a chain of events that she hoped would end some of the madness in the Badlands.

When she answered the call from Raven, he was breathing hard on the other end. "They got them."

"Sam, calm down. Tell me what happened."

She nearly dropped the phone when she heard Yoon was dead. And Calvin probably too. The Reapers had taken him. To make it worse, Calvin had told Raven the Reapers seemed to be a group of Iranians. He told her about the Siegler Pharmaceuticals cargo too. There was little doubt in her mind that this was all connected to Wild Fire. That these were the people responsible for beginning to spread the engineered plague.

"I need backup," Raven said. "Now that they know we're onto them, you got to get here before the Reapers leave. We could lose them and Calvin."

"Where are you now?"

"I'm in a hotel room just a few blocks away. There are twenty Reapers. Maybe more."

"Get out of there, Raven," Lindsey said. "I'm going to send backup right now, but they won't be there for a few hours."

"I can't leave. We lost Yoon. We lost Molina. I was supposed to have their backs. I might be able to still save Calvin."

"There's not a thing you or he can do against twenty-plus armed men. It's suicide. Just... just stand down until reinforcements get there."

The line went dead, Raven shutting down the conversation.

Lindsey wanted to curse and scream with frustration. At this point, she was both worried sick and furious with Raven. She had to take a few deep breaths to calm herself after he had hung up on her.

She had to trust he wouldn't do anything stupid and take on this small army by himself. She had already lost two of her best Rangers, men she cared about, and if Raven died too...

Hell, there was no way she was letting these guys leave. If Raven and the team were right, then all of the train ambushes, the Siegler Pharmaceuticals, the Wild Fire came right back to this group of Iranian paramilitary terrorists.

Of course, as soon as Uwase realized she and her Rangers were headed to Moab, he would warn the Reapers.

She ducked away from the entrance to Fort Golden,

standing between a couple of Colorado Ranger SUVs. The first thing she did was call Palmer to get a group of Rangers and the chopper ready and told him to get someone to immediately arrest Uwase. He had to be contained.

"Isolate him immediately," she said. "Do not let him make any calls on radios or phones either. We cannot let the Reapers know we're onto them."

"You got it, ma'am," Palmer said. "I'm on it. See you soon."

But the Rangers couldn't do this on their own; they needed help.

Lindsey dialed the perfect person for that job.

"Blair, here."

"It's me. Lindsey. I've just confirmed Uwase is leaking intel to a group of Iranian terrorists who call themselves the Reapers Militia. We believe they're responsible for the train attack, and worse, they look like they've got something to do with Wild Fire too. Just now, Raven Spears and his team found the Reapers Militia hideout in Moab. Raven estimates well over twenty armed men. I'm going out and would like your Marines with me."

"I'm with you, Sheriff. I'll make a call to get the boys ready."

"Good, thank you."

She hung up the sat phone and entered Fort Golden, rushing up the stairs to the helipad.

Her heart pounded in her chest with each passing second, knowing Raven and Creek were out there, their lives at risk.

In minutes, she, Palmer, and a small team of three Rangers were loaded up and flying over the Rockies. The thrum of the Bell 407GX helicopter's engines reverberated throughout the chopper. Lindsey and Palmer were seated in the main cabin with the other Rangers.

As they raced over the darkened mountaintops, passing

over tree-lined rivers that were barely visible in the moonlight, another chopper roared beside them. The helicopter was the crowning glory in British Marines rotor wing aviation. It was the Merlin Mk4, recently converted and delivered to the Royal Marines stationed in Colorado.

While Lindsey only had access to the humble Bell chopper that had been requisitioned from the Denver Police Department, Blair had convinced his superiors to bring the Merlin. Something that wasn't approved when the Angel Line was attacked.

She was glad to have them with her now.

The sleek gray chopper was barely visible against the star-studded sky. It carried twenty-five Royal Marines, each fully outfitted and armored, ready for a bloody fight against the Reapers.

The Rangers were also ready. She had chosen them for their military backgrounds. They checked over their M4s that Lindsey had authorized for the mission. These men didn't have to rely on using their personal weapons like most Rangers during their day-to-day operations. The Royal Marines had managed to scrape together just enough extra NVGs and masks for her team to borrow for the mission. It was another valuable gift that she vowed to use to its fullest.

She prayed they would all be coming home tonight. But each of these men knew the risk of this mission. She had already briefed them about what had happened to Yoon and Molina.

They were all upset with the news, but instead of grieving, they used their loss to give them the strength to avenge their fallen brothers in what would most likely be a difficult fight.

Lindsey took a moment to think of Yoon and Molina.

The pain of seeing Vicky mourning her husband's death

was still raw. So was the pain of visiting the families of Ferris and Cranston, who had lost their lives days earlier.

Yoon hadn't had a spouse or kids, but he had been solely responsible for taking care of his two elderly parents who now lived outside Fort Collins. They had no one else to provide for them, and Lindsey was going to do her best to make sure they were taken care of.

"We're not losing anyone else tonight," Lindsey said over the open channel. It was more of a statement to herself than them. A reassurance to herself that they would come out of this mess victorious.

That would be her primary goal.

Raven. Calvin. The Rangers in this chopper with them. No more would fall victim to the Reapers and whatever nefarious plans they were enacting.

They had been soaring over the mountains for a good hour and a half now.

Lindsey called Blair on the radio. "We're about forty-five minutes out, so long as the weather cooperates."

"Copy that," Blair said.

"Unless conditions on the ground change, I'm going straight into the Moab fire station to pin down the Reapers and find Calvin. I want your men to create a dragnet, clean up the town, and round up every Reaper we find."

"You got it," Blair said.

They churned on through the night. Lindsey wanted desperately to reach out to Raven, but she couldn't risk trying to contact him. Breaking radio silence could inadvertently cause him harm.

She just hoped Raven kept his promise to stay put until she arrived. She also hoped the Reapers hadn't already picked up their supplies and headed out of there. They had Uwase secure in a jail cell back at Fort Golden, but there was no telling if that alone might be enough to spook the Reapers.

Lindsey found herself repeatedly checking her watch, as if doing so would get them to Moab sooner.

The seconds ticked by agonizingly slow. They were still flying over the Rockies, but they were nearing the desert.

Her satellite phone suddenly started buzzing. She unclipped it from her tactical vest, plugged it into her headset via the aux input, and answered it.

"Sheriff Plymouth here," she said.

"Lindsey, it's Raven."

His words came out at a whisper.

"Raven, what's going on there?" she asked.

"How much longer?"

"Thirty, maybe forty minutes away at worst," she said. "We're almost there. Just hold tight."

Raven was silent for a moment.

"I stayed back, like you said, but they have Calvin," Raven said. "I heard some screams. I think they are torturing him."

"God." Lindsey looked out the window. The calm night sky belied the horrible nightmares taking place in Utah.

She turned to the pilots. "We've got to go faster!"

"This is our max speed, Sheriff," one of them replied.

Lindsey brought the phone back up to her lips. "Stay put, Raven. You can't go in there on your own. Calvin is trained for this, and we're almost there."

"We got another problem. More than Calvin. I can see them packing up their cargo into three box trucks in front of the fire station. They might be leaving any minute now."

"Shit, do you know where?" Lindsey asked.

"I've tried to listen from here, but I can't really understand them. They're all speaking Farsi."

Lindsey held back another curse. "How far is your truck? Do you think it's possible to tail them at a distance?"

"By the time I get back to the Tahoe, the Reapers would have at least a thirty-minute start on me," Raven said. "Plus, I don't think I have the gas to tail them long."

Lindsey could sense that Raven was itching to do something.

"Raven," she said, "you have to hold tight. You told me there were at least twenty men out there. You're alone."

"I'm not alone. I've got Creek."

"Jesus, Raven. You can't be serious. Look, we've got reinforcements. We can track them from the sky."

"Yeah, and what if they shoot you down? They have a lot of firepower," Raven said.

"Rockets?"

"Maybe. I haven't seen any, but they have automatic weapons and flash grenades. My feeling, though, is that they're armed to the teeth, especially considering what happened with the Angel Line. Listen, we got one shot at this, Lindsey. If these people really are responsible for Wild Fire, we can't let them get away."

The math was clear. Raven was right.

The United States had already lost so much thanks to North Korea and their crippling EMP attack. Would there even be anything left of the United States if these Reapers were allowed to continue spreading the Wild Fire, especially with as much stock and supplies of the weapon as Raven's team had reported?

Still, what could Raven do alone except throw his life away? The Rangers needed him, and they needed him alive. *She* needed him alive.

"Raven, if they leave before I get there, try and follow, but don't risk your life," Lindsey said.

"Okay."

The call ended.

She leaned back and tapped her head on the hull out of frustration.

"That was Raven?" Palmer asked her.

"Yeah, the Reapers are packing up and preparing to leave."

She called Blair and updated him on what Raven had told her.

"So we've got to change our plans," she said. "It looks like our prey is on the run, and we're going on the hunt. We're going to need to hit hard and fast."

"Understood," Blair said.

As soon as she was off the call, she placed another to Utah Scouts Command and Fort Golden. She wanted every available armed and medical unit to start heading into the Utah desert, ready to back them up in case the Reapers did somehow have rockets or a way to take out the choppers.

She had a dark feeling that this race to find and stop their enemy was not going to be easy.

23

CALVIN WOKE TO ANOTHER COLD BUCKET OF WATER thrown in his face. His head throbbed. Every vertebra in his spine was on fire.

His chest heaved, and he tried to gulp down air. Even though cold water had been dumped on him, he felt like he was burning up. At the same time, chills shivered through his arms.

A hacking cough began. He felt it deep inside his lungs. Once he started coughing, mucus dripped from his nose in long ropes. He couldn't wipe it away.

His hands were tied behind his back, and ropes were wrapped over his chest. His ankles were secured to the legs of the chair he sat in.

The single yellow light hanging overhead scorched into his eyes with a violent intensity, making the pain throughout his body only that much more excruciating.

Distant, indistinct voices echoed.

A few more blinks, and Calvin saw men carting out barrels through the fire station's front garage door. The sound of thrumming engines rumbled through. It seemed like the men were loading vehicles waiting outside.

There'd been so many barrels, so many crates, that these people had stored them both outside and inside the station. Not far from him, canisters of ammunition lay open next to a rack filled with weapons.

A nasty coughing fit tore up through Calvin's lungs again until he drooled over the floor.

One of the Iranians stomped toward him with a bucket of water and a rag. "Good. You are awake again."

The Iranian's long black sleeves were rolled up to reveal veiny arms thick with muscle. He had cauliflower ears like he'd spent a lifetime fighting and wrestling.

Calvin felt a cold ball of dread settle into his stomach.

It was this man's fault he'd gone unconscious just moments ago.

"And who are you, my friend?" the Reaper asked in a thick accent. He leaned down until he was right in Calvin's face, his foul breath smelling of cloves and cigarettes. "Will you finally tell me?"

"I'm the guy that is going to kill you, *friend*," Calvin said through clenched teeth.

The Reaper started laughing and set the pail down. "By now, you know how this goes. I put this rag on your face. Pour the water over it, and you suffocate. All the while, you still think you're somehow going to kill me?"

The man pulled up another folding chair from a nearby table. He sat down in front of Calvin, the bucket on the concrete floor between them. "Let's do this differently this time. Maybe that will help you cooperate. My name is Amir. Now, I am very good at having conversations with new friends. I hope you can learn to be very good at it too. Because if not, I am also very good at *convincing* friends to talk, and you and I... we've only just begun."

Calvin didn't say a word. He just kept his lips straight and focused on fighting back the pain and dread echoing through his body.

"Let us try again," Amir said. "Maybe you'll be more cooperative now. What is your name?"

"Michael Jordan."

Amir grinned diabolically. "You think you are funny, don't you? Well, Michael Jordan, let us try again. What is your name?"

"Michael Jordan, asshole."

Amir shrugged. "Last chance."

"My name is Amir—"

The man turned and kicked Calvin in the chest, knocking him backwards. His head thudded against the concrete, and his hands were smashed beneath his own weight.

All the pain in his body flared like someone had poured gas on his nerves and lit it on fire.

"I'm gonna..." Calvin's lungs were caught in another agonizing coughing fit for a second. "Kill ... you."

Amir pressed his combat boot over Calvin's chest. "I know who you are, Calvin Jackson. I hoped you would be a good friend, but you failed my test. I have friends in your government. Friends who tell me about you and your Steel Runners and the trains. Are you surprised?"

Calvin said nothing, still struggling to recover from the coughing. Another shiver tore through his body, followed by an intense wave of heat.

He tried to focus on what Amir had just said.

If he knew Calvin's name, why did he want more information?

Calvin's only hope was that maybe, just maybe the guy had lost contact with their mole in the Colorado Rangers. Either that, or Lindsey's attempts at keeping his and Raven's operations a secret from her FAC had worked. This guy had only old intel.

Not enough to know what was really going on.

"You are a former Navy SEAL, no?" Amir asked.

Calvin coughed.

"You are good at holding your breath, then. This is also good." Amir gestured toward the barrels. "This last time you were unconscious, I dipped a cloth into our stock of the KB-399 biological weapon. All it took was holding it over your face for a couple minutes."

"What the fuck is KB-399?"

"You people call it Wild Fire," Amir said. "It is an engineered plague, originally created by the old Soviet Biopreparat program. You know what this is, don't you?"

Of course, Calvin knew. The old Soviet-era bioweapons program was notorious. They had developed all manner of nightmarish weapons ranging from engineered plague to anthrax, smallpox, and many other frightening pathogens.

Biopreparat was disbanded, and all their research stopped. But there had always been rumors that wasn't the case. Yes, the old Soviet facilities had fallen during the collapse of the USSR. However, it was no secret that far too many biological samples were only poorly secured at best in all the chaos.

It wouldn't be hard to imagine a group of terrorists getting their hands on the old weapons. Furthering research on them, maybe even through funds funneled by antagonistic governments.

Was that who these people were? Crazed extremists who wanted nothing more than to watch America burn? To kick her while she was already down?

The legacy of bioweapons programs like these was one reason he'd been inoculated against so many diseases when'd he joined the SEAL teams. But even so, no vaccine for the plague existed.

"I can see by your face you understand," Amir said.

"Why does Iran want this? Why are they doing this?"

Amir grinned wickedly. "The Ayatollah knows nothing about what we've done. What we do is for the glory of Allah and no one else. Our small group has been blessed with this jihad mission." He leaned in closer. "Do you know why I'm even telling you this?"

Calvin said nothing as another four men lugged a crate outside. He could still hear idling truck engines and panicked shouts. These men were in a hurry to leave Moab. Which meant whatever information they wanted from Calvin, they wanted it quick.

That did not bode well for what Amir had in store for him.

"I'm telling you all of this because you will die a very painful death if you do not cooperate. The KB-399 will leave you a wreck of a human being. You will be in agony in your last hours of life. Surely, by now, you've heard of the hundreds infected in these mountains. All we had to do was poison the water supplies of a couple small communities. It has been so easy to get desperate people barely surviving in these wild lands to work for us. They've been willing to turn their weapons against Americans. Imagine, now that we have received this shipment, what will come next. How much of America we can poison. We've only just begun this jihad."

Amir poked Calvin's chest with a finger.

"But you can be spared this misery if you just cooperate," Amir said.

Someone across the fire station said something to him in

Farsi, and he snapped back a response. It looked as though his people were getting impatient with him.

"If you know I'm a SEAL, then you know I will never help you, motherfucker," Calvin said in a raspy voice.

"Oh, but that is where you are wrong," Amir loomed over him. "Let us start with something easy. Tell me now. How many others came to Moab with you? How many others are following us?"

"No one."

"You're already lying. We killed one of your friends right next to you."

"No one besides us," Calvin said.

"Oh, okay, so a crippled Navy SEAL stumbles in with a Colorado Ranger, somehow managing to find us all by themselves?"

Calvin thought back to what Jeff had said. The Reapers knew they were coming to the Mesa. Chances were good he knew about Raven already, but if he didn't, Calvin certainly wasn't going to give him up.

He just had to buy time for reinforcements to get here. To delay if he could so these men didn't escape.

"Well?" Amir asked. "I personally know that a Colorado Ranger team entered the New Frontier just hours ago with reinforcements and fresh supplies. We heard this from our sources inside your government. But when we went to meet these new Rangers, they never showed up where they were supposed to. So where are they?"

Calvin had no idea what he was talking about at first. Then he remembered Sheriff Plymouth's trap she had set to find the traitors. This man thought the reinforcements had actually arrived. Reinforcements that didn't actually exist.

"Imagine the plague that is coursing through your body," Amir said. "Soon it will fill your lungs with fluid. You will not be able to breathe. No, no, no, even an elite Navy SEAL cannot breathe with fluid in his lungs. Calvin, I can help you recover from this plague. I know secrets that your doctors do not. All you must do is tell me the truth."

"I told you," Calvin said between gasps. The pain of breathing was enough to tempt him. Given Amir wasn't wearing a mask, the man must not be lying. He must have a cure or vaccine or something if he thought he was protected from the Wild Fire.

But Calvin wouldn't betray Raven.

"Yoon, the man you monsters killed, and I... we came... alone," Calvin said.

"I do *not* believe you."

Amir disappeared for a moment, opening a door that let in more sounds of machinery. They were definitely getting ready to bug out. But it seemed Amir was intent on getting Calvin to speak.

When the man came back, he dunked a rag in the bucket of water.

Calvin knew what came next. He tried to regulate his breathing.

Because even the hardiest soldier, even the most well-trained SEAL could hardly withstand the pain and deep psychological distress that came with waterboarding.

Calvin had been through this before in Survival, Evasion, Resistance, and Escape training. And even in a controlled environment, it was one of the most awful experiences of his life.

Having his fingernails pulled out would have been easier to deal with. Maybe have Amir rip out some teeth with a pair of pliers. Even the shock of electricity would be a welcome alternative.

But being waterboarded struck at something deep within

the human consciousness, a primal fear that was more than just physical agony. One he'd already endured with Amir, and one he did not look forward to experiencing again.

"Last chance," Amir said. "Who else came with you to Moab and where are they now?"

Calvin saw desperation in Amir's eyes. The man did not want to be followed. He must've known that this operation and his unholy terrorist actions would come to a disastrous end now that they'd been discovered.

"Your mother," Calvin said as he lifted his head. "She sucks a mean—"

Amir punched Calvin in the face with a crunch.

"Hossein, help me with this infidel!" Amir called.

A huge, lumbering man with a black beard lumbered over. He pressed his hands over Calvin's shoulders, ensuring Calvin could hardly struggle against his restraints.

Amir draped a wet rag over Calvin's face. Then came the water dripping into his nose.

He'd already endured one round of waterboarding from Amir and Hossein. In his mind, he knew he could survive another.

But then came the choking and coughing.

It felt like he was on the ocean floor, trapped in darkness with no oxygen tank, no diving mask.

He thrashed against Hossein's grip, head smacking against the floor, and his limbs pulling and straining against the ropes. Hossein held his chin in place with brutal strength, ensuring Calvin couldn't whip the rag off.

Distant memories reminded him there had been an end to this before.

But those memories were overwhelmed by the voices in his mind screaming that he was drowning. That he was going to die.

His nasal cavity was on fire and his throat swelled up.

All the animal instincts in his mind exploded at once. He lost control of his body, a victim to pain and intense terror.

Then the light came back.

He started coughing. His lungs heaved. He gulped down precious oxygen.

"Thirty seconds," Amir said. "That was fun, no?"

Hossein merely grunted, nostrils flaring as he looked at Calvin with an expression of hate.

Calvin could say nothing. His mind screamed at him to tell Amir that he had come here with Raven and his dog. Or that Lindsey was coming with reinforcements.

To fight back those urges, Calvin bit the inside of his cheek. He focused on the pain. Tasted the blood.

Keep quiet. Buy time. Survive.

Another man yelled at Amir and pointed outside the garage door, as if he was beckoning Amir to hurry and load up into the trucks. Calvin thought he saw them ushering out two other people with blindfolds on, an adult and a child.

What the fuck? Who are they?

But Hossein pushed him back to the ground before Calvin could see much else.

"Did you decide who else came to Moab with you?" Amir asked.

Calvin said nothing.

"Let's try this again, then."

Hossein put his weight on Calvin and the agony repeated. The sense of helpless desperation. The drowning. Then the cloth came away. Coughing and more fear.

Calvin vomited water.

He thought he had refused to answer Amir's question, but his mind was muddled.

The cloth came back with the water.

The cycle repeated. Over and over.

Calvin fought, squirmed, and cursed all that was holy.

At some point, Amir and Hossein took another break. Just enough time for Calvin to recover his breath and sanity.

He could hear more shouts outside and another set of truck engines growling to life. Panicked voices, all yelling in Farsi, called out. The sounds of crates and barrels clunking into the back of trucks echoed through the open windows of the fire station.

A group of men came back into the station to take out the last few crates.

These people sounded like they were almost ready to flee. To escape into the desert to renew this apparent biological weapons operation.

But right when Calvin was able to breathe normally again, the waterboarding continued.

The fact that he was infected with the Wild Fire plague no longer mattered. The fact that his body was a painful wreck didn't matter either. None of that felt as bad as nearly drowning then being brought back to breathe and recover just enough to repeat the cycle.

All Calvin could think of was that he wanted Amir to mess up. To suffocate him for good. To make this process stop.

And when it didn't happen, when he was welcomed back to the world, he screamed.

24

Adjusting the straps on his gas mask, Raven crouched at the hotel window with Creek, both of them looking out over the street just a couple blocks down from the fire station.

Lindsey was maybe thirty minutes away now. Only twenty or so if they were lucky.

Fifteen minutes ago, the Reapers had started loading up four large box trucks with the crates and barrels they'd stored under the tarps. Five minutes ago, Calvin had stopped screaming.

Now Raven hoped to hear him call out in agony, just to know he was still alive.

But he heard only the engines gurgling and the shouts of men. If he had to guess, the Reapers were nearly ready to take off. A few smaller SUVs and pickup trucks were loading up men outside a motel adjacent to the fire station.

Raven couldn't wait for Lindsey's reinforcements.

He owed it to Calvin to try and save him if he was still alive, and Raven was going to be damned if he let these extremists get away and vanish into the desert. All those barrels and crates of what were almost guaranteed to be components of the engineered Wild Fire pathogen—a biological weapon by all the evidence they'd uncovered—could not continue to be loosed on the country.

"You ready, boy?" Raven strapped his pack on and checked his dog. "We're going in."

Even Creek seemed uncertain, rearing back slightly.

If the dog could talk, he would have probably agreed with Lindsey.

To take the Reapers down, they needed an army.

But since Raven didn't have one, then he was going to have to be a ghost and channel the trickster spirit Iktomi.

He quietly moved out of the room and down the stairs with Creek. At the bottom floor, he looked out another window. Two men were patrolling between an old school bus and a semitruck. They appeared to be watching for anyone traveling down the street toward the convoy.

Raven went outside with his Akita behind him and prowled toward the end of the school bus and paused.

The two Iranians walked toward him, their feet falling heavily on the asphalt. Each had a pair of night vision goggles.

Those would be useful, Raven thought.

He kept back, out of view, listening to their hushed voices, each word getting louder as they got closer. Raven cradled his crossbow, then took a deep breath.

The pair of Reapers started past the front of the bus on the passenger side. Raven stalked around the other side, toward the driver's side wheel well. The men continued along the road, their backs to Raven and their rifles roving the darkness.

He motioned for Creek to stay, then aimed the crossbow and fired. The bolt tore silently through the air and punched straight through the back of one Iranian's neck.

Clutching at the fatal wound, the man crumpled to his side. The second Reaper was staring down at his comrade when Raven let one of his hatchets fly.

The heavy blade cracked right into the man's cheek. He let out a muffled, gurgling cry, wobbling on his feet as blood gushed from the wound and poured over his chest.

Raven ripped the arrow out of the dead Reaper's neck, then jabbed it into the neck of the man with the hatchet sticking out of his face.

After a brief struggle, the man collapsed. Raven collected his arrow, reloaded it, and then plucked his hatchet free.

He also removed the night vision goggles, placing them over his own head. They didn't fit perfectly over his gas mask, but it was better than nothing. The world suddenly came alive in an array of green, white, and black. He could see the whole street and neighboring blocks clearly.

Other soldiers were patrolling the next street over, headed in the opposite direction. They escorted a few other men using handcarts to load supplies. Everyone seemed to be in a hurry. But they weren't working with the urgency Raven would have expected if they had known reinforcements were imminently on their way. That told him Calvin had kept quiet during his torture.

Raven would use this to his advantage and make sure any pain his friend had endured would be repaid in spades.

Raven counted the troops utilizing his new optics, coming to twenty. Two more than he had estimated after killing the first two. There were probably a few more he couldn't see from his vantage.

With such a small force, it was taking the Reapers a while to load their supplies into the trucks. No wonder they had conscripted criminal groups from the Badlands to help them pull off other heists. It was the manual labor they needed, plus they were easy scapegoats to hide what the Reapers were actually up to.

So far, none of the men had noticed him. He patted down the dead Iranians for more useful supplies.

Between them, he found a pair of flash grenades like the one they'd used on Calvin.

I'm coming, brother, he thought.

Working quickly, Raven dragged the bodies under the bus to hide them, then started east toward the fire station, navigating through a clutch of two-story homes with Creek.

He paused in one yard, hiding behind some bushes directly across from the fire station. Two SUVs drove away from the motel and parked in front of the three box trucks. An additional SUV and pickup parked just behind the trucks.

All seven vehicles started down the road. His heart thumped in his chest. At first, he thought they were leaving, before he realized they were simply moving closer to another parking lot, two blocks farther west, where they had more supplies to load up. They halted alongside the right side of the road.

He and Creek continued between neighboring houses southward to get closer. They emerged in the front yard of a home across from the aptly named Rustic Moab Motel and hid behind a sedan parked in the driveway. That was where the Reapers had come pouring out when they'd discovered Yoon and Calvin.

Three SUVs were still in the parking lot.

Unlike the abandoned vehicles in the streets, these had fully inflated tires and clean windshields free of dust. All details his night vision goggles allowed him to see clearly now.

When he judged it safe, he led Creek along the cover of the vehicles into the motel's parking lot. Just to their west, straight down the street, was where the convoy was finishing their last preparations. He paused a moment as the Reapers shut the doors on two of the box trucks.

Crates nearly filled the third truck, and it looked as if a couple more loads from the handcarts would do it. Then these terrorists would be off, no doubt.

It was time to play dirty like Iktomi would and stop these monsters right here and now... by any means necessary.

Raven drew on some of his criminal skills back before he'd pulled his life together. First, he checked the gas tank of an early 1970s Chevrolet Blazer. He could smell the odor of gasoline, so at least it wasn't empty.

From his pack, he drew out a long rope of gauze and dipped it into the tank, then left it hanging out.

Moving to the front of the vehicle, he used a knife to pry at the seal between the window and the door. He tripped the locking mechanism with a click and pulled the door open gently. Instead of getting in, he moved on to the next idea.

None of this would be perfect, but it just might work if he was lucky.

With the Reapers ready to leave, there was no time to set up all the traps he had in mind, but at least he could cause some damage and hopefully stall the convoy. Then he would go find Calvin.

He pulled out another tool he always kept in his survival kit: fishing line.

After tying the fishing line to the pins of each flash bang, he stretched the lines taut across the parking lot and the street alongside the motel.

As soon as he was finished, he ducked back toward the SUV with Creek.

He took several deep breaths. His goal wasn't to stop the Reapers or even get into a fight with them. All he wanted to do was distract them, confuse them, slow them down, and if he was lucky, see if there was any possible way he could save Calvin.

"Get ready," Raven whispered to Creek.

He thought about Lindsey asking him to stay put. To stay out of danger until she got there. She wouldn't be far now. Only minutes away if everything went smoothly.

But the enemy had just shut the door on the third box truck. The men were now loading up into the two SUVs at the front of the convoy and the pickup and SUV at the rear.

Time was up.

They were heading out.

"Okay, boy, let's do this," Raven said quietly.

He ducked into the Blazer and pulled open the plastic over the ignition with his knife. Once again, his former criminal past came into practice as he hot-wired the SUV. It took him a few moments before the engine coughed to life.

A chime sounded. The fuel gauge was near empty, but it would be plenty for what he had to do.

Stepping back onto the asphalt, he used a lighter from his pack to set the fuel-soaked gauze hanging off the tank on fire. Then he went back to the driver's side door, propped a rock on the gas pedal, and put the SUV into drive, aiming it straight toward the convoy. He jumped back from the Blazer as it took off.

Raven motioned for Creek, and they ran around the backside of the motel. He looked over his shoulder as the driverless Blazer sideswiped the pickup truck at the back of the convoy, knocking the SUV off its trajectory.

A couple of Reapers started firing at the Blazer as it swerved wildly.

The vehicle scraped into an abandoned minivan on the left side of the road, sparks flying where metal ground against metal. Bullets pounded the vehicle as it twisted to the right, slamming right into another abandoned car parked in the road at the front of the convoy. Raven could vaguely see the burning gauze from the fuel tank.

A few of the Reapers started to approach the stopped Blazer, holding their fire. One of them must have seen the flaming gauze. He began to wave and shout. But it was too late for those men to escape. Flames burst outward as the Blazer exploded in a brilliant blast, nearly blinding Raven. He flipped his optics up, watching the fireball.

Pieces of the charred SUV slammed into the convoy. Raven slowly got back up as billows of dark smoke rolled from the inferno. Panicked and angry shouts filled the night as the Reapers started reorganizing the convoy, reversing the trucks away from the fire, and pulling their injured away.

Raven had bought maybe a couple more minutes.

He didn't have long to consider what to do next, though. A group of four Reapers began firing blindly into the night, forcing him and Creek to sneak behind the motel. They stuck to the cover of the bushes to make it into the parking lot of the fire station.

As Raven crept his way toward the rear wall of the facility, he heard a deafening pop. A brilliant flash of light tore through the night for a second near the motel.

The Reapers had tripped the first flashbang, again buying Raven precious time.

Not long after, someone tripped the second.

Raven used that opportunity to rush toward the fire station, chest heaving as he ducked low into some bushes, Creek at his feet.

While the enemy yelled in confusion, the truck engines still growling, he watched the door to the fire station that the Reapers had pulled Calvin through before. Raven hadn't seen them take Calvin out of the fire station yet. Maybe he'd missed them loading the Steel Runner up in the chaos or maybe they'd left Calvin—or his body.

Was he too late?

He paused at the door, listening just under a slightly open window. Two urgent voices speaking Farsi drifted out just as he was about to move around the side and look for Calvin.

He stopped when he heard footsteps and a voice in English.

The door to the fire station burst open.

Two Reapers strode out, dressed in black fatigues. One had his sleeves rolled up, revealing lean muscles; the other looked like a rhinoceros with a dark beard.

They dragged a beaten man that Raven recognized only by his wiry black hair and dark skin. It was definitely Calvin, and despite his condition, he was kicking, trying to free himself, as the two soldiers hauled him out into the road.

Creek's fur stood straight up across his back, but Raven motioned for the dog to hold.

More voices called from the other side of the motel, where the convoy had been repositioning. One of the radios crackled to life with Farsi.

The two men suddenly dropped Calvin, speaking rapidly in panicked voices.

The smaller of the two pulled a pistol and aimed it at Calvin.

"Your time is done," the man said. "I underestimated how many of you there are, but they will die, just like you, soon enough."

Calvin spat at the Reaper.

The other boulder of a man kicked the Steel Runner in the stomach. Raven aimed his M4 at the guy as he bent down over Calvin.

Someone from near the trucks shouted a command in

Farsi. Whatever it was, these guys sounded worried. Like they were more than ready to get the hell out of here.

Raven prepared to fire, but his targets had hauled Calvin up in front of them like a human shield. Plus, the gunfire would give away his position. All the Reapers trying to escape might converge on him.

But he had the drop, and he had Creek.

Slinging his rifle, he pulled out his hatchets.

The man with the pistol pulled the slide back, chambering a round, but the larger guy loomed over Calvin, holding him down.

"Goodbye, Calvin Jackson," said the man with the pistol.

Raven couldn't let Calvin die.

He ran forward, throwing a hatchet that hit his first target in the back, forcing the Reaper to drop his pistol. The other guy got off Calvin, both looking just as surprised to see Raven.

25

Calvin couldn't fucking believe it.

Like a ghost from the night, Raven appeared with a gas mask and night vision goggles, just in time to save his ass.

Hossein got up with a knife that he slashed to keep Raven back.

Calvin squirmed on his stomach toward the pistol that Amir had dropped. The terrorist was on his back, groaning with the hatchet buried into above his shoulder blade.

If it weren't for his hands bound behind his back, Calvin could've scooped up the gun to help Raven, who swung his axe at Hossein. The big man thrust his knife at Raven, and then grabbed him by the arm, tossing him to the ground with the force of a gorilla.

Creek suddenly lunged up and latched onto Hossein's arm. The dog ripped into his flesh as Raven tried to get up.

Hossein shook the dog, and then went to stab him when Raven grabbed his wrist. He used his other hand with the hatchet to smack Hossein with the back of the blade. The big man hardly seemed to react and tossed the dog to the ground.

The Akita yowled in pain as the big man used his knife to slash at Raven again.

Calvin pushed up to his feet. Dizziness threatened to take him. He could feel the fluid gathering in his lungs. Just like Amir had promised.

Every breath he took, his throat rasped. He still hadn't fully recovered from the waterboarding either.

But then Mouse's voice sounded in his head.

It's just a mind game.

"Mother fu..." Calvin lowered his head and charged like a defensive lineman going in for the sack. He threw all his power into ramming his shoulder right into Hossein's gut.

The huge man tumbled backward, his back hitting the wall of the fire station.

All the while, the sound of truck engines roared from the street. It sounded like they were heading away now, or maybe his ears were playing tricks on him. Maybe something had spooked them?

For a second, he thought he heard the thump of helicopter blades in the distance.

Calvin wanted to believe that meant reinforcements had been spotted and were on their way.

Either way, for now at least, he and Raven were on their own with Creek.

Calvin kicked a boot hard into Hossein's groin. The man let out a yowl of intense pain. Raven suddenly pointed.

"Calvin, watch out!" he yelled.

Calvin turned to see Amir had somehow gotten up on a knee, and he was holding his dropped pistol. He aimed it right at Calvin with a shaky hand.

In the heat of the battle, Amir made a grave mistake.

He hadn't finished off Creek.

The dog lunged from behind Amir, leaping onto the man and sinking his teeth into his neck.

Gunfire cracked, and a bullet cut past Calvin's head as Amir went down. Stunned, but uninjured, Calvin kicked Hossein in the head with all his might.

"Calvin!" Raven said. He tossed a knife to Calvin. Somehow, Calvin managed to catch it. He sawed through the bindings around his wrists while Raven helped Creek with Amir.

Hossein managed to get back up and knock the knife from Calvin's hand just after he had cut his bindings. Free now, Calvin backed away and then ducked below a punch. He came up behind Hossein, wrapping an arm around his neck and taking him down.

Working his legs up and over Hossein's legs, Calvin then tightened his chokehold.

The burly Iranian bucked and tried to roll over, but Calvin used all the strength he had, all the power left in his diseased body to hold him down.

Every fiber of his muscles strained with the effort. Hossein tried to butt him away with his head and threw his elbows into Calvin with desperate vigor.

Each impact sent another shudder of fiery pain through his damaged body, but Calvin held strong.

But before Hossein succumbed to oxygen deprivation, he swung his hands up and grabbed Calvin's face. His thumbs found Calvin's eyes and he began to press down.

Agony swelled from the pressure. Calvin jerked away, loosening his grip.

As soon as he did, Hossein broke free and jumped back to his feet. Even as he gasped for air, he raised a boot to crush Calvin's skull into the ground.

Calvin rolled to the side just as the Reaper's boot smashed against the concrete. Again and again, Hossein went after the

Steel Runner, finally catching him on the shoulder with one heaving stomp. Pain ignited from the violent attack.

It's just a mind game, Calvin thought again.

Pain was nothing. It was just in his mind.

Hossein raised his boot again to crush Calvin's face when a blade suddenly *thunk*ed into the side of the huge man's head. He collapsed sideways, landing with enough force to send a tremor through the ground.

Raven approached and bent down to his friend. "You okay?"

Dazed, Calvin managed to nod, but said nothing.

When he did open his mouth, he started coughing. Blood came up with mucus in his saliva. He looked over at Amir and his lifeless eyes.

Creek trotted over with a limp, and Raven checked over the dog.

"Keep away," Calvin said.

Raven turned his gas mask back to Calvin. There was a crack in it that must've happened during the fighting.

The sound of helicopters came again, and this time, Calvin was sure the noise was real.

"I'm infected," Calvin finally managed to choke out, dragging himself away from Raven. "I'm going to die. You have to get out of here."

Raven motioned for Creek to get away.

Then he reached for his sat phone, pulling it out. It was broken, destroyed in the hand-to-hand combat. "Son of a bitch."

The helicopters blazed overhead, undoubtedly chasing after the departing convoy.

"Those are Lindsey's reinforcements," Raven said. "They'll come back for us. You're going to be okay. They'll find a cure."

They'll find a cure.

Those words seemed to echo in his brain. Calvin started coughing again. The fight had drained him, and try as he might, he couldn't catch his breath.

"Don't move," Raven said. "I'm going to make sure the Reapers are all gone. I'll be right back."

Raven got up and ran with Creek.

Calvin tried to raise himself up to his knees, but he was growing weaker. It felt like he'd sprinted a whole marathon, and he was still struggling to take in oxygen. It reminded him almost of being waterboarded. The quiet desperation of just trying to take a breath.

He collapsed again, coughing.

Blackness started to creep into his mind. The headache and fever swirled through his skull, accompanied by sheer exhaustion from the plague tearing through his body.

His eyelids were too heavy. The pain swelled in the back of his skull. His senses faded in and out, like his mind was slowly being sucked through a black hole.

Raven returned a few minutes later.

"We're clear," he said. "Just hold on, brother."

Calvin continued to cough, his lungs burning.

Heaving out a cough, Calvin turned on his side toward Amir. Seeing his maskless dead face reminded him of something during his torture.

Then the realization hit him.

Something he'd noted earlier.

Maybe there really was hope.

"They have a cure, Raven," Calvin said in a raspy voice.

"What?" Raven asked.

"The Reapers infected me... but they didn't wear masks... didn't protect themselves."

Raven looked at Amir, and then Hossein. "Oh shit."

Standing, the tracker looked toward the sky.

"It's up to Lindsey now," he said. "The fate of the New Frontier is in her hands."

————

Lindsey peered out the window of the helicopter. They had just passed Moab. During their brief flyover, all she had seen was a burning SUV blocking one of the streets. But if there were any other signs of life, she didn't see them.

No trucks. No convoy like Raven had described.

Which meant the Reapers had already left with the Wild Fire.

The longer it took to find out where they had gone, the more likely the enemy would disappear into the desert.

Palmer looked at her nervously as the other three Rangers checked their weapons over.

"Raven, do you hear me?" she called on the radio.

She hadn't heard from him since he'd warned her that the Reapers were preparing to leave. Now with the enemy gone, she feared the worst.

But while she worried for Raven and Calvin, she had a mission to protect the people of Colorado. For that matter, she had to protect the people of the United States.

"Do we have eyes on that convoy yet?" Lindsey asked the primary pilot.

"Negative," he called back.

"Damn it," Lindsey said under her breath. Then she called Blair. "We need to split up. Cover more ground."

"Copy that," he replied "Just tell us where to go."

After considering the most likely options, Lindsey gave Blair's team directions along with her pilots. She had the

Royal Marines follow US-191 north as her team broke off westward down State Route 313.

The seconds turned to minutes as they blasted away from Moab.

"Look!" Palmer said, peering out the window. "Is that them?"

Lindsey looked out the window, squinting. She could barely see the glint of moonlight on metal in the distance, right along the 313.

"Got 'em," the primary pilot said. "I got three big box trucks. Plus, two SUVs up front, and an SUV and pickup truck behind."

"Send those coordinates to Blair," Lindsey said. "Let's tail these bastards until the Marines catch up."

Blair called her a moment later. "On our way, Sheriff."

"Race ahead and block them off on the west," Lindsey said, knowing the Merlin was faster. "We'll take them from behind. Once we cut them off, we go in, weapons hot."

They started after the convoy, tearing through the night. Lindsey felt like a falcon swooping down on hapless prey. Their enemy had nowhere to go now. No way to outrun them or escape.

"We have these assholes finally," Palmer said.

Lindsey scanned the landscape below. Moonlight revealed the rocks and shrubs across the rolling desert. The Royal Marines caught up in only a few minutes, racing ahead of the Rangers.

The two helicopters closed in on the convoy.

At the same time, the convoy was accelerating. A last desperate attempt to run away.

Sparks of gunfire exploded from the pickup and SUVs escorting the convoy, forcing the Bell Chopper to back off.

But the Merlin continued forward, soaring straight to the

front of the convoy. They were better able to withstand the small arms fire.

"The Marines are about to cut them off," the primary pilot said. "We'll catch up again and begin our descent."

"NVGs and masks on!" Lindsey said to her team.

She fidgeted with both until they were comfortable and she could see.

The Bell started to twist as it lowered to the highway, giving Lindsey a perfect vantage across all seven vehicles and the Merlin.

Ahead of the convoy, moonlight reflected off the long barrel of a machine gun mounted on one of the Merlin's side doors. A Royal Marine gripping the viscerally terrifying weapon unleashed hellfire on the lead SUV. Flames spurted from under the hood of the vehicle as it careened off the road and into the ditch.

The Merlin lowered to the highway, forcing the convoy to slow, as the door gunner opened up on the next SUV in front of the first box truck. Tracer fire raked back and forth, slashing out at the enemy. The SUV skidded to a stop.

Return fire slammed into the chopper as it lowered, pinging off the armor.

The entire convoy had stopped but the box trucks started to reverse. The Bell Chopper caught up to the rear of the convoy and started to lower to block their path. For a moment, Lindsey thought this would be easy. Cut off the Reapers and kill those that didn't surrender.

But that hope vanished when a sudden flash of light flared from the stopped SUV at the front of the convoy. A finger of smoke lanced away from an RPG launcher held by a Reaper.

"Blair!" Lindsey shouted.

The Merlin lurched sideways, but they were too close to avoid the rocket. It slammed into the rear section of the chopper with an ear-shattering explosion. The big bird went into a spin, its tail blown into shreds of scrap metal.

The belly rammed sideways into the ground, grinding against the asphalt. Fire and smoke plumed from where the rocket had struck.

Gunfire burst from the enemy vehicles as disoriented Royal Marines climbed out of the wreckage.

Lindsey watched in horror as all hell broke loose. They had lost control of the situation in a single horrifying moment.

She snapped out of the shock.

"We have to help them!" she shouted. "Take us down!"

Gunfire streaked in their direction, the pilots banking away from it. Several rounds punched into the hull.

Even as they jerked, Lindsey could see the surviving Royal Marines rushing for cover, some of them dragging injured with them. Despite the disaster, they worked with expert precision, several of them putting down covering fire that kept the Reapers from pursuing.

"Blair, do you read?" Lindsey said on the radio.

Platoon sergeant Michael Aitken answered with their call signs. "Coyote One, Wolf Two here. At least four Marines down. Blair is unresponsive."

Lindsey felt the familiar tendrils of fear threatening to wrap around her heart. She would not let terror win today and braced herself for the fight ahead.

"Copy, Wolf Two, we're on our way," Lindsey said. Then she turned to her men. "Get ready!"

Palmer and the other three Rangers stood from their jump seats. Each had one gloved hand on the rail along the ceiling of the cabin and another on the M4s strapped over their chest.

"We've got to move fast," Lindsey said to her men, then she turned to the pilots. "Put us down and immediately get the hell out of RPG range."

The SUV and pickup truck at the end of the convoy had both stopped, guarding the box trucks. Two Reapers with AK-47s fired at the chopper as they lowered.

Bullets cracked against the windshield.

Lindsey braced herself as the skids thudded against the asphalt with a heaving jolt. Palmer cranked open the side door.

"Go, go, go!" he bellowed.

"On me!" Lindsey yelled.

She hopped out as Palmer provided covering fire, beating the Reapers back. She ran with the Rangers and slid into the ditch on the right side of the road for cover. Palmer leapt out after them, and the chopper took back off in a hurry.

Lindsey and the Rangers moved into position, crawling up to the side of the trench. Palmer was the first to open fire, and the other Rangers joined in. Their rounds pinged against the SUV and the pickup, shattering the windows and deflating tires. Bullets tore into the sides of the vehicles.

A Reaper opened one of the rear doors of the SUV. He aimed an RPG launcher at the escaping Bell chopper.

"No, you don't," Lindsey whispered under her breath. She lined up the man in her sights and let loose a three-round burst.

The terrorist fell back, firing the RPG at the same time. It tore off into the sky, smoke trailing after it.

Thanks to her quick actions, it just missed the bird.

But there was no telling if more men would try launching rockets at the only surviving chopper they had. They needed to work quickly.

Return fire hammered their position, kicking up geysers of sand.

"Wolf Two, status?" Lindsey asked, straining to listen over the comm.

"*Five* of ours now KIA," Aitken called back, nearly breathless. "At least four Marines injured. Wolf One included. We're pressing the advance."

The Reapers around the SUV and the pickup were firmly entrenched behind the open doors of the vehicle. Lindsey aimed for one of the men's feet and fired into his boot. The man fell with a yowl, but his comrade yanked the injured man up into better cover behind the SUV.

As the firefight raged on at the front of the convoy, Lindsey motioned for Palmer to follow her in the ditch. They kept low as her other Rangers provided suppressing fire.

Once she was in parallel with the pickup and the SUV, she peered over the edge. Two of the Reapers were sprawled across the road. Two more were still sheltering behind the open doors of the SUV, one of them with the injured foot.

Lindsey thought briefly of taking these men prisoner to question them. But she wasn't willing to risk more of her Rangers or the Royal Marines. Plus, these terrorists had murdered many of the Steel Runners and countless others.

They had no interest in surrendering, even now, when the tide had obviously turned against them.

So she pressed her rifle tight against her shoulder and nodded at Palmer. Three rounds from each of them tore through the sides of the two men.

"Keep moving," she said.

They traveled up the ditch, covering each other. The flames from the burning Merlin flickered, casting long shadows from the wreckage. She could just see four Royal Marines walking at a hunch down the ditch toward them.

A Reaper suddenly appeared out of smoke drifting across the road. He limped, nearly dragging a bloody leg. He raised a pistol in a shaky hand and aimed at the Royal Marines, who didn't seem to notice him. Lindsey didn't cry out a warning.

Instead, she aimed and took the injured Reaper down with a burst to his head.

The guy slumped into the ditch, sliding down the dirt.

Lindsey swept the road for more contacts, but didn't see any.

Only a couple more sporadic gunshots went off toward the front of the convoy.

Aitken's voice came over her comms. "Coyote One, Wolf Two. Clear here."

"Clear back here, as well, Wolf Two," Lindsey replied.

The Rangers' chopper was circling at a farther, safer distance.

"Condor One, got eyes on hostiles?" she asked.

"Condor One here, we don't have any contacts," the primary pilot of the Rangers' bird replied.

"Aitken, stabilize your wounded," Lindsey ordered. "Any spare men you got, start searching the convoy, but watch out for potential Wild Fire exposure. And keep an eye out for Raven Spears and Calvin Jackson. They could be prisoners."

"Copy that," Aitken replied.

Lindsey held hope she would find the men alive but knew the chances were unlikely considering how the Reapers seemed to operate, killing anyone and everyone that got in their way.

While Aitken sent seven uninjured Royal Marines to take care of their casualties, he led the other eight in, clearing the destroyed SUVs at the front of the convoy. Lindsey and her Rangers converged on the pickup truck at the rear. They approached slowly, covering each other, until Palmer reached the pickup.

He tore open the front passenger door as Lindsey aimed her rifle into the cab. Nothing remained inside the cab except for spent brass shells and a single dead Reaper slumped in the driver's seat with a rifle next to him.

The truck bed had only a few containers of ammunition alongside two Siegler Pharmaceutical crates.

When they reached the next bullet-scarred vehicle, an SUV, the story was the same. A couple more Siegler crates stuffed in the back. Ammunition. Weapons. Food and water supplies, even some packages that had the silver star of the Colorado Rangers logo.

"This is stuff from the Eagle Restoration Site," Palmer said.

"All from those groups they've been making work for them," Lindsey said. "To the box truck. Hurry."

She and her men cleared the cabin of the first box truck they encountered. Then they moved to the rear. As soon as they opened it, they revealed barrels and crates all marked with the Siegler Pharmaceuticals logo.

"Palmer, put in a call to Doctor Wheeler," Lindsey said. "We're going to need his closest USAMRIID teams here. I don't want anyone to touch this stuff until his people arrive."

"On it," Palmer said.

Lindsey rounded the box truck to get a view of the other two remaining trucks. Six of the Royal Marines had surrounded the first truck. From what Lindsey could see, all they'd found was more crates and barrels. There was no sign of Raven or Calvin.

As six Marines lined up along the rear of the last box truck next, her hopes were reaching new lows.

"Clear it!" Aitken said, tearing open the rear door. It retracted up toward the box truck's ceiling to reveal more crates and barrels.

But that wasn't all.

"We've got people!" Aitken called out. "Noncombatants!"

Lindsey rushed to join the Marines. She stood next to Aitken, expecting to see Raven and Calvin back there, tied up.

Of course, the two people she did see were indeed tied up, hands bound by ropes. Their eyes were wide with fear as the Royal Marines shone their tac lights at the people's faces.

But neither were the hardened warriors she expected to see.

She recognized them almost immediately.

"Oh my God," she whispered.

It was Agathe, Uwase's wife, and Emmanuel, their six-year-old son. Each had a cloth pulled tight over their mouths as a gag.

Lindsey's stomach twisted in a painful knot. She called the Utah Scouts Command immediately. She gave them her coordinates. "How soon until we get air medivac?"

There was simply no way she could get the injured Royal Marines and Uwase's family to safety in the cramped Bell.

"We have both our Sikorsky S-76Cs rerouting your way," a comms officer replied. "We can be there to evac all causalities in about ten minutes."

"Copy that. Thank you for the support," Lindsey said.

She directed Aitken to send the rest of his men to do everything they could to help Blair and the other injured Royal Marines.

Palmer returned after making the call to Doctor Wheeler. He and Lindsey removed the gags and the ropes around Agathe's and Emmanuel's wrists. They helped the mother and son away from the truck toward the side of the road. Emmanuel began sobbing immediately, holding on to his mother. She held the boy close.

"Where is Uwase?" she asked. "What's happening?"

"It's all right, ma'am," Lindsey said, trying to sound as

calm as she could. "You're safe now. I'm with the Colorado Rangers, and we've got the UK Royal Marines with us. We're going to get you back to Golden."

"These people... these terrorists... they took us from Golden," Agathe said. "We're not safe there."

"You will be now," Lindsey said. "You have my word."

All the puzzle pieces were clicking into place. Now she understood why Uwase had been feeding the Reapers intel. He had betrayed her because they'd kidnapped his family and held them hostage.

She felt bad for the man, but she wished that he'd told her instead of acting from a place of pure fear. So many lives could've been saved. She might have been able to help him.

"We're not going to let anyone hurt you again," Lindsey said.

"Thank you," Agathe said.

"I'm sorry, but I need to ask you something, and I need answers quickly. Did you see any other prisoners?"

"What?" Agathe asked. "Prisoners?"

"Any other hostages like yourselves in Moab?"

Agathe shook her head, tears glistening. She hugged Emmanuel closer to her chest.

"No, they kept us back in the fire station in the old bunk room," Agathe said. "They never let us out unless we were blindfolded. Tonight, though... tonight, we heard screams, but... but that's it."

"Okay, thank you." Lindsey was doing everything she could to remain calm. She wanted to be a centering force for this poor woman and her crying child. "You're doing well. Now do you know if you were exposed to the plague? A bioweapon? Any diseases?"

Agathe trembled. "They told us if we didn't cooperate, they'd make us sick."

"Do you feel sick at all?" Lindsey asked.

"No," Agathe said. Her son also shook his head.

"Good. Just stay right here, and we'll have a medic look at you both."

Lindsey took a few steps back from Agathe and her son, then ran to the Royal Marines. She steeled herself against the sight of the men rushing between the injured, doing their best to tie tourniquets, apply bandages, and reassure their brothers-in-arms.

She spotted Aitken kneeling next to Blair. The lieutenant was on his back, but his eyes were closed.

"How is he?" she asked, trying to see if there was anything she could do to help.

"Alive for now, but he needs medical attention fast," Aitken said.

"Medivac is only a few minutes out now," Lindsey said. She squeezed Blair's hand, wondering if he was even aware enough to receive any comfort from her grip. "Aitken, please make sure you watch over Agathe and Emmanuel until Utah Scouts Command reinforcements and medical evacuation teams arrive. Then make sure everyone gets home safely, okay?"

"Will do, Sheriff," Aitken said. "What are you going to do?"

"As soon as the medivac takes your people away, I'm headed out again. We're still missing two men, Sergeant. This mission isn't over until I find them."

26

RAVEN PEERED OUT THE WINDOW OF THE FIRE STATION. He listened to every sound since the choppers had gone by.

Would the Reapers return to kill him when they realized that Hossein and Amir had failed? Or had they simply fled, racing as far and fast as they could?

Without a working sat phone, he had no idea if Lindsey had caught up to the enemy. Nor did he know if help would find them.

Even if someone did come for them, would it be in time?

Creek whined. He was still favoring his right front paw when he walked, but Raven didn't see anything broken or fractured when he checked the Akita.

Mostly, the dog just seemed like he'd gotten bruised from the fight. But Raven did worry Creek had contracted the plague from Calvin. He kept thinking of that wolf in La Sal.

So far, Creek didn't show any signs of sickness.

Calvin, on the other hand, looked terrible.

Raven went back over to check his friend, who lay curled up on a mattress with an oxygen mask over his face. It was connected to a tank Raven had found stowed away... and might be the only reason Calvin was still alive.

Calvin took in a raspy breath, struggling for air.

Raven pressed a finger against the man's neck, feeling a small almost imperceptible thump. His pulse was racing, but it was weak, like his heart was giving up.

Calvin was unconsciousness now. He didn't have much time, even with the oxygen.

"Hang on, buddy," Raven said.

He considered trying to move him in a vehicle, but there was no way he would make it to help in time. Even if he could find a working car or hike to the Tahoe, he didn't want to leave Calvin alone.

Raven knew that the best thing to do when you were lost in the wilderness was exactly what Lara's dad had told her: Stay put.

He had to trust that Lindsey would return to Moab. Assuming she survived the attack against the Reaper convoy.

Calvin started to rasp for breath again. The small oxygen tank was almost out of air, and Raven didn't have another.

Plus, for all he knew, with his cracked gas mask from the fight with the two Reapers, he had been infected. If he started to develop symptoms as bad as Calvin's while wandering out into the desert, he'd be dead sooner than a deer with an arrow through its gut.

Creek suddenly perked his ears, standing above Calvin protectively. His good eye shot toward the window, and he let out a growl.

"What is it, boy?" Raven whispered, shouldering his rifle.

Then he heard it.

The familiar thump of helicopter blades sounded in the distance.

He reached into his pack and pulled out a flashlight to signal the aircraft. For a second, he wondered if this might be the Reapers. Did they have access to helicopters?

Calvin let out another gasping breath. Raven readjusted the oxygen mask.

No, it was extremely unlikely that the Reapers had a helicopter. Not out here. Not when they'd been using ground vehicles, as far as he'd seen.

He had to risk it for Calvin.

Creek followed him as he ran out the front of the fire station and stood in the middle of the street. He flicked the light on and off, signaling SOS in Morse code. To his surprise, the helicopter blinked its lights back in response.

His heart started beating so fast, he thought it would explode through his chest.

Maybe they were about to be saved after all. It took only seconds for the chopper to lower toward him. He ducked under the rotor wash.

A man leapt out of the chopper wearing a gas mask. It took him a second to recognize Palmer. Then Lindsey hopped out, her red hair draping behind her mask.

"Lindsey!" Raven called.

Lindsey ran toward him. Three more Rangers came out of the helicopter after her and Palmer, all wearing gas masks. She gestured for them to spread out into combat intervals.

Raven resisted the urge to hug Lindsey when she got to him with Palmer.

"Where's Calvin?" Lindsey asked.

"He's inside," Raven said, holding up a hand before she could get too close. "But he's not in a good place, Lindsey. The Wild Fire... I think he got hit with a huge dose. He needs oxygen."

"Shit. We've got to get him back to Golden."

"Lindsey, I need you to know I was probably exposed. My mask is busted. I know you guys have masks, but..."

"We'll be cautious. Take me to him."

Raven led her and Palmer through the open garage door of the fire station. Calvin lay on his back, still unconscious.

"There's something Calvin said before he passed out," Raven said. "He was trying to warn me about the Wild Fire."

"What?" Lindsey asked.

"He told me the Reapers *knew* he was infected. Hell, they were the ones that infected him, but they weren't wearing any masks or anything," Raven said. "Nothing to protect themselves from the plague."

"Which means they have a cure. A vaccine, maybe," Lindsey said.

"Yeah, there's got to be something the Iranians were using so they didn't catch Wild Fire. All the communities like the Brigadiers and the Rattlesnakes that were threatened, the ones they got to do their bidding, the Reapers promised they would share a cure if they succeeded."

Lindsey looked at Raven with disbelief in her eyes. "You think it's true?"

Raven paused, looking over at Calvin's still form.

"Maybe they weren't lying after all. Maybe there's something on their convoy."

Lindsey called Aitken right away, telling him what Raven had said. "Blair told me you Marines are trained to deal with biohazards, so you've got to search the convoy immediately."

"The USAMRIID teams will be here within an hour or two."

"We've got to get a head start on this. Find out if there's anything in there that looks like a treatment or vaccine."

She turned back to Raven.

"If there's a cure, if there's a treatment the Reapers had that we don't know about, we'll find it," Lindsey said. "Wheeler's teams will help us find it."

"Hopefully soon," Raven said.

He thought he could feel fluid filling his lungs already. The urge to cough. His body heating up.

Maybe it was the flagging adrenaline. Maybe it was all in his head.

The thump of helicopter blades still churned outside the fire station where the Bell was idling.

"We got to take Calvin back now and get him on oxygen," Lindsey said. "Maybe the people back home can stabilize him enough until we find that cure. This mission isn't over until we get you two home safely. That was the deal."

The helicopter engines grew louder outside.

"Condor One, we've got a casualty that needs immediate evac. Confirmed Wild Fire exposure," Lindsey said over the radio.

Raven had never seen Lindsey so fierce. Even when she'd been on the battlefield.

"You got it," Raven said, rushing back to Calvin. Lindsey gestured for Palmer to help. The three of them picked up their ailing friend as gently as they could. Raven never realized just how solid the Steel Runner was built until that moment.

Together they lugged the former SEAL outside. Raven was absolutely beat, exhaustion tugging at his limbs. But he had made a promise to get Calvin out alive. And that was exactly what he was going to do.

They pushed out into the desert air. The Rangers Lindsey had left outside the fire station twisted, watching the streets, as the group carried Calvin toward the bird. Its rotor wash kicked up waves of grit, forcing Raven to bow his head. Creek followed along, padding over the concrete, until they made it into the main cabin.

As soon as they had Calvin lying down on the cabin floor, Palmer grabbed the first aid kit and passed a headset to Raven. Creek nestled next to Calvin, trying to comfort the man. The partition between the passenger cabin and cockpit was closed to prevent the pilots being exposed.

The other Rangers boarded the cramped cabin.

"Condor One, we're ready," Lindsey said.

The helicopter lifted away from Moab a moment later.

Lindsey put a hand on Raven's shoulder.

"Thank you, Sam," Lindsey said. "We wouldn't have stopped the Reapers without you and Calvin."

Raven examined the injured and infected Steel Runner. He was in bad shape, and Raven wasn't sure he would even survive the ride to Golden. Hell, Raven wasn't sure he and Creek would either. Maybe he was being paranoid, but he could feel something changing in his body. He could only hope it was just his mind and not Wild Fire beginning to blaze through him.

As the chopper left Moab long behind them, the first rays of the early morning sun crept over the horizon. Raven welcomed the warmth, staring for a moment before turning back to Calvin.

All Raven could do was pray to the animal council and ask for their forgiveness for any pain that he and any other humans had inflicted on them. He thought back to those poor suffering wolves in La Sal and again asked for mercy, knowing that this engineered disease had infected not only his kind, but theirs.

"Please show Calvin mercy," Raven whispered over his

friend's body. He knew it might seem farfetched, but he hoped the animal council, if they were out there, heard him.

If his prayers failed, then maybe the plants—or USAM-RIID now—would provide the cure to the Wild Fire.

There was nothing else he could do.

27

ONE DAY AFTER THE ATTACK ON THE REAPER CONVOY,
Lindsey was out of quarantine. She was now at the jail in Fort
Golden with Palmer at her side. She was finally free to visit
someone who was most definitely not free.

A guard stood in front of the cell. At Lindsey's nod, he
opened the door for her, and Palmer waited outside.

Uwase was sitting on a cot, his head in his hands, and his
elbows resting on his knees. Her people had already inter-
viewed him, but she wanted her own shot to see if there was
anything they missed.

He didn't even glance up at Lindsey when she sat on the
cot beside him. Palmer remained outside at her order.

"Uwase, I wanted to let you know that your wife and son
are still healthy," she said. "They haven't shown any sign of
Wild Fire infections, and the doctors are giving them a clean
bill of health."

"Praise God," Uwase said. He finally looked up at her.
"What's going to happen to me now?" he asked.

Lindsey took a moment before she answered.

For the past two years, she had spent too much time being

judge, jury, and executioner. This time, deciding Uwase's fate wasn't her job.

"What happens next isn't in my control," she said. "That's for a tribunal to decide."

His bottom lip trembled. "Whatever happens to me, just know Agathe and Emmanuel have nothing to do with the Reapers or my actions. They're innocent."

"I know," Lindsey said. "They'll be looked after."

"I know you won't believe me, but I was on your side, Sheriff. I never would have betrayed you if they hadn't gotten my family. I'm so, so sorry."

He put his face in his hands again.

"You should have come to me," Lindsey said. "I know they threatened your family, but how many other families do you think were threatened because of the spread of Wild Fire?"

Uwase looked up at her, a tear falling from an eye.

"If you're truly on my side, I need you to tell me everything you know about the Reapers," she said.

"I already told your people everything I know."

"Which seems to be nothing," Lindsey said. "I need to know if the Iranian government was involved or if these were just some lone actors."

"I am not part of their government. I work for the UN."

Uwase looked up at her again and straightened when she didn't respond.

"All I know is that the Reapers were threatening other groups around the New Frontier," he said. "That group that attacked the Steel Runners in Iowa? They were from the Rockies."

"How do you know?" Lindsey asked.

"The Reapers told me that because I think they wanted to show how powerful they were."

"What else?"

Uwase sighed. "All I knew was that they took my family, and that was enough for me to give them the information they wanted. I wish I could make up for it. I wish I could tell you more."

Lindsey started to stand.

She could only hope the Reapers were a terrorist cell acting alone. If not, and this was a sanctioned hit from the Iranian government or other larger group, there would be more of these slimebags out there, and more attacks.

Though she was more than glad they were all dead now, it did mean there weren't any left alive to talk.

"Tell my wife and son I love them," Uwase said.

"I will," Lindsey said with a nod.

She left the prison cell. The guard closed it, and she headed toward the office wing of Fort Golden with Palmer.

"Time to speak to Secretary Montgomery," Lindsey said as they walked.

"Here's the sat phone, ma'am." Palmer held it out.

Lindsey took it and dialed a number she'd memorized.

"Lindsey," answered the Secretary of Defense. "You learn anything more?"

"I'm afraid not, ma'am. We've recovered plenty of things from the Reapers' convoy, but intel isn't one of those things."

"We're still working on our investigations, so much of the work is classified. Rest assured, the president is keenly interested in resolving this matter as quietly as possible."

"Right, because it's an election year."

"Yes," Charlize said. "President Diego does want you to know he is proud of your successes and said he'd personally visit soon to thank you and your people."

Lindsey held back a snort. She knew she wouldn't be seeing him anytime soon.

"As for the Reapers, by all accounts, I think you've wiped

out the whole group," Charlize said. "We believe these men came over on a recent humanitarian airlift from Europe. The passenger manifest had twenty-seven men that fit the description of your Reapers. Men who were supposedly part of that shell company they created, Siegler."

"And Iran's involvement?"

"It's not exactly clear where the funding for the Reapers' operation came from. We couldn't get Iran to admit to anything, and I believe they're trying to avoid an international incident. They assured us that they aren't trying to take advantage of the situation here."

"Of course they said that. But even if we don't believe them, I guess there are plenty of other groups that would like to take a stab at us right now."

"That's why we're turning our eyes toward all the rogue states and organizations that funneled money into ISIS, Al Qaeda, and other terrorist groups over the years."

"What about Siegler?"

"We're still tracing the ownership, but again, I suspect we'll find common terrorist backers for the shell companies. Rest assured, we will do everything we can to bring the responsible parties to justice on the international stage. In the meantime, you focus on keeping Colorado safe."

"I plan on that. Which leads me to another question. Did you speak to President Tso of the Navajo Nation?"

"Just this morning. He hasn't heard anything from Eddy Nez or the Rattlesnakes. It's unclear if Eddy is still alive, and if he is, what the group plans to do next. You'll have to keep an eye out for trouble."

"I always am."

"Thanks, and again, great work, Lindsey."

"I'm so glad to have you on our side. Couldn't have done it without your help."

Lindsey ended the call and handed the sat phone back to Palmer. The Secretary of Defense wasn't the only ally she had to thank for the successful operation.

She directed them toward another hall past a guard station. One of the guards hit a button at a desk, and the doors opened to a corridor that led to the rest of Fort Golden.

They headed outside into the hot sun.

Palmer put on his aviator glasses before they got into Lindsey's white Ford Bronco.

"So how long until the next bomb goes off, so to speak?" Palmer asked.

"Well, we still have Wild Fire to worry about." Lindsey started the engine. "And I'm afraid the whole Badlands is still a powder keg waiting to explode. All it's going to take is a single match."

She drove out of the lot to the Red Rocks Medical Center for a meeting with Doctor Wheeler. It was a bustle of activity inside. Medical personnel in personal protective equipment rushed new patients into the hospital.

A gaggle of civilians congregated outside the front doors. They clamored around a trio of nurses with clipboards trying to triage the patients. Each of those civilians was lining up for help, coughing or looking scared.

"Damn," Palmer said. "Place is chaos."

"Yup," Lindsey replied.

"Like you said, it's a powder keg."

They bypassed the panicked crowds of people out front by showing their badges to a pair of guards at the center's entrance. Once they had donned face masks and made it to the laboratory wing, Lindsey spotted Doctor Wheeler and his puff of gray, wispy hair at the end of the hall. When he saw her, he waved her over.

Dark bags hung under his eyes, apparent even behind his thick-framed glasses.

"Sheriff, come with me," he said. "It might be better if your deputy waits outside."

Lindsey nodded and Palmer stood outside while she followed Wheeler into a room with banks of computers and a window that looked into a laboratory. Past the window, researchers in white bunny suits and safety goggles worked at microscopes and other equipment.

She and Wheeler weren't alone.

Divekar and Blair were already waiting at a table between the desks.

The Royal Marine wore a sling to hold his left arm in place, and his face was covered in bandages.

"Sheriff Plymouth." He rose from his seat. "Good to see you're still healthy."

"Thank you, how are you feeling?" she asked.

"Mild concussion, contusions, stitches, and some light burns," he said. "I might not be out in the field for a couple weeks, but I can still serve in the FAC."

Divekar offered a sympathetic smile. "He's honestly lucky it's not worse."

"We're lucky too." Lindsey paused. "I can't tell you how thankful I am for everything you and your men have done."

Blair nodded, his eyes growing watery. They had a joint memorial service scheduled in two days for the Rangers and the Royal Marines. Somehow, to Lindsey, that ceremony didn't seem like it would be enough to honor all these men's sacrifices. The best thing she could do was carry on the mission they'd started and protect the New Frontier.

"I truly am glad for what you all have done," Wheeler started, "because I admit, my USAMRIID field teams wouldn't have found half the answers we needed without your help. I know that you two each lost good men securing this information, and the nation will forever be in your debt." Wheeler dropped into a seat beside Blair. "With that in mind, good news or bad news first?"

"Good," Lindsey said.

Wheeler motioned to Divekar, and she began to speak. "The supplies you recovered in Moab contained a medicine and dosage instructions that were successful in treating our first batch of patients."

Lindsey felt a massive burden fall away from her shoulders. "That's fantastic news. What about the bad news?"

Divekar's expression dropped. "The cure is not a normal antibiotic. At least, not one we normally use."

Wheeler tapped his fingers across the table as if he was nervous. "To put it simply, it's a toxin produced *by* bacteria to kill off other bacteria. This specific bacteriocin is derived from *Y. enterocolitica.* Unfortunately, we don't have a supply on hand, and we don't have a stock of *Y. enterocolitica* with which we can produce the bacteriocin."

"That's a big problem," Lindsey said.

"A big problem, indeed," Wheeler agreed. "Wild Fire was engineered from a specific strain of *Y. pestis*, which is already extraordinarily resistant to antimicrobial agents. We searched our databases at USAMRIID. This particular bacterium is related to a weapon first engineered in the USSR's old bioweapons program, Biopreparat. It appears some extremists from Iran got hold of this research and kept it alive, fine-tuning it over the years. Evidently, *someone* engineered the bacteria to increase its antibiotic resistance—and the only thing we've got on hand that works against it is that bacteriocin."

"How much of the bacteriocin did we recover?" Lindsey asked.

"Enough to treat forty more patients," Divekar replied.

"But now we're looking at well over a hundred sick people."

"Two hundred, in fact, yes." Divekar had a pained look on her face. "The numbers have increased since my last report."

A tightening knot twisted Lindsey's insides. "So, what do we do?"

Blair chimed in again. "Our government has secured a stock of medical supplies in our Defense Chemical Biological Radiological and Nuclear Centre that contain the bacteriocin. Tiankai also appears to have access to some Chinese stock as well. I've already begun arranging shipments."

"How soon will they get here?" Lindsey asked.

"The first emergency air shipments will arrive tomorrow," Blair said. "However, from what Doctor Wheeler described, treating the patients in your clinics might not be enough."

Lindsey shot Wheeler a look. "What's that mean?"

"It means that we know the reservoir of Wild Fire thanks to your people," Wheeler said. "There may be stocks of it still left unsecured in the New Frontier. That Angel Line train wasn't the only train that contained Wild Fire, of course."

"Of course," Lindsey said. "The disease was spreading a couple weeks before then. It sounds to me like the Reapers were testing it out. You think that's true?"

"Perhaps the Reapers Militia snuck in smaller shipments of the Wild Fire to test on populations in the New Frontier," Wheeler said. "If your team hadn't stopped them in time... well, the amount of Wild Fire they smuggled in would've been enough to bring down the entire Western United States once they started distributing it."

"Jesus..."

"Unfortunately, that's not all," Divekar added. "The problem is that there are probably plenty of people living in the Badlands who might carry and help spread this disease. Doctor Wheeler and I had a few lengthy discussions on this issue. The only way to truly rid the United States of Wild Fire is to proactively find and treat infected people throughout the New Frontier."

A leaden weight settled over Lindsey as she realized what that meant. "We're going to need more trackers and military action to contain the disease."

"Yes, we have to fight this aggressively," Wheeler said. "Just because we found a cure does not mean it's over. Far from it, in fact."

"What in the hell have these terrorists started..." Lindsey massaged her forehead. "We've got a load of work ahead of us."

"I will be glad to organize my men to help distribute the antibiotics throughout the New Frontier once they arrive," Blair said, "but we're in for a fight. I've read some troubling reports about various parties competing for control over the New Frontier now that the defeat of the Reapers has left an opening. It sounds like your Rangers will be busy."

"Of course," Lindsey said. "Although they won't be the only ones involved in this effort. We're going to need more allies and more soldiers to win this fight."

"The Royal Marines are with you, Sheriff," Blair said.

Lindsey nodded her thanks. But it would take more than that to keep the Frontier from turning to complete hell.

―――――

Raven sat in a hospital room at Estes Park Medical Center wearing a hospital gown and surgical mask. The nurse had given him a plastic face shield too. He had asked the staff to let Creek stay with him. They had been insistent they absolutely could not, especially with all the quarantine measures in place from the plague.

So instead, the dog was faithfully guarding Sandra's home as Allie took care of him. And despite being exposed to Wild Fire, Creek had tested negative.

Unfortunately, Raven had not been so lucky.

He hoped it wouldn't be long until he saw his best friend again. According to the doctors, he would be out soon, but Raven never trusted doctors.

He did trust he was getting better, though. Especially after he had been administered the cure, the bacteriocin, which prevented him from too much physical suffering. But he had plenty of mental torture watching yet another person he'd served beside teeter on the edge of death that pained him to his core.

An EKG beeped in a low rhythm next to an adjacent hospital bed. Though the doctors no longer believed he was contagious, a clear plastic curtain traced the perimeter of the bed to isolate Calvin Jackson from the rest of the room. The Steel Runner lay beneath a shroud of white blankets. Tubes snaked into his nostrils and sutured-up arm. His chest rose and fell slowly. Bruises covered his face.

It was a miracle Calvin was still alive after all he had been through. From the train wreck to the torture, not to mention the Wild Fire.

Any normal man would've given up. Would've let death take him.

But Calvin had survived.

No wonder the guy had made it as a SEAL.

There was a knock at the hospital room door.

At first, Raven thought it was another nurse checking on Calvin.

Instead, Sandra came in, dressed in a gown and mask like

him. Lara followed her inside sheepishly.

"Still doing okay?" Sandra asked.

"So far," Raven said. "How about you two?"

"We're holding up," Sandra answered. "Busy as hell, but what's new?"

Lara nodded, but remained quiet.

"You know, your father and mother would be so proud of you," Raven said to Lara. "You came back from the mountains, and already you're taking care of other people."

"My grandmother said I survived for a reason, and that's why." Lara perked up, more confident. "Those days when I was taking care of my dad... I had a goal. A focus. I realized I needed to help him, that was my purpose, and now I've got a chance to help other people."

Sandra put a gloved hand on Lara's shoulder. "And she's doing great at it." She nodded back toward the hall. "Thing is, we didn't come to chat. Got to get back to some other patients. But someone came to see you. Catch you later, Raven."

As soon as Sandra and Lara disappeared into the hall, someone else came in.

She was dressed in a white bunny suit and mask too, but he recognized her green eyes and fiery red hair immediately.

"Lindsey," he said. "What are you doing up here?"

"Looking for you. Started at your old room and had to find Sandra to tell me where you went. I should have known you would be here with Calvin. Guess you guys are buds now, yeah?"

"I couldn't leave him here alone," Raven said.

Lindsey came into the room and sat in the empty chair beside him.

"You really shouldn't be here," Raven said. "It's not safe."

"Nowhere is safe right now, but Doctor Wheeler told me if I take the right safety precautions, it's okay. You and Calvin shouldn't be contagious any longer. Besides, I wanted to see how you were doing and thank you."

"No need for thanks. We did our jobs. Nothing more."

"You're either modest or cocky as hell, Sam."

Raven chuckled.

"Truth is, the Reapers would still be out there without your help," Lindsey said.

"We got lucky, finding them."

Lindsey scoffed. "You know as well as I do that it wasn't luck."

Maybe it was the wolves that had led him to it after all, Raven thought. But he kept it to himself, instead stewing in silence.

She walked over to Calvin.

"What's the latest update on him?" Lindsey asked.

"Yesterday, the docs said he had a fifty-fifty shot," Raven replied in a low voice. "But today, they seemed more optimistic. The plague isn't the issue anymore. He had some other complications. Other respiratory infections, I think the docs said, as a result. His body is just... exhausted. The next day will be telling. If he doesn't wake up..."

Raven couldn't finish the thought.

"I'm sorry, Raven," Lindsey said. "You did everything you could to save him. It's up to medicine now."

Raven shook his head. "We've lost so many people, Lindsey. So many. Every time I work with someone, it's a death sentence for them."

Lindsey reached out to him with a gloved hand and laid it over his. "We're making progress. I wish I could take the pain away. I really do. After we lost Colton, I didn't think I could do *this* whole sheriff thing without him. Whenever I'm not sure what the right decision is, I want to pick up a phone and call him."

"Yeah, I hear that," Raven said. "I miss Colton too."

He looked over at Calvin. In some ways, the retired SEAL reminded Raven of the late Police Chief of Estes Park.

"Funny thing is, I've only known Calvin for a few days, but he risked everything just to save me and Creek. He is so much like Colton."

"They were... are both great men."

"I think I underestimated him," Raven said. "Calvin, I mean."

"Me too. He's rough around the edges but has a huge heart. I hope he pulls through, because this country needs more good men like him *and* you. We're a long way from healing the West."

"Getting rid of the Reapers and those Brigadiers should help."

Lindsey sighed. "I wish that were true, but in some ways, it's going to be worse."

She told him everything Doctor Wheeler had found out about Wild Fire since the last time they'd talked.

"Sounds like I'm not getting a vacation." Raven said.

Lindsey let out a soft laugh. "Only if you consider working with me a vacation."

She crouched in front of his bed.

"I'm sorry for the past, Sam," she said. "I need you for whatever comes next."

"I'm sorry too. I guess working with you isn't the worst thing..."

But all the same, he hoped that didn't mean she would join him out in the Badlands. Not after all he had seen, from the train wreck to Moab. He could picture his sister's face if she found out he would be going back out there.

Death seemed to follow Raven wherever he went, and he

was doing everything he could to keep it from taking the last of the people he loved.

Sandra, Allie, Creek, Lindsey...

He couldn't stand to lose any of them.

Raven wanted to tell Lindsey how he felt. More than just about the death too, he had suppressed his feelings for her. But like so many times, this wasn't the right moment.

Before he could say anything, Lindsey gasped.

"He's opening his eyes," she said.

She ducked out into the hall, calling for a nurse.

Raven stood and stepped up to the plastic curtain around Calvin's bed.

The SEAL's eyes fluttered open slowly. At first, his gaze seemed unfocused, his pupils directed at the ceiling.

Then they slowly found Raven.

"Calvin, man, you're awake," Raven stuttered, still in shock.

The SEAL seemed to study him for a few seconds.

Calvin's lips moved, and it seemed like he was trying to say something.

"What is it?" Raven asked.

"I'm... starving..." Calvin managed to say.

Raven almost laughed. "Lindsey's called a nurse," he said. "They'll bring you some food."

"Only you can bring me food..." Calvin grimaced.

"What?" Raven asked. Now he wondered if Calvin was hallucinating or delusional.

His dry lips cracked into wicked, shaky grin. "Got any crayons you can spare, Marine?"

"You bastard," Raven said.

"How's... how's Creek?"

"He's all right. Recovering at home."

"And the cure... did you find it?"

"Thanks to you, yeah," Raven said. "Lindsey's team recovered something that helps against the Wild Fire. Look, man, I'm sorry about what happened to all the Steel Runners. As soon as you're better, Lindsey can get you back to San Diego."

"Good." Calvin licked his cracked lips. "So I'm... I'm not going to die..."

"No, man. You're getting the hell out of here."

"I'm going to see Mouse's kids. Tell them what their dad did for this country."

"Give them my condolences," Raven said.

"I will."

Raven cocked his head toward the hall. He heard the footfalls of a nurse rushing toward the room.

"I know you don't like to work with people." Calvin paused, taking a deep breath. "But... I don't know where I'm going now. Y'all need help out here. You think... when I get better, I can join you?"

A voice ingrained in Raven's head wanted to say no. To insist that he worked alone.

But after what Calvin had done, he figured it was time to give someone a chance again.

"We can make room," Raven said. "Of course, you'll have to get Creek's approval first."

"I would... expect nothing less."

The hospital door opened again to Sandra and a doctor. Lindsey followed them inside. They sanitized their gloves and gowns before slipping into the partition around Calvin's bed. The doctor gave Calvin water and quizzed him with a bevy of questions as Sandra checked his vitals.

Lindsey stood beside Raven as they watched. Raven reached out with a hand, unsure how she would react. To his surprise and elation, she squeezed his hand back.

Sandra didn't seem to notice, too busy working on Calvin.

The New Frontier was still as wild as the day the nukes exploded over the US, casting it into literal and figurative darkness. They had discovered the source and potential cure to the Wild Fire, but it was still spreading through the Badlands, true to its namesake.

The disease might not have been caused by the animal councils, but he had no doubt it had upended the natural order. Iktomi wouldn't be the only one seeking revenge on the humans responsible for the devastation and perversion of nature.

Raven would continue to face the fires of disease and mankind. But at least he wouldn't do it alone.

The End of Book 1.
Thank you for reading new Frontier: Wild Fire. Look for Book 2, Wild Lands coming this fall.

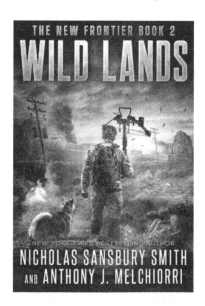

-ABOUT THE AUTHORS-

Anthony J Melchiorri is a scientist with a PhD in bioengineering. He used to develop cellular therapies and 3D-printable artificial organs. Now, he writes apocalyptic, medical, and science-fiction thrillers that blend real-world research with other-worldly possibility. When he isn't at the keyboard, he spends his time running, reading, hiking, and traveling in search of new story ideas.

Read more at https://anthonyjmelchiorri.com/ and sign up for his mailing list at http://bit.ly/ajmlist for free books and to hear about his latest releases.

Nicholas Sansbury Smith is the *New York Times* and *USA Today* bestselling author of the Hell Divers series, the Orbs series, the Trackers series, the Extinction Cycle series, the Sons of war Series, and the new E-Day Series. He worked for Iowa Homeland Security and Emergency Management in disaster mitigation before switching careers to focus on storytelling. When he isn't writing or daydreaming about the apocalypse, he enjoys running, biking, spending time with his family, and traveling the world. He is an Ironman triathlete and lives in Iowa with his wife, daughter, and their dogs.

14214451R00234